HIGH ROLLERS

Dean Parker

ISBN: 978-1-4802-4977-6
PUBLISHED BY CREATESPACE

www.amazon.com
www.deanjparker.com

Printed in the United States of America

To Jayson Stonne

*My best friend and the greatest "high roller" I've
ever known!*

You make the impossible possible.

Also by Dean Parker

Hawaiian Heat

Acknowledgements

The following people have been a great influence, not only on my work, but in my life:

Literary agent Ken Sherman – your guidance and encouragement were invaluable in making this novel the best I could make it.

Aviva Layton – a marvelous editor and a true lady. Your tips on technique and suggestions for improvements have made me a better writer.

Jackie Collins – a brilliant author and a fascinating woman. Thank you for inspiring a crazy and wonderful career choice!

Joy Jamrok – expert proofreader and treasured friend. Joy is what you bring to everybody who meets you.

Chris Pow – Thank you for an excellent cover design and all your hard work.

Marcy Martin – a dear friend and an amazing woman. You've inspired me more than you know.

Vivian Parker – my mother, my friend. The angel who always stands by me. My life has been wonderful because of you.

HIGH ROLLERS

CHAPTER 1

MAY, 2011

She hurried down the elegant hotel corridor and stole a fast glance behind her.

The entire hallway was deserted.

Even though she was seventeen-years-old, her opal eyes betrayed a maturity that soared far beyond her age.

Reaching into her white Dior purse, she grabbed her phone, pulled up a number, and hit CALL.

There was only a slight pause before she heard the other line ringing.

"Miami Beach Police, what are you reporting?"

"You've got to help me," she gasped into the phone, trying to keep her voice low. "He's keeping me prisoner here, and he won't let me out."

"Where are you calling from?"

"The Fountainbleu Hotel. Tresor Tower. Room 1208. He's got a gun! He said he's going to shoot anybody who comes through that door!"

"Who's 'he'?"

"My boyfriend," she whimpered. "Frank Dinato. He's a drug dealer. He works for Luca Santinello."

"What's your name?"

"Gina..." Closing her eyes, she started to cry. "He said he's going to kill me. Please..."

The woman's voice was kind, yet assertive. "Gina, I want you to listen to me. I have help on the way, but I need you to stay on the line with me - "

Gina held the audio piece closer to her lips and shouted, "Frank! No!" Then she disconnected the call.

She turned the phone off, placed it back in her purse, took a deep breath, and started down the other end of the hall.

When she reached the door to Room 1208, she inserted a card key into the reader, opened it, and breezed in. "Hi, honey," she greeted the nineteen-year-old guy lying on the bed. He was suntanned, with jet hair, iridescent eyes, and a sexy smile. "Hey, babe." His attention was diverted by the football game he was watching on the large plasma T.V. "I thought you were going to buy a swimsuit."

She held up her purse before setting it down on the bureau. "Would you believe it fits in here?" she joked, laughing softly.

He leered, patting the space on the bed beside him. "C'mere."

Gina slowly approached the bed, gazing at him lovingly. Then she lay, quite naturally, beside him.

He slipped his arm around her. "I'm glad you're here."

"Me, too." Worry creased her porcelain features. Her eyes darted around the room. "I loved Disney World," she simpered.

"Uh-huh," he grunted, eyes still intent on the T.V.

Her voice was shaking. "I hope we can go back there again sometime."

He barely seemed to have heard her. "Yeah, babe."

"Frank," she said sharply. "I have to talk to you about something."

He didn't reply.

She turned away, her face contorted with anguish. "How can you do it...?"

"What's that?" Frank asked, still not looking at her.

Gina kept her own eyes straight ahead, and her voice was deathly calm. "I just want to know how you can push drugs on young kids like that."

He turned on her, his eyes mean, his face twisted with fury. Frank slapped Gina hard across her cheek, causing her to squirm away from him. "Don't ever say that to me. You don't know what yer talkin' about."

Her eyes were filled with fear, but she didn't back down. "Tell me it's not true. Tell me you didn't kill Holly."

He moved closer to her, but she rolled off the bed and stood glaring at him.

"Get back here," he growled.

She shook her head.

He sprang off the bed, grabbing her before she could run and throwing her hard against the wall.

"Frank! No!"

"If you tell anybody – anybody – where I am – you're dead! You understand me?"

She nodded, real tears rolling down her cheeks. Gina began to sob.

"Shut up!" he blazed, shoving her into the wall again. He banged his fist dangerously close to her head. "I'm not kidding, Gina! Don't make me hurt you!"

She stared at him silently, but she was still crying.

A thunderous pounding almost crushed the door to the room. "Open up! Police!"

Gina could see the fire in Frank's eyes. "You called the cops?" he whispered, gripping her by the shoulders and pushing her on the floor.

"No, Frank!" she screamed. "Please!"

The door flew open, and three of Miami Beach's finest burst into the room, guns drawn. "Police! On the floor! On the floor now!"

Frank hesitated only a split second before complying.

They had him handcuffed in seconds, roughly pulling him to his feet.

"Are you okay, ma'am?" one of the men asked Gina.

She nodded, trembling too violently to do anything else.

The officers had just gotten Frank to the door when he turned around and gazed at Gina. He was someone she didn't know. "I swear to God, I'll kill you!"

His eyes didn't leave her face until one of the officers pushed him hard from behind and snarled, "Get him out of here!"

Several hours later, Gina sat in a waiting area at the police station, staring numbly into space. Through an open door, from inside the room behind her, she heard the voices of two male police officers.

"Her name's Gina Moore. New York City. She's the daughter of some rich chick up there."

"She in with this guy?"

"They don't think so. She didn't know where the stuff was stashed or who the source was."

"Funny thing. 9-1-1 was all set to dismiss her call until she mentioned Santinello."

"Oh yeah? They think she was going to lead them to the big man himself?"

"I'd love to see *that, man*."

The first officer lowered his voice. "They contacted the mother. She's on her way down here to get her."

Six weeks later, Gina sat on the living room couch of her mother, Cynthia's, Manhattan penthouse.

Cynthia, an attractive blonde, was on the phone, her voice solemn. "I see. Thank you for calling." She slowly replaced the receiver, her hand shaking. "The warden confirmed it. Frank was...killed last night. By one of the inmates." Cynthia sat heavily beside Gina. "It's over."

Gina shook her head. "I don't think it is."

"Why?"

Gina swallowed hard. "Because I think I might be pregnant."

CHAPTER 2

SEPTEMBER, 2002

Gina's nightmare began when her father died. She had been eight years old and watching T.V. on the living room couch when her mother arrived home, sat down next to her and told her that Daddy wouldn't be coming home again.

It was beyond Gina's comprehension that anybody could take her father away. Daddy was the one person who understood her completely. Without him in the world, she had no world.

Mommy changed, too. Before, Cynthia had always been attentive, fun. Gina's mother was home more often now, but spent less time with her little girl. Most days, Cynthia remained locked in her bedroom while Gina picked at many a lonely dinner.

One memory kept coming back to Gina, although it was vague and blurred. It was the night after her father's funeral. She heard voices in the living room, grown-ups she didn't recognize. Gina quietly opened the door to her room and peered out. Unseen, she crept down the hallway.

Gina heard Cynthia's voice, raised and frantic. "How could you let this happen? You told me they wouldn't get to him!"

A man's deep voice, muffled and indiscernible.

Gina took another step closer.

Cynthia again. "You said that before! I can't believe *anything* you say!"

Gina heard Cynthia break down into sobs, and then the sound of another woman's voice, soft and comforting. Gina felt a chill go through her. Her mother's cries stabbed at Gina's heart. Fearful of being discovered, Gina turned and ran back to her bedroom, diving into bed and pulling the covers high over her head.

Sleep didn't come. Her mother's sobs and her father's soothing voice replayed over and over in her mind.

"Mom?"

Gina was twelve when she came home from school one afternoon and found her mother lying on the living room couch. Cynthia was breathing heavily and dressed in silk pajamas and a robe.

Gina nudged her shoulder.

Cynthia didn't move.

Gina shook her harder.

Cynthia rolled over and snored loudly.

Gina glanced around the penthouse living room and spied two empty liquor bottles on the glass coffee table.

She slowly backed out of the room and retreated into her bedroom.

The next morning, Gina brought Cynthia breakfast in bed – something she never did. Gina carefully entered her mother's room carrying a tray of buttered toast and orange juice.

Cynthia stirred, her head pounding, and sat up just as Gina reached her bed. "What are you doing?" she asked groggily, struggling to focus, her voice barely audible.

"I made this for *you*," Gina said proudly, holding the tray aloft and then gently setting it down on the bedside table.

"Thank you, sweetheart," Cynthia mumbled, reaching for the glass and taking a short sip of juice. She looked out the window, noticing the bright sunlight spilling inside. "Why aren't you at school?"

"It's Saturday." Gina sat on the bed. "I have to talk to you, Mom. I'm really worried about you."

Cynthia attempted a sick laugh. "I'm fine, honey. I had a few drinks last night, but I'm perfectly all right."

"It's not just that. When do you think you'll go back to work?"

Cynthia made no move to touch any of the food. "Work? I haven't made any plans. Actually, I'd like to travel for a while.

What do you say, for your next school vacation, you and me take a trip to Italy?" Cynthia's expression was gleeful.

Gina's was anything but. "I don't want to go to Italy, Mom. I want you to stop doing this to yourself!"

"What are you talking about?"

"You think I don't know what you're doing? You sit around here all the time. You never go out anymore. Last night, you were so wasted, I couldn't wake you up - "

"That is not true!" Cynthia raged, her eyes flashing. "Don't you ever talk that way to me! Ever!"

Gina got up from the bed and took two steps back. "I'm not taking any pleasure in this! I'm saying this because I care!"

"Get out of my room! Right now! And you can stay in *your* room until you start acting right."

Gina started for the door - then spun back around. "If you start drinking again, I'm not staying here."

Cynthia scowled. "And where do you think you're going to go?"

"I'll call Aunt Deidre, and I'll go live with *her*!"

"We'll see about that," Cynthia snarled, throwing the covers off of herself.

Gina marched over to the doorway and stopped again. "I'm glad Dad's not here to see you like this."

"Out!"

Gina darted down the hallway.

Two days later, Cynthia and her younger sister, Deidre, were having lunch at the Red Lobster in Times Square.

"Your daughter has a lot of sense, I think," Deidre said, slowly devouring a shrimp salad.

Cynthia stiffly looked down at her clam chowder.

"I'm not surprised," Deidre went on. "She always was advanced for her age."

Deidre was a younger version of her sister, with pale blonde hair and a flawless complexion.

"I know," Cynthia said softly. "It's not getting any easier. Steve was the only one who understood her. Our waiter is less of a stranger to me."

"What if she's right? Why *don't* you go back to work?"

Cynthia shook her head. "That's the last thing I need right now. Besides, Ryan Driscoll has a handle on everything."

"Then at least get back on the board again. You and Steve *started* that company. You should know what's going on."

Cynthia rejoined Moore Capital Holdings just in time. After meeting with Ryan Driscoll, an attractive red-haired man with a sharp mind for investments, she discovered that the company was losing money. Cynthia quickly petitioned to have herself re-elected to the board, and within a few months, was awarded the position of Chief Compliance Officer and Managing Partner. Cynthia was well liked, and most of the staff had been very helpful.

Gina was relieved to see the change in her mother. The two didn't see each other as often, but when they did, they had long talks and got along better than before. No subject was off limits – with the exception of Steven's death. Gina tried, but she could never get Cynthia to talk about it.

Without Cynthia's knowledge, Gina searched online for everything she could find about her father. One article in the *New York Times* explained everything.

NEW YORK – SEPT. 19, 2002 Steven Moore, founder and CEO of Moore Capital Holdings, was fatally shot yesterday while exiting the Union World Building in midtown Manhattan with Senator David Coulter. Mr. Moore reportedly defended Senator Coulter by pushing him to the ground when the Senator was allegedly fired on by an unknown assailant. Mr. Moore was struck by a bullet to the chest and transported to Riverside Hospital, where he was pronounced dead shortly afterward. The assailant has not yet been found. Manhattan police are still questioning witnesses.

"I'm not going!" Gina insisted.

"Don't give me a hard time," Cynthia retorted irritably. "We've talked about this, and this is the best thing for you."

The two stood facing each other in the living room of the penthouse.

At fifteen, Gina was much more confident and self-assured. "*You* talked about this," Gina fired back. "Since when do you ever ask *me*?"

Cynthia's head was spinning. Was she being punished for something? "Gina. This is about your education, and your future. You just have to trust me that I know what's best for you."

"This is *high school*, Mom! It's important! I don't wanna go to Connecticut!"

"It's one of the best boarding schools in the country."

"It's a prison for stuck-up girls! And no boys!"

Cynthia's lip curled in disgust. She shook her head dismissively as she headed down the hallway. "You don't need to worry about *that*. You're going, and that's all there is to it!"

Gina glared defiantly. *Wanna bet?*

The private girls' school was located in Darien, Connecticut, seemingly in the middle of nowhere. Pristine Colonial buildings situated on acres of green, connected by gleaming white walkways, and surrounded by rolling hills.

"C'mon, honey," Cynthia said excitedly when she and Gina arrived. "This is gonna be great!"

Gina looked around at all the other girls in their starched blue uniforms and frowned. *For you, maybe.*

A week later, Gina was sitting in a history class when the girl behind her pushed her desk into the back of Gina's chair. The first time, Gina ignored it. Their teacher, oblivious at the front of the room, continued talking. The girl did it again – harder. Gina turned and gave her a look, not quite making eye contact. The third time, Gina shot out of her chair and whirled around.

"Do it again!" Gina taunted her belligerently. "Go ahead! Try it!"

The girl pretended to look offended, but Gina stood her ground.

"Ms. Moore!" the teacher commanded. "Take your seat! Right now!"

The girl smiled thinly, triumphantly.

Gina shoved the girl's desk right into the girl's stomach and glared.

"Enough!" the teacher scolded. "You just bought yourself detention."

Gina scowled as she sat back down. *Whatever.*

Gym class was worse. Sports weren't Gina's strong point, but she good-naturedly changed into her gym clothes and joined the other girls in a vigorous game of soccer. It started off fun, but the girls on both teams zeroed in on her quickly. Anytime the ball came anywhere near Gina, it was kicked away from her. For no reason at all, Gina found herself kicked in the shins and knocked over on the field. One of the girls even kicked dirt in her face after she'd fallen. Gina returned to the locker room with murder in her heart, only to find that her locker had been opened and all the buttons from her blouse had been torn off.

She was in her room packing when her roommate from India, Sonaca, came in and stared at her in horror. "Gina! You must not go! You will fall into trouble!" Sonaca immediately crossed the room and started taking Gina's things out of the suitcase. "Quick! Put all this – "

"Sonaca. I know you mean well. But I'm not staying here another damn minute!"

Sonaca's eyes were wide. "You have no choice. They will throw you out. You must study."

Gina took the confiscated articles from Sonaca and tossed them back into the suitcase. "Do you really think anything we learn here is going to help us in the real world? I've had enough. I knew this was a bad idea when I came here."

"Where will you go?" There was real panic in Sonaca's voice.

Gina smiled as she closed the suitcase and zipped it up. "Wherever the hell I want."

Cynthia gripped her cell phone so tightly she almost broke it in half.

"Understand me, Mrs. Moore," said the woman's voice. "This is not a typical occurrence at Briarwood Academy."

"Principal Baker – could you explain to me how you can loose track of one fifteen-year-old girl?"

"Our school is not a prison, Mrs. Moore. The girls are free to make their own choices. However, leaving school grounds without permission is a violation of our policy and will not be tolerated - "

"What happened to make her go?" Cynthia asked suspiciously.

"I haven't the vaguest idea," came Principal Baker's uncaring reply, "But I can assure you, when she returns, she will be severely dealt with. If you remember, in our Code of Ethics - "

"Thank you, Mrs. Baker, I'll take it from here."

Cynthia disconnected and tried Gina's cell phone. Voice mail. Cynthia left a typical mother's message.

"Gina, where the hell are you? So help me, when I find you, I'm going to kill you!"

Gina got as far as a truck stop off the interstate highway before she realized that she'd have to start making plans. Pulling her suitcase behind her, she took a seat at the counter and glanced around the tacky diner. It was early evening, and there were only a few truck drivers in the place.

Upon closer inspection, she also discovered that her funds were getting low. She hadn't made any decisions beyond getting away from that school. Now that she was on her own, the world looked a little more dangerous.

The waitress spotted Gina immediately. In her mid-fifties, Mabel Adler possessed twinkling blue eyes that had seen it all. She approached Gina casually, pad and pen ready to go. "Hiya, honey. What'll it be?"

"I – I really didn't come in to eat. Do you know when the next bus comes through here?"

"All the time. Mostly charters. Where ya headed?"

Gina lowered her eyes, thinking quickly. "Detriot. I'm trying to get to the bus station, but I think I got lost."

"It's about fifteen minutes from here. I can call you a cab if you want."

Gina thought about her short supply of cash. "Yes. Maybe, first, I'll have something to eat."

"You want a menu?"

Gina consulted a list of prices over the grill. "Could I have a cheeseburger?"

"Sure can." Mabel brought Gina a greasy cheeseburger, fries, and a free mug of hot chocolate. When she gave Gina her check, Mabel watched her polish off the last of the fries. "Where ya from?"

Gina panicked. "Right here. Darien. We're moving," she added quickly.

Mabel nodded wisely. "With your folks?"

Gina nodded, staring at her plate.

"That's nice," Mabel said sweetly, clearing the dirty dishes. "Family must be a blessing."

"Don't you have any?" Gina asked curiously.

Mabel shook her head. "Never had the time, honey. Found out a long time ago I was better off on my own."

"You don't have any kids?"

Mabel shrugged. "What would I want with kids? I have everything I need." She was balancing the heavy tray in one hand. "You mark my words, honey – depending on your family is the worst thing you can do." Mabel gently patted Gina's hand. "You're better off by yourself."

Gina watched Mabel disappear into the kitchen, then dug in her purse for some loose bills. When Mabel returned, Gina handed her the check and some money.

"Thanks, darlin'." She consulted the large clock on the corner wall. "Hey, you better be gettin' to the station if yer going to catch that bus."

Gina nodded and slipped off the stool. "Right." She grabbed her suitcase and started out the door. "Thank you."

When Gina was gone, Louie, the head cook, who was at least ten years older than Mabel, stepped out from behind the grill. "Hey, Mabel, your son just called."

Mabel smiled. "Thanks, hon. He's supposed to bring my granddaughter over tonight."

Gina was sitting on the living room couch texting when Cynthia marched into the penthouse and saw her. Cynthia's purse and briefcase slipped out of her hands as she stared, wild-eyed. "Gina!"

"Mom..." Her voice was soft, cowering, her gaze intent. She started to get up from the couch when Cynthia exploded.

"Where the hell have you been?? What did you think you were doing? If you ever do that to me again, I'll break you in half!"

Gina ran to her mother and hugged her – almost too tightly. Cynthia held her tenderly, fighting back tears.

"I'm sorry, Mom...I tried, but those girls are horrible! Please don't make me go back. I'll do anything..."

Cynthia nodded and reached to close the front door, which she'd left open. Then Cynthia cleared her throat, took Gina by the shoulders and looked her full in the face. "Go get washed up for dinner...then you can watch T.V. for a while...but tomorrow we have to get up early..."

Gina's face fell, knowing exactly what her mother meant.

"Kenter High School still has open registration. And it's right here in the borough, so you won't have to leave home..."

CHAPTER 3

It was as if Gina's life had changed from a nightmare into a dream. High school became a wonderful adventure that she enjoyed most days, and she and her mother became even closer, more like friends. Gina had her own circle of friends, which mainly revolved around shopping and similar tastes in music. The girls she was closest to were Shannon Damon and Terry Harmon, whom she'd met before school one morning when she'd hung around the loading dock trying to work up the nerve to talk to a senior boy who wasn't interested. The three girls launched into a discussion about clothes and never looked back.

Shannon, a slender blonde, and Terry, a sturdy brunette, found Gina's personality fascinating. They found her even more fascinating once they learned of her background.

"Steven Moore was your *dad*?" Shannon asked in disbelief.

Gina nodded, her gypsy eyes studying her new friend.

"I'm sorry about what happened," Terry said softly. "I can't imagine what that's like..."

Gina inhaled deeply, feeling both horrified and relieved to be talking about it. "I really don't remember that much. It was eight years ago, and most of it is from what people have told me."

"You remember *him*, though," Terry said. "Right?"

It was as if a weight were being lifted off of Gina. "Some things. Just little things. Good feelings." A smile touched her lips. "He was a terrific dad."

*   *   *

Cynthia still refused to talk about Steven's death, although she did start to mention him more frequently around Gina and telling her more about what he'd been like.

Gina felt strangely close to him, as if a part of him lived inside her.

In fact, it *did*!

It somehow made the relationship Gina had with her mother stronger.

Cynthia continued to do well at Moore Capital Holdings. She had definitely found her calling. Even though Gina had become a blessing, Cynthia's work satisfied a need and kept a small part of Steven close to her.

Once a month, Cynthia and Gina participated in a ritual that consisted of lunch and shopping. It was fall in New York, but the weather was still pleasant, and Gina was excited about starting school again.

"I want to get you some skirts," Cynthia said happily as they sat enjoying lunch in the Olive Garden on Avenue of the Americas. "I saw some in the online catalogue that you'll look great in."

Gina wrinkled her nose and shook her head. "They're really not doing skirts this year. Most of the girls at school are wearing faded jeans."

Cynthia's face fell. Then she brightened. "You could start a trend! You don't always have to be like everybody else."

Gina rolled her eyes and pretended to be very interested in her salad.

"We at least need to get you a dress for your birthday party."

"Mom, that's not until April!"

"You want to wait until the last minute?"

"Fine. If it'll end this conversation, whatever you say."

Cynthia stifled a laugh. *She sounds just like Steve.* "All right. Well, since the party is a formal affair, have you thought about a date?"

"Again – not until April."

"I was just wondering if there's anybody at school that you like."

Gina shrugged. "Not right now."

"What about that boy on the swim team who took you out this summer?"

"Ted Casey? That's over."

"Since when?"

Since I wouldn't go all the way with him. "I just don't like him that way." Gina cagily sipped her Diet Coke. "What about *you*, Ma? You and *Ryan Driscoll* have been spending a lot of time together lately."

Cynthia nearly choked on her soup. "*Ryan*?? Oh, Gina! He and I are just friends."

"Uh-huh," Gina said coyly, unconvinced. "Well, so you say."

"Gina, I mean it. We work together. That's all."

"You're trying awfully hard to convince me, aren't you?"

Cynthia laid her spoon down on her napkin and looked at Gina earnestly. "Honey. You know if I were serious about *any* man, I wouldn't keep it a secret from you."

"I know," Gina said, then, teasing, "But if you keep trying to set me up, you better believe I'm going to return the favor!"

It was a cold February morning in 2011, and Gina was strolling toward the front steps of her high school with Shannon and Terry. All three wore heavy winter coats and carried their books as they strode past the snow banks between the sidewalk and the street.

"I'm meeting Brett in the gym before homeroom," Shannon said matter-of-factly, her exquisite face impassive. "He's taking me to the winter dance."

Terry made a face. "I thought you said he was all body and no brains."

Shannon allowed herself a slight smile. "Maybe that's just what I'm looking for."

Gina couldn't help shaking her head and laughing. "You guys are too much..."

As the girls reached the front steps, they heard the revving of an engine and looked up just in time to see a black Trans-Am careen around the corner.

The car jerked to a stop right in front of the entrance, and a pretty yet overly made-up brunette alighted from the passenger side. Slamming the door behind her, she bounced over to the other side with her books, leaned in the driver's side window and jauntily kissed the guy behind the wheel.

The driver caught Gina's eye immediately and held it prisoner. Black, wavy hair. Iridescent opal eyes. And a confidence that drew every inch of her to him.

"Gina!" Shannon called from the top of the stairs.

She turned.

"You coming?"

Terry and Shannon both looked at her expectantly.

Gina hesitated and took a deep breath. "No, you guys go ahead. I'll see you later."

Her friends understood immediately and smiled secretly.

Shannon swiped her card to let her and Terry in the front door.

The girl who'd gotten out of the Trans-Am turned and waved at the guy in the car before following them inside.

"Carmen!"

Gina jumped when she saw her jet-haired Adonis racing up the steps with a textbook in his hand.

He got to the front door just after it closed, pulling on it hard several times.

"Damn!"

Gina slowly ascended the stairs and called out to him. "You need a keycard to get in."

He turned and looked at her. Really looked at her. And liked what he saw. His face flushed, he quickly calmed down. "This place is like Fort Knox," he said finally, averting his eyes.

Gina was standing right in front of him now. "They should really worry more about keeping people *in*," she said sardonically.

He smiled then – and longer than he would've wanted to.

She smiled too. It was all she could do to keep breathing.

Gina indicated the book in his hand. "I can give that to her...if you want."

He looked at the book and politely handed it to her. "Yeah – sure. Thanks."

"What's your name?" She felt naked under his stare.

"Frank."

"Yeah?" she asked teasingly. "Frank what?"

"What are you, the FBI?" he asked, trying to make light of it.

"No," she said playfully, lowering her eyes demurely. "I just - "

"Or are you Hall Monitor?"

"Please!" she spat, rolling her eyes. "That's not me at all!"

"No," he said slowly. "Didn't think so."

"I'm Gina."

"Yeah? Gina what?"

She couldn't stop smiling. "Wouldn't you like to find out?"

"Maybe later." He started down the steps. "See ya around, Gina."

She watched him get into his car and roar off.

"He actually asked you out!" Terry's eyes and mouth were wide open.

Gina proudly held up her phone, which displayed a new message. "Yes he did! Here's the text he sent me confirming our date for Saturday night."

"What's his number?" Shannon inquired, trying to get a closer look at the screen.

Gina snatched the phone away.

The three girls were riding a city bus to school and huddled in some seats near the back.

Shannon looked at Gina in surprise. "I can't believe you're dating Carmen Esquivel's boyfriend!"

"*Ex*-boyfriend," Gina corrected. "He told me he broke up with her."

"Even so, you better hope she doesn't find out. She beat the crap out of this one girl for just giving her a dirty look!"

Gina shivered, but tried to act cool. "I'm not gonna worry about it," she said quickly, pretending to check her messages. "Besides, it's only one date."

"Where's he taking you?" Terry asked.

"All he said was that we would grab something to eat and hang out."

"That could mean anything," Shannon murmured.

"What are you talking about?"

"Gina," Terry said condescendingly. "Frank Dinato graduated last year. He's dated college girls!"

"I know."

"Do you know what you're going to do Saturday night?" Shannon asked seriously.

"I just told you."

"She means afterward," Terry chimed in. "I've heard he has his own apartment.

"If he asks you back there," said Shannon, "I don't think he's going to be happy with a handshake."

Gina hadn't thought of that. She looked at her two friends, who were genuinely concerned for her welfare, and she feigned a confidence she didn't feel. "Do I look like a preschooler? I wouldn't be going out with him if I couldn't handle it." Half-joking. "And if you think he's going to grab one of you on the rebound, forget it."

Gina didn't dream of telling Cynthia where she was really going that night. "Me and Shannon and Terry are going to catch a movie in midtown," Gina said innocently.

"Okay, honey. Keep your cell phone on."

Gina stifled a laugh. *Only my cell phone?*

She met Frank at a subway entrance a few blocks from Times Square, and together they headed to a nearby Italian restaurant. He looked about the same as the first time she saw him, only he was better dressed and had shaved. She had never met anyone so sexy. It was all Gina could do to remain cool during dinner. Frank seemed to be intimately acquainted with the staff, and she could've sworn his brooding eyes were reading her mind.

"How do you like being out of school?" she asked casually.

"Happier than hell," he smiled, downing a gulp of his Pepsi. "It was like gettin' out of prison."

"Yeah?" She tried to tear her eyes away from him as she rolled some spaghetti onto her fork. "I can't wait till *I* graduate!"

"Yeh?" His intimate smile sent a charge of electricity through her body.

Gina could barely taste her food. "So, you work now, or go to school, what?"

Frank burst out laughing. "I don't believe this! You're interrogatin' me!"

"I am not!" she said defensively, unable to stop herself from blushing. "I'm just asking – a couple normal questions – that's it!"

"Sure you are," he teased, drawing her into his smoldering stare. "You sure you're not doing a report for school?"

Gina felt the happiest she had in years. "I'm sure!"

Frank held her hand as they strolled down 36th Street. Gina floated as if she were on a cloud, and her mind was on automatic pilot while they made idle conversation.

"Wanna see where I live?" He turned to her expectantly.

"Where you live?" she repeated.

"Yeh. I'm over on 68th Street. We can hang out, relax. Whaddaya say?"

"Oh – I don't know. I can't be out too late - "

"I know, Gina. I wasn't plannin' on keepin' ya out all night. I just thought we could go someplace where we could be alone, ya know?"

Her heart seemed to stop as she carefully weighed the decision. "I'd like to – really – I just don't think tonight is a good - "

"It's okay, Gina," he said dismissively. "Don' worry about it. I'll take ya home." He turned in the other direction. "Come on - "

"Wait."

He stopped and looked at her intensely.

Her penetrating gaze laid her soul bare, leaving no mistake as to her intention.

"You said it's not that far, right?" Her voice was breathy, like a wisp.

He grinned broadly and took her gently by the arm. "Naw. A quick cab ride and we're there. Let's go!"

Frank's apartment was a small loft in an older tenement building, with sparse furnishings and a high ceiling.

Frank stood behind Gina as she took in her surroundings. He smiled as he removed his heavy winter jacket. "Make yourself at home."

Frank vanished into the kitchen, while Gina moved over to one of the large windows, which were big enough for someone to actually step through. "I think I can see the East River from here," Gina called.

Frank returned with two cans of beer and offered one to Gina.

"Thanks," she said, accepting it from him and sipping it gingerly. She looked around her. "You are so lucky to have your own place. My mother is driving me crazy! I just want to get the hell out."

"I like being on my own," Frank admitted, swigging from the can. "I need my privacy."

"Yeah?" Gina asked, rubbing the top of her beer can with her index finger. "What for?"

His voice was low. "Lots of things."

"Oh yeah? I'd like to hear about some of 'em."

He moved closer to her. "I'm ready to show you. Whenever you want."

"I'm ready to..."

His warm lips were on hers, crushing her mouth and exploring her essence with a heat that set all of her senses on fire. She struggled to breathe as he pulled her closer to him and undid the top two buttons on her blouse, softly massaging her breasts with the tips of his fingers.

She couldn't stop herself from crying out as his hand moved lower. She pressed herself tightly against him, enjoying the sensations of his tongue lightly caressing her neck.

He smiled, and they both set down their beers.

She allowed him to lead her into his bedroom, where he gently brought her down on the bed and kissed her again, unleashing a reckless passion that climbed higher every second. Her body relaxed, and she opened herself up to him freely and happily.

"Damn it!"

She sat up, startled. Only the light from the living room illuminated the darkened bedroom. "What is it?" she asked meekly, searching his face for a clue.

His voice was controlled. "I wanted to make love to you tonight. I didn't know it was your...time of the month."

She wanted to die. "Oh, God. I'm sorry..."

He shook his head ruefully, shoring himself up. "It's okay."

She placed her hand on his arm. "I want to. Next week, there won't be any problem."

His face clouded over. He turned away from her. "We're obviously not gonna be doin' anything tonight, so...why don't I take ya home?"

"Why?" she asked, a hardened edge to her voice. "I thought you wanted me to spend the night."

He threw her a lilting look. "What for? We can't do nothin'."

"Au contraire, my friend," she corrected. "There's only one thing we can't do. There are a lot of other things we *can* do that you'll like even better...I bet."

"Oh yeah?" he grinned, definitely catching her meaning. "Like what?"

Her eyes sparkled devilishly. "I'll show you..."

Gina's seventeenth birthday party was held in the Empire Room of the Waldorf Astoria Hotel. Cynthia had arranged a lavish party and invited over a hundred of Gina's friends and family. Included was Debbie Monroe, Deidre's daughter and Gina's fourteen-year-old cousin from Newport, Rhode Island, whom Gina hadn't seen since they were kids.

"You look pretty, Deb," Gina smiled, admiring Debbie's long pink gown.

"You, too," Debbie replied shyly.

Gina's dress was white, clingy, and complimented by diamond earrings. Her rich brown hair was swept up with a clip, and her eyes brimmed with excitement.

Frank arrived right after the party started, dressed in a plain brown suit. He immediately noticed the expensive tuxes and evening gowns surrounding him but remained undaunted. He greeted Gina with a big smile, and Cynthia with an awkward handshake.

"So nice to meet you," Cynthia said stiffly, not even attempting to smile.

"How ya doin'?" Frank replied, as if everything were fine.

Gina scarcely left Frank's side all night. To Cynthia's annoyance, Gina ignored most of the adult guests, but introduced Frank to everyone who approached their table. Shannon and

Terry sat with them with their respective dates, fascinated by the edgy, slightly older man Gina was with.

"Do you go to college?" Shannon asked sincerely.

Frank shook his head. "I have my own business. On the net."

"What kind?" Terry asked eagerly.

"Marketing. Different kinds of stuff."

Shannon's face seemed to be glowing. "That's cool."

"Yeh. You know those pop-up ads you see on different sites? I get paid to post those."

"You guys," Gina said, "Do you mind if we *not* spoil this party with boring talk about work?"

Frank looked at her meaningfully. "Okay by *me*, babe."

Immediately after dinner, a huge cake was wheeled out for Gina to blow out the candles, and then the live band launched into energetic rock songs. Even though the lights were low, everyone noticed Gina and Frank suggestively gyrating as they danced. Cynthia, who was respectably dancing with Ryan Driscoll, scowled.

Gina and Shannon were on their way to the ladies room when Cynthia cornered them.

"I need to talk to you," Cynthia said to Gina.

Gina's smile vanished. "What's wrong?"

Gina reluctantly trailed her mother into a corner of the adjacent Vanderbilt Room, which was not currently in use.

"What do you think you're doing out there?" Cynthia demanded. "Are you *trying* to embarrass me?"

"What?" Gina shot back, genuinely not understanding.

"There are important people out there, Gina! People from Moore Capital, our friends – and our family!"

"I knew you'd do this – that tonight would be all about putting on airs and impressing people!"

"Don't you care what other people think about you?"

"No I don't! This was supposed to be *my* birthday party – not a photo opportunity for you and your stuck-up friends!"

Gina started out of the room.

"Where are you going?"

Gina spun around and glared contemptuously at Cynthia. "It's obvious tonight's all about *you*. If you want it – you can have it!" She turned and retreated.

"That's smart!" Cynthia called out venomously. "Just act like a spoiled little girl, that's the right thing to do!"

Debbie was just coming out of the ballroom as Gina stormed past her. "Gina!" she started to say excitedly. "This is so - "

"Not now!"

Gina kept going until she was out the side entrance of the hotel and standing in the pouring rain on Park Avenue. The door opened again seconds later, and Frank found Gina leaning against the wall of the building, sobbing. He gently took her in his arms and held her.

"It's okay," he soothed. "Don' worry about it."

Sick with frustration, Gina managed, "She had to ruin my night...she always does this..."

Realizing the emergency door had locked behind them, Frank put his arm around her shoulders and led her down the street. "C'mon. You can stay with me. We're done here."

Gina didn't get back to the penthouse until two o'clock the next afternoon.

Cynthia was waiting for her. "Where the hell were you??"

"I was with Frank," Gina said quietly, laying her purse down on the table in the entry hall.

"I don't know what's gotten into you, Gina, but it's going to stop right now!"

"What do *you* care?" Gina snapped. "All you're worried about is how everything *looked* to your stupid friends! Half of them, I didn't even know - "

"What about *your* friends? You embarrassed yourself, and me, in front of them, too!"

"We were having a *great* time until you started playing your little game - "

"And then staying out all night and not calling me!"

"I wasn't in the state of mind to *deal* with you last night!"

"Then let's talk about that piece of garbage who showed up as your date! I *never* want to see you with him again!"

Gina smiled spitefully. "You won't."

"I mean it, Gina! Never! And you are grounded until the end of the school year. Don't even *think* about going anywhere."

"Why don't you just lock me in a prison cell?"

"If I could do that, I would! You will never disrespect me like that again, ever!"

"Then buy a monkey and teach it to do all the things I won't. You're through telling me what to do." Gina started down the hallway.

"Don't you walk away from me!"

Gina stopped. "I don't care what you do, because as soon as I'm eighteen, I'm out of here!"

Cynthia's mouth dropped open. "And live on what? Don't come to *me* for money."

"I'd rather live under a bridge than ever live with *you* again."

The following day, Gina spoke to Frank on her cell phone. "She's at work now, so I can talk."

"Maybe we should lay low for a while."

"Are you kidding? I'm not going to give her the satisfaction of controlling my life."

"I just don' want you in any trouble 'cuz of me."

Lying on her bed, Gina glanced around her immaculate bedroom. "This has nothing to do with you. It's all her. I just can't wait to get out of here!"

"I feel ya. I could tell when she first saw me she didn't like me."

"I don't care. What's important is that *I* do." Her voice turned sweet as syrup. "Meet me on Friday night?"

He hesitated. "I thought you were grounded."

"That's what *she* said. I make my own decisions."

"No can do. Remember I told you I was goin' out of town tomorrow?"

Surprise. "You're not still going?"

"I have to. Some friends invited me down to Florida for a coupla days."

"Don't you know that *I* need you?"

"What you need is to stay off your Ma's radar and play the *good* girl for a while."

"I don't think I'd be very convincing. Where in Florida?"

"Er...Orlando. Got some buddies down there."

"Take me with you," she said urgently.

"Oh no you don't. Your ma would hunt me down and kill me. I'll be back next week."

She was silent for a moment, not wanting to show her disappointment. "Okay. She would just give me a hard time, anyway."

"That's my girl."

Gina smiled at the thought of him. "So...your friends putting you up?"

"Naw. Booked myself a hotel room."

"Disney World?"

"Yeah, right! Naw." He sounded as if he were reading it. "The Quality Inn on International Drive."

"Sounds cozy. You'd have more fun with *me* there."

"I'll have more fun if yer waitin' for me when I get back."

"You can count on it."

Gina reluctantly went back to school the next day. The environment was somber, almost dismal. Gina was sure no one in her classes felt as bad as she did.

By lunchtime, the school cafeteria was noisy and crowded. Gina fought her way through jostling students as she carried her tray over to the table she shared with Terry and Shannon.

"What's up, guys?" she asked off-handedly, unenthusiastically removing a straw from its wrapper.

She failed to notice the tight-lipped expressions Terry and Shannon wore.

"I feel like crap today."

"You should," Shannon murmured.

"Don't give me a hard time. I feel bad enough about the other night." Gina looked up, absently popping the straw into a carton of milk.

Neither of the two girls looked at Gina, and their faces were ashen.

Gina stared at them pointedly. "What's going on?"

Terry spoke up first. "You knew Holly Drummerman, right?"

Knew? Gina thought a moment while she started in on her salad. "I have Algebra with her. Why?"

"Well...Holly...died last night."

Gina's eyes widened. "What! How?"

"They think she...OD'ed."

Gina looked at Shannon. For the first time, she realized that neither of her friends had touched their food. "Drugs?"

Terry nodded, clearing her throat. "Coke."

"There's no way!"

"Why not?" Shannon asked gravely.

Gina faultered. "Because...she just doesn't seem like the type to do that, that's all." She laid her fork down. "I can't believe it..." Her lip curled. "I hope they nail the creep who gave her the stuff."

Terry and Shannon exchanged glances.

Shannon's glare was protruding. "You got something you want to tell us?"

Gina's stare was equally intent. "No. Like what?"

Gina watched her friends carefully.

Their expressions gave away nothing.

"Gina..." Terry's voice was strained. "Do you know where Frank is?"

Gina picked up the cookie on her tray and began munching on it. "He's out of town. Florida."

"Figures," Shannon muttered, scowling.

"Do you want to tell me what your problem is?" Gina shot back, her eyes blazing at Shannon.

"Gina..." Terry began.

"What?"

"They think Frank...sold her the stuff."

It took a few seconds for it to sink in. Gina looked at Terry and Shannon like they were strangers. "If that's supposed to be a joke, it's not very funny."

"Do you really think we'd joke about something like this?" Shannon asked coldly.

"Well you guys have your facts wrong, because I know Frank's not a drug dealer."

"Gina, will you use your head? You've been hanging around this guy for three months. What do you really know about him?"

Gina rose from the table, her brain seething. "I know all I need to know."

"Why is he in Florida?" Shannon demanded, attempting to keep her voice down. "Hiding out? Because he knows the cops are after him now?"

Gina shook her head. "I'm not listening to any of this."

"We're just telling you what we heard," Terry said defensively. "We were worried about you."

"Well, don't. I can take care of myself."

Gina turned to go, but Shannon continued, "Gina, if they charge Frank with drug trafficking, they will nail you as an accessory. The cops won't believe you."

Gina took a deep breath, fighting fury. "Then I guess I'll have to prove that you two don't know what you're talking about. I can't believe you'd say this about Frank!"

Other students were beginning to stare, but the three girls didn't care.

"Will you just stay away from him?" Shannon insisted. "Before something happens to you, too?"

Gina's heart was pounding, but her voice was even. "You know what I think? I think you're both jealous – because I have a great boyfriend, and you guys are stuck with these little boys!"

"We're your friends!" Terry said heatedly.

"Not anymore. I'm done with you two bitches!"

Gina stormed out of the cafeteria and headed out of the school.

Cynthia wasn't home when Gina returned to the apartment around 1:30 P.M. Her mind was churning, but she knew what she was doing.

Gina strode purposefully into Cynthia's bedroom, opened the desk, pulled out a black leather wallet, and searched until she found Cynthia's credit cards.

A few hours later, at JFK, Gina accepted an airline ticket from a friendly reservations clerk. "You're all set, Ms. Moore. Your flight to Orlando leaves in two hours."

CHAPTER 4

Gina knocked on the door to the hotel room several times.

"Yeah?" he called warily.

"Room service," she replied cheerily.

"No, thanks," he called back gruffly.

Gina knocked on the door again. "C'mon, Frank."

Frank Dinato cautiously opened the door and stared at her open-mouthed. "Gina! What the hell are you doin'?" He took a quick look around, pulled her inside and shut the door. "Just what the hell do you think you're doin'?"

Her eyes were full of questions. "I thought you'd be glad to see me."

"What!" Recovering, he reluctantly touched her shoulders. "I mean – yeah, I am glad to see ya, you just...took me by surprise, ya know?"

"That's the whole idea," she smiled, inspecting the room. "One bed? That's a good start."

"So...uh...why *are* you here?"

She set her purse and small suitcase down on the bed. "I decided I needed a break, and that my mother should pay for it."

He inched toward her. "You shouldn't be here."

"Why? It's okay, isn't it?"

His eyes were clouded. "It's dangerous...I mean – does anybody know you're here?"

She happily shook her head. "Just you." Gina threw her arms around him and held him tight. "I just really needed to see you, Frank..."

"We're together *now*," he said softly, rocking her in his embrace.

      *   *   *

Later, they sat up in bed watching T.V. and eating popcorn.

Frank was bare-chested and watching the screen intently.

Gina wore a white silk slip and sat curled up next to him.

"I'm sick of this Griffith guy on *Right On*," Frank was saying, referring to the popular one-hour drama on the CW he was watching. "The guy can't act. Hear more about the Lamborghini he drives than the show."

Gina brightened. "*You* should drive a Lamborghini."

"Someday, babe. Someday."

She glanced around the room. "Is the a/c on? I didn't know Orlando was so hot!"

Frank nodded, eyes still on the screen. "Tell me about it. I'm supposed to meet some buddies tomorrow. We're goin' down to Kissimmee."

"I can't wait!"

Frank hesitated. "It's...kind of a 'guys only' thing."

Gina pouted.

"But I'm all yours at night."

She lightly massaged his chest. "I'm glad to hear *that!*"

The next morning, Frank found Gina out by the Quality Inn's pool. She was lying on a lounge chair and reading a brochure.

"Why didn't you wake me up?" he asked.

"I couldn't," she smiled, squinting up at him. "You looked so cute."

They kissed, and he sat facing her on the lounge.

Gina began, "There's someplace I've wanted to go since I was a little girl..."

He groaned. "I know where this is leading..."

"Can we go, Frank...? Please...? Take me to Disney World...?"

He gazed at her thoughtfully. "Okay. But it can't be tomorrow..."

"The day after?"

He fidgeted, not looking at her. "Yeh. Okay."

She hugged him. "I'm so happy! This is going to be the best week of our lives!"

Frank looked over Gina's shoulder.

A young dark-haired man in a tank top was glaring at them.

The man answered the door to the upscale high-rise apartment. Frank stood outside holding a small cardboard box. His eyes darted everywhere as he stepped inside and handed the man the box. "Here's your package."

The man closed the door and sneered. "I should kick your ass."

"She's nobody. Don' worry about it - "

"I *am* worried!" The man was only two years older than Frank but sounded light years wiser. "This isn't play time, this is business!"

"I know. I know, Joe. She's already gone."

Joe appeared to relax – somewhat. "She better be." He placed the box in a cupboard and secured it. "The next pick up is in Miami. I need you there the day after tomorrow."

Frank's face gave away nothing. "No problem."

"And whatever you do, don't be late. This guy doesn't like to be kept waiting."

The Walt Disney World Magic Kingdom was crowded with tourists and kids young and old. Gina and Frank took the elevated monorail across the man-made Seven Seas Lagoon to the main entrance. They rode Space Mountain, Splash Mountain, and even the Haunted Mansion.

The two strolled in front of the spectacular Cinderella Castle holding hands and admiring the botanical beauty surrounding them.

Frank laughed. "You're like a kid again! You sure you're old enough to drive?"

Gina threw him a look. "I will *try* to forget you said that."

Frank stared pensively down Main Street, U.S.A. "I'm glad ya showed up here. I really needed ya."

Gina beamed, then turned serious. "You were the only one I could talk to."

They shared an intimate look. Then they stopped and held each other.

"This place is so beautiful," Gina said wistfully. "I wish we could stay here forever..."

*   *   *

Back in their hotel room, Frank, his back to Gina, was packing his suitcase, when he stopped and said, "I gotta go to Miami tomorrow."

Gina, lying on the bed checking her text messages, looked up, her eyes wide. "What? Why?"

He shrugged, trying to make his voice sound casual. "Gotta see some friends. I'm on vacation, remember?"

Gina made her own attempt at casual. "How come you didn't ask me to fly down here with you?"

Frank's smile was genuine as he turned to her. "You're supposed to be in school. I kinda didn't want you to get in any trouble. So you should go back."

"But we're having such a great time!"

"Your mom and your school are looking for you. And you're a minor, so if they catch up with me, *I'm* in the big house."

"I have to lay low myself. If my mom doesn't cool off before I go back, it'll be even worse." She stood, running her hands down his chest. "Please...I want to go to Miami...I've never been there before..."

"Gina...you're makin' this really hard..."

She moved her hands lower. "Oh, I haven't even *started* yet..."

He took her face in his hands and kissed her, pushing her down on the bed and climbing on top of her. She surrendered fully, giving herself up to his fiery heat and well-toned body. She felt her clothes slipping off her, his hands everywhere, his tongue trailing down her neck.

"Do ya want me to do it?" he gasped, moving back and forth on top of her. "Do ya want me to stop?"

"No!" she managed, arching her back, her eyes tightly shut. "Do it...please, Frank...please..."

His movements intensified as their bodies intertwined. She resisted at first, holding back just enough, then welcoming him – fiercely and completely. Frank's rhythm increased. Gina responded powerfully, moving her body with his, drinking in every inch of him. A fire burned deep within her. Then there was a sharp pain. It grew stronger as Frank pushed harder, and Gina froze.

She lay there, weakly, but Frank didn't stop. He moved faster, more forcefully, until he broke through her barrier and she felt him filling her completely.

She cried out loudly, flushed at the sounds of her own screams, and found she couldn't stop. She joined Frank as he took her higher and farther, thrashing mercilessly into her until he couldn't stop himself from finishing.

Every sense shattered, Gina laid beside to Frank, breathing heavily, her face glowing.

He looked at her, sliding his arm around her waist. "All this time...you were waiting for me?"

Her eyes widened as they met his. "What do you mean?"

"I just figured you had some experience..."

She lay staring up at the ceiling. "Well I *do*. There are just certain things...I never..."

They kissed, melting into one another.

Gina murmured, "I was wrong about you..."

"What?" he asked casually.

She hugged him tightly. "Nothing. Nothing at all."

Miami was hot in more ways than one. The beaches of the Gold Coast were besieged with muscled, oiled bodies, young and old, and the hotels behind the warm sands, gleaming in the sunlight, were flooded with wealthy tourists.

Gina smiled as she lay next to Frank on a beach towel, her eyes shaded by dark mahogany sunglasses. The black bikini she wore left little to the imagination, but her great curves allowed her to carry it off – and keep it on.

Frank wore dark sunglasses also, and when he spoke, his voice was grave. "I gotta get back to the room."

Gina nodded absently as she watched two young men in Speedos carrying surfboards. "What time do you meet your friends?"

Frank was looking behind him. "Four o'clock."

"And I suppose it's one of those deals where it's 'guys only.'"

"You're supposed to be keeping a low profile, remember?"

"What has *that* got to do with it? I don't see why I can't meet your friends."

"Only *one of* 'em is my buddy, and they're a little older. I think you might feel out of place."

"You're not *that* much older than me," Gina pointed out, not looking at him.

He lightly touched her shoulder. "Gina...I'm sorry. But it's not like I knew you was gonna be here."

She still didn't look at him.

He forced a note of pleasantness into his voice. "I won't be gone long. And as soon as I get back, we'll go eat. Okay?"

He fingered her chin, turning her face toward his. "Okay??"

She couldn't help smiling, even giggling. "Okay. But stop tickling me!"

He played along. "Oh, yeah. I'm gonna tickle ya!" His hands roamed up and down her body, until she yelled uncontrollably. "Ya like that? Huh?"

"No! Frank! Stop it! I mean it!"

"That's not what ya said last night!"

No one took any notice as she continued to shriek.

The limousine stopped in front of a wrought iron gate leading to an impressive sun-drenched mansion. Frank sat in the car between two swarthy men, staring straight ahead and saying nothing.

The gate opened slowly, and the limo sped up the long driveway to the house.

Frank was led into a room that looked like a small library, where two older men were seated behind a long table. They glared at him as one of the other men closed the door and, along with his partner, stood on one side of Frank.

Frank looked at the two young men on either side of him, then at the men at the table. "What's goin' on?"

"Who's the girl?" one of them asked unpleasantly. "You were told to come alone."

"I did," Frank said quickly. "I mean, she didn't come with me. She followed me here. She's my girlfriend."

"What the hell do you think this is?" the other man at the table demanded. "A vacation?"

"How do we know she's not a cop?" the other asked. "Or a reporter?"

"She's not," Frank said hoarsely. "She's in *high school.* She's a rich chick from Manhattan. She thinks I'm on a vacation. She followed me here to get away from school."

"Mr. Santinello's not gonna like this," the older of the two men stated darkly. "The cops could be lookin' for her right now."

"And she's a minor," the other added. "This whole thing could blow up."

"It won't," Frank said, waving his hands emphatically. "We drove down here from Orlando, so no one knows where she is. That's why I didn't send her away, so she couldn't tell no one."

"You dumbass," the older man growled. "How do you know she's not callin' the cops right now?"

"'Cuz she'd be in a lot more trouble if she did."

The other man shook his head. "We can't let you take that shipment."

"Please!" Frank pleaded. "I can do it! I can't go back without it! Just let me handle it. It'll get there, I guarantee it."

The two men stared a few moments. Then the younger pulled a midsize traveling case from under his chair and opened it on the table. Inside were several white cellophane bags filled with cocaine. "This is the Grade A stuff. We just got it in from Havana. Your boys'll know how to refine it. You just have to move it."

"No problem," Frank smiled, moving closer to inspect it. "No problem at all."

Gina and Frank entered their room at the Fontainbleu together, and Frank immediately flopped on the bed.

"Long day, honey?" Gina teased gently.

"That was a hell of a meal!" Frank groaned lazily. "I'm done eatin' for the week!"

Gina lay her purse on a nearby bureau and studied Frank through the large wall mirror. "Frank? Do you know Holly Drummerman?"

Frank lay on his stomach, barely moving. "Who?" he mumbled.

Gina moved closer to the bed. "Holly Drummerman. She's...a friend of mine."

He sat up, concentrating for a moment. Then he shook his head. "Doesn't ring a bell. Why?"

"*She* knows *you*."

"From where?"

"She said she met you a few times," Gina said lightly, turning and starting for the window. "At some girl's party."

"'Some girl's'?"

Gina looked at Frank again and shrugged, carefully watching his reaction. "I'm just telling you what she said. *I* wasn't there."

"I wasn't, neither." Frank grabbed the remote and clicked on the T.V.

Smiling, Gina grabbed her purse and started for the door. "I'm going to go down to the gift shop."

"What for?" Frank asked, alarmed.

"I saw a swim suit that I'd like to buy," Gina replied, keeping her voice casual. "It's a two-piece," she continued sexily. "I think you'll like it."

"Don't be gone long. We gotta get packed tonight."

"I won't," she said breezily, heading out.

No sooner had the door to the room closed behind her, she stopped and turned around again. "Duh. Credit card."

She pulled out her passkey and had just opened the door when she heard Frank's cell phone go off and him answer it. "Naw...the shipment's all ready to go...What...! Holly Drummerman...! I don't believe it...how could she OD...?? I sold her the best stuff... Naw, they ain't gonna find me...and you tell Luca Santinello he'll get his money..."

Gina turned white, slowly backing into the hallway and letting the door close as quietly as she could. She stood there for a moment, looking as if she were going to be sick. Then she turned and ran down the corridor.

CHAPTER 5

Cynthia sank onto her living room couch next to Gina. "What do you mean you think you might be pregnant?"

"That's what the test says."

"What test?" Cynthia asked in disbelief.

"It's in my room, Mom," Gina spat, on the verge of tears. "Do you want me to go and get it?"

Cynthia took an uneasy breath and held Gina close. "We'll see Doctor Jennings in the morning. Just to be sure it's true."

"And if it is?"

"Well...then we'll deal with this, honey...whatever you want to do, I'm behind you."

"I can't get rid of it, Mom," Gina said quietly. "It's not about Frank. This is a part of me."

Cynthia took her hand. "Then we'll handle it together. Whatever else happens, you're not alone."

Gina hesitantly touched her stomach. "I know..."

Several months later, Cynthia was awakened by an insistent knock at her bedroom door.

"Mom?" Gina called from the other side. "Mom, I need you! Can you come out here?"

Cynthia's eyes flew open and she jumped out of bed, raced to the door and opened it.

Gina stood in the hallway, clutching her slightly protruding stomach in distress. "I think it's coming!"

"Are you sure?" Cynthia asked, starting to shake.

Gina doubled over and moaned loudly.

Cynthia gently took Gina by the arm and guided her into the living room. "It's time! Come on! We've got to get a cab!"

*   *   *

Gina couldn't stop the tears from flowing as she was wheeled into the Emergency Room. She barely heard the man and woman on either side of the gurney as she stared helplessly up at the ceiling.

"What have we got?"

"Eighteen-year-old female. Premature labor. BP rising."

"Contractions?"

"Seven minutes apart."

A bright light blinded her, and she could hear a woman's soothing voice.

"Gina...just stay calm and try not to move, okay?"

"My baby - "

"You're going to be just fine, but I need you to stay still."

Gina's cries subsided as the doctor and nurses hovered.

"Patient status?"

"Vitals are dropping..."

Gina drifted into unconsciousness while the team continued to work.

Gina's eyes opened gradually. She was in a private room with sterile white walls and austere furnishings. It took her a few moments to realize Cynthia was sitting at her bedside. The color returned to her mother's face as Cynthia rose and stood over her. "How are you feeling?" Cynthia asked, her voice strained.

It was an effort for Gina to speak. "What happened?"

"The doctors...they said you're going to be fine..."

Gina's eyes searched her mother's. "My baby...where is my baby...?"

Cynthia fought to remain in control.

"No...!!"

It was like a dark cloud had descended on Gina's life. She barely passed her sophomore year and had lost the baby right after Thanksgiving.

"I'm very sorry, Ms. Moore. The baby was born stillborn. We did everything we could."

Going back to school in January, 2012, she tried focusing on her school work to escape the pain. At various times throughout the day, she would start to cry for no reason. Terry and Shannon saw Gina through her worst days, and a lot of long talks at lunch and after school were her only solace. Gina found it hard even talking to her mother about the demons that tortured her.

That summer, Debbie came to stay with Gina and Cynthia at the penthouse. At first, Gina was uncomfortable with her younger cousin's presence. Neither Gina nor Cynthia made a habit of long-term guests intruding in their private world. Debbie's sweet personality and caring disposition won them both over, and by the fall, Gina didn't want Debbie to leave.

Gina was, however, feeling better about her senior year, which was just about to start. Debbie, who was entering her sophomore year in the private school she attended in Rhode Island, was less than enthusiastic.

"I'm the only one of my friends who doesn't have a boyfriend," she confided to Gina.

"Now it's a *requirement*?" Gina asked sarcastically, thinking her cousin's worrying was beyond unnecessary. "You make it sound like it's something you need for school."

"In a way, it is!" Debbie looked forlorn. "How is it going to look that all my friends have boyfriends, and no boy is interested in *me*?"

Gina understood, but was unsympathetic. "If you keep talking like *that,* no boy ever *will* be. It'll happen. Most likely when you're not looking for it. I'm sure there's a guy out there for you somewhere. Probably several." Gina's face fell. "You couldn't do any worse than me."

Debbie's voice was soft. "What about you? Are you interested in anybody these days?"

Gina rose from her bed and paced her room restlessly. "I can't even think about that. That's the farthest thing from my mind."

"It'll happen again someday."

Gina stared out the window, her back to Debbie. "I can wait. Believe me."

Gina did better in her classes during her last year of high school. Terry and Shannon relentlessly tried to fix her up, but the more of an effort they made, the more Gina resisted. Since everyone at school knew about her involvement with Frank and her subsequent pregnancy, her reputation was mixed, depending on who was telling the story. The boys who were worthy of her attention steered clear, and the ones who wanted her were too eager for the wrong reasons.

Gina's predicament changed when Shannon invited her and Terry to a bar and grill near the Merrick University campus on Long Island. It was a sports bar filled with great-looking college guys and their sexy female counterparts.

Gina surveyed the room critically, as if she were performing a professional assessment. "There's definitely a good selection here tonight."

"Better than what we get in school," Shannon agreed.

Terry grinned. "You guys make it sound like you're looking over a buffet!"

"That's right," Gina said. "And if it's good, we'll go back for more."

An athletic-looking guy in tight jeans and a polo shirt asked Gina to play darts. She spent over two hours with Jimmy, throwing darts and sipping beers, until he casually asked her if she wanted to hang out in his dorm room.

"Who else is there?" she asked cautiously.

"Nobody," he replied smoothly. "Got it all to myself."

Gina smiled mischievously. "Okay."

Terry and Shannon watched in stunned amazement as Gina waved to them as she left with Jimmy.

Still naked, Jimmy sat up in bed and stared. "That was awesome! Where did you learn that?"

Gina almost laughed as she finished getting dressed. "Public television."

He looked at her cheerfully. "You sure you don't wanna spend the night? I've got room."

Gina shook her head. "I live with my mom. And I don't need her to give me a bad time."

"Can I call you?"

Gina grabbed her purse off of the bureau, and as gently as possible, said, "I'm kind of seeing somebody. But thanks."

He followed her to the door and forlornly watched her leave.

*   *   *

The next one was a shy and studious guy named Brandon. Gina met him in the university library while doing research for a term paper. She accompanied him back to a room he was renting in a house off campus and quietly initiated him into the joys of physical stimulation. Gina was gone before he could mention anything about getting together in the future.

Her next conquest was a male sales associate in his early twenties who worked in a midtown department store. She flirted with him as she sauntered through the men's department, then returned to the store just before closing. He met her outside after everything was closed up and invited her back inside.

The huge store was faintly illuminated with minimal lighting and appeared to be deserted. He took her hand as he led her into the fitting room area.

This guy's the dumbest one yet. For all he knows, I could have a gun in my purse.

He had no problem getting completely naked, even in such an austere setting. She made sure he enjoyed every minute, but didn't allow him to stop until he'd given back at least as much.

Gina never returned to that particular store – despite the great service she'd received.

2013 started out gloriously. The girls went on a fun ski trip to Vermont in February, and then took a trip to Orlando for spring break. This time, they took Debbie Monroe with them, who was a lot more fun to be with since she'd turned sixteen.

It was a little strange for Gina being back in Disney World and the places where her troubles with Frank had occurred, but having her friends around her helped her bury the memories deep enough. While the four girls were in Orlando, Debbie brought them to meet Lisa McClure, a painfully thin, shaggy-haired brunette whose occupation was head groupie for Steve Riken, the lead singer for X-Rated Run, a wildly successful heavy metal group. Steve, Lisa, and the rest of the guys in the group were staying at a huge house in a gated community in Bay Hill while on break from their national tour. The house was large enough to accommodate the four girls with two guest rooms of

their own. After they'd talked with Lisa and briefly met Steve
Riken and his group, Terry and Shannon brought their suitcases
upstairs, unpacked, and wandered into Gina and Debbie's room.

"Are you guys ready to party?" Terry grinned, excitedly
throwing herself across the bed.

"Make yourself at home, Ter," Gina said dryly.

Terry stretched lazily. "I wish this *was* my home."

"She's turning into a metal head on us," Shannon joked.

Gina thoughtfully folded a skimpy blouse and slipped it
into a bureau drawer. "You guys. I was thinking tomorrow, we
could go to Daytona Beach. Maybe stay overnight."

"Another hotel?" Shannon groaned. "We just got here."

"Yeah, Gina," Debbie agreed. "Lisa said we could stay as
long as we like."

"I know," Gina said, purposely keeping her voice down,
"But I don't want to impose on this guy any more than we have
to."

Shannon looked at her in disbelief. "I honestly don't think
he cares. He's been stoned since we got here."

Terry motioned toward the window. "The guys and their
girlfriends are in the pool *now*. They didn't have any swimsuits
on."

"What are we waiting for?" Gina shuddered.

"You're not the least bit interested?" Shannon demanded.

Gina grimaced and shook her head. "Skinny, long-haired
guys aren't really what I go for."

Terry sat up eagerly. "That means you're looking again?
What *are* you going for?"

Gina thought about it. "Maybe a blond. How about a
Swedish guy?"

"Seriously?"

"Yeah. Only he's gotta know how to yodel!"

Daytona Beach was hot. Gina drove the other girls in the
car she'd rented at the airport and took I-4 East until they were
almost at the water's edge. It was unlike any beach any of them
had ever been to before. The sand was pure and powdery, without
so much as a pebble or an ounce of seaweed anywhere.

Gina, Debbie, Terry, and Shannon spread some towels
over the sand, lay in the sun for a while, then wandered into the
cool, clear water. Gina returned to the beach first, spreading some

suntan lotion over herself and lying back down on the towel. She lay there, contemplating her life and her future, when she looked up and saw a tall, bronzed god coming out of the ocean and carrying a surfboard. He had dark hair, a smooth body, and returned her prurient gaze with a smile.

Naked, he moved on top of her on the soft bed in the air-conditioned hotel room. He kissed her hungrily, his hands roaming all over her body. Although he was moving a little too fast for her tastes, she was enjoying the intense heat of his attention.

He was just moving into position when she stopped him. "Wait a second. Where's your protection?"

He'd barely heard her. "We don't need it. It's okay." He lowered his head and pressed more tightly against her.

"Hold it." She pushed him away, and he stopped. "We're gonna do this right, or not at all, okay?"

He looked at her in bewilderment. "Okay."

"Hand me my purse?"

"Why?"

She looked at him expectantly.

He reluctantly climbed out of bed, grabbed Gina's purse off of the bedside table and gave it to her.

She opened it, fished inside, and pulled out a wrapped condom. "I take it you know how to use this."

He looked less than thrilled. "Do we have to?"

Her expression said it all.

He nodded resignedly and took the condom from her. "Okay."

Her smile was filled with satisfaction. "Good. Let's rock and roll!"

Gina and Debbie sat side by side in their first class seats on the flight back to New York.

"What are your plans for the summer?"

The question caught Gina off guard. "I haven't made any, really."

"Why don't you come to Rhode Island?" Debbie suggested excitedly. "Newport is awesome in the summer!"

"Sure, Deb," Gina said unsurely. "It sounds great."

"Why not?" Debbie smiled, opening a packet of peanuts. "You owe yourself some fun before you start college."

Gina looked over at the seats across from them. Shannon and Terry were both sound asleep. "That's the thing, Deb. I'm not going to college."

Debbie was genuinely surprised. "What!"

"At least, not right now. I'm gonna take some time off for a while."

"What are you going to do?"

"I haven't decided yet. But whatever it is, it's going to be exactly what I want and not something my mother forces me to do."

Debbie nodded, her mouth full of peanuts. "I know what you mean." She took a sip of her ginger ale. "You know, Lisa asked me if I had a boyfriend yet."

Gina laughed. "Yeah! From someone who has one every hour..."

"I was tempted to lie. She doesn't rub it in my face or anything, but it still would've been nice to say something other than the usual 'not yet.'"

"Come on, Deb," Gina said comfortingly. "It'll happen."

"Who am I kidding? No guy's gonna ask me out. I mean, if it was meant to be, it would've happened by now. Right?"

Gina sighed wearily. "Is there anybody that you like?"

Debbie blushed. "Sort of."

"Why don't you ask *him* out?"

"He would only say no."

"I can't win with you." Gina looked up and noticed a sexy Hispanic guy on his way to the lavatory. "You see that, Deb? *That's* my type."

Debbie nodded in understanding.

"Oh, yeah," Gina said hungrily, as if she were selecting an item in a store. "I'll take one of those home. Wrap him up!" A wicked grin. "I'll *unwrap* him myself."

Gina went to her senior prom with Antonio Ramirez, a boy from her school. Terry and Shannon, along with *their* dates, took one of Gina's limos to the Marriott Marquis Hotel in Times Square, where Kenter High School's prom was being held in the Broadway Ballroom.

Once inside, the girls greeted their other friends, had a soda at the bar, and then sat down to dinner. Antonio didn't say much as they ate, but Gina sat listening as Terry Harmon and Lori Mancini talked excitedly.

"Have you been accepted anywhere yet?" Terry was asking.

"Warner College," Lori replied happily. "I'm starting their nursing program in August. You?"

"N.Y.U. I think I wanna major in psychology."

"You ready for graduation?" Antonio asked.

"Huh?" Gina looked at him blankly.

He barely noticed she hadn't been paying attention. "I can't wait to get the hell out."

Gina took a sip of her water. "What are your plans?"

"This summer? I'm gonna work in my uncle's garage."

"You good with cars?"

He shrugged. "Sorta."

Servers were starting to come around to the tables with food trays.

"What about the fall?" Gina pressed.

His eyes seemed to sparkle. "City College."

The D.J. started up immediately after dinner, and the soon-to-be former seniors of Kenter High hit the dance floor. Fast, upbeat rhythms that melted into hypnotic romantic ballads as the lights grew softer. The dance floor seemed to be bathed in blue as Gina clung to Antonio, letting the song wrap her in warm feelings. A smile touched her lips as she glanced over his shoulder, and then her eyes flew open wide.

He was standing in the entryway to the ballroom looking more handsome than she'd ever seen him and dressed in the same brown suit that he'd worn to her birthday party. His stare appeared mixed with hurt and anger, and the longing in his eyes sent shivers through her soul. "Frank..."

"Huh?" Antonio questioned, trying to read her face.

Two couples obliviously danced in front of Gina, blocking her view of the entrance.

"What happened?" Concern filled Antonio's voice, and he didn't let go of her.

"I..." Gina could see the entryway now. There was no sign of Frank. "Nothing."

*   *   *

"Will you tell her how ridiculous she's being?" Terry tried to keep her voice down, even though they were the only ones in the ladies room.

Shannon stared at Gina intently, worry creasing her perfect features.

"I know it sounds crazy," Gina said calmly, "But I could've sworn I saw Frank."

"Gina..." Shannon murmured. "He's dead..."

"I know. I know that. I've just been thinking about him so much lately. I've tried not to."

Terry placed a comforting arm around Gina's shoulder. "Of course. All those songs just stirred up some memories, that's all."

"Are you going to be okay?" Shannon asked sympathetically.

Gina nodded, clearing her throat. "I think I just need a soda or something."

"That's a good idea," Terry agreed, starting for the door.

Shannon handed Gina back her purse. "If you're sure you're all right, you better get back out there before Antonio thinks there's something wrong."

"There isn't," Gina assured her. "It was just my mind playing tricks on me. I'm all right."

Gina sat watching Antonio dance with Maria Diaz, a friend he'd known since fourth grade.

Terry and her date, Doug Holloway, returned to their table after several dances in a row. "You checking out on us?" Terry asked Gina jokingly.

A smile lit Gina's striking face as she indicated Antonio and Maria. "They've been buds forever. Besides, she likes girls. It's not like she's going to steal him away."

"You wanna dance, Gina?" Doug asked politely.

"Maybe later. Right now, I just want to chill."

Antonio returned to the table a few minutes later coated with sweat. "I need a breather. You wanna go take a walk, Gina?"

"Definitely."

*   *   *

The balcony wrapped around almost the entire ballroom. Gina and Antonio gazed at the enormous jumbo video screens against the buildings that lit up Broadway brighter than the sun. As they stood at the edge, Gina looked up into the night sky and then down at the taxis on the street far below.

"You having a good time?" Antonio couldn't stop himself from asking.

"Of course," she replied, wishing she could reassure him more.

"I wasn't sure. You looked like you were zoning out before."

"I was just thinking about graduation. Nothing's going to be the same again."

"Yeah, but it's gonna get better. It's not the end. It's just the beginning!"

"I know. I just don't want things to change..."

He put his arm around her and held her. "C'mon, Gina. Don't stress about it. It's gonna be an awesome summer! Don't mess it up before it starts."

She was still staring out over the city. "It's not the summer I'm worried about. It's afterward."

"So what do you wanna do? Plan out the rest of your life?"

Gina burst out laughing. "No! That's more my *mother's* style."

"So you *wanna* be like your mother?" He was grinning.

She faced him, a gust of wind rippling through her hair. "You're right. Tonight's gonna be the most amazing night of our lives. Let's make the most of it!"

Couples started leaving after midnight.

Jared Cook, Shannon's date, asked, "Did you guys get it?"

"Gina took care of it," Shannon responded softly, absently searching through her purse.

The six of them left together. Only instead of departing out the main exit with everybody else, Gina and her friends took one of the glass elevators up to a suite Gina had reserved near the top floor. The view was staggering and the suite luxurious. Each of the girls giggled excitedly as they all piled inside and took in their surroundings.

"I wanna order room service!" Terry chirped. "Champagne for everybody!"

Gina rolled her eyes. "On my tab, of course."

The boys shed their ties and jackets, and everyone got comfortable.

Terry kicked off her very uncomfortable high heels. "You guys, I can't believe we're actually going to be graduating next week."

Jared had unbuttoned most of the buttons on his white tuxedo shirt. "Worst four years I ever spent."

"I had a great time!" Terry blurted, her voice rising an octave above the others. Off their condescending looks, she insisted, "I did!"

After a while, Gina wandered out onto the balcony.

Antonio followed. "You okay?"

"I'm fine. I just needed some air."

"So...did you want me to go...soon...or...?"

"What are you talking about?" She caught the expectant look in his eye, and smiled. "Check out is at noon. You guys can stay as long as you like."

He visibly relaxed. "Great! I was thinking, it would be fun...to hang out."

Gina took his hand and led him back inside. "Yeah. We can hang out."

Gina awoke by herself the next morning. For a moment, she was disoriented, the sound of distant car horns and people shouting drifting into her subconscious. Then she sat up in the large bed and looked around. The lights in the master bedroom were off, and it looked as though she were completely alone.

Gina stepped out into the living room. Shannon sat on the couch texting, and looked up as her friend entered.

"What happened?" Gina asked groggily.

Shannon continued her texting. "Terry and Doug left last night, and the boys left a few hours ago. I didn't want to leave you here by yourself."

Gina sat down, collecting her thoughts. "Why didn't you tell me?"

"I didn't want to wake you up."

"What time is it?"

"Almost eleven."

Gina shook her head in disbelief. "Figures everybody would cut out."

Shannon smiled. "Antonio said he'd call you later. He's dropping by the school to pick up his cap and gown."

Gina nodded slowly. "This is it, isn't it?"

Shannon stopped her texting. "We knew the day would come."

"It doesn't mean we're ready for it."

"But what you're forgetting is that things are going to change for the *better*. We've got the rest of our lives. There's a great big world out there."

Gina's voice was strained. "I know. I just hate to say goodbye."

"Then don't. We're only going off to college, not off to war."

"You're right." Gina looked at her earnestly. "Do you think life will always be this good?"

"You haven't been listening." Shannon hugged her. "*Better*."

Gina's graduation day was emotional. First, she and Cynthia took forever getting ready, so she was running late to start. Then she couldn't find the tassel that went with her cap, so she spent a half hour looking for it. Cynthia came into Gina's bedroom carrying a similar tassel that was over twenty years old. "This was mine," Cynthia explained.

Gina shook her head. "That one's black and white, Mom. Mine is black and *orange*. It won't match."

Gina was just on the verge of using Cynthia's when she finally found hers on the floor of her bedroom closet.

The ceremony was held in Kenter High's auditorium, where over a thousand people were in attendance. As Gina and her identically dressed classmates marched inside to *Pomp and Circumstance*, Gina realized that this was the last time they would all be together as a class. When the march finally ended, everyone took their seats.

There were speeches from the principal, the senior class president, and the valedictorian. During the speeches, Gina texted several of her friends confirming their attendance at her graduation party the following evening. Before the diplomas were handed out, she even managed to hook one of her girlfriends up with a guy who was also coming to the party, whom the girl was too shy to ask out.

Gina hated to throw her cap up in the air with everyone else, but she realized that it was tradition. It was a life she didn't want to say goodbye to, wasn't ready to say goodbye to. High school was past her. The future excited and terrified her. She really didn't know what she wanted her life to be.

Gina had two graduation parties – one at the penthouse for all her friends on Saturday, and the other in the ballroom of the Plaza for all of her family and mother's friends on Sunday. Debbie and Deidre were in town for the week visiting, and for once, Cynthia actually seemed relaxed.

Gina left the penthouse at about ten o'clock on Monday morning and headed down Fifth Avenue. She was dressed conservatively in a white blouse and black skirt, and a brimming confidence had overwhelmed her.

Gina stopped on the corner of Broadway and W. 43rd Street, glanced up at the flashing lights of the huge billboard in Times Square, and surveyed the action around her.

She barely waited for the light to change before she hurried across the street.

"What can I do for you?" Matt Duran asked amiably.

"I want to close out the mutual fund account that my father put in trust for me" Gina replied.

"Do you have the account number?"

She handed him a bankcard, and he took it from her and typed a number into his desktop. Matt was in his mid-twenties and movie star handsome. Gina looked around the tastefully furnished office and wondered what he looked like without that expensive suit on. "Can you tell me what the balance is?" she asked stoically.

Matt nodded and searched his screen. "Just a little over two-hundred and sixty-thousand. You want to close out the whole amount?"

"Yes. And transfer it to my savings account, if you would."

"I can. But there are a few documents that have to be signed first."

"Sure. What do you want me to sign?"

Matt rose and stepped over to his printer, which was already humming and spitting out a sheet of paper. "Not you. Your mother. She's the executor of the account, and she has to sign off on it before we can release the funds."

"But that was supposed to be turned over to me when I turned eighteen!"

He blanched. "Twenty-one."

Gina sunk back in her chair, fuming.

"You can still withdraw them. We just need her signature on these." He handed her the offending documents.

"Yeah," she said dismally. "That'll happen. Are you sure there isn't any other way?"

He shrugged helplessly. "Sorry."

Gina scanned the documents and looked at him defiantly. "Fine. Challenge Number One."

Cynthia stared at Gina incredulously. "You want to do what?"

Gina took a deep breath. "I want to move to Los Angeles. Permanently."

It was early evening and already dark outside. The two faced each other in the penthouse living room, and Cynthia looked as though she'd been slapped in the face. "What do you mean, permanently? Why do you want to move?"

"To live on my own. To start a new life. *My* life."

"Why can't you do that here? What's in California?"

"I think there might be an opportunity there for me."

"For what?"

"I'm not sure. Maybe something in the film business."

"Which you know absolutely nothing about."

"I can learn! I just think it would be the best thing for me right now."

"How can moving three-thousand miles away from home be the best thing? Do you have any idea what can *happen* to you out there?"

"I'm not a baby. And I have to start learning how to take care of myself. You even said so."

"I know, but...this is not exactly what I had in mind."

"Please, Mom. It's important to me."

"I can see that," Cynthia said slowly, her mind racing. "I just don't know..." She paced the room, trying to will a solution to come to her. "What about your education? What are you going to do without *that*?"

"School will still be there," Gina said gently. "Maybe I could even go to school out there."

"No. I think that would really be a mistake, because the best schools are on *this* side of the country."

"But I don't even know what I want to do yet. I think it would be good for me to get on my own for a year and decide what that is before I start college."

Cynthia felt her insides turning to water as she watched her world crumbling in front of her. "A year..." Then she somehow regained her assertiveness. "Okay. I think it's the worst idea I've ever heard. But if you really want to do this, then you *will* have to take care of yourself." Cynthia's voice grew excited, and Gina became more apprehensive. "I'll give you twenty-five-thousand out of that account. That's more than enough to get you out there and get you settled. But you'll have to make your own money. Find some kind of work to support yourself. If you can do that – for a year – then we'll both decide what you'll do next. Do you still want to do it?"

Gina's heart was pounding so fast she could barely breathe, but she refused to back down. She also searched her heart, which told her what she really wanted. "Okay. That sounds fair. And you're right. I should make my own money."

Cynthia's voice was soft. "Oh, God...you actually agreed..." The lump in her throat made it hard to talk. "I don't know how to handle this...you're growing up so fast..."

With a rush of sympathy, Gina hugged Cynthia, but not before tears threatened both of them. "It's okay, Mom...I didn't want to hurt you...I want to make something out of my life and be a big success. Just like you."

"No," Cynthia smiled. "Your dad was the smart one. Not me."

"Shut up," Gina said warmly. "I don't want to hear that kind of talk, okay? He would be so proud of you. I know *I* am."

Cynthia was crying now, but she'd never been happier. "I have to tell you. I don't want you to go."

"Well I'd be worried if you *did*. This is something I have to do. For me."

Cynthia nodded, almost unable to speak.

Gina attempted a smile. "You can always come visit me."

"You know I will..."

"Is that a threat or a warning?" Gina quipped.

"Both."

Gina hugged her mother again, holding her close. "I love you, Mom."

"I love you, too."

They drew back and looked at each other.

Cynthia quavered. "When...do you think?"

Gina hesitated. "The end of the month."

It was like a stab. "That soon?" Half joking. "You're not running away from something, are you?"

Gina's eyes sparkled. "Not anymore."

Later, Gina was hanging up some clothes in her bedroom closet when Debbie came in. "I can't believe you're actually doing it. This is the craziest thing you've ever done."

"Thanks for your support, Deb."

"You know what I mean. Why L.A.?"

Gina finished with her clothes and spun happily around. "Why not? I think it's the perfect place for a brand new start."

"Did you forget about our plans? I thought we were going to hang out this summer."

"I know. And I wanted to. But this is the best time for me to go. Before something happens and gets in my way."

"Like what?"

"Like my mother thinking of a way to trap me here."

Debbie stared morosely at the floor. "I wouldn't mind if she did."

"Or..." A smile lit Gina's sharp features. "You could come with me."

"Come with you?"

"For the summer. You wanted to hang out. Why don't you help me get settled in L.A.?"

Debbie's mouth opened wide, and she was bouncing up and down. "That would be so awesome! Yes!" Then her face fell. "No."

"No?"

"My mother. She'll never let me."

"You guys are here for a few more days. We'll work on her. Wear her down."

Debbie happily threw her arms around Gina, nearly knocking her over. "Oh, Gina! Thank you so much!"

"Deb...?" Gina begged. "I can't breathe..."

The last week of June, three nights before she left, Gina had a going away party at the penthouse. Shannon, Terry, and all of Gina's friends from school were there. Cynthia enjoyed the party, too, although she became concerned when the music reached blaring proportions. Carrying some extra food out of the kitchen, Cynthia passed Debbie on the way into the living room.

"This is a great party, Aunt Cynthia!"

"What??" The music coming from the sound system in the living room made it almost impossible to hear.

"I said – THIS IS A GREAT PARTY!"

Cynthia smiled weakly. "Oh, yes. I hope everyone's enjoying it."

By some miracle, there were no noise complaints from any of the residents below, and the party finished around eleven o'clock. Afterwards, Gina sat on the living room couch with Shannon and Terry, talking in hushed tones.

"You are so lucky," Shannon said. "I wish *I* was moving to L.A."

Gina smiled. "You can go in *my* place. I still don't know if I'm doing the right thing."

"You are," Terry assured her. "You're going to take Hollywood by storm!"

"What are you going to *do* out there?" Shannon asked.

Gina smirked. "I don't know yet. First I want to see what it has to offer."

Terry shook her head. "That means she's going to start jumping surfers."

"Not!"

"Oh, so yes."

"If I'm going to have a career, I guess that means I'm going to have to get a job."

Shannon threw her a look. "You? Get a job? That, I would pay money to see!"

Gina giggled. "Great! The bucks are rolling in already!"

The ride to the airport Monday morning was uncomfortable. Cynthia disguised her pain by making idle conversation with Deidre. Debbie did most of the talking as they sat in the back of the limo. Gina mainly looked out the window and listened to the talk around her, her mind churning with apprehension.

It was harder once they got inside the airport. To their total amazement, despite the heightened security, the attendant who checked the girls' luggage asked Cynthia and Deidre if they wanted to accompany Gina and Debbie to the gate. The attendant gave each of the mothers a special pass, which would allow them to go through the security checkpoint, and off they went.

"I'm going to come out next week," Cynthia affirmed as she hugged Gina for the fourteenth time.

"No! I need some time to get the apartment ready. Just before Debbie leaves, you guys can visit. It'll be more fun that way."

"Fun for *you*."

"Besides, you've got work – and so will I."

"I never thought I'd hear you say *that*."

The girls didn't get on the plane until final boarding call, leaving Cynthia and Deidre staring wistfully after them.

"Did you tell her?" Deidre asked, not looking at her older sister.

"Hell, no."

Deidre shook her head ruefully. "She would have to choose Los Angeles, of all places."

A worried look crossed Cynthia's face. Then she shrugged. "It's a big city. What are the chances of her ever running into *him*?"

CHAPTER 6

He climbed naked out of the L-shaped swimming pool and sauntered over to the nubile girl lying on the chaise longue. "Could you hand me a towel?"

She adjusted her mirror-tinted shades. "Why bother? You'll just get all wet again, anyway."

He reached down, took her hand, and pulled her to her feet. "I have to go pretty soon. One more time?"

A devious smile lit her California blonde features. "Okay. Let's go to my room."

He stopped her. "Actually, I was thinking someplace... different."

She stared at him. "You mean right here?"

He shook his head and indicated the pool.

"Scott!"

"C'mon, Christine, life is short. I have to be at the studio in an hour and a half, so..."

Christine Whittaker regarded the picturesque swimming pool, then turned back to Scott.

Smiling, she peeled off her one-piece swimsuit.

Now nineteen, Scott Griffith had been a working actor since he was ten, and a star since he was fourteen. The Griffith family had moved to L.A. in 1994, shortly after Scott was born. His father, Robert Griffith, had owned part of a television station there until Robert's ambition grew. Robert started off by going to work for WXLA, a local network, before joining one of the major networks as a show runner, and later, a producer.

*   *   *

When Scott was eight, and his sister Heather barely four, the Griffiths lived next door to a woman whose friend was a talent agent. The neighbor commented on Scott's blond good looks and asked Scott's mother, Tracy, for some photos of Scott to pass on to her friend.

Joyce Gilpen asked Tracy and Scott to visit her office, and looked over the attractive young boy with interest. "I'd like to try him for one year," Joyce told Tracy. "He has a quality that I think would come across in commercials, and the right look. I think I can get him some work."

Scott got the first job he went out on, which was for a breakfast cereal. He was turned down on the next four auditions, then landed two more commercial spots, after which he booked a supporting role in a T.V. movie. He was almost eleven by this time and starting to fill out physically – too much so.

Joyce pointedly told Tracy, "If he gains any more weight, I won't be able to send him out for a lot of things."

Tracy kept a sharp eye on what Scott ate, but like most boys his age, Scott gravitated toward junk food and items with high fat content. Tracy also tried getting Scott into sports, but he showed no interest in most kinds of exercise, only video games and acting.

Auditioning for various roles, Scott saw the same faces over and over. His competition. One boy he saw continuously was around his own age. Jason Kellner was good-looking in an all-American way. Sandy-brown hair, amber eyes, and an impish smile. He and Scott were almost always up for the same roles. Scott won most of them.

On the few occasions they worked together on the same jobs, Scott attempted conversation. Jason usually responded by disagreeing, or with a goading, sarcastic remark. Even when Jason seemed to be friendly, Scott had the feeling that Jason was mocking him, as if he were secretly scheming to make Scott look foolish.

Scott told Tracy all about Jason, as he usually confided everything to his mother.

"Why don't you invite him over here to play?" Tracy suggested.

Scott nodded, liking the idea immediately.

"He sounds like he'd be a good friend for you. Trust me, Scott. Kids are different off the set than they are when they're working."

Two weeks later, Scott booked a commercial for Lego toys along with two girls and one other boy – Jason Kellner. Scott planned to wait until the lunch break before asking Jason if he wanted to hang out. Before he could, they were playing with some of the toys while the crew was setting up the next shot, and Scott was pretending to use a Lego crane to hoist a genuine-looking pretend crate.

"Mine's the strongest," Scott said, getting into the game. "I can move an entire building with this one."

Jason regarded Scott through narrowed eyes. "I heard your mom needs a *real* one to pick *you* up."

The girls laughed, and Scott was immediately uncomfortable.

Scott glared at Jason, too angry to say anything.

Any idea of inviting Jason to the Griffith house was swiftly forgotten.

When Scott told Tracy, she was livid. "I have his mother's phone number," Tracy said. "If you want, I can call her."

"No, Mom. I don't want you to do that." Scott stared down at the kitchen table miserably. "Just forget about it."

"To hell with him," Tracy spat, putting her arm around Scott. "There'll be other jobs. You'll have a *lot* more jobs. I doubt you'll see *him* again."

Six months went by. Joyce didn't call Scott for one audition. Tracy called Joyce and asked why they hadn't heard from her.

"It's slow right now," Joyce responded, sounding hurried. "I'll call you as soon as I have anything."

The holidays came, and Scott found himself too occupied by school and social activities to even think about another acting job, until the spring pilot season of 2006 rolled around. Joyce seemed to have forgotten that Scott existed. Tracy called the agency again but was unable to get Joyce on the phone.

Robert was perturbed when Tracy told him. "I'm going to take off work early tomorrow," he said pensively. "Let's me and you take a ride down to her office."

*   *   *

Scott and Heather were playing in the living room the following afternoon when Robert and Tracy arrived back home around four o'clock.

"We went to see your agent today," Robert announced gruffly.

Scott immediately looked to Tracy. She didn't appear happy, either. That was when Scott knew he was in trouble. "What did she say?" Scott asked anxiously.

Robert sounded more disappointed than angry – which troubled Scott even more. "She said you were bothering people on the set."

Scott's eyes widened. "What! No!"

Robert nodded grimly.

"They said you were bothering the other kids," Tracy said sharply, her tone accusatory. "Talking when you weren't supposed to be."

"I was not!" Scott blurted, his face turning red. "We were *all* talking! Jason was the - " Scott's features clouded over. "It was Jason! He's trying to get me in trouble!"

"Why would he do that?" Robert asked seriously, unconvinced.

"I don't know! He hates me for some reason. I didn't bother anybody. He's a liar!"

Robert didn't look like he believed Scott.

Tracy softened, realizing that there might be some truth to what Scott was saying.

"You know I don't misbehave on sets," Scott said hoarsely, his heart pounding. "Did you ask Joyce *who* said these things?"

"She's not going to tell us *that*," Tracy said condescendingly.

"We told her," Robert said, "That we would talk to you, and that if she started sending you out on jobs again, there wouldn't be any more problems. So she agreed."

Scott's mouth dropped open. He felt dizzy.

"She said she has an audition for you next week, so she'll call us."

"Thanks, Dad!" Scott threw his arms around Robert and Tracy.

"Just watch your step from now on," Robert said with more sternness than he felt.

Scott never had a problem on a set again after that. He ran into Jason a few months later at an audition. Jason smiled his fake smile, as if they were the best of friends and nothing had happened. Scott became more wary of Jason Kellner than ever.

Scott's big break came when he auditioned for a series called *Right On* for the CW. After the audition, Scott had two callbacks, and then was asked to read in front of seventeen network executives. The part he was up for was smart aleck Cal Anderson, a student at Richfield High School, the setting for the teen drama. After weeks of waiting, he was awarded the role, and he and the rest of the cast went immediately into production that June.

Joannie Kellner, Jason's younger sister by three years, was cast as Casey Larson, one of Cal's friends at school. At first, Scott was unnerved, fearful of Jason frequently visiting the set. Scott needn't have worried. Jason was cast as the son of a cop on *Blue Shield*, a new one-hour drama for Fox. And as Scott got to know Joannie, he found her sweet, trustworthy, and genuine – nothing at all like Jason. Scott was immensely relieved, although his work schedule left him no time to even hang out with friends.

Right On hit its unsuspecting public in the fall of 2008 and was an instant hit. Scott Griffith became a celebrity almost immediately, along with his fellow cast mates. *Right On*, referred to by critics as "the rebirth of *Beverly Hills, 90210*," identified with the young and older demographics alike. Most of all, Scott had a blast doing the show.

By right, because he was fourteen, Scott should have been starting high school. The show's production schedule wouldn't permit it. He was tutored on the set whenever he wasn't able to attend classes at Beverly Hills High School, which made it hard to be like a regular kid. And contrary to what was written about him in teen magazines, his experience with girls was practically nonexistent.

Scott's first crush came on the set of *Right On*. Sandy Ettensberger was the daughter of one of the camera operators. As they were both fourteen, Scott and Sandy's first date consisted of an early dinner with the cast and crew under a tent out on the back lot, followed by Scott's first kiss behind one of the sets.

Their "relationship" lasted a whole two months before it faded into a casual platonic friendship. Scott was devastated because he was sure Sandy had lost interest because he was overweight. Of course, in the film and television business, being anything but emaciated was considered overweight.

Soon Scott's cast and crewmembers became his friends and extended family. Since he worked almost forty hours a week and spent the rest of the time being tutored, he had few friendships outside of *Right On*.

The exceptions were two slightly older boys whom he'd hung out with since the sixth grade - Joe O'Reilly and Sean Goldstein. Sean had his driver's license and the use of one of his dad's cars, so he'd pick up Joe and Scott at their respective houses, and the three of them would go cruising to different places – the mall, the beach, and an occasional party.

One night after the three of them wandered the halls and knocked on suite doors at a posh hotel in Santa Monica, Sean stopped on the side of the 405 Freeway, and he and Joe got out, grabbed a toolbox out of the trunk, and told Scott to stay with the car. Scott waited for over half an hour, wondering what the hell they were doing and afraid that the car might get hit by one of the hundreds of other cars flying by.

After what seemed like an eternity, Sean and Joe returned carrying a *SPEED LIMIT 55* sign, and demanded that Scott help them place it in the extra large trunk. Somehow the boys fit the sign inside, and they sped off. Tracy Griffith was more than a little surprised when Scott came rushing into the house that night and insisted she come outside. When the two of them reached the driveway, Sean and Joe were hoisting the *SPEED LIMIT 55* sign out of the trunk and positioning it next to the car. Scott even had Tracy take a few photos of them standing next to the sign before Joe and Sean took off with it. Tracy was just glad Robert was working late.

As part of his association with *Right On*, Scott attended several network parties and publicized events, where he and the other cast members were photographed and interviewed.

One party that didn't make it into the media was held one summer night at a sprawling beach house in Malibu. Sounds of the raucous rap music could be heard from outside, and thanks to one entire wall of the living room being made of glass, anyone on the water could've seen all of the scantily clad teenagers dancing and partying inside.

Scott arrived at the party with Joe and Sean. Observing everyone else around them, Scott tried not to let it bother him that both his friends were considerably thinner than he was.

The beach house was swarming with very attractive, nearly naked teens, and the three boys could barely hear each other over the music.

"Did I tell you guys or what?" Joe shouted gleefully, kicking off his sneakers and unbuttoning his jeans.

"Oh yeah!" Sean agreed excitedly, pulling off his shirt and gawking lustfully at the female eye candy. "Don't let the flesh parade pass you by!"

"C'mon, Scott," Joe urged, tugging at his friend's shirt. "You ain't gonna score any honies like *this*!"

Scott looked around self-consciously. "I thought we were goin' swimmin'."

Sean grinned at Joe. "Yeah. Skinny-dipping."

Both boys high-fived just as an exotic-looking girl in a white bikini sauntered by.

She favored them with a smile, but didn't break stride.

"Whoah!" Joe gushed weakly. "I wouldn't mind gettin' some of *that*!"

Sean's eyes followed the girl out of the room. "No way, dude. She's out of your league." Off a look from Joe. "Okay, mine, too!"

The three boys headed out to the back patio.

Joe and Sean helped themselves to whatever alcohol was available.

"Scott!" Sean called. "You want a beer?"

Scott shook his head. "Maybe later."

Sean glared at him. "Dude, what is your problem? You're gonna make us sorry we brought you!"

Scott stared awkwardly at the two of them and accepted the beer can from Joe.

He took a sip and nearly gagged.

Joe shook his head in disgust.

Sean noticed a group of guys and girls in the hot tub off of the kidney-shaped pool. "Hey! They got a Jacuzzi! Let's go!"

"I'll be right down," Scott called as he watched them run off.

Scott ambled back into the living room.

The music was deafening, although none of the model-perfect teens dancing around seemed to care.

Scott leaned against the far wall when he noticed the girl they'd seen earlier undulating around the room wearing nothing but her skimpy bikini.

She was dancing by herself, but still attracted the attention of many of the guys gyrating around her.

Scott realized that the girl was staring at him as she swayed her magnificent body around the room.

He attempted a smile, hoping that his shirt concealed the bulge of his stomach.

She shimmied over to him and gave him an inviting smile. "Hi."

"Hi," he croaked, trying not to stare at her glorious figure.

Raquel Morollan motioned for Scott to join her, performing a series of suggestive dance moves in front of him. Placing both her arms around his neck, she leaned into him and said, "You're a good dancer."

He blushed and looked down at the floor. "Thanks."

"My name's Raquel."

He could barely look her in the eye. "I'm Scott."

"Scott?" she teased. "As in 'Scotty the Hottie'?"

He smiled weakly, unable to take his eyes off her body.

"Do you like to play?" she asked, her eyes challenging his.

"Er – sure," he responded, uncomprehending.

"Yeah?" she husked. "What do you like to do?"

"What do you mean?"

She rolled her eyes. "I mean," she chided, "Behind closed doors."

Again he stared at her, uncomprehending.

She giggled and took his hand. "Follow me." She led him up the carpeted stairs to an upstairs bedroom, where she closed and locked the door. They could still hear and feel the vibration of the music through the walls, but it was a great deal more private.

"I like this better," he mumbled. "It's a lot easier to - "

She was kissing him on the mouth, slowly, sensually, passionately. When they finally broke, she looked at him seriously, her expression intent. "You need practice."

Scott went red in the face. "What do you mean I need practice?"

Raquel laughed. Her tone was affectionate. "Don't worry about it. It's okay if it's your first time."

"It's not my first time," he lied, rolling his eyes. "Give me a break."

She smirked, undoing her bikini top and letting it fall to the floor. "So why do you still have your clothes on? Are you afraid?"

He struggled to take a deep breath. "No way!"

Later, lying in bed, she ran her hand down his smooth naked body.

"You'd look better if you lost weight," she commented.

His voice hardened. "What's that supposed to mean?"

"Nothing," she groaned. "I just think you need to tone up, that's all."

"Yeah," he muttered, getting out of bed and reaching for his clothes.

"You were great," she simpered.

He stopped. "Really? I was okay?"

"Better than okay. I'll bet with some practice, you could be even better."

"You think so?"

"You have a lot to learn," she said matter-of-factly. "But I can teach you. Call me?"

He turned his back to her and slipped on his underwear. Then he faced her again, staring at her for a long moment. He nodded unsurely. "Okay."

She watched with amusement as he fumbled into the rest of his clothes.

He kissed her slow and sensuously before he left, then stepped out into the hallway, closing the door behind him.

It was quiet now as he hurried along the hallway and down the stairs into the living room. The house was nearly deserted, and Scott searched every room of the ground floor.

He opened the door to what looked like a den. All the lights were off, but the open windows allowed him to see by faint moonlight.

He found Joe and Sean lying on the floor, still in their swimsuits.

"Guys...you ready to go?"

They didn't respond.

On closer inspection, Scott could see that Sean's eyes were open, staring up at him.

"Guys?"

He moved closer to Joe.

Scott shook him, but his friend didn't move. "Joe, c'mon! This isn't funny!"

He looked over at a cellophane bag of white powder on the floor next to Sean.

Scott stood, his eyes growing larger. "Oh, God..."

He took a step backward and nearly tripped over a chair. "Oh my God..."

He turned to see a desk by the window and immediately reached for the phone.

"9-1-1, is this an emergency?"

The words barely came out. "Yes...yes..."

"Where are you calling from?"

"I don't know...I didn't drive here..."

Scott heard the clicking of computer keys. "Are you at 15716 Beach Colony Road?"

"I think so..."

"What is your emergency?"

"My friends...they're lying on the floor...they're not breathing - "

"What's your name?"

Scott hesitated. "Sean."

"Sean, where are you in the house? What room?"

"I don't know...I think it's the den."

"Sean, I'm sending the paramedics. Can you tell me what happened?"

"I think it's...drugs..."

"What drugs were they taking?"

He had to take a deep breath just to enunciate. "Cocaine."

"Cocaine? Anything else?"

"No..."

"All right, I want you to stay on the line with me...Sean...? Sean...?"

Scott hung up the phone and took one last look at his fallen friends.

He slowly backed out of the room.

Scott was making his way over a sand dune when he heard the ambulance sirens. He hurried toward the Pacific Coast Highway and looked helplessly around. Shivering in the cold night air, he started up the treacherous road, then stopped and pulled out his cell phone.

Robert Griffith answered the phone, sounding groggy.

"Dad...? It's me..."

"Scott? What's wrong?"

"I need you to come and get me. I'm in trouble. Something happened..."

"Where the hell are you?" Robert's deep voice was almost a growl.

"The PCH and Malibu Canyon." Scott was crying. The hand he held the phone with shook. "I need your help, Dad...please..."

He sobbed so hard he almost collapsed.

Scott would've been grounded for the next several years if it hadn't been for his commitment to *Right On*. Robert and Tracy were paranoid about every place Scott went. It didn't ease their fears when he turned sixteen-and-a-half and was insistent about getting his driver's license.

When they were alone, Tracy discussed it with Robert. "I've been looking forward to him driving for the longest time, so he could drive him*self* to work. Now, it terrifies me."

"We can't keep him at home forever," Robert admitted. "Seeing what happened to Joe and Sean scared the hell out of him. It scared the hell out of *me*. If one good thing came out of it, Scott knows now to stay away from that."

Scott got his driver's license in the fall of 2010.

"Your dad and I want to buy you a car," Tracy announced happily. "What kind do you want?"

"A Lamborghini," Scott said without hesitation.

She shot him a withering look. "Don't hold your breath for *that*."

"You are *not* gettin' that car," Robert grumbled.

"Why not?" Scott countered.

"Because I said so. I would buy you a house with that money before I spent it on something foolish like *that*."

"*I'll* buy it," Scott insisted.

"*That's* what you want to spend your money on??" Tracy demanded in disbelief. "If you do, you're crazy!"

"You know I'm in the magazines all the time," Scott retorted. "Do you know how much publicity that would create?"

"What about the insurance?" Robert questioned seriously. "You think *I'm* gonna pay that?"

"I'll pay it," Scott boasted, not at all sure that he could do so.

"Forget about it," Robert warned. "There's no way you're gettin' that car."

Scott got a good deal on the Lamborghini he bought from a local dealership in Beverly Hills. Robert reluctantly signed the necessary papers for the ownership as well as the insurance, as he knew there would be no living with Scott or Tracy if he didn't agree. Scott practically bounced out of the office as he and Robert headed to the parking lot to wait for Tracy.

"You know I don't agree with what you're doing," Robert grumbled, absently shoving his hands in his pockets.

"It's my own money, Dad," Scott replied, equally stiff.

"I know, but you don't know how long this series is going to last. If it's canceled, you don't know when your next job'll be."

"Thanks a lot!" Scott spat. "The top network and producers in Hollywood think I have what it takes, but not my own father!"

"Hey – I'm on your side, kid. But you don't know what's gonna happen. I don't wanna see you throw your money away."

"You really think I'm that stupid? Don't you think I've thought of that?"

Robert shook his head, staring unseeingly out at the traffic on Olympic Boulevard. "I think it's too much money, Scott. I'd rather see you buy a house."

Half-joking. "You trying to get rid of me?"

Robert stared at his son and fought not to smile. "I tried. But your mother wouldn't let me."

Tracy came out of the dealership office then and joined Scott and Robert in front of Scott's new fire-engine-red dream machine. "You two ready?"

"*I* am!" Scott beamed excitedly. "Whaddaya say, Dad? You wanna ride with *me*?"

Mock panic. "*I'm* not getting into that thing. I don't even think I would *fit* in that thing!"

Devilish grin. "Mom?"

Tracy's eyes were wide. "Don't look at *me*."

"Go ahead, Tracy," Robert said casually. "The life insurance is paid up."

"Oh, thanks a lot!"

"Come on, Mom." Scott managed his most pious expression.

Tracy looked, outraged, from one to the other, then scowled in resignation. "All right. I guess I've lived a full life."

Scott jumped excitedly behind the wheel and started up the Lamborghini's motor.

"No thrill rides," Tracy warned as she warily climbed in beside him.

Scott revved the engine and noisily shot out of the parking lot.

Buying the Lamborghini turned out to be a brilliant career move as well. It was photographed, published, and publicized, until Scott was known more for his car than for his work on *Right On!* Before the series wrapped its second season, Scott was receiving offers to do feature films, and was constantly hounded by the teen magazines for photos and interviews.

Scott lay on the bed in his room one afternoon studying a new *Right On* script when his cell phone went off. Without looking at the caller I.D., he answered it.

"Hi!" A disturbingly familiar female voice.

"Who's this?"

"You can forget me after the fun we had at the beach?"

He sat up straight. "Raquel??"

She giggled. "Who else? I thought you were going to call me."

"I did. I mean, I would've...I got in trouble after that party."

"You did?"

"Don't you know what happened?"

Her tone grew serious. "No."

So she didn't know. Scott decided not to go into it. "I couldn't get a ride home, and my parents found out..."

"You see?" she said triumphantly. "You should've come with *me*."

"I thought I had."

"Good one. Why didn't you tell me you were a T.V. star?"

"I didn't know I was."

"Yeah, right. Hey! Why don't you come over tonight?"

"Over your house?"

"Duh."

"I guess. What'll we do?"

Suggestively. "Anything you like."

Raquel lived in a beautiful home on Georgina Avenue in Santa Monica. Scott found his way there with little trouble.

Her parents weren't home. And she looked beyond glad to see him.

"Oh my God!" Raquel shrieked when she saw the Lamborghini.

It was love at first sight.

"I'll get my purse!"

She couldn't have been more in a hurry to go.

Scott showed off his new toy to the fullest – racing the motor, fast starts, sharp stops. The only thing he wasn't comfortable with yet was the speed. It amazed him how much power the compact vehicle contained, so he still drove carefully on the rare occasions he was in high gear.

"Let's go on the freeway!" Raquel suggested excitedly.

Scott liked the freeways better than the surface streets because it involved less shifting and it was easier on the car.

"Is this the fastest you can go?" Raquel taunted, disgust creeping into her voice. "You don't know how to drive!"

Scott reluctantly drove faster, which seemed to please her, even though it made him uneasy. He soon learned that he didn't dare slow down unless he wanted to incur more of her insults.

"I'm in the mood to go to the beach," Raquel purred, so of course, that's where they went.

When they returned to her house, Raquel led Scott into her bedroom. She turned on her stereo, and the two of them listened to music for a while until she playfully started groping and tickling him. Then she grabbed him in a kiss fast, and they were naked and making love, united in an athletic teen frenzy.

When they finished, she lay beside him, flushed. She turned to him with a grin. "I see you've been practicing."

Raquel's father was a development executive for ABC Television, so Scott had the honor of escorting Raquel to a number of industry events. Always, the evening was laced with the promise of another hot time in bed. Scott and Raquel barely got through an evening or a dinner without Raquel fondling him under a table, enticing him in an elevator, or exciting him on the drive back to her house.

Scott, of course, was having the time of his life.

Raquel's scrutiny of his physical appearance bothered Scott more than he let on to her. She was a natural beauty. Her body was so perfect. Scott was good looking. He knew that. But out of his clothes, his stomach protruded, and he lacked any muscularity or definition. He was painfully aware of this every time they were in bed.

Scott started out by limiting the portions he ate. This was difficult for him because he seemed to have been born with an enormous appetite. Then he switched to eating healthier foods – a habit that baffled his parents.

"Is that all you're eating?" Tracy complained. "Cereal and tuna fish?"

"It's enough," was Scott's reply.

He did lose some weight – even went down a pants size – but that still wasn't enough. Scott bought an expensive weight set, and then a home gym, setting it up in one of the house's smaller guest rooms. He worked out just about everyday, as much as his shooting schedule permitted, until his body looked closer to the image he aspired to. Even though he appeared more toned and had developed some muscular definition, he was never satisfied with what he saw in the mirror.

Of course, Raquel was just as vocal with her *positive* comments. "You are looking *hot!*" she would tell him, running her hands down his newly enhanced pectorals. It was the kind of praise and reassurance he needed.

The producers of *Right On* noticed the change in Scott's appearance as well. The script of one episode contained a scene where he appeared briefly in his underwear, and two months later, he did his first bed scene where he was shown bare-chested with a female guest star.

One night in the summer of 2011, Scott and Raquel attended an informal gathering some of their friends were having on Santa Monica Beach. It was nine o'clock at night, and all of them were either lying or sitting around the crackling fire, while R & B music blasted from a nearby boom box. Two of the guys were using a beach grill to cook cheeseburgers and hot dogs.

Scott and Raquel were lying on a large towel, each propped up on one elbow and staring into each other's eyes. Scott only wore white Speedos, which not only emphasized his firm legs and buttocks, but also his muscular upper body.

"I'm cold." Raquel pouted.

Scott moved closer to her on the blanket and put his arms around her. "Well come over *here*. I'll keep you warm."

He kissed her.

She looked at him mischievously. "You know what?"

"What?"

Lasciviously. "I'm hungry."

"Again?"

She stretched, proudly exhibiting her finely toned stomach and endless legs. "What can I say? You make me work up an appetite!"

He laughed, shaking his head in disbelief.

Suggestively. "You know what I want?"

"What?"

Making it sound dirty. "A cheeseburger! Would you go get me one?"

He groaned.

"Please..."

He nodded and leapt to his feet. "All right. Be right back."

En route to the grill, he noticed a beautiful blonde girl, who looked to be no more than fifteen, eyeing him with fascination. Her smile was big and wide, reaching all the way to her eyes. He caught her looking him up and down, and she blushed and resumed talking to the other young girl next to her.

"Can I have a cheeseburger?" Scott was standing at the grill watching one of the guys make the burger, when he looked up and saw the blonde girl standing next to him.

She beamed. "Hi!"

He managed a polite smile and looked away. "Hi."

"You're Scott Griffith, aren't you?"

Feigning discomfort. "Who wants to know?"

Her laugh was like a song. "You're on that new show *Right On!* I love that show!"

He was afraid to look at her, but he couldn't help smiling. "Thanks."

"My name's Maryann. Maryann Davis."

He turned to her and almost fell into her deep, widely spaced blue eyes. "It's nice to meet you."

"Likewise. Are you here by yourself?"

He opened his mouth to speak, but the words barely came out. "No, I...came with a friend."

"Me too!" She indicated the girl she had been talking to earlier. "See? That's my best friend over there. Amanda."

The girl Maryann had pointed to was looking at them and waving.

Scott tentatively waved back.

The boy behind the grill handed Scott his order on a napkin. "One cheeseburger."

"Thanks." Scott turned to Maryann.

She smiled nervously. "Well, I guess you better go eat your cheeseburger."

"Oh...it's not for me. I mean...I've gotta get back."

Her eyes never left his face. "Whatever you say."

Scott turned and headed back to where Raquel laid waiting on the towel. "It's about time!" she teased.

Scott faltered. "Well...I had to make sure they made it just right." He joined her on the towel.

She reached for the cheeseburger, took a bite, and offered it to him. "Have some."

"No, thanks. I'm good."

"C'mon!" she pressed. "Eat!"

"No, really, Raquel. I don't want any."

She didn't give in. "You have to eat."

"I'll have some yogurt later." He looked down at the sand. "You know I'm trying to stay in shape."

She eyed his well-toned body appreciatively. "You sure are."

He smirked and leaned into her. Kissing, they fell back on the towel.

An hour later, the informal gathering was more like a party. The music was louder, bottled beer had appeared, and groups of teens were all dancing together.

Raquel and a friend of hers, Sara, were each helping themselves to a beer out of a nearby cooler, barely able to hear one another talk over the music.

"I like Ross and all," Sara was saying, "And he's a nice enough guy, but...he just doesn't...do it for me. You know what I mean?"

"Hey," Raquel boasted, "I'm with Scott Griffith, so that is something I know *nothing* about."

"Where is he, anyway?"

A look of concern creased Raquel's exotic features as she looked around. "I don't know. Didn't I just see him talking to Jeff and Lee?"

Sara smiled impishly. "Maybe they all went skinny dipping."

"Without us? They better not have!"

Scott and Maryann were strolling along the water's edge just a short ways down the beach. The tide lapped at their bare feet as they moved side by side, their bodies illuminated by the pale glow of the moonlight.

"What's it like being famous?" she asked.

"It's awesome," he admitted weakly.

"I want to be famous someday."

"No you don't. Don't get me wrong. I wouldn't give it up, but some days, I wish I could just be a normal person." His tone grew ominous. "When someone recognizes me on the street, I never really know if they like the show, or if they just want to get close to me so they can hurt me."

Maryann shivered.

Scott put his arm around her.

"I don't want to hurt you," she smiled.

He relaxed. "I know you don't. But sometimes – when people come up to me – it freaks me out, you know? They act like they know me, and that I should know *them*, but I don't, and it's just...really weird."

She looked at him slyly. "You must admit, you like it most of the time."

He allowed himself a slight smile. "Most of the time...I guess."

They turned and faced each other. The noise of the party loomed in the air, and Maryann snuggled closer to Scott. "I'm cold."

He held her gently in his arms. "Well...we'll have to do something about that, won't we?"

Their kiss was warm and wet and long. When they broke, Scott gazed at her tenderly, holding both her hands in his.

"That was really great," she breathed.

He looked mesmerized. "It was, wasn't it?"

Both looked up to see Raquel standing only a few feet away, staring at them, her eyes blazing. "You son of a bitch!" She turned and stormed up the beach toward the parking lot.

Scott ran to catch up to her. "Raquel! Wait! It's not what it looks like! Please!"

She spun around and faced him, her voice shaking. "Just stay...away...from me." She kept moving.

"Raquel! Listen to me! You know you're the one I want to be with! I didn't mean for this to happen, I swear! Please!"

They had reached his car. She laid her hands against the edge, her back to him, and she seemed to have trouble breathing. "I want you to take me home."

He stared at her a long moment, pain twisting his face. Then he looked down at the ground, and nodded slowly.

As soon as Scott pulled up in front of her house, Raquel leaped out of the car, slammed the door as hard as she could, and strode briskly toward her front door.

Scott was right behind her. "Can't we at least talk about it? I don't even know her! She doesn't mean *anything* to me!"

She didn't stop, not even to look at him. "Oh, that makes it all right! That just makes it...so much better!"

They'd both reached her front door.

"All right!" he admitted. "I made a mistake! I'm sorry. I didn't mean to hurt you. Can't you forgive me? Please?"

She turned to face him. He could see that her whole body was trembling. "As far as I'm concerned...you don't exist. I never want to see you again!" She started to unlock her door.

"Raquel...I'm really sorry..."

"Good. Get out!"

She marched inside and slammed the door in his face.

He stood there, dazed.

Scott faced his parents in their living room and smiled proudly. "Mom. Dad. This is Maryann Davis."

Robert and Tracy Griffith beamed at the angel of a girl with the silky blonde hair and widely spaced aquamarine eyes. She looked to be no more than sixteen, although her innocent demeanor betrayed a glimpse of childlike maturity.

"It's very nice to meet you," Tracy said warmly, her hands clasped in front of her.

"Hi," Maryann said timidly.

"Where did you two meet?" Robert asked. "School?"

"No," Scott said.

"Actually, I go to Malibu Canyon High," said Maryann brightly.

"We met at the beach," Scott supplied. "That party I told you about."

Robert nodded, but his expression was hard to read.

"I hope you like lasagna, Maryann," Tracy said pleasantly, starting out of the room. "It'll be ready in about fifteen minutes."

"Thank you, Mrs. Griffith," Maryann called out politely, as Robert trailed Tracy into the kitchen.

Grinning, Scott took Maryann in his arms. "I think they like you."

Her smile was intoxicating. "I'm glad."

He stole a quick glance in the kitchen and kissed her lightly on the cheek.

She slipped her tiny hand in his, and he led her from the room.

Scott's bedroom was in total darkness as he lay next to Maryann, cupping her face with his hand. They were both naked as they faced each other, and her eyes bore deeply into his.

"I love you." He couldn't stop himself from saying it.

"I love you, too," she said meaningfully.

He ran his hand through her luxuriant hair. "Are you sure you want to do this? Are you ready?"

There was slight amusement in her voice. "I am if you are."

"Yeah," he managed. "My parents won't be home for hours, so we have plenty of time."

"Cool," she simpered. "So what are we waiting for?"

They kissed, and Scott felt another amazing trip beginning.

Maryann was Scott's date for the Emmy Awards ceremony in the fall of 2012. Light bulbs flashed and camera crews surged as the stunning couple paraded across the red carpet and into the Nokia Theater.

One aggressive male reporter rushed forward. "Scott, do you think your chances are good for winning the Emmy you're up for?"

Scott deliberately blushed. "It doesn't matter to me if I win. I'm just glad to be here and to have been nominated."

Maryann proudly held Scott's hand as they sat in their aisle seats throughout the elaborate proceedings. Fiona Turner, the young pretty star of the supernatural teen drama, *Sorcery*, was presenting. "The nominees for Outstanding Lead Actor in a Drama series are...Mike Connor, *Underworld*...Andrew Caffrey, *Arbor Ridge*...Scott Griffith, *Right On*...Peter Hatch, *Extreme Heat*...and Jason Kellner, *Blue Shield*..." She hastily fumbled with the envelope. "And the winner is...Scott Griffith, *Right On!*"

Scott was barely aware of anything else after his name was called. His legs felt weak as he made his way onstage and accepted the gold statuette. The words of his acceptance speech poured out of his mouth effortlessly, although his heart was pounding so loudly he could hardly hear himself think.

When Scott left the stage and reached his seat again, Robert rose, and he and Scott euphorically high-fived and hugged, surprising both of them.

Tracy couldn't help but turn to Maryann and say, "I wish they were like that *all* the time!"

Scott was equally congratulatory later when one of Robert's shows, *Valets,* won for Best Original Comedy Series.

Sitting in his own seat, Jason Kellner appeared to be genuinely happy for Scott.

The entire entertainment community had underestimated Jason's acting ability.

Along with Robert and Tracy and most of the other A-Listers, Scott and Maryann attended the "after" party in the Sky Bar of the Mondrian Hotel. Maryann stood gleefully by Scott's side as he was besieged with congratulations from friends and acquaintances alike – all people she recognized from film and television. From time to time, he would take her hand, affectionately squeeze it, and give her a knowing smile.

Maryann was admiring the view from one of the large windows when she noticed Scott checking his phone. "What is it?" she asked.

"A text from Heather," he replied, typing back. "She's watching at her friend Lynda's house. 'Congrats, bro.'" Scott grinned as he slipped the phone back into his pocket.

"She's proud of you," Maryann smiled. "Just like I am." She kissed him on the cheek.

Scott and Maryann waited with his parents while the valets retrieved Robert's car.

"I don't know why you parked in the garage," Tracy said to Scott. "I don't think it would've done any harm to have it parked."

"I told you," Scott said. "Nobody drives that car except me."

The valet arrived with the Griffith's Cadillac, and Robert collected his keys.

Tracy hugged Scott. "All right. We'll see you at home. I'll leave your award on the dining room table." Choked. "I'm proud of you, Handsome."

Scott blushed for real. "Thanks, Mom."

"Don't stay out too late."

Scott shrugged. "I should be home by...Thursday."

Maryann rolled her eyes at Tracy. "He's always fooling."

"Oh, I'm used to it," Tracy said as she climbed in beside Robert, and they drove off.

Scott took Mulholland Drive to the canyon. The lights of L.A. lay spread out below them as Scott expertly navigated the endless twists and turns of the road. Maryann beamed as Scott revved the engine and raced along the mountain ridge.

Scott didn't see the next bend in the road in time. He slammed on the brakes, skidded against the guardrail, and careened into a tree. His first thought was Maryann. Shaken as he was, he looked over to where she sat, her head slumped against the window. She wasn't moving. "Maryann!"

Despite her horrible head wound, she still looked like an angel. Scott tried desperately to wake her, but he couldn't.

"Maryann!" It was a scream. As he tried to get her seatbelt off, he muttered, "Come on, honey, don't do this to me..."

She still showed no signs of consciousness, so he called 9-1-1. The police and paramedics arrived ten minutes later. Scott stood on the side of the road crying as the medics transferred Maryann into the ambulance. He rode with her to the hospital, where the medical examiner pronounced Maryann dead upon their arrival. Cause of death was massive head trauma.

Scott was in a daze as the police questioned him and gave him a Breathalyzer exam. He thanked God that he didn't drink. The police officers took him home around 4 A.M., where they woke up Robert and Tracy and questioned *them*. Even after the officers left, Scott's parents were too stunned to say anything, although they looked at him like he was someone they didn't know, someone they dreaded. Only Tracy regarded him with so much as an ounce of compassion.

Scott struggled to find his voice. "Mom..."

"Don't say anything!" Robert barked, unable to look at his son. "Don't say a damn thing! You're lucky I don't kill ya! Just stay out of my sight..."

Tracy solemnly followed Robert into the kitchen.

Scott burst into tears again, his entire body racked with sobs. He glanced briefly at the Emmy he'd received at the ceremony, now sitting regally on the dining room table. The sight of it made him sick.

It was two weeks before Scott could return to work. The official excuse for his absence was illness. Scott barely ate or slept, despite his family's best efforts to be sympathetic. Even Tracy couldn't get through to him. Robert and Tracy briefly discussed having Scott see a therapist.

Scott didn't go to Maryann's funeral. He couldn't face anyone. It was hard enough focusing on his work on *Right On*. He managed to keep his grief hidden from almost everybody. Only Joannie Kellner sensed that something might be wrong and tried to get him to open up, but Scott didn't crack. For what he'd done to Maryann, he didn't *deserve* any comfort or relief. And he never would again.

Scott arrived home from work one evening, opened the gate that blocked his parents' driveway, and drove Robert and Tracy's Cadillac inside. He was just turning off his CD player when he looked in his rearview mirror and saw a large balding man moving swiftly up the driveway and heading straight for him. Scott got out of the car and recognized the man, simultaneously starting toward the side door of the house. "Mr. Davis..."

Cameron Davis grabbed Scott and threw him against the side of the car. "No good bastard! You killed my little girl!" The force of the blow laid Scott out on the hood, clutching his jaw and blinded by searing pain. "You killed her! It's because of you she's dead! I'm going to kill *you*!" Scott felt the kicks to his legs and stomach as he crumpled to the ground, vainly holding up his hands to defend himself. The middle-aged man standing over him was a relentless deadly force, tirelessly kicking and striking in a blaze of fury.

Through the haze, Scott searched for an escape and managed to roll away from his attacker. Scott was just about to get to his feet when Cameron Davis was pulled off of Scott and roughly turned around by Robert. "What the hell do you think you're doing?" Scott's father demanded of the crazed man.

"He killed her!" Cameron shouted, equally fierce. "He won't get away with it!"

Cameron swung at Robert, who ducked and punched Cameron hard in the face. Cameron reeled backwards and stared at Robert in amazement.

"I'll kill you, too!" Cameron raged, charging at Robert.

Robert grabbed Cameron roughly and held him fast against the car door. "Will you listen to me!" Robert shouted. "It was an accident! A damn accident!" His voice was strained. "I am so sorry about what happened to your daughter, but this will not – bring – her back!"

Cameron's eyes were wide, and Robert could see the fury and pain inside the tortured man. "That's easy for you to say," Cameron hissed. "My little girl is where *your* son should be!"

Robert caught his breath as he glared at Cameron, watching the shorter man's every move.

"I hate you!" Cameron blazed. "I hate you all!"

Cameron stared at the ground miserably, blinking away tears, before turning and starting back toward his car.

When Cameron was gone, Scott took a deep breath and came up behind Robert. "Dad..."

Robert couldn't look at him. "Just get in the damn house," he growled disgustedly. "Go!"

Scott had never felt worse in his life than when he sat in the detective's office at the Hollywood police station while a stenographer took down his every word.

"Had you consumed any alcoholic beverages at any time that evening?"

"No."

"Were you under the influence of any narcotics or any illegal substances while you were operating the vehicle?"

"No." Scott cleared his throat, but he still found it difficult to speak.

"What street were you driving on just before the accident?"

"Mulholland Drive."

"Do you know what the speed limit is on that road?"

Scott paused unsurely. "Forty, I think."

"And how fast would you say you were going?"

Scott hesitated again, thinking hard. "I'm not sure."

The detective grunted with controlled anger. "The speed limit is actually thirty on that road, and you were going almost fifty around that corner. We measured the skid marks from when you hit the brakes."

It was all too vivid in Scott's mind. Images he could never block out. He looked to the detective for understanding, some sympathy, a sign of absolution for the pain that plagued him. There was none.

"Not many kids your age can afford the kind of car you were driving," the detective went on tonelessly. "Just because your car is fast doesn't entitle you to disregard the rules of the road."

The detective pulled some 8 x 10 photos out of an envelope and tossed them on the desk in front of Scott. The photos were of Maryann after she'd been brought into the morgue.

"Look what it cost you." The detective's voice was deliberately non-accusing. "Take a *good* look."

Scott turned away, feeling as if he were going to be sick. "I can't..."

"You'd better. It could've been you."

Scott could barely stand as he faced the imposing judge in the closed courtroom.

"The defendant is charged with reckless endangerment and is ordered to pay two-hundred and fifty-thousand dollars in punitive damages to the Davis family, and is also ordered to serve two years' probation. License is suspended for one year, at which time this case will be subject to review." The older man expertly disguised his contempt as his eyes rested on Scott. "Mr. Griffith. I hope you'll think about the results of your actions. Your negligence. And the loss that the Davis family has suffered at your hands. I'm sure that loss will remain with you should you ever decide to drive a car again." Dismissively. "And I never want to see you in my courtroom again."

Scott, Robert, and Tracy stood facing Robert's attorney, Troy McClendon, outside the closed courtroom doors.

"You handled that exactly right, Scott," Troy was saying. "And I think I can get your license reinstated in a couple of months - "

The courtroom doors opened, and Scott and Robert turned to see Maryann's parents exit the courtroom with their own attorney.

Cameron glared at Scott with a hatred so fierce that everyone felt it. "You got off easy, you little bastard." The Davis' attorney rested a hand on Cameron's arm, but he shook it off. "Your daddy *giving* you that money you've gotta come up with?"

"I am *not* paying for my son's mistake," Robert said firmly.

Cameron's disdain shifted to Robert. "Two-hundred and fifty-thousand dollars. That's probably pocket change for you. Is that the going rate for my daughter's life?"

Robert's eyes flashed. "Why do you insist on making this more difficult for all of us, Davis? I loved Maryann, too, like she was my own daughter - "

"But she wasn't." Cameron's voice was soft. "How about you keep your lousy money and I take your son's life instead?"

Davis' attorney stepped forward. "Cameron..."

"Shut up."

Robert's tone grew sympathetic. "Do you really think this is what Maryann would want? Would she want to see you acting this way?"

"Don't you ever talk about my daughter - "

"The case has been heard! And Scott's guilt is going to punish him far more than any court could! It's over."

It looked as though Cameron were going to hit Robert. Only he didn't. "This ain't even *close* to being over."

Scott sat next to Joannie Kellner on the set of *Right On* one day while they were waiting for the crewmembers to reset the lights.

"Hey, Emmy winner," she teased. "How come I haven't seen that machine of yours on the lot lately?"

"Too many tickets," Scott lied smoothly. "My old man's making me sell it."

Joannie was genuinely disappointed. "Oh, no. You never even took me for a ride in it."

Scott grinned sexily. "Be grateful. At least you didn't have to put out."

*   *   *

Robert, Tracy, Scott, and Heather sat at their kitchen table, barely able to digest one of Tracy's splendid homemade dinners.

"If *anybody* finds out about what happened to Maryann," Tracy said to Scott, "Your career is over! They'd never keep you on the show! And this new *movie* you just got offered!"

"Will you stop worrying," Robert commanded. "Part of the agreement they signed when they accepted that check was that they couldn't disclose any of our names or the cause of Maryann's death to *anyone*. Especially the media."

"And you think that's going to make a difference?" Tracy snapped.

"It better. As sorry as I am about what happened to that poor girl, I am not going to let them destroy our lives."

"Oh, God," Scott murmured, truly wishing he were never born. "Why did it have to happen...?"

Robert caught Tracy's look of warning before guardedly responding, "It didn't. But it has. And I hope you learned a valuable lesson. Because I agree with Maryann's father one hundred percent. But you're still my son. And nobody's going to hurt you."

In a daze, Scott slid out of his chair and stumbled upstairs.

Scott checked the caller I.D. on his cell phone before answering. "Hey, Sandy."

"Did you forget about me?" she teased.

"Never."

"Okay." Coyly. "I just thought you were ignoring me because we used to date."

Scott grinned broadly. "Don't you know you're my best bud?"

"Aw, you're sweet. What's going on with you? You've been like a recluse for the last few months."

"The show's been keeping me busy."

"Sorry your dad made you get rid of that car."

Scott tried to sound appropriately blameless. "Me, too."

Sandy hesitated. "Scott, I'm not asking for myself, but are you seeing anybody right now?"

"Not seriously. Why?"

"Because I have a friend named Rose. She watches *Right On* all the time, and she would love to meet you."

Scott sighed deeply. "Yeah...I really can't these days, Sandy - "

"I wouldn't ask, but her parents live in Holmby – kind of close to *you* – and I think you'd really like her. Bottom line: she won't stop hounding me until I arrange for you two to meet. So you'd be saving my life."

Scott beamed. "Saving your life, huh?"

"She's eighteen, and definitely your type. I'll e-mail you her picture and her phone number, and *you* decide."

When he and Sandy disconnected, Scott opened Sandy's new message and pulled up the photo. What he saw was an innocent-looking girl with a voluptuous figure, cascading black hair, and deep blue eyes set in a kind, fresh face. Her mischievous grin brought such a smile to his lips that he saved the number in his phone and called it. Voice mail. He listened to her perky personal greeting before disconnecting.

No. I definitely want to talk to this one in person.

Scott came downstairs one morning to find his mother waving an envelope at him. "What is it?"

"Troy got your driver's license reinstated. Did you want to drive your*self* to work today?"

Scott stood there for a moment contemplating. "No. Not yet. I'm not ready for that."

"Rose?"

"Yes?"

"This is Scott Griffith."

Her gasp was almost childlike. Over the phone, Rose Leoni sounded sweet and innocent – nothing like the kind of girl he usually dated. Not since Sandy, anyway. Even though Scott had yet to meet Rose, he liked her almost immediately. "You're so handsome," she trilled. "I can see why you're such a big star."

"Would you like to go out sometime?" He surprised himself by saying it, but he didn't regret it.

She giggled girlishly. "Sure!"

Rose was prettier in person than in her JPEG. Scott drove Tracy's Cadillac to pick Rose up at her parents' house on Delfern Drive. Meeting Rose was a delight. Meeting her parents felt like a police interrogation. Ed and Judy Leoni questioned Scott about himself, his career, his education, his parents' background, and even asked if he was currently involved with anyone.

He hesitated appropriately. "No, I'm not. My schedule on the show doesn't leave me much time. But Rose just sounded so nice on the phone...I wanted to meet her, and get to know her a little bit." He smiled politely at Rose, who sat across from her mother in the Leoni's tastefully decorated living room.

Ed Leoni regarded his wife thoughtfully. "Well...he obviously comes from a good family and has a strong work ethic. I think we can allow him to take Rosie out for the evening."

Scott actually thought Mr. Leoni was making a joke. Sadly, he wasn't. Scott was relieved to finally get out of the house. Once he and Rose were by themselves and on their way out, things went much better. They had dinner at Il Pastaio, a fashionable Italian restaurant on Canon Drive, and were immediately at ease with one another. Rose had an honest, wicked sense of humor, which was totally refreshing for Scott. Instead of going to a movie, Scott drove to the beach, and they held hands while strolling along the walkway. It was the kind of date he hadn't had since he'd received his high school diploma.

On their fourth date, Rose asked Scott to her senior prom.

He looked uncomfortable. "I don't think that would be a good idea."

"Oh." Her disappointment touched him.

"I just mean – I'd have kids coming up to me, we wouldn't have any privacy..."

"I just thought it would be so romantic. And there's nobody else that I'd rather go with. I'll probably stay home."

"You shouldn't do that. You should go. I never got to go to a prom. It's something special."

Rose was astounded. "Why didn't you go to your prom?"

"Because I got my high school diploma through an on-set tutor. I stopped going to regular school when I was fourteen."

Rose regarded Scott meaningfully. "Then it'll be your prom, too. The one you should've had." She threw her arms around him. "It'll be *our* night. And nobody will take it away from us."

It was a magical night that Scott had thought could only be created on television. Scott picked up Rose, and then Rose's friend, Jennifer, and Jennifer's date, Jay. The four of them sat at the same table in the International Ballroom at the Beverly Hilton. Jennifer was sweet, and Jay was down-to-earth and easy to talk to.

Many of Rose's classmates did approach Scott and nervously asked him questions about himself and *Right On*, but Scott wasn't mobbed like he'd feared. He and Rose slow-danced on the dance floor, staring dreamily into each other's eyes, and it was like they'd known each other their whole lives. Later, they strolled along the patio overlooking the pool.

Rose held onto Scott tightly. "Do you think we'll *always* be like this, Scott?"

The wind whipped through Scott's fine blond hair. "Kind of doubt it. Sooner or later, one of us'll have to go to the bathroom."

She completely ignored his joke. "Don't leave me... please..."

"Hey," he teased, trying to get her to smile. "I'm not going anywhere."

Their night didn't end after the prom. Scott, Rose, Jennifer, and Jay stopped at the Denny's on Lincoln Boulevard in Santa Monica for a late-night snack and some laughs. Scott was amazed that he was hungry again after such a short time. He and Jay even bonded, cracking silly jokes at Rose and Jennifer until they were all hurtling funny insults at each other and laughing loudly.

Afterwards, Scott dropped Jennifer and Jay off at Jennifer's house, and then stopped in the darkened parking lot of a lonely closed shopping center. They started to kiss, slowly, and Scott began to unbutton his tuxedo shirt. The glare of a flashlight and the sharp tapping on the window stopped them. Both looked up to see a large male police officer standing on the driver's side and a police cruiser parked next to the Cadillac.

His heart pounding, Scott reluctantly opened his car window.

"You kids can't be here," the cop said gruffly. "What are you doing here?"

Scott's voice cracked. "We were just...sitting...and talking..."

"No way. You've gotta leave. Right now." The cop shined his flashlight through the front and back seats. "Either of you been drinking any alcoholic beverages tonight?"

"No, sir."

The cop looked at Scott accusingly, then appeared satisfied. "All right. I'll cut you a break. You leave right now. I catch you back here again, you're both going to jail."

Scott barely disguised his relief. "Yes, sir. Thank you."

Scott and Rose drove around until they found a secluded glade behind some trees in a park in Santa Monica. Rose happily joined Scott in the backseat, where they made love uninterrupted, although Rose had some difficulty removing her heavy white dress. When they were finished, Scott drove her home, returned to his own house, and gratefully collapsed into his bed.

Scott met Christine Whittaker a few weeks later at a network wrap party. Christine's father was the technical advisor for a top medical show. Blonde, sinewy, and extremely sexy, Christine intrigued Scott from the moment he first laid eyes on her, and they began dating almost immediately. The two of them went out occasionally, although their relationship was mostly physical, much like it had been with Raquel. Scott genuinely cared for Rose, but he couldn't handle a serious relationship. He was still getting used to driving a car around, although Robert and Tracy had recently taken him to a Porsche dealership, where Scott had purchased another car with his own money.

He rarely drove fast, even on the freeway, and he never drove carelessly again. Maryann was still in his thoughts, although Scott's family never mentioned her name. Tracy had wanted to display Scott's Emmy in their living room, but he had refused. The trophy remained on a shelf in Scott's closet, where he seldom had to look at it. He knew he didn't deserve it. Sometimes he felt like he didn't deserve to be alive.

Scott left Christine's one morning after a passionate night of lovemaking and a playful swim in her pool. They were drawn to each other but not in love. As much as Scott cared for Rose, he had to admit to himself that he wasn't in love with her, either.

As Scott drove to the studio that morning, he acknowledged the ugly truth.

He'd killed the love of his life.

CHAPTER 7

The black stretch limo sped furiously down the quiet street of gated mansions in Long Island, New York.

Coming to an abrupt stop in the drive of one of the more impressive homes, the driver of the car lowered the tinted window and spoke into a callbox next to the gate.

"I'm back. I got him."

From the balcony overlooking his front lawn, Larry Mitchell observed the black limousine pass through the gate and whisk towards the rear of the compound.

An astute-looking man in his late fifties, Larry possessed a full head of silver hair, a square jaw, and a cleft in his chin. The tailored gray suit he wore blended incongruously with the warm sunny day.

His mouth was set in a thin line as he turned and went back inside the house.

Larry was sitting in a large red leather chair in his ornate study, when two young muscular men, also in suits, entered and stood at attention.

"We've frisked him, sir," one of them said. "No weapons."

Larry waved his hand dismissively. "Fine. Send him in. And leave us alone, will you?"

"He's dangerous, Senator."

Annoyed. "I don't care."

The two men nodded and stepped aside.

A robust man in his late fifties entered. He had shaggy white hair, sharp opal eyes, and wore black-rimmed glasses and brown sports clothes.

Two more solemn young men stood behind him in the doorway. The first two reluctantly joined the second pair and closed the door behind them.

"What the hell do you want, Camarari?" Larry demanded.

"Watch your mouth," Caesar Camarari responded roughly. "'Cuz if I wanted to blow you away, I wouldn't need the piece your boys just took from me."

Larry rose from his chair. "I know. You wouldn't even have to leave L.A. to do that."

"I came right to *you*, Larry, 'cuz I couldn't say nothin' on the phone, and you're the only one who's got the kind of pull to make sure that the bastard goes to trial."

Larry turned and paced toward the window. "So you want me to go up against the biggest mafia boss in the country just to settle this vendetta that you two have?"

"The bad blood between me and Santinello ain't got nothin' to do with it. The scum peddles drugs to young kids. He needs to be put away for good. And I want *you* to make it happen. You *owe* me."

Larry nodded thoughtfully. "It's a good thing Santinello doesn't know you're in town."

Caesar made a face. "What are you? Stupid? 'Course he knows I'm in town. Probably been tailin' me from the airport."

Caesar was standing so close to him now that the two men were practically on top of each other.

"Just get him this time, Larry."

Luca Santinello lumbered out of the Luna Restaurant in Little Italy, and into a waiting limo parked curbside on Mulberry Street. Accompanied by three of his bodyguards, he settled himself in the backseat, and the car glided off in the direction of Chinatown.

A large man in his mid-fifties, Luca almost always dressed like he was going to a funeral. His wizened, hooded eyes observed everything, and his hardened features betrayed no sign of what he was thinking or feeling.

Sandwiched between two of his lieutenants now in the back of the limo, Luca flinched when he heard a cell phone go off.

One of his most trusted men, Sal, caught Luca's look. "Sorry, Mr. Santinello. It's mine." Into the phone. "Yeah...? Uh-huh...He's right here." To Luca. "For you, Mr. Santinello. It's Aldo."

Luca took the offending instrument and regarded it with disgust. "I'll never get used to these damn things." He spoke guardedly into the phone. "Uh-huh."

"It's Aldo, Mr. Santinello. I wouldn't bother ya if it wasn't important, but I thought you'd wanna know. Camamrari came in on a flight this morning. We tailed him from the airport. He went to see the senator. We don't know what about."

Luca's voice was cold. "And you're waitin' until just *now* to tell me?"

"Sorry, Mr. Santinello, but we had to move fast. There was no time."

"Well you got time *now*. Get somebody on it. Find out what he's here for and what he's doin'. I wanna know. ASAP."

Luca snapped the phone shut and tossed it on the floor.

Caesar Camarari returned home from his trip at 10:30 P.M. the following night. Home was an opulent fortress near the top of Bel Air Road.

From the living room window, his wife, Carol, an attractive woman in her mid-fifties, watched as the limo passed through the gates and headed straight into the garage. The huge door came down immediately.

Seconds later, she heard the kitchen door open, and Caesar entered the living room looking tired and sullen.

"How did it go?" she asked.

Caesar heaved a sigh. "Mitchell's gonna cooperate. He's finally going to put that lowlife away. Or I'll put Mitchell away. For good. Put the security system back on."

A menacing German Shepard bounded into the room and playfully jumped up on Caesar.

"Nina! How ya doin', girl? Ya miss me? Huh?" Caesar gently petted, patted, and slapped the big animal around.

Nina responded with only affectionate whimpers and licks with her enormous tongue.

Caesar turned and lumbered up the large staircase, Nina right behind him.

Carol made her way into the kitchen and was just about to arm the alarm system when she heard a discreet knock at the door. Seeing who it was on the other side, Carol cautiously opened it and allowed the kind-looking elderly woman to enter.

"Mom, what are you doing here?" Carol asked, quietly closing the door and lowering her voice to a hush. "Go back to your part of the house before he hears you."

"It's a fifteen-minute walk to my part of the house," Alice Benson snapped. "What did you find out?"

"Not a lot. But the senator *is* going to help."

Alice took a seat at the kitchen table. "Thank the Lord for that. Finally. After all these years, Santinello is going to get what's coming to him."

Carol sat across from her mother. "Well, the state is only going to indict him. It doesn't mean they'll get a conviction."

"They'd better. Who knows how many other lives he's ruined? On top of ours?" Alice looked sharply at Carol. "Enough time has gone by. Why doesn't Caesar have him taken care of permanently?"

Carol's gaze was level. "I never question him on those things, Mom. I'm sure there's a very good reason why he hasn't. The same reason there's always been."

"To protect *us*." Alice nodded gravely.

"Yes. He's always been able to do it. We just have to trust that he knows what he's doing."

Gina knew who was calling before she even checked the caller I.D. "Hi, Mom!"

"Did you forget my number? It's almost a week you've been out there, and *I* have to call *you*?"

"I'm fine, Ma. Really. Me and Deb have just been busy getting stuff for the apartment."

"And hitting the beach, I imagine."

"Well I can't be seen without a tan. I won't be able to show my face."

"Have you given any thought to what we talked about?"

"I'll get a job eventually. I'm just not sure what I'm suited for."

"Would you be interested in doing something in television?"

Gina grimaced. "You mean acting? That's definitely not for me."

"What about *behind* the camera? Maybe working for a studio?"

"I don't know. Why?"

"Because a friend of mine out there has some influence at Paradigm Studios, and she says she can get you a job working on a T.V. show, if you want it."

Gina liked the idea right away. "Which one?"

"I have no idea. Do you want me to call her and tell her you're interested?"

"Sure! I wouldn't mind giving it a try."

Driving through the main gate of Paradigm Pictures was surreal. Gina gave her name to the guard and was directed to park in the nearby south parking lot. She was driving a new white Mercedes convertible that she'd just purchased, and it gleamed in the bright sun as she quickly located a parking space. The entire studio lot seemed to be populated with huge buildings that looked like aircraft hangers, and with the help of a map the guard had handed her, Gina painstakingly found her way to Stage 21.

"Gina?" The woman was blonde, pretty, and looked to be about Cynthia's age.

Gina nodded eagerly.

"Susan Lowry."

They shook hands.

"Are you ready to start work?"

"Yes."

Gina followed Susan inside the enormous soundstage and past several constructed sets. A family living room. A male teenager's bedroom. An outdoor basketball court.

"This production is the series *Right On*. Have you seen it?"

"No," Gina said sheepishly. "Sorry."

"That's all right," Susan said amiably. "Your job as a production assistant entails doing practically everything."

"I won't have to act in front of the camera, will I?"

Susan smiled. "Everything except that."

Susan's description of the job had been accurate. Gina found herself all over the set, preparing the craft services table, setting props, handwriting fake "homework" papers for the actors to use. That morning, the producer's assistant even allowed her to drive some extras in an electric golf cart across the lot to New York Street, where a second unit crew was shooting.

When Gina returned to Stage 21, the assistant director demanded, "Have you seen Scott?"

"Who?"

"Scott Griffith. He plays Cal."

She had no idea who he was talking about. "No."

The man handed her a sheaf of blue papers. "He's probably in his dressing room. Bring him these new script pages. And make sure you put them in his *hand*. I don't wanna hear that he didn't get 'em."

Heather Griffith tried to ignore the stares she was getting from the cute blond boy sitting across the quiet classroom.

She smiled at him, blushed, and then turned away.

Keeping one eye on her teacher, she carefully checked her latest text message.

I THINK HE LIKES U.

Heather looked up. Her best friend, Lynda Seville, a large-breasted brunette, smiled knowingly.

Heather shook her head emphatically.

The boy continued to stare.

Heather continued to play it cool.

Another text. U GONNA LET HIM TO 2ND BASE?

Heather shook her head again.

This time, her teacher, Mr. Katz, noticed.

Once the bell rang, the students of Beverly Hills High filled the halls in a wave of teenage bodies.

Outside the classroom doorway, the blond-haired boy caught Heather's eye, smiled shyly, and disappeared down the corridor.

"Another one bites the dust?" Lynda had come up behind her.

"I don't understand it. He didn't even give me a chance to say anything."

The two girls started down the hall.

"It's your family, Heather. They intimidate people."

"If I could, I'd change my name and move someplace else where nobody knows me!"

"What are you complaining about? I'd be thrilled if my dad were a hot producer. But I wouldn't want Scott as my brother..."

"I know. Because you're totally into him. Just like the rest of the country."

"Do you have to go to your locker?"

"Yes."

They turned a corner.

"You act like all of this is a bad thing," Lynda went on. "It's not! You can have any guy you want."

"I don't want just any guy. He's gotta be absolutely amazing!"

"Boyfriend material?"

Heather shrugged. "I suppose."

Lynda smirked. "Yeah. The guy you have your first time with should be the man of your dreams."

Heather stopped and pulled Lynda to one side. "What?"

"Heather, c'mon. We've been friends since grade school. Do you really think I don't know you're still a virgin?"

Heather gripped Lynda's arm and hissed, "Cool it, will ya! And just because we're friends doesn't mean I tell you everything."

Lynda regarded her knowingly. "Heather. It's me you're talking to. The time has come for you to kiss your virginity goodbye. You just have to choose which guy gets the honors."

Gina hurried down the carpeted hallway behind the main sets, glancing at the names on the dressing room doors. JANICE LINDEN. JOANNIE KELLNER. RORY THOMPSON. When she came to SCOTT GRIFFITH, she knocked confidently on the door. No response. She knocked louder. Gina heard a man shout from inside, so she hesitantly turned the doorknob and entered.

The dressing room was more spacious than she'd anticipated. Nicely furnished, with a long make-up counter, mirrors with light bulbs along the top, and two director chairs. Gina heard water running from an adjacent cubicle, so she called, "Mr. Griffith? I'm supposed to give you these pages!"

She glanced around the room again, noticing some wardrobe on a rack and some clothing carelessly thrown around. The running water stopped, and Gina jumped when a man's voice behind her yelled, "I said I'll be right - "

She turned and saw him. He was looking toward the door, but his eyes bulged when he noticed her there. She couldn't tear her eyes away. Blond, muscular, naked, and dripping wet, he was so surprised, it took a moment before it occurred to him to try to cover himself. "I'm sorry," she gasped, trying to look somewhere else. Gina weakly held up the pages in her hand. "I – I was supposed to give you these..." She reluctantly turned her back to him.

"You can just leave 'em on the table." He grabbed a towel and wrapped it around his waist.

"Okay," she said apprehensively. "But I'm supposed to put them in your *hand*."

He slowly stepped up behind her and took the script pages out of her hand. She flinched, still keeping her back to him. "It's okay," he said kindly. "They're in my hand. Look, I didn't mean - "

"I'm sorry," she said, still flustered, darting out the door and nearly running over Joannie Kellner. Joannie stood in the doorway and stared at Scott in mock surprise.

Pointing at Joannie, Scott half-jokingly warned, "Don't even say it!"

The first scene to be shot that Gina had to assist on that morning couldn't have been more ironic. Scott and three other male actors assembled on a locker room set and shot an entire dialogue scene wearing nothing but towels around their waists. Of course, Gina knew that the boys had to be wearing shorts underneath, but it didn't stop her mind from wandering. And remembering.

From time to time, Scott looked over to where she stood behind the camera and gave her his warmest, most knowing smile. She fought to meet his gaze, but still had difficulty maintaining the stare.

Gina didn't realize that Joannie Kellner was standing next to her. "These are the scenes I *love*!" Joannie smirked. She motioned to Scott. "So...you were helping him rehearse?" she asked, throwing Gina a knowing look of her own.

Gina widened her eyes and shook her head emphatically. "Definitely not." She quietly stepped away from Joannie and busied herself at the prop table.

*   *   *

"You saw Scott Griffith naked??" Debbie shrieked.

"By accident," Gina insisted, sipping a soda and reclining on their living room couch. "He told me to come in, so I did. I didn't know he was in the *shower*. I didn't even know he *had* a shower back there!"

Debbie eagerly sat down next to her. "And?"

"It's not funny, Deb. I was afraid they were going to fire me or something. This is my first job. I don't want to blow it."

"You won't."

"I don't know what *he'll* say."

"Yeah, but from what you told me, he wasn't that put out by it."

"How am I supposed to face him every day?"

"Like a grown-up. This is the real world. Things like this happen."

"Only to me."

"I just have one question."

Annoyed. "Shoot."

"Can I go to work with you tomorrow?"

Gina had just come out the door to Stage 21 when she saw Scott heading her way.

He stopped her as she reached the bottom of the steps. "Can I talk to you?"

She squinted up at him in the bright sunlight. "I have to bring in the extras from Central Casting."

"It can wait," he said gently. "What's your name?"

She fingered the studio badge on her shirt. "Gina. Gina Moore. Look, Mr. Griffith, I'm really sorry about - "

"You don't have anything to be sorry about. I've been looking for you because I wanted to apologize to *you*. I was trying to tell you that I'd be right out because I didn't want you to leave with those pages - "

"I shouldn't have come in there. I thought you were telling me to come in, but I couldn't be sure, and I didn't want to get in any trouble - "

"You sound like me." He grinned. "Every time I try to stay out of trouble, I end up finding it. More than my share, usually."

She visibly relaxed. "You're not gonna have me fired?"

"Fired? I wouldn't do that. I just didn't want you to think I was some kind of a nut. I am, but I didn't want you to think that."

She surrendered the tiniest of smiles. "Thanks, Mr. Griffith. That's very nice of you."

"Another thing. You keep calling me 'Mr. Griffith,' I'm gonna start looking around for my *father*. After what we've been through, you can at least call me Scott."

Her eyes softened. "Okay. I'll remember." She looked startled. "Oh. I'm sorry. I've gotta go get those extras!"

He lightly touched her arm and deadpanned. "Background Artists."

She tried not to smile as she hurried off.

Mesmerized, he watched her disappear around the corner.

Gina handed Debbie a VISITOR badge and led her through the main studio pedestrian entrance.

"This is so incredible!" Debbie beamed. "How did you manage it?"

"You're in luck. Our second A.D. is from Rhode Island, too."

"A.D.?"

"Assistant Director. Don't you know anything?" Gina grinned.

Debbie looked around the studio lot in awe. "I feel like I'm dreaming. Have you seen anybody famous?"

"Only the cast of *Right On*. They don't really let me go around wandering."

Impishly. "Is Scott Griffith going to take off his clothes again?"

"Not if we're lucky."

"Speak for yourself!"

Gina escorted Debbie past the soundstages and toward the main administration building.

"We don't have much time," Gina said. "You have to leave right after lunch."

"Don't remind me."

They were just about to enter the building on their left when Gina saw Scott Griffith strolling toward them. "Hey!" He looked glad to see them both.

Debbie's mouth dropped open. "Oh my God!"

"Oh, come on," Scott joked. "I can't look *that* bad. I took a shower today especially!"

"Hi, Scott," Gina greeted him. "Lunch isn't over yet, is it?"

"No, no. I was just wondering who your friend is."

"You're Scott Griffith," Debbie announced, wide-eyed.

Gina sighed. "Scott, this is my very star struck cousin, Debbie Monroe. She's staying with me for the summer."

"Nice to meet you," Scott smiled, taking Debbie's hand.

Debbie struggled to breathe and smiled back.

"Did you need anything?" Gina asked Scott.

"Actually, yeah," Scott replied. "Are you guys going into the commissary?"

Gina nodded.

"Would you mind if I joined you?" he asked hesitantly. "I hate to eat alone. Most of the time, that's what I end up doing." He looked at Debbie. "That's if you don't mind."

Debbie felt like she would faint. "Mind?"

"I think she's trying to say she would be thrilled." Gina shrugged. "And it's okay by me."

The three of them sat at a window table in the studio commissary.

"I loved your last movie," Debbie gushed.

Gina looked at the two of them in momentary confusion.

"You haven't seen *Wacky Wednesday*??" Debbie was staring at her incredulously.

Gina sighed. "I can tell I'm not very popular at this table."

"It was really cool!" Debbie enthused. "It's about this father and son who switch bodies for a day, and then all this crazy stuff happens!"

"I play the son," Scott explained earnestly.

Gina couldn't help smiling. "I figured." Her smile vanished. "Wait a minute. Isn't there already a movie like that that came out a long time ago?"

"Yes," Scott admitted, looking away. "*Freaky Friday.* It was a Disney movie."

"I thought so. Except it was with a mother and daughter, wasn't it?"

Scott grinned. "Right again. I get it. You know about all kinds of movies - as long as they're not one of mine."

Gina glared at him. "That's not true!"

"I think it is," Scott teased.

"Is not!"

Scott escorted Gina and Debbie toward the main studio entrance.

"Debbie," Scott said, "There's a tour of the studio lot you might like. Would you like me to put your name on the list?"

"Yeah," Debbie answered immediately. "Sure. If it's no trouble."

"I'll take care of it right now."

After they left Debbie, Scott accompanied Gina back to Stage 21.

"Well, we got through a lunch," he commented dryly. "Are you still feeling weird around me?"

"I don't feel weird around you," Gina replied honestly. "For some reason, I feel like I've known you a lot longer."

"It *is* a lot longer. It's been two whole weeks."

"Do you *always* joke around?"

Scott looked at the ground. "No."

"Yes," Gina affirmed, sure she was right.

"I was gonna say...we got through a lunch...how would you like to try dinner?"

Gina looked away. "Oh. I'll tell you what. I will have lunch with you any day you want. I don't think I'm ready to do dinner yet."

Scott was genuinely amazed. "You're turning me down?"

"No. I'm just saying that this work schedule is very demanding, and we shouldn't let anything distract us. Besides, I just moved out here, and I really can't make any plans right now." She looked at him uncomfortably. "Is that okay?"

"Fine," he said, still in shock. "Where did you move from, anyway?"

"New York. Manhattan."

"Ah. New York City girl. Cool."

She rolled her eyes. "Thanks. I can't get that worked up about it." Gina stuck out her hand in a mock gesture. "Friends?"

He shook her hand, equally mocking. "Friends."

"Great. I'll catch you later." And she was gone again.

He stared after her with a longing he hadn't felt in years. "Yeah. I hope so."

Joannie Kellner sat in one of the director chairs on the *Right On* set, thoughtfully studying her script. The main stage lights were down, and most of the cast and crew were still at lunch.

A good-looking brown-haired guy wandered into the soundstage and casually snuck up behind her. "If you want, sis, I can help you with the big words."

"Jason, what are you doing here?" she asked, pretending to be annoyed. "I thought the guards were supposed to keep *out* lowlife."

"I'm not shooting today, and I didn't feel like listening to Mom's whining, so I thought I'd check out the action *here*."

"You're not missing anything."

Jason glanced towards the *Right On* classroom set and spied Gina setting some cards on the set furniture that read *Hot Set, Keep Off.* "Oh, hel*lo*," Jason muttered, eyeing Gina like she was a delicacy on a menu. To Joannie, "I see they're improving the look of the show."

Joannie dismissively turned a page of her script. "She's one of our new P.A.s."

"We all have to work our way up."

"You're a little late, brother. *Scott* already has something going on with *that* one."

"Scott? How many times do I have to tell you, Joannie? He's *gay!*"

"He is not!"

"I'm serious," Jason said, looking uncomfortable, and almost convincing her. "I've caught him checking me out a few times."

And he was off. Jason was standing in front of the set when Gina looked up and saw him. Hands in the pockets of his khaki pants. Subtle gaze. Innocent smile. She immediately recognized him as a familiar face she'd known more than half her life.

Gina returned his smile politely. "Hi."

"Hello."

She found it hard to ignore his guileless gaze. "Don't I know you?"

"I wish you did."

Recognition hit. "I do know you! You're Joannie's brother."

His face fell. "'Joannie's brother.' Wow. Haven't gotten *that* one in years."

She blushed as she took a step toward him. "I didn't mean it that way. You're on *Blue Shield.*"

"Jason Kellner," he affirmed amiably.

"And you did two sitcoms before *that.*"

Jason was genuinely surprised. "That's right. Didn't think anybody remembered."

Gina turned her head in a manner that was uncharacteristically shy. "Some people, I don't forget easily."

"I couldn't forget *you*. Except you haven't told me your name."

Even more uncharacteristic, she became self-conscious. "Gina."

"Nice name." *Nice body.*

"But if I've said anything to offend you, then my name's Tara."

The twinkle in his eyes reassured her. "You haven't said anything to offend me."

She grinned. "Guess there's hope for me."

He lowered his voice and leaned in close to her. "I can't believe I'm about to say this, but I have to get to know you, Gina."

"You *have* to?"

"Yes," he said seriously. "You're not like any woman I've ever met before." He looked away, but she could see the embarrassment in his eyes. "What I'm trying to say is...would you like to go out with me sometime?"

"How do you know I don't have a boyfriend?" she asked, his intense look unsettling her.

"I don't. Wishful thinking."

They stared at each other for a few moments. Gina was the first to look away. "We're gonna be shooting all this week..."

"So am I. The weekend?"

"I just moved out here...I have a lot of stuff to - "

"You have to eat. And I'd like to have dinner Saturday night with something else besides another script to learn."

She tilted her head to one side. "Are you actually trying to get me to feel sorry for you?"

He struggled to keep a straight face. "If it'll help."

Gina sighed, trying without success to look annoyed. "Oh, all right. If you promise not to call the suicide hotline, it's a date."

From her seat behind one of the cameras, Joannie monitored Jason's progress.

Three minutes and eight seconds. He's catching up to Scott.

Gina and Jason had a table on the patio of the Warehouse Restaurant in Marina Del Rey.

"It was actually my mom," Jason said, absently pushing the food around his plate. "It wouldn't have happened without *her*. She got me and Joannie into acting classes by the time we were five. I did commercials until I was eleven, and then I got the part on *Total Strangers*."

"The sitcom," Gina nodded, starting in on her salmon. "I *liked* those sitcoms with the studio audience. Me and my friends used to watch them all the time."

Jason shrugged. "They're just not doing 'em anymore."

"How come *you're* not on *Right On*?"

Jason exaggerated a surprised reaction. "Me and Joannie on the same set? I would smack her, and she would end up calling the cops on me."

Gina gazed at him, not buying a word. "She says the same kind of crap about *you*, and I can tell neither one of you really mean it."

She had him that time. He reluctantly cracked a smile. "She's okay. I'm proud of her."

Gina picked at her vegetables, although her mind was far away. "Is it more *fun* working on *Blue Shield*?"

Jason nodded eagerly. "*I* like it. It's a good fit for me."

"That's important."

He sat back pensively. "I don't think I'm the right type for *Right On*."

His comment snapped her back to the moment. "What's the right type for *Right On?*"

"You have to appeal to young girls. I appeal more to old ladies."

Disbelief. "Old ladies??"

"Yeah." Jason affected a high-pitched old woman's voice and motioned with his hand like he was pinching a child's cheeks. "Oh, you're so cute, let me give you a quarter!" He scowled. "I'm great with the Over Seventy set."

"I'm sure you're exaggerating."

"It's just how people see me."

"Are you and Joannie the same age?" Gina couldn't help asking as they strolled down Santa Monica Pier.

"She's sixteen. Three years younger than me. She still thinks she's smarter."

"I don't have any brothers or sisters."

"Are you studying?"

"Studying what?"

"Acting. Is that your aspiration?"

Gina widened her eyes in genuine surprise. "Me? No way. I'll do anything but that."

"You're kidding. A woman who looks like you. I thought for sure you came out here to be an actress."

Gina shook her head. "A friend of my mom's got me the job. I still don't know what I want to do yet."

Jason almost didn't believe her. "Really?"

Gina nodded. "That's what I moved out here to find out."

Jason was driving Gina back to her apartment in Westwood when he asked, "Have you ever been to a mixer?"

She frowned. "I don't think so."

"It's what you would call a Hollywood party. A lot of celebs host them for publicity."

Gina smiled knowingly. "Of course."

"I got invited to one next week at Laurel Gillis' house."

"*Laurel Gillis?* I *love* her songs."

"Yeah? Would you like to go with me?"

"It sounds great! Thanks." Gina's smile vanished. "I just feel bad about Deb."

"Who?"

"My cousin. She's here visiting me."

"Oh, right." Jason thought quickly. "Would she want to come?"

"Are you kidding? She'd be thrilled to death!"

"Okay. I can get her name on the list."

"Seriously?" Worried. "Are you sure?"

"Why not? It'll be fun."

Jason pulled into the semicircular driveway of Gina's apartment building on Wilshire Boulevard. Inside the lobby, a uniformed doorman watched Jason's car expectantly.

Gina debated what to do. "Would you like to come in?"

His soft brown eyes were shining, but he appeared uncertain. "It's only our first date. Definitely next time. Okay?"

Gina smiled warmly. "Okay. I had fun. Thanks."

They were still looking at each other, and they leaned in at the same time and kissed. His lips were hot on her lips, and he seemed to touch a part of her soul where few others had been allowed. It was over too quickly, and the kind expression on his face reassured her. "Pick you up around seven?"

Gina nodded and got out of the car.

Jason watched her step into the lobby and disappear inside the elevator.

He thought about her all the way home.

Cynthia Moore wore a pair of white silk pajamas as she sat in the living room of her New York City penthouse sipping her morning coffee.

The phone on the coffee table buzzed, and she immediately checked the caller I.D.

FRONT DESK.

Sighing heavily, she picked it up.

"It's David, Ms. Moore. Down in the lobby."

A sleepy, "Yes?"

"The same process server is here. I told him you weren't home, but he's been waiting outside the front door for the last two hours." David lowered his voice. "I'd call the police, but technically, he's on public property - "

"I know. Don't say anything to him, David. But from now on, let me know whenever you see him around here."

"Yes, ma'am."

*   *   *

Cynthia checked carefully to make sure the parking garage was deserted before she slipped out of the stairwell and headed towards the rear exit. She was dressed in a pair of slacks and a blouse, her Prada purse slung over her shoulder.

She stole another glance behind her. Nothing. She could only hear the clicking of her own shoes against the pavement.

Cynthia turned to see two tough-looking women upon her, flashing badges and expertly blocking her way to the exit.

"District Attorney's office. Cynthia Moore, we'd like to ask you a few questions."

The three women sat in the back of a stationary limo parked just a few feet from where the two plainclothes officers had cornered Cynthia.

"What is it you want?" Cynthia asked softly.

Office Schroeder, who looked to be no more than a few years older than her partner, spoke up. "For the past month, we've been trying to serve your daughter, Gina Moore, with a summons. We understand she still lives here."

Cynthia opened her mouth to answer, then changed gears. "What is this all about?"

"Her testimony is vital in a case we're preparing against Luca Santinello."

Cynthia's eyes widened. "We don't know anyone by that name."

"Mrs. Moore," Schroeder's partner said tersely, "It's a matter of record that your daughter was involved with one of Santinello's top drug pushers."

Schroeder nodded. "That's why we believe she may have information that could help convict him."

Cynthia's mouth dropped open. "You want her to testify against him??"

"If she doesn't, Santinello could walk away clean again."

Schroeder's partner affirmed, "Gina is the only link between Frank Dinato and Luca Santinello. If we can prove the two of them were connected, we can make the charges against Santinello stick."

Cynthia shook her head, her expression pained. "What difference does all this make now? Frank Dinato is dead."

"Yes," Schroeder agreed, "But Santinello and his organization are still alive and well. And if we don't put him away, countless other young kids and teenagers will fall prey to drugs and the damage they do. Do you and your daughter want to live with that?"

"And it doesn't just affect the kids," Schroeder's partner added. "It destroys entire families and devastates the parents." Pointedly. "But we don't have to tell *you* about that."

Officer Schroeder could see the agony in Cynthia's eyes, and her tone softened. "Please, Mrs. Moore. Where is your daughter?"

CHAPTER 8

Scott Griffith awoke early Saturday morning feeling incredibly good and unusually happy.

Slipping on a pair of red shorts and a blue t-shirt, he went downstairs to find his mom and dad and Heather eating breakfast at the kitchen table.

Tracy had made her own specialty, blueberry pancakes, and was serving them when Scott strutted into the kitchen.

"His Royal Highness is up," Tracy teased, placing a pancake on the plate she had set for him at the table.

"Morning, Mom," he greeted her warmly, giving her a quick hug and sitting down.

"Hey, bro," Heather smiled. "How's work going?"

Scott sipped his orange juice. "I can't wait until we're done shooting this season finale. I can use a break."

Tracy deposited a small stack of envelopes next to Scott's placemat. "Your mail. I thought you'd want to open some of it."

"I haven't had time. This week's been hectic."

"Just be happy your *fan* mail isn't delivered here," Heather quipped. "Otherwise we wouldn't be able to get into the living room."

Scott opened a festive-looking envelope, pulled out the card, and read it with amusement. "Oh, yeah. I heard about this."

Heather looked up. "What is it?"

"It's an invitation to Laurel Gillis' party. She's having a bash to kick off her national tour. It starts next week."

"When is the party?"

"Next Saturday."

"Who's Lori Gillis?" Robert asked, looking up from his laptop.

"*Laurel* Gillis," Tracy corrected, replacing the orange juice carton in the refrigerator and sitting down at the table herself. "I've heard one of her CDs. She's not too bad."

"Laurel's big right now," Scott remarked.

Robert shook his head. "She won't last. A lot of these young girls come along and try to be singers. They all think they're gonna be the next big sensation. They're hot for a while, and then they're forgotten after a year."

Scott held up his invitation. "Check out the address of her house. It's right here in Bel Air."

"Yeah. And most likely it's rented. Do what I told you, Scott. Focus on your acting. Stay with *Right On* until you're offered more features."

Scott nodded and started in on his pancakes.

"Are you going?" Heather inquired.

"I might," Scott mused. "Should be fun."

"Is there any chance that you could take me and Lynda with you?"

Scott stopped mid bite. "You and Lynda?"

"Yes! You said that when the next big party came along, you'd take us with you."

Scott grimaced. "I did say that, didn't I?" He paused dramatically and took a deep breath. "Okay. I think I'll take Rose to this one. If you and Lynda want to join us, it's okay by me."

Heather leaped out of her chair and flung her arms around Scott's neck. "You're the best brother!"

"Heather – off. Now."

She kissed him on the cheek. "I love you."

"Whatever."

Raquel Morollan went shopping for a dress on Rodeo Drive by herself. She'd been to many celebrity-filled parties in the past, but the event at Laurel Gillis' house tonight was especially important. She knew that Scott Griffith would be there, and she didn't want to look anything but her absolute best.

One of the memories she cherished most was the two of them swimming in her pool one night when her parents were out of town.

She clung to him in the water, never wanting to let him go.

"I wish it could be like this all the time," he husked, staring deep into her eyes.

"I know," she said, the thought filling her with elation. "Someday I want us to live in our own *house, with our* own *pool, and cars with matching license plates that say 'Rocky' and 'Rambo.'"*

He grinned. "That sounds great! As long as mine's red!" Scott pulled away from her, slid his hands under the water, and proudly laid his sopping wet Speedos by the side of the pool.

Raquel's eyes widened. "Oh my God!" Her mouth was still agape as he took her in his arms and kissed her neck. "What's gotten into you? I've created a monster!"

"That's right," he said between kisses, "You have. So you better enjoy it..."

The chiming of her cell phone snapped Raquel back to the present.

It was her current boyfriend, Shawn Carrigan. "You all set for tonight?"

"Just about," she said thoughtfully. "I'm doing some last-minute shopping."

"What else is new?" he retorted good-naturedly. "I just got done working out and I need a shower. I wish you could join me."

"Maybe I can stay at *your* place tonight, and we can get really dirty."

"Now yer talkin'!"

Smiling, Raquel hit CALL END and slipped the phone back into her purse.

I've got to find some way to get Scott alone tonight. We have a lot of lost time to make up for.

Scott was right in the middle of a barbell rep when his cell phone went off. Returning the barbell to the rack above his head and sitting up on the bench, he reached for the phone.

"Scott!" scolded the childlike female voice on the other end. "Where've you been?"

"Rose!"

Annoyance. "Yeah, who'd you think?"

"Well, I was expecting a call from Miley Cyrus..."

"What!"

He grinned. "Just kidding."

She giggled girlishly. "Oh, Scott. I don't know why I put up with you."

"I think we both know why."

Pretending to be offended. "Scott! You're terrible!"

"That's not what you said the other night."

Loving every minute. "You're disgusting!"

"I know. Are you all set for the party?"

Panic. "No! It's tonight, and I don't have a thing to wear!"

He rolled his eyes and shook his head, almost smiling. "I'm sure you'll look great – just like you always do."

"It's a very important decision," she said seriously.

"I understand," he said, not really understanding at all. "I'll talk to you later."

Scott disconnected and looked out the large plate-glass window of his family's home gym. The room was so pristine, it looked as though it had never been used. Fully equipped with a rack of silver hand weights, barbells, ellipses machines, and nautilus weight machines, the gym had three walls that were completely mirrored, and a built-in, high definition sound system.

He had just set the phone down on the bench when it went off again.

UNKNOWN.

Scott frowned and hit TALK.

The voice on the other end was a mature, confident, and very intelligent woman. "Scott? It's Ellen Stellar."

He almost dropped the phone. "Ellen! Hi! How ya doin'?"

"Good, sweetie. I need to meet with you. Are you free to drop by my house sometime today?"

"Yeah," he croaked. "Sure."

"Oh, good! Is one o'clock okay?"

"Perfect," he managed.

"Great! I really appreciate this, honey. See you then."

Scott pulled up in front of a manicured driveway blocked by a large iron gate on Bellagio Road in Bel Air. He stopped next to a keypad callbox on the driver's side, pushed the call button, and waited. A beep sounded, and Ellen's guarded tone crackled through the speaker. "Hello?"

"Ellen, it's Scott," he called.

Her voice warmed up considerably. "Oh, hi, honey! Just park next to my town car. I'll be right there."

He waited until the gate slid all the way open before pulling into her driveway and parking.

Ellen's house was a magnificent Colonial-style mansion that looked almost a hundred years old but was in beautifully maintained condition.

Scott leaped out of his car and bounded to the front door. He pressed the doorbell and waited.

The door was opened by a striking woman of forty-two, with keen, intelligent eyes, a sinewy body, and beautiful suntanned skin. The conservative blouse and slacks she wore didn't do her figure justice, but her personality radiated energy and enthusiasm.

"Scott! It's good to see you!" She swept him into a hug, then closed the door behind him. "How've you been, sweetie? You look *great*! Every time I see you, you look more handsome."

He blushed slightly and stepped into her elegant living room. "Thanks."

She gestured to the couch. "Have a seat."

He did so. "Is there a problem with *Wacky Wednesday?*"

Her face registered surprise. "Oh, no. Not to worry. The movie's doing great, and the video distribution deals are all in place."

He nodded, relief flooding him. "Good to hear."

"No, what I wanted to talk to you about is another project I'm working on. A big action movie. One that'll make *Wacky Wednesday* look like a sick student film."

He leaned forward eagerly. "I'm all ears."

"We're talking a mucho budget on this one, Scott. Big action sequences, *some* stunts, depending on what you're comfortable with. And – you're going to love *this* part – location shooting in Las Vegas and four European countries!"

Scott's eyes widened. "You want me to star in an action movie?"

Ellen hesitated. "Well...not exactly star. More *co*-star."

"Oh. You want me to share 'above the title'?"

"Exactly. The part I have you in mind for is Todd Everett. He's the *younger brother* of the leading man."

"Who's *that* going to be?"

"I've already signed Jerry Garnett."

"You're kidding! Jerry? He's done everything from action to Shakespeare."

"Have you two met?"

Scott was duly impressed. "No, but...I never pictured myself doing a film alongside *him*."

Ellen smiled. "Well picture it now. I'm offering you the part."

"Wait a minute. I've still got *Right On* to think about. If I said yes, when would shooting start?"

"In about six weeks."

"What!"

"Right when your hiatus starts. Do you have something else lined up?"

Scott's mind was racing. "No, but I haven't even read the script yet! And we've got to talk details. Why didn't you just send an offer to Maureen?"

"Because I wanted to get your reaction first, before I started getting involved with agents and contracts. I wanted to see if it was something you *wanted* to do."

"Definitely. I just want to read the script first and find out more about it before I commit."

"Of course."

Confusion. "One thing, though. If I'm supposed to be Jerry's younger brother, how do you explain the fact that he has an Australian accent and I don't?"

Ellen gazed at Scott levelly. "You grew up apart, but are brought together after your father's death, because your dad was a government agent whose secrets were leaked to foreign enemies."

Scott's grin grew broader. "I can see you've thought of everything."

"The secret of my success, 'dahling,'" she quipped.

"So...do you have anyone else in mind for this part?"

Ellen shot him a look. "Scott. I wouldn't have called you if you weren't my first choice. To be honest, I wrote the character with you in mind."

"You're the writer on this, too?"

Ellen pretended to be affronted. "Hey, don't look so surprised, kid. I came up with most of the concepts for my early movies – long, long ago – back in the silent era," she joked, taking his laugh as a good sign. "I need an answer right away.

I'm going to give you a copy of the script, and I want you to read it and get back to me as soon as possible."

"Ellen, I need time to think this over. I won't stall, but I want to talk to Maureen first – and my dad, too."

"I understand, sweetie. And hey – I wouldn't ask you to say yes without consulting *them*. In fact – I'm going to send Maureen an offer and a copy of the script right now. At least this way, you can get a jump on it."

When Scott stepped outside Ellen's front door, he had a copy of the screenplay in his hand and a look of uncertainty on his face.

"Thanks, Scott," Ellen said. "Tell your mom and dad I said hi."

"Will do."

As soon as she closed the door behind Scott, Ellen picked up her cell phone, searched for a number, and hit the call button. "Rachel? Do me a favor, honey, and send a copy of *On the Verge* with the offer for Scott Griffith over to Maureen O'Malley at CAA. Send it by courier tonight. I want her to get it first thing Monday."

Lynda Seville was standing in the center of her bedroom when her cell phone chimed.

Grabbing the treasured instrument off her bed, she checked the caller I.D. "What's wrong?"

Heather, riding in the passenger seat of her father's Cadillac next to Scott, took a deep breath. "Nothing's wrong, honey, would you relax?"

Lynda glared at her reflection in a full-length mirror. "How can I relax? I can't go in this dress! It makes me look fat!"

Heather had to raise her voice, as Scott was in the middle of a conversation on his own cell phone. "You do not look fat. You look great!"

"How do *you* know? You're not here!"

Into his phone, Scott was saying, "We're on our way, Rose. We're just heading down Sunset now..."

Focusing on her own call, Heather said to Lynda, "Stop it! Everything's going to be great, so don't worry."

Together, Scott and Heather chorused, "We'll see you in a few minutes."

*   *   *

Gina was a vision in a tight black strapless dress and her hair swept up, as she emerged from her bedroom and stepped out into the sumptuous living room of her apartment.

Jason Kellner, standing next to Debbie, stared in genuine admiration and grinned. "Whoah! You're gonna outshine everybody else there!"

Gina rolled her eyes and inspected her appearance in the mirrored living room wall. "Hardly."

Jason stood behind her. "You look totally different than when we first met. I think you'd look just as good in *jeans*."

She smiled at him. "Has anybody ever told you that you're full of it?"

"All the time. But I don't listen to my sister anymore."

Debbie looked stunning herself in a beautiful pink gown. "I still feel like a third wheel. What should I do when we get there?"

Jason shrugged. "Smile for the photographers. Mingle. Just like you would at any party."

"This doesn't sound like 'any party.'"

"Deb, stop worrying," Gina assured her. "It's gonna be fun!"

"Yeah," Jason agreed. "And instead of escorting *one* beautiful girl, I get to escort *two*. I'm gonna be the envy of every other guy there."

Debbie blushed.

Jason checked the time on his cell phone. "We should get goin'. You girls ready?"

"Yes!" they replied in unison.

The three of them started for the door.

Gina grabbed up her tiny purse. "My mom's gonna flip when I tell her about this."

"No worries," Jason said smoothly, opening the door. "Only a dufuss would have to ask his parents' *permission*."

Scott sat facing Rose Leoni's parents, a sincere and humble expression on his face. "Honest, Mr. and Mrs. Leoni. This is a respectable gathering Laurel Gillis is holding in her home. Only the industry's highest-level professionals will be there. A lot of media will be there, too, so it's not the kind of party where anything inappropriate is gonna happen."

Ed Leoni hesitated. "It's still a Hollywood party. And I've heard about what goes on at some of these Hollywood parties."

Scott shrugged. "It's actually more a promotional mixer than a party. For publicity. Laurel's doing it to launch her national tour."

Judy Leoni stared at Scott accusingly. "Won't there be alcohol there?"

"Yes," Scott admitted. "But we're all under age. And there'll be security there to monitor everybody's activities."

Heather, who was standing by the chair Scott was sitting in, added, "Security and *police*."

This seemed to make Judy Leoni relax.

Ed still held back. "You'll have Rosie home when we say?"

Scott looked at Rose and smiled. Then he turned to Ed. "Absolutely."

"Because there was that time a few weeks ago when you didn't."

Scott and Rose looked at him in surprise.

"We told you to have her home by eleven o'clock," Ed went on, "And you didn't get back until almost eleven-fifteen."

Heather burst out laughing.

A stern look from Ed silenced her.

Heather stared. "Oh. You're serious."

"It'll never happen again," Scott said sincerely. "And it would be my honor to escort Rose to the party tonight."

Rose beamed.

This did not go unnoticed by Ed. "All right," he conceded. "We trust you both. Have a good time. Just make sure you're on time tonight."

Scott stood up – immensely relieved. "Yes, sir."

Scott, Heather, and Rose bounced out of Rose's house as if they'd been let out of a cage.

"Oh God!" Rose groaned. "That was so embarrassing! I am so sorry, you guys."

"No problem," Scott said easily, gallantly opening the passenger side door for her and allowing her to step in. "Just remember you owe me."

Rose giggled as she got inside and Scott shut the door.

Heather smirked at Scott knowingly. "I heard a little bit of Cal Anderson coming out there, bro."

Scott grinned devilishly. "Who says I can't act?"

Laurel Gillis' house was situated on a private road off of Linda Flora Drive in Bel Air. Even from a distance away, loud rock music could be heard echoing throughout the canyon as a long line of cars inched their way up the steep hill.

Off-duty police officers stood at the entrance to Laurel's street checking IDs and searching vehicles. From the back of the house, multi-colored klieg lights shot beams into the night sky that moved almost in time to the music.

Scott, Rose, Heather, and Lynda entered Laurel's backyard through the side gate. Passing through security, they stepped onto the patio, which had been transformed into an elegant tented garden, complete with statues, fountains, and illuminated palm trees.

In the far corner of the backyard, five good-looking young men stood on the bandstand pushing their instruments and voices to the limit.

A banner above their heads read WEST COAST THUNDER.

"I feel like I'm at the Academy Awards!" Lynda chirped happily.

Scott nodded, looking around intently, scanning the crowded patio. "Maybe the Emmys, mixed with a little bit of the Grammys."

"It's a celebrity party," Heather stated. "What do you expect to find? Unknowns?"

Rose was literally bobbing up and down. "Oh, Scott! Oh! I think I'm going to faint!"

"Don't do *that*," Scott warned. "There're photographers behind us." He steadied her with his hand. "Be cool, okay?"

She nodded, still beaming, her face flushed.

"Now we all stay together," Lynda affirmed. "Right?"

"Rose and I will," replied Scott. "Heather, it would probably look better if you and Lynda separate from us."

"I know," said Heather, taking her friend's arm. "Don't worry, Lynda. You look gorgeous!"

"Oh my God!" Rose shrieked, causing Scott to literally jump. "Scott...it's Jason Kellner." She clung to Scott's arm. "And he's coming this way!"

"Rose, calm down," said Scott. "He won't eat you." Under his breath, "At least, he better not try to."

Scott steered himself for the confrontation. He turned, saw Gina, and nearly double-taked.

"Dude," Jason greeted Scott casually. "What's goin' on?"

"Hey," Scott replied tightly.

Gina's smile was both knowing and reassuring. "Hi, Scott."

"Oh, that's right," Jason said, feigning ignorance. "You two know each other, don't you?"

"Of course," Scott smiled, looking directly at Gina. "You look beautiful." Acknowledging Debbie. "*Both* of you."

Debbie and Rose were watching Scott and Gina closely.

Jason's eyes surveyed the party. "My agent told me tonight was a hot ticket. I thought he was exaggerating, but I guess not."

Heather smiled. "It must mean we're in with the cool kids now."

"Heather??" Jason laughed and looked at Scott. "You gotta be kiddin', man! You brought your *sister* as your date??"

Scott's eyes flashed. He rested his hand protectively on Rose's shoulder. "*She* is my date. And for some reason I can't fathom, she wanted to meet you."

"Naturally," Jason smiled, extending his hand. "Jason Kellner."

"Hi!" Rose gasped, unable to stop beaming.

"Rose Leoni," Scott supplied.

"A pleasure, Rose," Jason said smoothly, executing a very obvious fake laugh at Scott. "Sorry about that. I just can't believe you brought your sister."

Scott flushed. "I thought Joannie was coming, too."

"She is," Jason said, restlessly glancing around. "We just don't make entrances together."

Heather smirked. "She probably just didn't want to be embarrassed."

Jason glared at her. "Funny."

"It's true," Scott said, locking eyes with Gina and motioning to Jason. "I hate to say this – but he's *your* problem tonight."

Scott, Rose, Heather, and Lynda moved off.

"You're really funny, Scott!" Jason called out after them, fighting to stay in control. "You're almost as funny as that blond hair of yours!" His face went red as he looked from Gina to Debbie. "It's probably Born Blond #42."

From the top of the steps leading from the patio into the house, Laurel Gillis and her manager, Jimmy Montana, observed the party like they were appraising a diamond necklace.

"So far so good, Laurie," Jimmy commented, nodding his approval. "This is just what we wanted. By tomorrow morning, the trades'll be proclaiming that 'Laurel Gillis can bring the stars down from the heavens!'"

"Oh, sure," Laurel replied. "If you spend enough money, you can get *anybody* to come to your house."

Jimmy, an attractive black man in his early forties, turned to her sternly. "What is that, a joke? Girl, look around you! These people are here to see *you*! To check out *your* digs – because of who *you* are!"

She nodded, unconvinced. "If you say so, Jimmy."

He put his arm protectively around her. "I say so. I also say you look smokin' tonight."

She smiled weakly. "Thanks." Realization. "Oh, Jimmy. Did you remember to add Jerry Garnett's name to the guest list?"

"Now don't I always remember to do what you ask me to?"

"Only when there's something in it for *you*," she replied affectionately.

"Of course, girl! That's what makes me a great manager!"

As soon as Raquel and Shawn entered the party, she immediately searched for any sign of Scott. Famous faces were everywhere, but not the one she most wanted to see.

"You okay?" Shawn asked, looking at her with concern.

She manufactured a sexy smile. "You bet! Let's check this party *out*!"

"I thought you and Scott were friends," Gina said.

Jason looked sheepish. "Not really." With a rush of indignation, "I tried to be friendly to him! Did you see how he just started cracking on me when all I did was say hello to his date?"

Debbie had wandered off by herself, and Gina and Jason found themselves by the bar next to the swimming pool.

"I don't know," Gina said reproachfully, "It sounded like you started in on him *first*."

"I didn't realize you were part of his fan club," Jason said stiffly.

"No, I just wondered what you don't like about him, that's all."

"Why do *you* like him so much?"

"I work on his show. That's it."

"Yeah?" Jason sounded dubious. "For your sake, I hope that's *all* it is."

"What's *that* supposed to mean?"

Jason glanced around and leaned closer to Gina, his voice low. "It means don't let him screw you over. Give him the chance, and he will do it without blinking an eye."

"I still can't believe I'm here!" Rose insisted.

Scott smiled proudly, pulling her closer to him and checking out the action around them. "I can pinch you, if you want."

She turned to him, annoyed. "Scott! Why do you say things like that?"

"I'm just kidding."

She sighed dramatically. "You're always kidding. I never know when you're serious."

He stopped, his eyes intently searching the crowded patio. "I...I need to use the bathroom. I'll be right back." He started off.

Rose clung desperately to his arm. "You're leaving me? Here by myself? You can't!"

He looked at her seriously, disengaging himself from her grasp. "You can't follow me into the bathroom, Rose." Leering. "It's not that kind of party."

Gina stood next to Jason as he spoke to three other young actors in front of the buffet table off of Laurel's living room.

"Working on a series is like being in prison. Seriously. I had to turn down this great part in a feature film because my schedule is *locked*. Unless I can fit a project *right* into my hiatus, it's a no-go."

After a few minutes, Gina began to wonder if he'd forgotten that she existed. She glanced idly around. Most of the young people there, she recognized from film and T.V. Gina was dying to meet more of them. Debbie had been gone more than half an hour.

Gina turned back to Jason. "I'm gonna see if I can find Deb."

Jason nodded absently. "Okay."

Laurel watched her guests mingle as a very attractive guy in a tuxedo stepped up behind her and put his arms around her. "Having fun?"

"Miles!" She jumped, spinning around and facing him. "I was beginning to worry."

"Worry about me?" His long brown hair fell past her face as he leaned in to lick her earlobe.

"Wait a minute!" Tensing up, she pulled away from him. "Not here! This is my *party*!"

"Exactly. *Your* party. You can do anything you want."

She sighed. "I wish it really worked that way."

He moved closer to her, his eyes sparkling intimately. "So if I were to take you in my arms and kiss you...right now...what would you do about it?"

She took a deep breath, looking slightly flushed. "I would remind you that there are photographers with cameras everywhere."

He feigned confusion. "I've performed on camera before."

She couldn't help smiling, glancing around her. "Not like these - " Something at the patio entrance caught her attention. "Miles...excuse me a minute, baby, I'll be right back."

He followed her gaze over to the sight of a very handsome, dark-haired man who had just passed through security. "Hey...that's Jerry Garnett, isn't it?"

"It is." She patted his hand. "I won't be long."

Laurel almost ran in Jerry Garnett's direction, leaving Miles standing by himself, scowling.

*   *   *

Gina sat on one of the couches in Laurel Gillis' two-story living room alongside two very well dressed young actresses. Several guests in the group were making conversation while MTV played on the large plasma T.V. screen.

Gina looked up to see Scott moving towards her.

He smiled, perching himself on the edge of the couch. "I can't believe you're here!"

Gina's face was flushed. "That makes two of us."

"It's good to see you. Off the set, I mean."

"It's good to *be* off the set. I can't believe you guys work such long hours."

Scott nodded ruefully. "Tell me about it."

"Where's your girlfriend?"

He looked as though he'd been stung. "Rose? She's not my girlfriend. We're just friends..."

Her eyes seemed to bore into his soul. "If you say so."

"What reason would I have to lie?"

Gina started to get up. "It's really none of my business."

He stopped her with a gentle hand on her arm. "Who says it isn't? We're friends, right?"

"We *work* together. I don't think we should take it beyond that."

"Look, if this is about what happened in my dressing room - "

"It's not. I just think we should keep our relationship professional, that's all."

When Raquel spotted Scott in Laurel Gillis' living room, she was dismayed to find him on the couch speaking with a beautiful dark-haired girl.

No. Now wasn't the time. She had to catch him alone. *Alone at a star-studded Hollywood party?* When would that possibly be?

Shawn was still at her side.

"Honey," she said sweetly, "I need to find the ladies room. Will you wait for me down here?"

"Sure," he said easily, impressed by all the young celebrities that were passing by.

"Thanks." She squeezed his hand and quickly headed upstairs.

"How do you know Jason?" Scott asked stiffly.

Gina intrepidly met his gaze. "I didn't until about a week ago. He came by the set to visit Joannie."

Scott nodded. "I heard about that."

"I didn't know you guys don't get along. I'm sorry."

"It has nothing to do with you. I just don't want you to be sorrier."

"What does *that* mean?"

"It means I've known this guy for a long time. And he's a brilliant actor. I don't trust him as far as I can throw him, and I wouldn't believe a word he says."

Gina almost burst out laughing. "You are incredible! Don't you think you're taking this too far?"

"If I didn't care, I wouldn't say anything."

"No. You two are turning this thing into some sort of contest, and I don't like it."

"That's not how it is. By right, I should've been here with *you* tonight."

Gina shook her head in disbelief. "That's exactly what I'm talking about!" She turned and stormed off.

Scott went red in the face and followed her. "Wait a minute!"

Heather came down the long white-carpeted staircase amidst a sea of people, and edged her way through the living room.

Various beautiful young girls sauntered by wearing daring and innovative fashion creations that Heather couldn't resist checking out.

Craning to see over people's heads, Heather spotted Lynda in a far corner of the room engrossed in conversation with a slim brown-haired guy who was leaning cockily against the wall. He looked as though he were ready to pounce on her.

On closer inspection, Heather realized that it was Jason Kellner. Whatever Jason was saying to her, Lynda seemed to be loving every word.

"Lynda!" There was more disappointment than agitation in Heather's voice.

Dismay hit Lynda's face when she saw Heather. "Excuse me," she quickly said to Jason, stepping around him and glaring at Heather. "What is it?" she hissed.

"I thought you were behind me in line for the bathroom. I turn my back for two seconds, and you're getting busy with *him*?"

"We are having a *conversation*! That's *all*!"

Jason had come up behind Lynda. "It's starting to get crowded in here. I'm gonna go get another drink."

"I'll go with you" Lynda said sweetly.

"You know what?" Heather exploded. "Fine! If you think he's such a big deal, you be my guest!"

Heather turned and marched out.

Jason shook his head, sneering. "Everybody in that family is uptight. Why do you hang out with them?"

"Heather's my best friend. She's really cool – most of the time."

"Scott thinks he's some big movie star now. Have you *seen Wacky Wednesday*?" Jason made a face and wrinkled his nose. "I wouldn't take my *grandmother* to go see it!"

Heather was standing by herself next to the swimming pool when she heard a young girl's voice call out to her. "Aren't you having fun?"

Heather turned to the speaker. It was one of the girls who had arrived with Jason Kellner. "I'm sorry?"

"You just don't look like you're having a good time."

Heather sighed. "I've had better."

"I'm Debbie Monroe." They shook hands.

"Heather Griffith."

"Me and my cousin, Gina, had lunch with Scott at Paradigm Studios a few weeks ago. He's awesome!"

Genuine surprise. "How do you two know Scott?"

"Gina works on the set of *Right On*."

Heather digested the information slowly. "And she's dating *Jason*?"

"Well...I don't think they're dating. This is only the second time they've been - "

"I could kill him!" exclaimed Rose Leoni, rushing up to the two girls. "I could just kill him!"

"What's wrong?" asked Heather, alarmed.

Debbie only looked on in astonishment.

"Your stupid brother!" Rose blazed. "He took off on me again and I can't find him anywhere! Do you know where he is?"

"I haven't seen him."

Fuming, Rose spoke almost to herself. "Honest to God, this is the last straw! I'm gonna kill him. It's as simple as that."

She flounced off.

"What was all *that* about?" Debbie couldn't help asking.

Heather seemed unconcerned, smiling secretly. "I have some idea, but I want to see how it all plays out."

Scott kissed her so hard, she felt like she would faint.

Gina couldn't see anything in the darkened bedroom as Scott kicked the door closed, locked it behind his back, and pushed her backwards towards the bed.

She tore at the buttons on his shirt, almost ripping it off him.

He nearly tripped as he stepped out of his shoes, keeping her lips a prisoner of his own as they tumbled onto the bed.

His hand strayed under her dress, exploring. His fingers moved gently, nimbly. She sighed in husky appreciation. His blue eyes were luminous in the dark as he bent to kiss her again. This time he slowed down all his actions, shifting his body to comfortably lie next to her.

She felt the material of his pants as they slid down his legs. His soft hands caressed her everywhere, and she barely noticed her own clothes slipping from her body. Only his underwear covering him, he moved on top of her, smoothly working his way down, kissing her all over.

Grabbing him roughly by the shoulders, she landed him on his back and pinned both his arms to the sheets.

"Stay down" she gasped. "And shut up."

Holding him firmly in place, she kissed him again, rubbing her body against his and attacking him in every place he seemed vulnerable. Raising his legs, he gripped her around her feline form and joined her in her rocking rhythm.

Shutting everything else out, she teased him until his own cries consumed him.

Debbie approached one of the portable bars on the patio and noticed the bartender immediately. This particular one was distinctly shorter than the others, about her height, with stunning red hair, crystal blue eyes, and a milk tone complexion.

He beamed when he saw her. "What can I get you?"

She was drawn to him almost magnetically, and for some reason, found it difficult to breathe. Debbie set her empty glass down on the bar and hoarsely said, "I'll have another one, please."

His soft eyes searched her face. "Another one what?"

She started to laugh, her body shaking as she stared down at the ground. "I'm sorry. I mean, I'll have another Coke."

He filled the glass with some ice. "Just a Coke?"

"Yes." She giggled, then realized how ridiculous she must've sounded. "It's my third one tonight."

His eyes hardly left her face as he used the bar's soda gun to pour her Coke. "Then I hope you're not driving."

Heather had wandered around to the side of Laurel's huge house, away from the party, where the catering trucks were parked and a tent where the food had been prepared had been erected.

She took no notice of the black-tie servers scurrying in and out of the tent with trays as she continued toward the front of the garage.

"You look about as bummed as I feel" a deep male voice called out of the darkness.

Heather spun around and peered intently into the shadows. She could just make out the form of a rugged, muscular man with long dark hair, perched on top of a beer keg and swigging from a longneck bottle of beer. On closer inspection, she could see that he was dressed in a tuxedo, and had the most incredibly handsome face she'd ever seen. His eyes seemed to glow as he stared at her through the opaque gloom.

"E-ex-excuse me?"

"You heard what I said." He hopped off the beer keg and moved closer to her – liking what he saw.

Heather took a step backward.

"Relax, cutie. I'm not gonna hurt you."

Exercising false confidence, she indicated the bottle he was holding. "Couldn't you get in trouble for drinking that?"

"Why?" He took another swig. "I'm over twenty-one. How about you?"

She started to say something, but nothing came out. Clearing her throat, she fought to regain her composure. "You should probably be with the other servers."

He shook his head, his face darkening over. "Oh, that's just great! Now I'm being mistaken for a waiter. What else is going to happen to me tonight?"

Heather realized he was telling the truth. "I'm sorry. I didn't know."

"I don't know why I'm surprised. I should be used to it by now."

Heather looked into his face. She could see the hurt and pain he was feeling. Forcing a note of cheerfulness into her voice, she said, "So...who are you here with?"

"Laurel Gillis. She's my girlfriend."

"What!"

He laughed sickly. "Not that you'd know it. She could care less that I'm even here." He swallowed hard. "She's probably making it with Jerry Garnett for all I know..." His face screwed up as he realized he was saying too much. "Okay. I'm going to shut up now."

"Don't you dare! I think that's awful!" She glanced back in the direction of the party, confusion clouding her features. "That doesn't gel. I've always heard that Laurel is so nice."

He grunted. "She's only nice if she likes you."

Heather smiled.

He looked at her, his cascading brown hair shining in the moonlight. "I shouldn't be laying this all over you. I don't even know you."

"I'm Heather," she said softly.

His gaze stripped her defenseless. "My name is Miles. Miles Morrison."

Gina fluffed out her hair as she came down the back stairs and entered the kitchen. She thought she was imagining it when she saw Jason and a large-breasted girl in the corner standing very close and discreetly fondling one another. She was just about to head out to the patio when Jason looked up and saw her, the smile fading from his lips. "Gina!"

She reluctantly stopped and faced him.

Jason left the other girl's side without a second thought and made a beeline for Gina. "Where the hell have you been?"

"I told you. I went looking for Deb."

"Your cousin's out by the pool, she's been there for the last hour. Where were *you*?"

"Looking for *you*." Gina motioned to where Jason had been standing. The other girl was long gone. "You looked busy."

"What's wrong with you? I brought you to this party as my guest. How do you think that makes me look when you just disappear?"

"You weren't worried when you were talking to all your friends." Gina waved her hands emphatically. "You're making too much out of this. I was just socializing – like you." She looked away. "Well maybe not like *you*..."

"You had me worried. I didn't know where you were."

"I'm not a child. C'mon, Jason. This is a great party! Why are you trying to spoil it?"

"I'm not."

"Prove it. Let's have some fun!"

"Now yer talkin'!" Smiling, he slid his arm around her. "Wanna get a drink?"

"Definitely yes! I could use one."

Miles stared at her in disbelief. "You're really Scott Griffith's little sister?"

Heather flushed. "Little sister? I'm not in kindergarten, for God's sake!"

He smiled. "Sorry. Still, that must be...pretty cool."

She shrugged. "Most of the time. I'm still trying to live down my name."

"Griffith?"

"Heather! I'm a blonde named Heather! Do you know what it was like going through school with that?"

He cast his eyes downward. "Couldn't be as bad as being a boy named Miles."

She giggled. "You're right. That is much worse."

He pretended to be insulted. "Hey – hey – what are you laughing at, little girl?"

She couldn't help herself. "You!"

Hard as he tried, he couldn't stop from laughing, too.

"Hello, Rocky."

Raquel spun around and saw him standing in front of her. It felt like a dream, but it was real. She had been leaning against the railing of the balcony of one of Laurel Gillis' guest bedrooms, absently staring out at the twinkling lights of the homes across the canyon. The noise of the party seemed to merge with her own thoughts, but looking at Scott, it was like all time was standing still.

She barely found her voice. "Nobody's called me that in years."

To his surprise, he realized he was trembling. "I thought *I* was the only one who called you that."

"That's...probably why."

He stepped onto the balcony and slowly moved toward her.

Now that they were standing face to face, all her strength was gone. She felt her legs go weak.

"It's good to see you," he murmured.

False confidence. "You, too."

He took a deep breath. "Still mad?"

"No." And she genuinely meant it. "I never was. I just missed you."

"I'm real sorry about the way things ended. I never wanted that to happen."

She looked away, struggling to control the rush of feelings that flooded her. "It doesn't matter now..." she said sadly.

"It does to me. I wanted to tell you that I'm very sorry...and I hope someday you can forgive me..."

Raquel folded her arms, still unable to look at him. When she did speak, her voice was choked. "Why do you have to be so damn nice...?"

He smiled warmly and took another step toward her. "It's not something I would want to get around. You can't tell any of the reporters."

Their eyes met. "I *tried* to stay mad at you," she said. "But I couldn't..."

"So...I see you're with someone."

Surprise. "You saw him?"

Scott nodded.

"Yes," she managed. "His name's Shawn. He's great."

"I'm glad."

"And...you, too?"

"Me? No, Rose is just a friend. I just don't have the time. My schedule is crazier than ever!"

"I know. I saw *Wacky Wednesday*."

"My condolences," he joked.

"We can be friends, can't we?" she ventured. "Lord knows I'm not your enemy."

"Yeah," he replied, the idea comforting him immediately. "I'd like that."

All the lights on Laurel's patio went down, and a strident drum roll permeated the night air.

"Ladies and gentlemen," a male voice boomed over several hidden speakers. "Your hostess for this evening – beginning her national tour here in Los Angeles – and sweeping forty cities across this great land of ours – the one – the only – Miss Laurel Gillis!"

Discordant cheers reverberated throughout the tented garden as Laurel Gillis took the stage, wireless microphone in hand. "Thank you," Laurel intoned above the cacophony of the crowd. "Thank you so much, everybody! It means so much to me that you could all be here...and this song...is for all of *you*!"

Right on cue, the band played the intro to *Crazy Kiss*, one of Laurel's high-energy dance tracks. She began to sing. Her voice was strong and clear. Superb – especially for a live performance.

By the time Laurel launched into her second song, *14-Karat Love*, her guests were dancing on her patio, and later, slow-dancing to her melodic romantic ballad, *If I Knew Then*.

Laurel performed for over an hour, one song after another, which surprised and pleased most of her guests.

"Are you sure you're not from a tabloid?" Miles asked playfully.

"Please!" Heather scowled.

The two of them were strolling down Laurel's street – a cul-de-sac with only two other houses. "Okay," Miles said. "Laurel would kill me, but here goes. It was her girlfriend's birthday, and she and her friends came into the club where I was working - "

"Oh, you're a bartender."

He grinned. "Not exactly. Dancer."

"Ballroom?" Heather's eyes widened, and she turned to him. "You're a stripper??"

He realized it was quiet at this end of the street, so he lowered his voice. "I'm an actor, FYI." Miles looked down at the ground. "I just do the dancing thing when work is slow. That's all."

They stopped, and Heather took a good look at him. "I'm sorry I mistook you for a waiter before. I have to say, though." She blushed. "I love the way you look in that tux."

"I was thinking about working it into my act. Everything comes off except the bow tie." He stared at her hungrily. "What do you think?"

She smiled nervously. "I wouldn't hate it."

He stepped closer to her and looked deep into her eyes. "What *else* would you like?"

"Pardon?"

He took her face in his hands. "Do you like me?"

Heather was breathless just looking at him. "Sure - "

He was kissing her. A long, lingering, probing kiss that made her body go limp in his arms.

When their lips finally parted, they were holding onto each other, and it seemed as if they were the only two people on the planet.

"Did you like that?" Miles asked softly. "*I* did."

Heather's eyes were shining as she gazed at him, but she could only nod.

Scott stood next to Laurel's pool, looking down at the water, his expression forlorn. He didn't seem to be aware of anything going on around him, and his sapphire eyes were sullen and empty.

"Scott?" Jason Kellner had come up behind him. He attempted to sound friendly. "What are you doing, man?"

Scott gritted his teeth, his voice barely audible. "What do *you* want?"

"I was just wondering why you were over here by yourself. Your date walk out on you?" Half teasing, half serious.

"Just get away from me!"

Fake concern. "Oh. I guess she did." Jason patted Scott condescendingly on the shoulder. "Better luck next time, pal - "

Scott spun around and got right in Jason's face. "What part of 'get away from me' do you not understand?"

Jason pretended to be surprised. "What's your problem, man? It's not like I stole your girl or something." Jason backed away from Scott, but his sneer remained. "Hey, what happened to that blonde chick you brought to the Emmys last year? You knock her up and pay her off?"

Scott grabbed Jason by the front of his tuxedo and threw him up against the wall of Laurel's pool house. "You shut the hell up!"

"Get off me, you queer!"

Scott punched Jason hard in the stomach.

Jason hit Scott in the mouth with a sledgehammer blow, causing Scott to reel backwards and clutch his cheek. "You wanna fight me?" Jason goaded Scott. "Huh? I'll freakin' kill you!"

Scott lunged for Jason, who deftly blocked Scott's move and landed a sidekick to Scott's stomach.

Scott stumbled back, temporarily thrown. He glared at Jason.

"I have a black belt in karate now," Jason boasted, raising his hands in a threatening manner. "You're not gonna mess with me."

Scott rushed forward and kicked Jason square in the groin.

Jason doubled over, his cry like a young girl's.

Scott grabbed Jason by the front of his shirt and forced him to look Scott in the eye. "You are a piece of garbage! You're not even good enough to speak her name!"

"Screw you!" Jason gasped, anger clouding his red face, struggling to force Scott to release his hold on him.

The two grappled, not looking where they were going.

Both tripped and fell head first into the pool.

When Scott and Jason surfaced, they were still taking swings at each other.

Several of the paparazzi leaped over the security ropes and snapped pictures of this ludicrous spectacle.

Three security guards darted down to the pool area and fished the expensively attired gladiators out of the water. "Break it up! C'mon! Get away from him!"

Gina and Debbie stood at the front of the crowd watching while the photographers' cameras captured every soaking wet moment.

The party broke up around one o'clock.

Scott used one of Laurel Gillis' bathrooms to dry off as best he could, while Rose, Heather, and Lynda waited for a valet to bring their car around.

"You still talking to me?" Lynda asked, discreetly taking Heather aside.

"Why wouldn't I be talking to you?" Heather asked, genuinely not understanding what her friend meant.

"I thought you still might be mad about before."

Then Heather remembered. "Oh. You could've at least told me you were going to talk to someone. It's a party, I would've been cool with that."

"I know" Lynda said softly, staring at the ground. "I was going to say something before, but then *you* disappeared."

Heather shrugged. "Forget it."

"Anyway, where *were* you all this time? You missed all the excitement!"

Heather giggled, her mind still on Miles. "You mean Scott falling into Laurel's pool?"

"Where is he?" Rose demanded to no one in particular. "I swear, if I'd known he was going to pull this crap, I never would've come tonight."

Heather sighed, by this time fed up with Rose. "You say it, but you don't mean it."

The valet arrived with their car just as Scott came out of the patio gate and started down the driveway. His clothes were completely soaked, and his blond hair clumsily towel-dried and sticking up. He looked even sexier than usual.

"It's about time!" Rose fumed, pretending to be more upset than she actually was. "I thought we were going to have to leave without you."

"I had to say goodnight to Laurel," Scott said defensively.

"I hope you apologized for ruining her party."

Scott shook his head wearily, tipped the valet, and he, Rose, Heather, and Lynda set off.

The ride home wasn't any easier.

"I can't believe you did that, Scott!" Rose chastised him. "How could you embarrass me like that?"

He looked at her incredulously. "I was defending myself."

"Well you didn't have to fall in the pool! I can't believe you made an ass out of yourself like that."

"Thanks for understanding," he muttered dryly.

"So how do you think that makes me look? You humiliated me, Scott. That wasn't very nice."

Scott tightened his grip on the steering wheel as he drove. "Rose...we're going to talk about something else right now, or nothing at all. Got it?"

"Fine," she said petulantly, staring angrily out the window.

"I start shooting a new movie next month," Scott continued in a more casual tone, his headache subsiding.

"That's interesting," Rose remarked sarcastically, not caring anything about that at all.

"It is!" Scott insisted, determined not to let her spoil his evening. "It's going to be really great, because we're doing some location shooting in Las Vegas..."

It was 2:30 A.M. when Gina and Debbie arrived back at their apartment.

"That was the best!" Debbie exclaimed excitedly. "Can we do this again tomorrow night?"

Gina shot her cousin a look, and with great relief, kicked off her shoes for the night.

"It was nice of Joannie Kellner to give us a ride home," Debbie went on.

Gina snorted. "Nice? Her and Scott Griffith work together. She just wanted the details of what happened out by the pool."

"I wouldn't mind having those myself."

A cell phone chimed from inside Debbie's purse.

"Oh! I don't believe it!"

"What?" Gina asked.

"It's Brian! The bartender I told you about! He's calling me already!"

Gina smiled. "He must be anxious."

Debbie pulled out her phone, checked the caller ID, and frowned. "Hello...?" she questioned uncertainly. "Oh, hi, Aunt Cynthia...sure." She handed the phone to Gina. "It's for you."

Gina sighed resignedly and took the sleek device from her cousin. "Hi, Mom."

Cynthia's tone was hushed. "Where the hell have you been? I've been trying to reach you all day."

Gina laughed. "It's been a crazy day, Mom!" Turning serious. "What is it?"

Cynthia's voice was so low that Gina could barely hear her. "I need you to come home. We've got trouble."

Gina was fighting panic. "What's wrong?"

Cynthia was deathly calm. "The same thing that was wrong two years ago. I need you back here."

CHAPTER 9

Robert Griffith threw the color-printed pages on the kitchen table and shouted, "I could kill you!"

"Bob, please," Tracy implored softly, "We can all hear you, you don't have to yell - "

"Yeah, I have to yell! It's the only way to make this kid understand!"

Robert stood over Scott, who sat at the kitchen table trying not to look at the printer-quality image of his brawl in the pool with Jason Kellner.

"You happy?" Robert thundered. "That's what everybody's talking about online! How my son couldn't keep it together for one night! You couldn't embarrass me in front of a small group of strangers! You had to do it in front of a dozen reporters! Thanks a lot!"

"He said something about Maryann," Scott growled.

"I don't care! You don't let guys like that get to you! Not in public. Especially that little weasel."

Tracy looked pointedly at Heather. "Where were *you* when all this happened?"

Heather stared at her mother wide-eyed. "Me and Lynda were just hanging out in Laurel's house. We didn't get outside until it was all over."

"*You're* lucky your *career's* not all over," Robert said to Scott. "That's all you need is to get fired from the show - "

"They're not gonna fire me," Scott said defiantly.

Robert's anger rose. "Oh, you don't think so, huh?"

"Scott," Tracy said sternly. "Any publicity you get reflects on the show and the rest of the cast. You don't think they're going to say something to you about it? Expect a call from Howard Aldrich, I'm telling you now."

"Fine!" Scott said, getting up from the table. "I'll deal with it. And thanks a lot! I can't even count on my own family to back me up!" He stormed out of the room.

"We'll back you up when you do things right!" Robert called after him.

"Mom?" Heather's voice was timid. "Lynda and her aunt are picking me up, so..."

Tracy nodded without looking at her, and Heather scurried out the back door.

Tracy glared at Robert. "You *know* Maryann is a sore subject with him."

Robert took a seat at the table and thoughtfully sipped his juice. His voice was low. "Yeah, well...that was hard on *all* of us..."

Tracy started to clear some plates. "I don't know why you're so hard on *him*. You two are exactly alike."

"Oh, don't start that now - "

"Both of you have that Irish temper and you know it! I've seen you when *you* get mad, Bob, and it's even worse! So don't act like it's all him, because he gets it from you."

"Yeah, but Tracy, I'm not in the press like he is. And if the producers think he's creating a negative image for the show, they'll can him without thinking twice. And good luck landing a deal *that* sweet again." Robert shook his head. "I don't want to see that happen to him. I'm on his side. Doesn't he know that?"

"Why didn't you tell him that just now?"

"He never listens. He's stubborn as a damn mule."

Heavy sarcasm. "I wonder where he gets *that* from!"

Gina cleared her throat and spoke nervously into her hands-free phone. "When is the trial...?" She stopped pacing the living room to write something down on a pad. "What day do I have to be there...?"

Debbie was watching her, and almost holding her breath.

"Yes..." Gina finished. "I understand...Thank you..." Gina disconnected, and for a moment she seemed disoriented. She turned to Debbie, took a deep breath, and said, "That was the Assistant D.A. They want me to testify on the thirtieth of next month. I have to be in New York on the twenty-third for preparations."

"You're really going to do it??" Debbie's voice rang with disbelief.

Gina sat next to Debbie on the couch. "I have to. If I don't, I'll be putting other people's lives in danger."

"What about *your* life! Don't you know what could happen to you by going up against somebody like him??"

"That's why I have to do it, Deb. To keep him from doing the same thing to other people. Besides, they're subpoenaing me. They're going to force me to do it whether I want to or not."

Scott was lying on the bed in his room when he heard a knock on his open door.

He looked up to see Tracy standing in the doorway, the screenplay to *On the Verge* in her hand.

"Hard at work, I see," she teased.

"What did you think?" he asked, indicating the script.

"Very good," she said, sitting on his bed and setting the screenplay down beside her. "It's the best script I've read in a while." Tracy shook her head in admiration. "Ellen Stellar – she just does it all, doesn't she?"

"How come Dad's never hired her?" Scott asked, sitting up.

"Because we can't afford her," Tracy said seriously. "Your father is head of Griffith Entertainment, not Paradigm Studios."

"I knew I got the wrong parents," Scott joked, grinning.

Tracy affectionately mussed his hair. "Somebody else's parents you want? Huh?"

Scott pretended to think about it. "Maybe Paris Hilton's."

Tracy shot him a dirty look. "How would you like Rose Leoni's father? *He'd* keep you in line."

Scott made a face. "No, thanks!" Lying back down. "Kill me first!"

Debbie drove the white Mercedes convertible down Westwood Boulevard, garnering a lot of attention from the U.C.L.A. students flooding the sidewalks – especially the boys. She pretended not to care as she moved carefully into the left lane and headed south toward Wilshire.

Her phone chimed. Earpiece already in place, she checked the caller ID on the dashboard.

CALABASAS, CA.

Oh, *that* was a clue!

She hesitantly pushed the TALK button.

"Is this Debbie?"

"Who is this?"

"Brian Bullens."

"Brian! How are you?"

There was genuine delight in his voice. "You remember me!"

"Of course I do." She checked out the phone number again. "Where are you calling me from?"

"Calabasas. I live with my parents."

"Where's that?"

"In the Valley."

"The Valley," Debbie said blankly. "Death Valley?"

His laughter brought a smile to her lips. "The San Fernando Valley."

"Well I'm sorry," she said helplessly. "I've only been here a month. I don't know where everything is yet."

"I know," he said tenderly. "So, how about I show you? If you're not doing anything Saturday night, maybe you'd like to get together?"

"Well, I'll have to check my busy schedule," she said sarcastically. "Actually, I don't have anything planned, so I'm wide open." She cringed. "I did not mean that the way it sounded."

She could hear the smile in his voice. "Pick you up around five?"

She grinned as she made a left onto Wilshire. "Perfect."

Cynthia was in an even worse mood than usual. "Are you out of your damn mind?? Why can't you just once do something that I ask? I told you to wait until our lawyer looked into this and let *him* contact the city attorney's office! No – you had to call them up and tell them where you are! Now you have no choice! Now you *have* to testify against this animal!"

"Damn it, Mom, it's *my* choice to make!" Gina was still typing on her laptop, but she stopped intermittently to focus on her phone call. "What good would it do to hide? They would find me eventually, and that would just make it worse!"

"Oh, God!" Almost to herself. "I can't believe I raised a daughter so stupid!" Fiercely, to Gina – "I never said we weren't going to cooperate with them! But we were trying to work out a deal so that you didn't have to testify before the grand jury. Right now, Santinello has no idea what you look like. If you appear in court, he will know your face and how to find you. And he will have you killed."

"But once they put him away, he won't hurt me or anybody else again."

"How naive can you be? Santinello can get at anybody – even from jail. And how long do you think he's going to stay there? Even if you testify, he's got a sharp team of lawyers who'll have him out in less than a year. Do you want to keep running for the rest of your life? Don't think the justice system in this country really works, Gina, because it doesn't. Not for people like him. I want you back here pronto!"

Gina's heart pounded wildly, but she was determined to remain placid. "Relax, Mom. This'll work."

Cynthia's voice was strained. "Our best hope is that he dies in jail. Like Frank."

"I know, Mom." Gina cleared her throat. "Anyway, I'm booking my flight to come back now. That detective said I would have police protection from the time I get off the plane, until Santinello is locked up."

"And are you going to have police protection the rest of your life? What are you going to do *after* the trial?"

"Mom...if I don't do this, his dealers are going to keep getting young kids hooked on drugs."

"Oh, come on, Gina! Even if Santinello died tomorrow – which, I wish to God would happen – his dealers are going to keep selling that stuff no matter where it comes from!"

"I have to try, Mom."

"Well, for God's sake, don't do anything else without checking with me first! I already lost the best man who ever lived. I'm not losing you, too!"

Debbie swiped her key card to open the gate to the pool area and immediately noticed that she was not alone. Swimming expertly under the water was a lean, well-built man with brown hair and tanned skin.

It was dawn, and the sun was only just starting to come up.

Smiling, Debbie found a deck chair and set her towel down on top of it. She was wearing a new black one-piece swimsuit, which fit her slender figure perfectly.

She heard a splash behind her and turned.

The man in the pool was hugging the side and leaning guardedly against the rim. He looked up at her with a nervous smile. "Hi."

He appeared to be only a few years older than she was. Striking. Deep, penetrating eyes. And a hint of danger in the way he carried himself.

For a second, she faultered. "Hi." She looked away briefly to make sure her keycard was tucked safely inside her towel. "I didn't think there'd be anybody else here this early."

"Yeah." His voice was tremulous. "I thought the same thing."

She extended her hand, slowly moving toward him. "I'm Debbie."

He held up a hand. "I'm Rick, and you might not want to come any closer."

She stopped, her eyes wide. "Why? What's wrong?"

He looked away, and he seemed to be short of breath. "Here's the thing: I know it's a communal pool, and don't freak out...I don't exactly have a swimsuit on."

Debbie's eyes grew wider, but she made no move to turn away. "Oh."

"I know I'm not supposed to do this, but I thought if I came early enough, when there's no one else around, it would be no big deal." He fixed her with a pleading stare. "You're not going to report me, are you?"

She backed away – but only slightly. "No."

"I'm sorry."

Now she did turn her head. "It's okay." Frowning. "Then how did you...?"

"I've got a robe. Give me...just a second."

He shored himself out of the pool and pattered swiftly toward the other side of the pool.

Debbie sneaked a peek at his bare feet and legs, her eyes involuntarily moving upward. When she'd seen all she dared to, she kept her back to him until she was certain that it was safe, then slowly faced him.

He was now clad in a white terrycloth robe which clearly covered the best parts of him, although it did make her feel more comfortable.

His tan seemed even deeper. "Better?" he asked, indicating the robe.

Debbie's eyes shone brightly. "Much," she managed, manufacturing a smile.

He looked down at the cement, then back up at her. Faking a smile of his own, he gathered his few belongings off the lounge chair and started toward the gate. "See ya."

She waited until he disappeared into the elevator before allowing the huge smile to spread across her face. "God, I love L.A.!"

Scott sat in a director's chair in front of the mirror in his dressing room, thoughtfully studying the script for the episode they were shooting.

Joannie Kellner appeared in the doorway and tapped on the open door. "Knock knock." Entering uninvited, she sauntered over to him and laid her own script on top of his table. "Wanna run lines?"

He looked up, not at all surprised to see her. "You never wanna run lines. You always wait until we're on the set, and then you wing it."

Mock outrage. "It's better than what *you* do. Always having your lines memorized, way ahead of everybody else. It's disgusting."

He set his own script down. "What's on your mind?"

"Did you have fun the other night?"

He frowned. "Oh, yeah. Right up until the finale. And please – no 'making a splash' jokes. I've heard it all."

Joannie leaned against the counter. "So what was it about?" she asked sympathetically.

"He didn't tell you?"

"He said you were 'acting like an ass.'"

Bitterly. "Oh, yeah. It was all me. It's never him."

"What did he say?" Joannie persisted, sure that she knew the answer.

Scott shook his head, not looking at her. "It doesn't matter. Something stupid." A suitable lie occurred to him. "He was just...making some cracks about my date."

Joannie rolled her eyes in disgust. "That sounds like him. Scott, you can't let my brother bug you."

Scott managed a smile. "I'll try harder next time. If there is a next time."

Joannie picked up her script. "There'll be a next time. Jason always has to tangle with somebody. It's like breathing."

Joannie turned to leave just as Gina appeared in the doorway.

"The gang's all here!" Joannie quipped.

Gina looked at Scott gravely. "You're wanted on the set."

"Did you hear that, Scott?" Joannie threw over her shoulder as she breezed out. "You're *wanted*."

Gina started off when Scott called, "Hey, wait!" He was instantly on his feet and by her side. "I just wanted to talk to you."

"I can't right now."

"Please – let me apologize."

"For what?"

"I don't know. For whatever it is I might've done the other night that you didn't like."

"You're not making any sense. I had an awesome time at the party."

He touched her shoulder. "I did, too. That's why I want to see you again. I *need* to see you again."

"Gee, I wonder why."

"Is that what you think it's all about?"

"You tell me."

"You want to know what I'm *really* like? Go out on a date with me. Give me a *real* chance."

Gina stood there, staring at the ground, thinking it over. "All right. This is already messed up, let's just mess it up some more."

Scott beamed. "Great!"

The walki-talki clipped to Gina's belt crackled. "A.D. to P.A.-2."

Gina grabbed the radio and pushed the TALK button. "P.A.-2."

"Did you find Scott?"

Gina grabbed Scott by the arm and propelled him down the hall. "Affirm," she said into the radio. "He's on his way."

"Wait a minute," Scott said, happily allowing himself to be manhandled. "What about our date?"

"Saturday night," Gina muttered.

"All right! What time do I pick you up?"

"Seven o'clock. And text me your address. I'll pick *you* up."

The Griffith's house was at the top of Stradella Road, overlooking a panoramic canyon and a picturesque ridge that barely concealed Century City in the distance.

A large gate obstructed the driveway, so Gina pulled up to the callbox on the left-hand side and pushed the button.

A moment later, a beep sounded, and a friendly older man's voice said, "Welcome to McDonald's. May I take your order?"

Gina looked up in surprise and stared at the box oddly. "*Excuse* me?"

Gina heard hushed voices on the other end, and then Scott came on. "Gina? Is that you?"

"Yeah," she said unsurely, her tone withering.

"I'll open the gate. Just pull inside and park anywhere."

The gate opened slowly, and Gina did just as she was instructed. She was just getting out of her car when Scott came out the front door of the house. A man and a woman stood in the doorway behind him, watching.

Scott's smile could've lit up the sky. "I can't believe you're actually here. It's wild! You know?"

Gina looked at him strangely, gratefully accepting the hug he gave her. "No. I *don't* know. What are you talking about?"

He couldn't stop smiling. "I'm just...glad you're here."

Gina acknowledged the man and woman standing in the doorway and politely waved.

Scott placed his hand on her shoulder and lowered his voice as he led her toward the house. "I'm sorry about that before. That was just my dad...acting like an ass. Don't pay any attention to him."

Gina stifled a genuine smile as she steered herself for the introduction.

"Mom, Dad. This is Gina Moore."

"It's very nice to meet you, Gina," his mother said pleasantly.

"If you've come to visit Panic Palace," his father said amiably, "This is it."

"Not intentionally," Gina replied.

"One thing we do have to tell you," Robert said seriously, and with some difficulty. "We have to approve of every girl Scott goes out with, so if you don't pass the test, that's it – you're scratched."

"Oh, will you stop!" Tracy scolded. "You're going to scare the poor girl off! Gina, please come in. And don't listen to him."

"That's right," Robert deadpanned. "I just live here."

The inside of the house was more magnificent than Gina could've imagined. Cathedral ceilings, large entryways, marble floors, and decorative potted plants. Two plate-glass doors in the living room led to a balcony with a sweeping view of the surrounding canyon.

"Wow!" Gina couldn't help saying. "This house is incredible!"

"You want the two-dollar tour?" Robert joked. "It'll cost ya."

The large plasma wall T.V. in the living room was on with the volume turned down. A segment on CNN caught Gina's eye. The news caption read DRUG LORD INDICTED. Onscreen a sour-faced man in his sixties was being led in handcuffs from a courthouse in New York City.

Gina forced a smile to her lips and said, "Sounds great."

Brian's parents were hosting a barbecue at their house in Calabasas. Friends and family, nothing formal.

Brian's parents were nice, friendly people. They liked Debbie immediately.

As the sun began to set, Debbie and Brian were in the pool. Debbie was lying on her stomach on top of a pool raft, and Brian was in the water holding onto the raft.

"I don't want you to go," Brian said softly.

"I know," Debbie said, staring forlornly into the water.

"This has been the best summer of my whole life!" His eyes twinkled.

"For me, too."

"How come Gina didn't come?"

"Gina actually has a date tonight." Dazzling smile. "So I'm all yours."

"Love the sound of *that*."

And he kissed her. Long and meaningfully. Slow and lovingly. She couldn't resist him. She didn't want to.

The Griffith's house was four stories high and built into the side of the cliff. The first level was actually the top floor, and down they went from there. The patio and swimming pool were right off the ground level, and a stairway on the side of the house led from the bottom, all the way to the driveway at the top.

Gina and Scott reached the edge of the pool area, where they had a bird's eye view of the houses trailing down Roscomare Road.

"I just wanna die," Scott muttered.

"Why?" Gina asked, genuinely puzzled.

"Why? You weren't even in the driveway when my dad started embarrassing me!"

Gina smiled. "I like your dad. He's cool. He's...real."

"A little *too* real."

"You want a nightmare? Try living with my mother. That'll make you wanna run away from home!"

"Is that what *you* did? You never told me. What brought you out here?"

"The weather, mostly. I just didn't want to spend another winter in New York."

"But why L.A.? Of all the places you could've gone? You have no desire to be an actress. I don't think you want to make a career out of being a P.A."

Gina shrugged. "I guess it's because L.A. seemed... exciting! I just wanted something better. But most of all, I wanted to be free from my mother."

"Oh yeah?"

Gina nodded. She looked at him pointedly. "What about *you*?"

"What?"

She gestured expansively. "You've obviously got money. I mean, you could live anywhere you wanted to. On your own. You're almost twenty. Why do you still live with your parents?"

He really had to think about it. "Because I want to. This is my home. And look at this place – why *wouldn't* I want to live here?"

Gina rolled her eyes. "Yeah, and having your parents watch everything you do. Monitoring you like you're in jail."

"I come and go as I please here, Gina. What's the big deal? I know I'll have to find my own place eventually. I'm just not ready to."

"You're close to your family," Gina stated, envy in her voice.

"Don't spread it around," Scott said gravely. "I have my reputation to protect."

They sat at a corner table for two at Spago.

Gina looked at Scott seriously. "And you think Jason was the one who complained about you on that commercial all those years ago?"

Scott shook his head ruefully. "I don't know who else it could've been. That, and I trust my instincts. Ever since then, there's something about him I don't trust."

Gina picked at her shrimp. "That's so weird. He seems so charming."

"He's an actor. Fooling people is what he does best."

"Oh really?" Gina asked playfully. "You're an actor, too. How do I know you're not fooling *me*?"

Scott started in on his breast of duck and sighed. "I guess you don't know. I'll just have to prove it to you."

Gina smiled as she nodded. "Good answer."

Gina and Scott were just coming out of the restaurant when the lights from several flash cams hit them in the face.

"Hey, Scott. How about a quote for *Tiger Beat*?"

"Scott, *Pop Starz* magazine. Are you two a couple now?"

"Are you doing a movie together?"

Scott held up his hand and spoke slowly and calmly. "I'm just out for the evening with a good friend. That's all."

"How about a couple of pictures?" one of the female reporters asked.

Scott hesitated, then turned to Gina and lowered his voice. "You don't have to."

Gina took Scott's arm and smiled for the photographers. "Why not?"

The reporters captured multiple shots of the two of them before departing.

Scott looked at Gina, his expression uncomfortable.

They started down Canon Drive.

"I'm sorry about that," he said.

Gina shrugged. "Do you hear me complaining?"

"Yeah, but I have no control over what they say about you in print. It might not be good."

"How are they going to know who I am?"

"You'd be surprised. All of a sudden, your name is splashed all over the tabloids, and you wonder how the hell it happened."

She took his hand and fixed him with her gypsy eyes. "I'll risk it."

The Griffith house was dark when Gina pulled into Scott's driveway.

"Guess Mom and Dad didn't wait up," Gina remarked dryly.

"You never know," Scott said ominously. "They might've planted hidden surveillance cameras." His eyes shone brightly in the dark. "You taking off?"

Gina shrugged, an invitation in her voice. "I don't have to."

"Great!" Scott beamed, opening the car door. "You wanna go for a walk?"

Gina stared. "A walk?"

Stradella Road was quiet as Gina and Scott strolled down the winding sidewalk.

"My mother lives to drive me nuts!" Gina confided.

Scott, his hands in his pockets, glanced into someone's empty living room. "She can't be as bad as my dad."

"I would take *both* your parents over her any day. She's not happy unless she's running my life."

"Join the club. What about your dad?"

Gina hesitated. "He's dead."

"I'm sorry. How did it happen?"

"He was shot."

He stopped and looked at her. "What?"

"He was walking out of a building with this senator," Gina said solemnly. "It was the senator they meant to get."

"You mean an assassin??"

She shushed him. "Why don't you say it a little louder?" They kept going.

"Sorry," he mumbled.

"It's all right. It happened when I was eight."

Scott couldn't get over it. "Wow. Do you remember him?"

Gina stared straight ahead. "I do. Mostly from what I've seen in pictures, though." A smile lit her exquisite face. "What I remember most is that he used to call me 'princess.'"

Scott bit back a laugh. "'Princess'? You?"

Her smile turned into a scowl. "Okay, maybe this date should be over right now."

His attitude changed, and he affectionately took her hand. "I will shut up now."

She allowed him to hold her hand as they continued down the well-lit road. "Smart move."

Debbie and Brian stood facing each other in his room.

Their wet bathing suits were still on.

He continued to kiss her, his hands straying down her body.

The lights were dim.

They could still hear the noise of the party downstairs, but they didn't care.

He stopped and looked at her for a moment, afraid to do anything.

Smiling, she peeled down her one-piece swimsuit and gracefully stepped out of it.

Brian could hardly breathe as he watched her.

She took his hand and guided him to the bed. Then she lay down.

He happily shucked off his trunks and joined her.

He was everything she wanted and more.

Gina and Scott stood outside the Griffith's front door.

"Maybe we shouldn't do this," Gina whispered. "What if your parents catch us?"

"They won't catch us," Scott whispered back, "'Cuz we're gonna be real quiet. Okay?"

Scott punched in a code on the keypad and the door opened.

A loud beeping from inside sounded.

"What's that?" Gina demanded, quickly following him into the foyer.

Scott flew over to another keypad on the foyer wall. "It's the security system," he muttered frantically. "I have to disarm it."

Gina closed the front door while Scott punched in a four-digit sequence on the panel.

The beeping continued.

Panicked, Scott punched in another code.

The beeping seemed louder.

Gina's eyes darted everywhere. "Why can't you turn it off?"

"I know what I'm doing!"

The air exploded with a piercing alarm that wailed throughout the entire house.

Robert, dressed in cotton pajamas and groggy, appeared in the entryway to the living room.

Tracy, obviously woken from a sound sleep, came up the stairs clutching her bathrobe around her.

Gina and Scott stared at them, open-mouthed, wishing they were someplace else.

Gina stopped at the door of her apartment and reached inside her purse. Producing her key, she inserted it into the lock and opened the door.

The apartment was completely dark inside.

She reached for the light switch when a man's hand pushed her arm down and behind her back. His other hand covered her mouth.

She tried to scream, but the sound was muffled.

He roughly pulled her inside and closed the door.

Gina wanted to bite down on his hand, but he was wearing heavy gloves.

His hand left her mouth long enough for her to inhale deeply, but the next moment, he held a switchblade to her throat. "Don't make me use this," he hissed.

She caught a glimpse of him in the mirrored wall. He was slender, only a little taller than she was, dressed all in black, and wearing a ski mask.

She could feel the blade of the knife digging into her skin. Just moving was painful.

Her voice was barely audible. "Please..."

"Shut up! Get away from that window!"

She obediently complied – afraid to breathe.

Gina could hardly see where she was going.

The intruder hit his knee on the glass coffee table, temporarily moving the knife away from her throat. With her free hand, Gina seized his arm and pushed it down as hard as she could, at the same time bringing her knee up and catching him in the groin with her heel.

He let go of her and wailed in pain.

Gina ran towards her bedroom, but in an instant, he grabbed her arm, turned her around, and propelled her back into the living room.

"Help!" she shouted. "Somebody help me!"

She screamed as he pushed her on the couch and jumped on top of her.

His hands were around her throat, squeezing tightly.

She gasped and spluttered, but the sounds died inside of her.

Gina was staring her attacker in his masked face now, her eyes bulging with terror.

She couldn't breathe, but her hands were free. Desperately, she brought both her fists up between his arms and fought to break them.

His hold on her remained.

Her hands flew to his hands and tried to pull them off.

His grip around her throat tightened.

Her arms flopped back down on the couch, then reached up and pulled at the ski mask.

It took more than one try, but Gina managed to get the mask off.

He released her.

Gina looked into the man's face and retched.

"Frank!"

CHAPTER 10

It was late afternoon when Heather trotted down Stradella Road and pulled out her cell phone. "It's me. Are you close?"

"Closer than you think, babe."

She turned to see a shiny black convertible pull up in front of her.

Miles was behind the wheel. The car's top was down, and Miles' was off, his glorious, well-defined chest on show.

Heather blushed as she opened the passenger door and got in. "I thought I told you not to call any attention to yourself."

He indicated the dark sunglasses he was wearing. "No one'll recognize me in these."

She couldn't help smiling.

He shifted the car and looked at her hungrily. "You ready to have some fun?"

She nodded eagerly.

Miles revved the engine and roared down the winding street toward Sunset Boulevard.

Heather and Miles sat on the ornate couch in Miles' living room. He was shirtless again, his arm was around her, and he was kissing her.

His free hand nimbly unbuttoned the top two buttons on her blouse and began exploring what was underneath.

She stopped him. "I'm sorry."

He fixed her with a humble expression. "I thought you liked me."

"You know I do. I...I'm just not ready...yet."

"Yet? Meaning...?"

"Meaning...I've been thinking about what we were talking about...and I want to...I just want it to be right."

"Oh," he said warmly, finally understanding. "Special?"

"Yeah," she said softly. "This is a big decision for me."

"I know."

"A girl only has her first time once."

He deadpanned. "I think it works the same for boys, too. But don't quote me on that."

She smiled, snaking her arm around his bare shoulder. "But I'm not with a boy. Am I?" she added huskily.

He shook his head and kissed her again. Wet, sucking ...hot!

She broke it off, barely able to catch her breath. "This time," she said, reaching for the button on his jeans, "I'm with a man..."

"That's right," he said, softly stroking her chin. "I can't wait to show you."

"Me neither!"

He looked at her. "Where?"

She met his gaze levelly. "Here."

"When?"

She bit her lip. "A week from tonight."

He nodded. "All right." His smile reassured her. "It'll be perfect."

She ran her hands down his chest as she returned his kiss with the same fiery passion.

Scott could feel his parents' anger as soon as he entered the kitchen. They were sitting at the table eating breakfast and looked up as soon as they saw him, lips pursed and eyes narrowed.

Scott looked away, ambled over to the counter, and took a cereal bowl out of the overhead cabinet.

"Thanks a lot!" Tracy spat.

Robert's voice was controlled but menacing. "You do some damned stupid things sometimes."

"It wouldn't turn off," Scott said weakly. "The code didn't work! It wasn't *my* fault."

"How long have we had that same code, Scott?" Tracy blazed. "How long? A two-year-old could turn that thing off, and you have to set it off in the middle of the night and wake the whole house up - "

"What were you doing with that girl in here?" Robert demanded. "Sneaking her up to your room? That *better* not be what you were planning to do!"

"We were just talking. That's all."

Robert finished and stood up from the table. "You gotta take more responsibility for what you do, Scott. *Think* before you do something. Damn it – you're nineteen-years-old. If you don't learn now, you *never* will."

Robert lumbered out.

Scott sat staring miserably into his cereal.

"When are you going to smarten up?" Tracy snapped.

"All right! I'm sorry! God – you'd think I did it on purpose."

"We're not doing it to be mean, Scott. The day's going to come when we're not going to be able to help you. You're going to have to handle your own problems."

"I *am* handling them." Scott shook his head in disgust. "He just doesn't like me."

"Oh, stop it - "

"He doesn't! If he wanted anything to do with me, he'd talk to me – not lecture me."

"Oh, yeah," Tracy said sarcastically. "He doesn't care about you. That's why he bought you that Porsche, even though we both agree it's the last thing you need."

He scowled. "Do we have to talk about the car again?"

"Well what the hell do you want from him, Scott?"

Scott sat with his arms folded. "I'd like him to be a father. I mean – take Jack Kellner. Joannie told me him and Jason go camping together."

Tracy looked at him in disbelief. "You? Camping? With all those mosquito bites you get? You were only out there a few hours that time when you begged us to take you home!"

Scott fumed. "Okay. What about my career? He never talks to me about *that*. If he cared, he'd give me advice – not tell me how stupid I am *after* I do something he doesn't like."

"Well you *do* stupid things sometimes."

He didn't look at her.

Tracy stirred her coffee. "He thinks you're doing very well with your career," she said seriously. "For one thing, he thinks you should do that movie."

"You told him about it?"

"Of course I told him about it! He says the script is very good."

"He looked at it?"

"He read it the other night."

"He *read* it? The whole thing?"

Tracy nodded.

Scott looked dumbfounded. "Wow."

"You see?" Tracy said softly. "He loves you, Scott. He wants nothing but the best for you. We *both* do."

Scott stood and moved behind her. "I'm sorry, Mom." He lovingly placed his arms around her. "Forgive me?"

Tracy feigned annoyance. "No!"

He snuggled close to her. "I love you."

She couldn't help smiling. "You're such a jerk, you know that?"

He put on his best pathetic face.

She tenderly hugged him. "I should've choked you when you were born!"

Beverly Hills High School. Monday morning.

The bell rang, signaling the start of the lunch period.

As the swarm of students filled the halls, Lynda caught up to her best friend. "Hey, Heather!"

"What's going on?" Heather asked casually, clutching the new suede purse slung over her shoulder.

"I didn't hear from you all weekend. It's like you dropped off the planet."

"I had stuff to do. Homework," Heather said quickly.

"Right," said Lynda in disbelief. "Is that what you were doing on Saturday?"

"Why?" Heather asked suspiciously.

Lynda shrugged. "No reason. I just thought maybe you were out partying without me."

"Why would you think that?"

"Oh, I don't know," Lynda replied condescendingly. "Probably because your mom called my house looking for you."

"What!" Heather and Lynda stopped and stepped aside so that the other stampeding students could pass by.

"Don't worry," Lynda said smugly. "I covered for you. I'd just like to know what I'm covering."

They resumed their trek down the hall and up the stairs.

"All right," Heather said reluctantly. "I had to go somewhere, and I didn't want her to know where I went."

"Well I figured *that*! Where did you go?"

Heather shook her head. "It's not important."

"Heather! If I'm going to be your alibi, I at least get to hear the dirt!"

Heather and Lynda sat having lunch on a planter near their school's front lawn.

"I can't believe you kept this from me!" Lynda exclaimed in amazement.

Heather silenced her with a look. "Will you cool it! I don't need the whole school to know."

"Oh, God! You can't expect me to sit on a secret like this!" Lynda became calm. "But I will."

Heather blushed as she beamed. "He is so terrific, too, Lynda."

"How old is he?"

"Twenty-four."

"Oh my God!" Lowering her voice. "Have you guys had sex yet?"

"No. But we're planning to. Next Saturday night. That's why you've got to cover for me."

"But Heather...if you go all the way with him, that'll make him guilty of..." Whispering. "...statutory rape."

"Only if it's non-consenting," Heather said casually, finishing the last of a bag of Fritos. "And I am not about to call the cops."

"But what if your parents find out?"

"They won't find out! And you can't tell anybody, Lynda. I mean it."

"Oh, God..." Lynda's expression became gleeful. "Okay. Answer me this: You said he's a stripper..."

"He's part of a 'male revue.' It's not the same thing."

"Whatever. So...has he ever...done his act for you in private?"

Heather nodded, glowing. "Part of it. Honestly – it's like unwrapping a Christmas present." Her face got even redder. "And on Saturday, I get to open the biggest present I've ever gotten!"

*   *   *

Heather regarded her appearance in the full-length mirror critically. Standing in the center of her tastefully decorated bedroom, she adjusted the straps on the black cocktail dress she was wearing and shook out her shoulder length blonde hair.

Outwardly she projected a young adult woman – sophisticated, mature, and beautiful. But even as she straightened the necklace pendant dangling between her budding breasts, her hands shook.

"Where are *you* going?"

Heather nearly jumped.

Her mother was standing in the doorway.

Tracy's expression was full of questions.

Heather forced a pleasant smile and strode over to her bureau to collect her purse. "Stacy Horwitz is having a party tonight, so me and Lynda are going to drop by."

Tracy looked at her reprovingly. "Heather, do you think I'm stupid? I know what you're really doing."

Heather's eyes were wide. "You do?"

"Yes," Tracy said condescendingly. "You think I don't know you're going there just to meet boys?"

Heather failed to disguise her relief. "Oh...yeah - "

"Just be careful," Tracy warned. "And keep your cell phone on so I can reach you if I need you. You know how plans change around here." She started down the hallway.

"Mom?"

Tracy turned back around.

"It might be after twelve when we get back, so I'll probably just stay over Lynda's tonight and come back tomorrow."

Tracy nodded. "Fine. Don't forget I'm picking you up at school Tuesday afternoon to get your learner's permit."

Heather beamed. "Like I'd forget *that*!"

"I'll be glad when you have your license so you can drive *yourself* around."

"I can't wait!"

Tracy smiled wistfully. "Don't grow up *too* fast, huh?" She was gone.

Heather whispered, "I won't, Mom."

*   *   *

Miles unlocked the door to his apartment and allowed Heather to enter first. He watched her as he closed the door behind them. "You want a drink?"

"No. Thank you," she added timidly.

He came up behind her, rested his hands on her shoulders, and kissed the back of her neck. "It's good to see you. I missed you. Did *you* miss *me*?"

The sensation of his kiss made her legs go weak. His lips were soft and gentle on hers as his tongue caressed the inside of her mouth, then slowly moved down her neck.

He started to unbutton her blouse when she stopped him and did it herself – and much faster. His hand traveled to her breast, lightly massaging it with the tip of his finger.

Unable to take any more, she grasped his hand and stopped to catch her breath.

"You okay?" he asked.

"Yes," she exhaled. "Definitely okay. Better than okay."

His smile reached all the way to his eyes. "Wanna go in my room?" he asked solicitously.

Heather looked away. "I want to. I just..."

"We don't have to go all the way." He picked a wrapped condom up off of the coffee table and fingered it thoughtfully. "I told you. I just wanna be with you. It doesn't matter what we do."

"Really?" Her eyes probed his, radiating relief.

Miles tossed the condom back on the table. "Really." He took her hand and held it.

"I want you to know..."

He was kissing her again – slowly, but at the same time, urgently.

Her whole body surrendered as she hungrily responded.

He broke and patted her shoulder. "C'mon. Let's relax."

Miles stood and strode into his bedroom.

"I should probably go home," Heather called out. "Unless you want to do something else..."

Heather heard one of Mile's shoes drop to the floor, then the other. She got up from the couch and followed him, her expression uncomfortable. "Do you want to go somewhere?"

When she reached his bedroom, Miles was peeling off his socks and grinning. "I don't wanna go anywhere. Let's just take it easy."

"Miles...I can't..."

He was unbuttoning his shirt. "I know you can't. So we won't. We can just hang out...do what comes naturally..."

"I know what comes naturally to you..."

He slipped his shirt off, revealing his chiseled pectorals and muscular arms. His brown eyes bore deep into hers. "Oh yeah? What's that?"

"You're making this so hard..."

"I could say the same thing to *you*."

She watched as he unbuckled his belt and slid his pants and underwear off. His bronzed nude body gleamed in the early evening light. He extended his hand to her. "Join me?"

She couldn't stop the smile from permeating her stern expression. "Why not...?"

He was warm and caring and so gentle that she wanted to cry out just from his touch. They were both naked now as he moved on top of her, the only light in the room from the moon shining through the window blinds.

His long brown hair fell in her face as his eyes rested on her exquisite innocence. He kissed her softly, slowly; making her taste him, savor him, hunger for him. Her tiny arms slid around his broad shoulders, and she brought her legs up and around his lower body.

Both were breathing harder as he moved back and forth against her.

His eyes were closed.

Her face was flushed.

"You got it?" she asked, moving her hands down to his waist.

"Yeah," he gasped, positioning himself carefully, then thrusting roughly inside her.

She yelped in pain, raising her hips and holding onto him tighter. Heather pulled away from him, unable to take any more, sinking deeper into the sheets.

Miles increased his speed, hurting her, causing sharp cries to escape her lips. She fought him, moving from side to side, pressing herself harder into him, until he tore through her resistance with one penetration.

Her screams excited him more. He was now way past the point of turning back. He couldn't hold back much longer.

Miles slowed down. Then he slowed his rhythm even more.

Heather responded more fiercely, pushing harder, faster.

The grinding he caused within her was pure torture. She felt herself slipping, losing control, holding him prisoner, until she wanted it to be over. The tension flooded her body so violently, she couldn't stop shaking even after he lay still on top of her and slowly withdrew.

Then she wanted the feeling to return again, but she knew it was gone. She felt only the most incredible release of being comfortable with her own womanhood.

Miles just lay next to her, holding her safely in his arms.

Heather stood looking out Miles' bedroom window. One of his robes was wrapped around her naked body, and the moon gently illuminated her pale, flawless complexion. Her arms were folded as she stared down at the empty street. She contemplated how her life had changed and what she would do next.

Miles came up behind her. He was nude, and looked even more handsome in the soft light. He slid his muscular arms around her and held her tight.

"Are you okay?" he husked.

"Yeah," she said dreamily. "I couldn't sleep."

He kissed her neck. "I missed you. I don't like to sleep alone."

"No?" she teased, turning her head to look at him.

"No," he asserted, taking her by the hand. "Come back to bed."

She willingly followed.

Heather and Miles sat having lunch at Le Petit Four on Sunset Boulevard.

As Heather nibbled on her penne pasta, she became aware of the attention Miles was getting from most of the women, and even some of the men.

She beamed at Miles as she watched him pick at his trout.

"This great photographer I found," he was saying, "He shoots models, mostly. He's gonna do a portfolio for me that I can send to talent agents."

"Cool!" Heather enthused.

"Yeah." His face fell. "Trouble is, most of the time, they won't look at you unless you have a ton of credits or someone gives you a referral."

"But you've done stuff. Right?"

He looked sheepish. "I did some extra work for Central Casting, and a couple of commercials."

"My brother started by doing commercials."

Miles studied her thoughtfully. "Yeah." He gleamed. "And look how far *he's* come!"

Heather nodded.

"Obviously he has an agent..."

Heather took a bite of her chicken. "Scott's with CAA. Maureen O'Malley, I think."

"Yeah. I'd have to know somebody to get somebody like *her*."

"Well..." Heather simpered. "You *kinda* do."

He failed to disguise his eagerness. "Really?"

She shrugged. "I *might* be able to get your picture to her. I'll see what I can do."

"Hey, that'd be awesome!" He leered. "Is there anything I can do to...show you my appreciation?"

Her tone was equally suggestive. "I can think of a few things..."

Their waitress stopped at the table. "Is there anything else I can get you?"

Heather shook her head.

"We're good," Miles said pleasantly.

She left the check on the table.

When she was gone, Miles opened the black booklet and looked at the receipt.

"How much is it?" Heather asked curiously.

Miles looked at her pathetically. "More than I got."

Heather shook her head again and took the booklet out of his hand. "I got it. Don't worry about it."

"You sure?" he asked, making no move to wrestle the check from her. "You make me feel guilty whenever you do this."

Heather rolled her eyes. "It's no big deal. Besides," she added coquettishly, "You can pay me back in other ways."

It was early afternoon when Miles slipped out of his apartment, checked both ends of the hallway, and started for the elevator. He pushed the call button, still looking around, waiting impatiently.

The doors opened, and he was almost prepared for the short, fifty-year-old Hispanic man who cornered him. "Miles," he said sharply in broken English.

Miles reluctantly stepped inside and pushed LOBBY.

"I need the rent money, and I have to have it today."

The doors closed, and the man stayed inside the elevator with Miles as it traveled downward.

"I know, Mr. Garcia," Miles said, summoning sincerity. "You know I'm always on time with it. I'll have it to you in a couple more days."

"The month'll be over in a coupla more days!" Garcia spluttered. "Then, you'll owe me two months' rent! I can't work that way, Miles, I told you before."

The elevator doors opened, and Miles started out.

Garcia didn't relent. "If I don't get it by the end of the day, I'm changing the locks. I mean it."

Miles was gone.

Out on the street, Miles scanned the list of names in his cell phone's memory.

LAUREL GILLIS.

CALL.

"You have reached a number that is no longer in service. If you feel you have reached this recording in error - "

"Damn it!" he raged, disconnecting, his grip on the phone tightening.

Aware that passersby on the sidewalk were watching him, Miles started down the street, his mind racing. He tried to shut out the sounds of traffic and people, but they were roaring in his head like jackhammers and freight trains.

Then he looked up at the Hollywood Hills and relaxed. Taking a deep breath, he grabbed his phone and searched for another number.

HEATHER GRIFFITH.

CALL.

The front entrance of Beverly Hills High School was moderately quiet at lunch period. Students could be heard shouting and chattering as they roamed the campus, the on-site security patrolling randomly in electric carts.

Miles leaned, arms folded, against his car, which was parked curbside on Moreno Drive. Despite the dark sunglasses he wore, he was still strikingly noticeable in tight white pants and a checkered shirt.

Heather checked to make sure no one was watching before slipping off school property and running over to where he waited.

"Thank you so much for wearing a shirt, by the way." She tugged at one of his sleeves. "I didn't want you drawing attention to yourself."

He smiled sexily. "It's the least I can do."

She reached into her purse, pulled out an envelope, and handed it to him. "Seven-hundred dollars. It's all the ATM would let me take out."

Miles opened the envelope and quickly counted the seven one-hundred-dollar bills. He fingered them carefully before stuffing them back inside. "I swear I'll pay you back."

She smiled sympathetically. "I know that."

Miles shoved the envelope inside his back pocket and looked at her lovingly. "I wish I could take you in my arms and kiss you right here."

"I know you do. I wish you could, too." She stole a glance behind her. "I better get back before somebody sees us." Heather started for the entrance. "Call me later!"

Lynda was standing behind the fence in the faculty parking lot, watching them very closely. She didn't like what she saw.

Slowly backing away, she turned and moved off before Heather saw her.

Heather's sixteenth birthday party was a fun, lively gathering held at the Griffith home the following Saturday night.

Heather wore an elegant red cocktail dress and had her hair up. One of her mother's diamond pendants completed the look, and she looked radiant when she finally emerged from her bedroom.

Before the party started, Heather, Scott, Robert, and Tracy stood in the kitchen. Tracy was checking on the food and the arrangements.

Heather looked at Robert imploringly. "Please, Dad – don't do anything to embarrass me when my friends get here."

Robert shook his head. "I'm not gonna do a thing to embarrass you – I'm just gonna lay down the law: No drinking - no drugs – no breathing - "

Heather didn't crack a smile. "Mom – make him stop."

Tracy shot him a look. "Bob..."

"This is important to me."

Robert nodded. "Okay. Fine."

Scott smiled proudly at Heather and outstretched his arms. "Can I have a hug?"

She was unenthusiastic. "I guess so."

They embraced tenderly.

"How do I look?" she asked.

"Stunning, as always," Scott replied. Then, staring at her hairdo, "Why didn't you wear your hair *down*? It looks so much prettier that way."

Heather made a face. "Give me a break!"

"It does!"

Tracy looked at Scott with disapproval. "There is nothing wrong with her hair." She indicated a covered bucket of ice on the kitchen table. "Now make yourself useful and put that at the bar."

Tracy headed into the living room with a tray of cold cuts, and Heather followed.

Scott reluctantly grabbed the bucket and was just about to take it into the other room when Robert quietly said, "I think her hair looks better the other way, too." He shrugged. "But what are you gonna do?"

The party started half an hour later.

Half the guests were Heather's friends, half various relatives. A sound system with speakers in every room issued forth melodic R&B, and people were eating, drinking, and having a good time on every floor.

*   *   *

Heather was talking to her grandmother and great-aunt when Lynda came up to her and placed a hand on her arm. "Can I borrow you for a second?"

"I'll be right back, Grandma," Heather said politely, following Lynda into a quiet corner of the living room. "What is it?"

"I saw you with him yesterday," Lynda said. "In front of the school. Miles?"

Heather went white.

"Why were you giving him money?"

"I'll tell you about that later - "

"Okay, Heather – he's hot. I'll give you that. But if you let him take advantage of you, you're insane!"

"Will you calm down," Heather said sharply. "He is not taking advantage of me. You don't know anything about it, so just stay out of it."

Heather started to move off, but Lynda pulled her back. "Don't you see what he's doing? He's using you! Heather – he's gonna hurt you. And I don't want you to get hurt."

Heather's eyes flashed. "I'll be fine. If I were you, I'd worry about yourself. I'm not the one with the reputation for being a skank."

Heather left Lynda staring after her, open-mouthed.

A few nights later, the Griffiths were all having dinner together at the same time – a rarity – when Tracy looked at Heather. "Did you tell your brother the big news?"

"What?" Scott asked, rolling spaghetti onto his fork.

"Check it out, bro," Heather grinned, reaching into her purse and pulling out a card. "I got my learner's permit!"

"Oh, Lord! The streets are no longer safe."

"I'll be a careful driver," Heather simpered. "I just need a responsible person eighteen or over to drive with me whenever I want to go someplace - "

"Forget it, Heather. No way. I don't care what you say, there is no way I'm going driving with you."

*   *   *

One hour later, Scott sat next to Heather in the passenger seat of their father's Cadillac. "Make sure you check your rearview mirror, and back out slowly."

"Okay." Heather gleefully started the engine and put the car in reverse.

The Cadillac sped out of the Griffth's driveway and nearly collided with another car.

"Whoah!" Scott yelled.

The other car sounded its horn and roared off.

"Damn it, Heather! Slowly!"

"Sorry."

The ride down Roscomare Road wasn't any easier.

Years later, they would both look back on it as quality time.

Many years later.

Things were uncomfortable between Heather and Lynda when they saw each other at school.

Third period, they had the same Geometry class. Both came from opposite ends of the hall and happened to meet outside the classroom door.

Heather looked away and Lynda brushed right past her.

Things weren't any better at lunch.

They skillfully avoided each other in the cafeteria and sat with groups they didn't ordinarily sit with.

The two girls exchanged dirty looks a few times, which caused the girls they were sitting with to murmur remarks to one another and watch them as eagerly as they would a new T.V. show.

Heather didn't care. Soon enough, everybody would target another victim to gossip about.

Miles sat across from Maureen O'Malley in her office at Creative Artists Agency. She was a stylish, attractive woman in her mid-forties, with red hair and intense blue eyes.

The room had floor to ceiling windows, which flooded the mid-size office with afternoon sunlight.

Maureen surveyed Miles intently as she politely greeted him. "I really have all the clients I can handle, Miles, but Heather Griffith recommended you so highly. And I can see why."

Appealing smile. "Thank you."

She scanned the resume on the back of his headshot. "I see you worked on two of Justin Timberlake's movies."

"Yes."

"Did you have any lines?"

"No. I was...an extra."

Maureen nodded and placed the resume on her desk. "The only thing I can send you up for right now would be commercials."

He leaned forward eagerly. "Great!"

"We're going to start you off in the commercial department for now, and we'll see how things go."

He almost jumped out of his seat. "Oh, thank you! Thank you very much!"

Heather had been consciously avoiding Lynda since her birthday party. Not that Lynda phoned or texted, but she and Heather couldn't help seeing each other in passing at school.

The following day, when Heather returned to school, she deliberately kept a lookout for her former friend – more out of curiosity than wanting to talk to her.

Lynda was absent. Heather didn't see her in any of their usual classes or at lunch.

Heather didn't think anything of it until the rest of the week passed.

Lynda did not return.

Heather asked around, questioning their mutual friends.

No one knew anything.

Miles had also been making himself scarce. Ever since CAA had signed him, he was either having new pictures taken, auditioning, or otherwise unavailable.

Heather decided to remind him that she was still alive.

She dropped by his apartment building that afternoon.

A crew was cleaning the lobby and the front door was propped open, so she just slipped inside and took the elevator up.

Heather got off on Miles' floor and headed down the hall. Just before she reached his apartment, the door opened and a mature-looking brunette stepped out. The brunette turned as Miles appeared in the doorway, clad in a flimsy silk robe and obviously nothing else.

Miles grinned as he took the girl in his arms and kissed her. By the time they broke, Heather was in sight, glaring at the two of them in disbelief, then in fury.

Miles turned and saw Heather.

He froze.

Heather's face was stone cold, her lips pursed in a thin line.

She fled.

CHAPTER 11

Gina and Frank stared at each other for a few moments in the dark, neither saying anything.

The room was flooded with light.

Both turned to see Debbie and Brian standing in the doorway.

"Who the hell are you?" Brian demanded.

Frank jumped off of Gina and stood glaring at them.

He hesitated only a split second before charging the open doorway.

Debbie darted out of Frank's path, but Brian stood his ground.

Frank rushed him, pummeling Brian in the face and sending him into the wall.

Brian grabbed Frank by the shirt and punched him hard in the jaw, which had little effect.

Frank landed a sidekick to Brian's stomach, and Brian tumbled to the floor. Only momentarily daunted, Brian leaped up and took off after Frank, who had disappeared down the long corridor.

"Brian!" Debbie called, her voice almost a screech. Then she turned to Gina, who was curled up in a ball on the couch, shaking and crying. "Gina!" Debbie was immediately at her side. "It's okay, honey. He's gone."

Debbie went to put her arm around her, and Gina jumped up and screamed.

Brian raced down the stairwell and bolted through the emergency door, which led out to an alley behind the rear exit of Debbie and Gina's building.

It was dark, with only a few streetlights illuminating the deserted area.

Brian looked in every direction, but there was no sign of Frank.

Breathing heavily, Brian spun around and returned inside.

Debbie's voice was soft, but full of growing concern. "Gina, what is it? He's gone now. It's going to be all right."

There were tears in Gina's eyes as she shook her head. "No...It's not...all right...he wants...to kill me..."

Debbie felt her heart stop. "You know him?"

Gina was struggling to breathe.

Brian appeared in the doorway.

"I lost him!" he gasped.

Debbie ran to him. "Brian!" She flung her arms around him and held him. "You scared me! I can't believe you did that!"

"I thought...I could catch him - "

"What if he killed you?"

He smiled weakly. "Relax. I'm here."

"Would you two shut up!" Gina hissed. "Close that damn door!"

Debbie and Brian looked at her. Gina was now remarkably composed.

Brian closed the apartment door. "Shouldn't we call the police?"

Debbie reached for her cell phone. "Yeah. I'm gonna do that right now."

"No," Gina said firmly, watching them both very closely.

"What!" Debbie's eyes bugged out.

"Shut off that phone."

The look in Gina's eye made Debbie comply. "You wanna wait?"

Gina rose and slowly paced the room.

Debbie was staring at her cousin. "Gina? You said you know who he is?"

"She does?" Brian was looking at Debbie wide-eyed.

Gina turned to them. She was still quivering. "Yes. It was Frank."

"Frank who?" Debbie asked.

"Frank Dinato. My ex."

"That was Frank!"

Gina's mind was racing.

"Gina, how is that possible? You told me he was dead."

"Yeah, well, that's what *I* thought."

"Then you definitely need to call the police!"

Gina had her back to Debbie and Brian, who stood looking at her for a long moment. She slowly turned to them, her expression intent. "It won't do any good."

Debbie looked down and gasped. "It's a knife!" She started to bend down. "Is this his?"

"Don't touch that!" Brian warned. "You'll smudge the fingerprints."

"There won't be any," Gina said dismissively, still deep in thought. Acknowledging Debbie and Brian, she sighed regretfully. "I hate to do this, but there's only one person I can call."

Cynthia was sitting on her bed and shaking so violently that she could barely hold the phone in her hand. "That's it – I'm coming out there!"

"To do *what*, Mom? You want him to come after *you*, too?"

"I'm not leaving you out there alone!"

"I'm gonna be back in New York in two weeks, anyway."

"You think you're going to make it back here alive? Oh, God!" Cynthia paced her room. "I wonder if you should try *driving* back...No, they could still tail you or trace the car...even if you rented it in Debbie's name..."

"Why would they tell us that Frank was dead if he wasn't?"

"I don't know!"

"Something's going on here, Ma. Why would Frank want to kill me?"

"Because you sent him to jail!"

"Yeah. But why now? If he's been out of jail for two years, why would he wait till now to do this?"

Cynthia was silent for a few moments as she thought it over. "You're right."

"Santinello..." Gina's voice wavered. "And he knows where I am...Oh, God, Mom, what am I gonna do?"

Cynthia struggled to calm herself. "All right. We need some help here. And I think I've got the answer."

"What?"

Cynthia hesitated. "Keep your cell phone with you. I have to make a call, and I'll call you - "

"What!"

"I will call you back," Cynthia said firmly. "Just answer when I do."

Cynthia reluctantly disconnected and stood there for a few moments, considering. She quickly searched through her phone log. When she found the number she was looking for, she stopped, took a deep breath, and stared at the phone. "God..." She paused for only another few seconds, and then pushed the CALL button. The other end of the line seemed to ring forever before it was finally picked up.

"Carol...?" She forced a note of brightness into her voice. "It's Cynthia...How are you...?" Her tone changed. "Oh, not very good...It's the reason why I called. I've got to talk to Caesar. It's extremely urgent."

Gina chose a simple skirt and blouse that looked conservative yet stylish. She drove through the East Gate of Bel Air and continued straight up Bel Air Road. As she navigated the narrow, meandering street, the phone conversation she'd had with her mother reverberated in her mind.

"There is someone who can help you, Gina. And he's right there in L.A."

"Who?"

She could hear Cynthia's hesitation. "Someone I should've told you about a long time ago."

Gina was almost at the top of the mountain when she found the address she was looking for. She stopped in front of the wrought iron gate, pushed a button on the callbox keypad and waited.

A minute later, the gates opened, and she drove right on through. She marched up the brick steps to the front door and pressed the doorbell.

After she heard the chimes ring inside, there followed the sound of a ferocious dog barking insanely.

The door was opened by a kind-looking woman in her late fifties. She smiled pleasantly. "Gina?"

"Yes."

"Come in."

As soon as Gina tried to step inside, a huge German Shepherd jumped in her path and barked menacingly.

"Nina!" the woman scolded the animal gently. Helplessly to Gina, "She's just not comfortable around strangers."

Pressing her back against the wall, Gina slowly edged her way inside. "We don't want her to be uncomfortable. Right?"

"Nina!" a man's voice commanded sharply. "Cut the crap!"

The enormous dog lowered its head and slunk to a far corner of the living room, where it remained, watching Gina warily.

Gina turned to regard the speaker. He was a large, imposing man who looked to be in his mid-sixties. He was wearing a button-down shirt, dress pants, and black-rimmed glasses.

"Come on in," he said, gesturing to the couch.

He followed her inside and took a seat opposite her in an old recliner.

Gina occasionally glanced over at Nina, who appeared deceptively innocuous curled up in the corner.

Gina remained perched on the edge of her seat, her trembling hands folded in her lap.

Carol stepped meekly forward. "Gina, would you like a drink or something? Some water, maybe?"

"No, thank you."

Carol caught Caesar's look. "I'll just leave you two alone."

As soon as Carol had gone, Caesar took a long hard look at Gina. He sighed deeply and shook his head, a broad smile creasing his weathered features. "Boy – this is a day I never thought I'd see."

Gina looked at him strangely. "Why?"

He was immediately apologetic. "Don't get me wrong – I ain't unhappy about it. It's just hard to believe." He was looking at her as if she'd come back from the dead. "It's real good to meet ya, Gina."

She attempted a smile, even though she was still very nervous. "It's nice to meet you, too...Uncle Caesar..."

Gina was finding Caesar's gaze unsettling.

"What's wrong?" she asked, wondering if he might be senile.

"Nothin'," he muttered, staring dreamily into her face. "Hmph...You just...look so much like your pop..."

"So you're his...brother...?"

"Yup. Older by ten years. You remind me of him when he was a kid. 'Course, the last time I saw you, you was in your crib."

"Okay, this is all really weird - " Gina stood, and immediately Nina was on all four of her legs and growling. Gina quickly sat back down again and grimaced. "She's good at what she does."

Caesar was unconcerned. "Who, her? She won't bite. She's friendly."

"Friendly?" Gina looked at him in disbelief. "I'd hate to see her mean."

"Gina, I know this is a lot to take all at once, but ya gotta believe me – all I wanna do is help ya. Yer mixed up with some pretty bad people. The fact that yer even walkin' around right now is a miracle."

"How is Frank alive and we never knew it?"

"Santinello arranged for him to disappear. That's why they told you he was dead."

"Why?"

Caesar paused a moment. "He's one of Santinello's top guys. Knows a lot of stuff. And a lot of people. If the Feds got to him first, there woulda bin a crack in Santinello's organization the size of the Grand Canyon."

Gina felt faint. "He wants to kill me."

"Dinato? Naw, I don't think that's it. Dinato ain't the one who wants you dead. It's Santinello."

Gina swallowed hard. "Santinello?"

"Dinato's been workin' for Santinello this whole time," Caesar explained. "Santinello sent Dinato to do the job because he figured Dinato knew you, could get to you easier. That's why Dinato didn't come after you until now – Santinello didn't need you out of the way until he found out you were gonna testify against him."

Gina was glad she was sitting, as she doubted she could summon the strength to stand right now. She happened to glance down at the dress shoes Caesar wore and wondered how he could stand wearing things that looked so uncomfortable. She took a deep breath and looked Caesar right in the eye. "What do I do now?"

"Nothin'," Caesar said, almost sounding happy about it. "I'll take it from here. The first thing I'm gonna do is call Santinello and his people off. Then they can't bother ya anymore."

Gina stared at him, uncomprehending. "What do you mean 'can't' bother me? What are you going to do?"

He smiled. "All it'll take is a phone call. Then you'll sit tight with me until this trial." He stood and paced the room. "Shame you had to agree to testify. That really made a mess of things. We could've arranged for you to disappear somewhere until things got quiet." He turned to her with a reassuring look. "Don't worry. I'll take care of it. Your mom did the right thing calling me."

Gina stood in the Camarari's kitchen with Carol and Alice. Caesar had gone upstairs, and Gina had just been introduced to the two women.

"It's so wonderful to meet you!" Carol said sweetly. "We've heard a lot about you – mostly from your mother!"

Gina faltered. "This whole thing is so weird. Now I have this family I never knew about."

"We've always been here," said Alice. "And now we're here whenever you need us."

Gina sighed. "I wish I didn't."

"Don't worry," Carol said. "Caesar knows how to handle these things."

"I'm so glad," Gina said, folding her arms across her chest. "I didn't know what to do..."

Carol touched her arm lightly. "He's going to do everything he can."

"And so will we," said Alice, taking Gina's hand. "And we don't expect you to be a stranger around here."

Gina smiled gratefully. "I won't."

Caesar lumbered down the stairs and came through the living room into the kitchen. The look on his face was grim. "I want you to sleep *here* tonight. Don't go back to your apartment. It should be safe by tomorrow."

"What about Debbie?" Gina asked, her voice rising.

"Call her. I'm gonna send a car for her in *one hour*. My driver will take her straight here. I can't run the risk of her being followed – even though I know the bastard knows where to find me. Tomorrow we'll talk about what yer gonna say at this trial. Capische?"

Gina nodded, not trusting herself to speak.

Gina and Debbie had dinner at Caesar's that night.

They sat at the large table in the dining room with him, Carol, Alice, and – of course – Nina.

"C'mon, girl," Caesar called, feeding the animal chicken from the table.

Gina indicated Nina and asked Carol, "Are you sure she wants me in the family?"

"'Course she does," Caesar answered. "She woulda eaten you by now. So if *she* likes ya, yer in."

When Alice finished, she dabbed her lips with a napkin and said, "I'm feeling a little tired. I think I'm going to go to my room now."

"Have a good night," Debbie smiled, finishing off the last of her spaghetti and meatballs.

Nina barked at Alice as she left the room, but remained loyally by Caesar's side.

Alice departed through the kitchen.

"Why does she have to bark at Mom?" Carol asked, carefully hiding her irritation.

"She won't hurt her," Caesar said, mopping up some marinara sauce with a slice of bread. He looked at Gina and Debbie with a sly grin. "She'll only give her a *little* bite!" He laughed, even though Carol knew that he loved Alice.

Gina and Debbie weren't so sure.

"He's kidding, right?" Gina asked.

"I'm dead serious," Caesar said, not meaning a word. Then he called out to the kitchen, even though Alice was long gone. "One of these days, Old Alice is gonna find out she ain't such a ballbreaker after all!"

Caesar was watching the large flat screen T.V. in his den when Gina stepped inside. She knocked tentatively on the mahogany wall. "Uncle Caesar? We're going to bed now. Good night."

Caesar muted the T.V. and motioned for her to enter. "C'mere, kid. I wanna talk to ya."

For some reason, she felt fearful as she moved closer to him. "Yeah?"

"Sit down."

She joined him on the couch.

"I just want ya to know somethin'. I wasn't the best brother to yer old man, but I don't turn my back on family. I swear to you – I'm not gonna let that son of a bitch get you."

Gina nodded, staring at him wide-eyed.

"Yer blood, and I'm gonna protect you. Got it?"

"Got it."

He relaxed. "All right." He took the T.V. off MUTE. "Get outta here. Get some sleep. Tomorrow's gonna be a long day."

Gina felt a little bit better as she headed up to bed.

The next morning, Caesar sat in his home office dialing his cell phone.

Miles away in Brooklyn, Mike Ortellani was stocking tomatoes in his family-owned grocery store when the phone clanged.

He grabbed it up and announced, "Gambino's Market."

"It's Caesar Camarari," said the voice.

"Caesar! How ya doin'?"

"Good, kid. Lemme talk to the old man. He around?"

"Yeh. Hold on a minute." Mike placed the call on hold and strutted into the back room.

At an old sturdy table sat an elderly man wearing a white shirt and suspenders.

"Grandpa?" Mike called. "You got a phone call. It's Uncle Caesar."

The old man barely seemed to have heard him as he regarded Mike, not comprehending.

"There's a phone call for *you*," Mike said, louder. "Here." He reached for the extension phone on the table, pressed the flashing light, and handed the receiver to the old man. "You can talk to him here, Grandpa."

The old man took the phone, and Mike left the room. "Yeah?"

"Peter! Hey!"

"Is that you, Caesar?"

"Naw, it's Al Pacino. How ya holdin' up, Pete?"

"Eh – any day my obituary ain't in the paper is a good day."

"Yeah, I hear ya. Listen, Pete, I need a favor. I got trouble. Santinello."

"Oh, boy..."

"He's after my niece – on account she's a witness for the prosecution. We didn't touch him before this. I want you to call him off."

"Caesar...ya know...we don't get involved with stuff like that."

"She's my family. And this ain't right."

Pete didn't want a confrontation. "All right. I guess... maybe just this one time..."

"I owe ya, Pete. He's been gettin' away with enough. I don't have to tell *you*."

"Yeah. I know. By the way, Caesar...my nephew's goin' to L.A. in a few weeks...he really wants to see the Dodgers..."

Caesar smiled broadly. "Tell 'im I'll get 'im box seats! Thanks, Pete."

When Caesar ambled into the kitchen, Carol was making scrambled eggs and toast. "The girls'll be down in a few minutes."

Caesar was pensive as he strutted over to the table. "Anything wrong?"

"That matter. It's been taken care of."

Carol brightened. "Well that's *good*."

"Yeah. For now."

The toast popped out of the toaster, and Carol placed it on a small plate. "What does that mean?"

Caesar's eye twitched as he stared solemnly into space. "It means if Santinello is ever a free man again, I can't do a damn thing..."

Debbie came into the guest bedroom Gina was using at Caesar's house.

Gina was texting on her phone.

"Are you sure it's safe to go back?"

Gina looked up. "Caesar's sure. He wouldn't send us back if it wasn't."

Debbie nodded uncertainly.

Gina finished her text and set the phone down on the bed. "Listen, Deb. This has gotten really out of hand, and I think it's better that you go back to Rhode Island."

"Gina, no! I don't want to go back. If you ever needed me, now's the time."

"I am not putting your life in danger over this. It's bad enough *mine* is!"

Debbie sat down next to Gina on the bed. "Gina. Please let me help. I'm not just your cousin, you know. I'm your friend."

"I know, Deb - "

"I can't let you go through this rough time alone. I plan on standing by you – no matter what. So like it or not, you're stuck with me."

Gina looked at Debbie for a long moment, a slow smile spreading across her face. "All right, Deb – you win. At least, with me. I doubt your *mom's* going to go for it."

Gina's cell chimed.

Debbie made a face. "I wish there was some way we could just *not* tell her."

Gina didn't recognize the number on the caller ID, but she pushed ACCEPT.

Scott was driving in his car. Hesitantly, he asked, "Are you still talking to me?"

"Barely," she joked, enjoying his discomfort.

"I just wanted to say I'm sorry about the other night."

"Ya gotta love technology," Gina said sarcastically. "It's okay. Really."

"I wanna make it up to you. The season wrap party for *Right On* is next Saturday. Would you be my date?"

Gina hesitated. "Next Saturday...? Okay."

Gina stood in front of the mirrored wall of her apartment's living room slipping on her earrings. "You sure you don't want to come with us, Deb? It's not too late to change your mind."

Debbie was sitting on the couch, admiring Gina's outfit. "And get in the way of your date? No way. Besides, I've gotta finish packing."

"Okay," Gina said, grabbing her purse. "I'll talk to you tomorrow."

★   ★   ★

Right On's season wrap party was held on Soundstage 21 at the studio. The entire interior was festooned with decorations, and elaborate buffet tables were set with every imaginable variety of food.

Scott couldn't have been more proud to have Gina by his side as the cast, crew and their families mingled. Heather was there with Robert and Tracy, and Joannie's parents arrived with Jason, who shot Scott and Gina venomous looks from across the room but did not venture near them.

Scott couldn't disguise his shock when Raquel Morollan entered with Wes Bingham, one of the show's other production assistants. Scott gave her a friendly hug and greeted them warmly, but Gina noticed the intimate way Raquel looked at Scott.

Debbie stepped into the building elevator and almost jumped when she saw Rick already inside carrying a bag of groceries.

He smiled. "Sorry. Didn't mean to scare you."

Debbie's face flushed.

Rick took in her workout clothes and towel. "What floor?"

"Eleven."

He good-naturedly pushed the button, and the doors closed.

Debbie drank in his exceptional good looks. "I like having a gym right in the building. I'm gonna miss this place."

"You're leaving?"

Debbie nodded. "My cousin and I are moving back east next week."

"That's too bad."

The elevator doors opened on the 11th Floor.

"Hey," Rick said, "How would you like to come to dinner? I can just as easily cook for the three of us. Are you busy tonight?"

"Gina's at a party. For work."

Rick pushed the elevator HOLD button. "You're on your own tonight?"

"Yeah," Debbie joked. "She abandoned me."

"Why don't you come over? Let me make you dinner?" His eyes pleaded. "To make up for the disastrous way we met?"

"Well..." She could hardly contain her excitement. "Okay."

"Come on up when you're ready. I'm in 1410."

"Will you stop pouting," Joannie admonished, smiling at the other party guests around them.

"You think it bothers me?" Jason retorted softly. "Seeing her and Scott together? Neither one of them are that important."

"Just go over there and talk to them. If you avoid them, they're gonna know they've beaten you."

"Nobody's beaten me. You have no idea what you're talking about."

"I know *exactly* what I'm talking about. That's why you're so upset."

"This is delicious!" Debbie raved, happily devouring her meal.

"There's more where that came from," Rick smiled, placing more tuna casserole on her plate, returning the pan to the stove, and joining her at his kitchen table.

Rick's apartment was distinctly a bachelor's pad. The furniture was dark, conservative, the décor sparse, and clothes and beer cans were littered about.

"If I eat any more, I'm not going to be able to breathe," Debbie complained.

"I don't think you have anything to worry about."

Debbie sampled another bite of her casserole, savoring it joyously. "When I get home, I'm going to ask our chef if he can make this."

He looked at her in surprise. "You have a chef?"

"Two of them. But Claudio only comes in on weekends."

"Oooh! Claudio! Pardon me!" he mocked.

She tried to sound angry. "You're really asking for it."

He grinned. "It beats begging."

"Don't I know you?" he asked politely.

Raquel smiled, immediately liking what she saw. "I don't think so."

"I'm Jason Kellner."

"Raquel Morollan."

His eyes twinkled. "You look very familiar to me. I know I've seen you somewhere."

"I was at Laurel Gillis' party last month."

"I knew it!"

She was still smiling.

"But I saw you at a network party a few years ago...You were there with Scott Griffith, weren't you?"

Her smile faded. "Yeah." She looked away, almost like a dark cloud had descended on her.

"Scott's a loser. You don't need him. But I can tell *you're* a winner."

Her smile returned. "Oh yeah?"

"I know about these things. I knew when I saw you tonight, I had to come over here and talk to you."

She subtlety looked him up and down. "Glad you did."

Jason scanned the room for Raquel's date, who was nowhere in sight. He lightly touched her shoulder. "I don't usually do this, but there's something about you I can't get out of my head. Would you like to go out with me sometime?"

Debbie and Rick sat across from each other in his living room, she on the couch and him in a chair.

"You've gotta tell me," Debbie said assertively. "Did you just forget your swimming trunks that day, or is there some other reason?"

Rick hesitated. "I didn't forget my trunks. I just don't typically wear them."

"Ever?"

"When it's necessary. I mean, if there were other people around, in the middle of the day, then, yeah, sure, but...I thought I'd have some privacy being there so early."

Debbie nodded in understanding. "Until I ruined it."

"You didn't ruin anything."

"Okay. But this is still kinda weird. Why do it at all?"

"It started with my parents."

"Your *parents* told you to do that?"

He laughed. "No. When I was a little kid, they used to take me to places on weekends where...people didn't wear any clothes..."

Debbie's eyes widened. "You mean a nudist camp?"

"They were called 'clothing optional facilities.' Actually, the clothing wasn't that optional. You had no choice."

"Oh my God!"

"Are you shocked?"

"Well...a little. Why did they do *that*?"

"It was just something they practiced. Still do. It teaches you not to be inhibited."

"Yeah, I would say *so*!"

He was enjoying her reaction.

"Couldn't they find *other* ways to teach you that?"

He shrugged. "I guess not."

"Looks like it worked, though."

"You get used to it," he explained earnestly. "Like you get used to anything. After a couple of days, it's weird when you have to put your clothes back *on*."

She was blushing. "I just can't imagine..."

"It's not a big deal, Debbie. That's why I'm very comfortable being naked around other people."

She raised an eyebrow. "You are?"

He nodded.

"So does that mean you're all dressed up just for me?"

He smirked. "Well, you're a guest. And I'm *dressed* because it makes *you* comfortable."

"So...if I told you that it *didn't* make me uncomfortable, you'd have no problem just hanging out in your birthday suit?"

"No. But it *would* make you uncomfortable."

She gazed at him levelly. "Maybe not."

"What are you saying? That's what you want me to do?"

Her eyes devoured him. "No, not right here. But what I would like...is for you to go into your room...take off all your clothes...and come back out here."

"Why?"

"Because..." She fumbled, quickly recovering. "Because I want to see just how comfortable you are."

"What about you?"

Debbie shrugged. "I'm fine with it," she lied.

There was a yearning in his voice. "*Then* what are we going to do?"

Her tone was equally promising. "Anything you want."

He pondered it. "I don't know..."

"Oh, now you're getting shy on me."

His eyes penetrated her. "Are you sure?"

"I wouldn't say it if I wasn't."

Now it was his turn to blush, but he rose from the chair and headed into his bedroom. "I'll be right back."

She watched him go into his bedroom and close the door.

She sat there for a moment, listening intently.

Nothing.

Then she heard the slight jingle of his belt, followed by his zipper being pulled down, and she began to visualize what was going on in that room.

She closed her eyes, almost praying, bringing her legs closer together.

She found it harder to breathe, and struggled to remain calm.

She stared intently at the bedroom door.

It was still closed.

Not a sound.

She began to wonder if he was coming out at all.

Debbie stared out the plate-glass door that led to his balcony, admiring the panoramic view of Westwood's high rises. The sun was going down, giving the sky a soft orange glow.

Fleetingly Debbie thought of Gina and what she would be doing right now. It was obvious Scott had feelings for her. Was Gina really planning on moving back to New York permanently?

Debbie heard the bedroom door softly open, and turned just in time to see Rick step out totally nude. He smiled self-consciously, but moved slowly toward her.

The daylight was nearly gone and there were no electric lights on in the living room, so he was gently silhouetted in the shadows of dusk.

Her excitement grew as he came closer, his bare feet nimbly treading the plush carpet.

When he was standing directly in front of her, he extended his hand to her, and she took it.

He pulled her to her feet, held her, and looked deep into her eyes. "I thought of something we could do..."

Scott felt like he'd been kicked in the stomach. "What about *us*? You just wanna throw that away?"

Gina struggled to stay composed. "We had fun, and it's been great, but it's over. What did you think was gonna happen?"

Scott shook his head, glad they were alone in his dressing room with the door closed. "I thought you were going to stick around, and we would get to know each other better."

"We have. And I'll never forget you and how great you are - "

"What is it you're not telling me? Why can't you come back to L.A. when your family emergency is over?"

"Because it was a mistake. I never should've come out here. I was running away from home, and from my problems. This isn't where I belong."

"Are you saying that you and me was a mistake, too?"

Gina looked at him. Her voice was soft. "It was about the only thing that *wasn't*. But it just isn't meant to be."

"You're wrong. It could've been good." He turned away from her.

"Yeah. For a while. These things don't last forever, Scott." Much as he tried to hide it, she could tell he was hurting. "Hey – it's not like we can't keep in touch. You're acting like we're never going to see each other again."

He turned back to her. "Oh, we will. Because I'm not letting you go."

She moved closer to him and kissed him. He responded, and the kiss grew hungrier. Scott broke it off first and held Gina tightly. "I love you..."

Gina stared at him in shock, shaking her head. "Don't say things you don't mean."

"I'm not."

She backed away from him, her expression pained. "I can't...I'm sorry..."

Gina opened the door and hurried out.

Luca Santinello sat facing Bobby Luchesi, a good-looking dark-haired man in his early forties. Bobby was attired in a well-fitting three-piece suit. Luca wore an orange jumpsuit and a livid expression.

The tiny prison room they were in had only one door and no windows. They sat at a long wooden table and spoke in hushed tones.

"What the hell is goin' on?" Luca demanded. "Why the hell am I still in here, Bobby?"

"Take it easy, Mr. Santinello. I'm doin' everything I can. It's the D.A. He's bein' an A-hole. Got the judge to deny bail."

"What!" Luca thundered, bringing his fist down so hard on the table Bobby thought he would split it in two. "No bail? They expect me to just sit in here?"

"The trial is two weeks away - "

"Two weeks!!"

"We're pretty sure we can get you a suspended sentence, and then you're outta here."

"What the hell am I supposed to do in here for two weeks?? I want outta here *tonight*, Bobby. Ya hear me?"

Bobby's voice quavered. "Can't do it, Mr. Santinello."

"Then get me a judge that's on the payroll. I don't care what you gotta do, just get it done!"

"I tried that. They wouldn't go for it. Even if I filed a continuance, it would raise a red flag, and they'd make you stay in here longer."

"Damn it!"

Bobby took a deep breath, unsure if he should go on. "I didn't want to tell you this, but we got a call from 'The Boy.'"

"Yeah?" Luca asked mildly, his mouth almost forming the beginning of a smile. "What did Gulietti want? To send me his regards?"

Bobby shook his head miserably. "Instructions. The Moore girl. She gotta be left alone."

Luca's face clouded over. "You gotta be kiddin' me..." he growled slowly.

There was real fear in Bobby's eyes now. "It came from the top. None of our boys had anything to do with it."

"I know who did it! Camarari!" Luca glared at Bobby. "Why are they letting him do this to me?"

Bobby was perspiring, but he kept his voice level. "He said there was an attempt on her life. They think you paid Frank Dinato to 'off' her."

Luca was a brilliant actor. "That's b.s.! I couldn't do nothin' from in here!"

Bobby projected agreement with Luca while still standing his ground. "I'm not tellin' ya what *I* think. That's what *they* think!"

"That bastard is screwin' with me 'cuz he thinks he's got the upper hand! Let me tell ya somethin'." Luca motioned for Bobby to lean in closer. "Nobody makes a dummy outta *me!*"

Luca smashed Bobby in the face with the full force of his strength, sending the smaller man to the floor, along with a sheaf of documents after him.

CHAPTER 12

"It's nice to see you." Rose Leoni smiled prettily.

Scott, sitting next to her on her living room couch, smiled back, even though he didn't really feel it. He rested his hand on her knee. "It's good to see *you*, too."

"It's been so long. I almost forgot what you look like!"

He threw her a look.

She burst out laughing.

"Thanks," he grinned. "You really know how to make a guy feel wanted!"

"I'm just kidding, Scott." She looked at him as if he were about to tell her something terrible. "I didn't think I'd see you again."

"Why?"

"I don't know. After that party...and then I didn't hear from you."

"I've just had my hands full with the show. Next month, I'm on hiatus, but then I start a new movie. Ellen Stellar's directing! If you can believe *that*."

Rose had no idea who he was talking about. "That's nice." She took his hand. "My mom and dad are out of the house – thank God! They won't be back until later. Much later." She giggled.

"Great!" Scott joked. "That'll give us a chance to do homework."

Rose looked at him condescendingly, then smiled appealingly. She pulled him up off the couch. "Let's go in *my* room."

"Yeah," Scott murmured. "I knew that's where we were heading..."

They had just reached Rose's bedroom when her cell phone went off.

She groaned impatiently.

"*Don't* answer it," Scott ordered.

She pulled away from him. "I have to. It might be somebody important."

"Like who?"

"*I* don't know!" Rose took the call. "Hi, Christine...! No, I'm not doing anything important." Off Scott's reaction, she motioned for him to be quiet. "Scott...? Why would I talk to *him*?" She giggled.

Scott shook his head and sat down on the bed impatiently.

Rose motioned that she would be right back, then disappeared into the hallway with the phone.

Scott sighed in disgust, debating what to do.

He checked to see if Rose could see him.

She was gone.

A mischievous smile lit his handsome face, and he once again checked the doorway before slipping off his sneakers, pulling off his shirt, and stepping out of his jeans. His underwear joined his socks on the floor, and he pulled down the covers on the bed and slid between the sheets.

Clasping his hands behind his head, Scott wondered how long Rose would take to remember he was there. He stared unseeingly out the beautiful bow window with its fine lace curtains and view of the garage. Two birds on a tree branch outside chirped happily as they kept watch over their home.

Rose returned a few moments later, the phone in her hand. "Sorry about that - " she started to say. Then she looked up and realized what he'd done. Her mouth opened wide when she noticed his discarded clothes on the floor.

"Scott!" she admonished, retrieving his jeans and draping them on the back of her desk chair. "Look what you've done! Why do you always have to make such a mess?"

"I'm a dog," he drawled sexily, fixing her with a smoldering stare. "Aren't you a dog lover?"

"You're so disgusting!" she said, joining him on the bed.

"C'mon," he said, lifting up the blanket and pulling the covers up around her. "I've missed you, Rose."

"I missed you, too..."

He kissed her softly on the mouth. His hand cupped her face, then moved down to her blouse and slowly unbuttoned it.

Rose was brushing her hair in her bedroom mirror by the time Scott finished getting dressed.

He leaned over and kissed her on the cheek. "Why did you wait so long to call me back?"

She shrugged and finished her hair. "Well, ya know...I've been busy..." Rose looked up at him in the mirror and grinned. She turned, stood up, and hugged him tightly. "I'm so glad you're here..."

"Thanks." Scott smiled warmly, holding her. He sighed happily and pulled away. "Well, I guess I better get going now - "

"No!" She gripped him in another vise-like embrace. "Don't leave me."

He laughed. "I'm not *leaving* you, Rose, I just have to go now." He looked her in the face. "In case you forgot, I have to get up for work in the morning."

"Don't go."

"And get fired?" he asked lightly. "I don't think so." He pulled away from her again and checked his pockets to make sure he had his wallet and car keys.

"I just don't want you to go," she said timidly.

He looked at her awkwardly, unsure of how to respond. "I'll be *back*. Right? Besides, it might be better if I'm not here when your mom and dad get home." He started out the bedroom door. "Especially your dad."

She followed him down the hallway. "I guess so. How about tomorrow? Can you come over when you get out of work?"

His pace quickened as he headed down the stairs. "I'll be tired. The weekend would probably be better for me."

They were in the living room now.

Scott turned to her. "I'll give you a call on Thursday."

He leaned over and kissed her.

She pulled away. "I can't believe you're leaving me."

He exploded, "Will you knock it off! I'm just leaving for the night. You make it sound like I'm running off to war!"

"You're *always* leaving."

"What's that supposed to mean?"

"You're not being very nice!"

"*I have to go*. What do you want me to do? Spend the night? With your parents in the house?"

"Don't be stupid," she said petulantly, turning and pacing toward the fireplace. "I just can't believe you're doing this to me. Especially after I told all my friends about us."

He moved up behind her. "That could be two people. What did you say?"

She faced him, her eyes wide with panic. "Nothing. I just told them about *us*. That's all."

"What 'us'? That we're dating?"

"Yeah...and more..." She scurried away from him.

"Spill it."

Annoyed. "What? I just told them that we're getting close, and that...we might get married..."

"What!"

She attempted a smile. "Was that the wrong thing to do?"

"You are unbelievable!" He fought to control his temper. "Do you know what the tabloids could do if they got a hold of a story like that? It could affect my job on *Right On*."

"I didn't know *that*."

"How could you not know that? I can't believe you would even say something like that – to anybody!"

"I thought it was what you wanted."

"What I wanted! Oh my God! Where did you even *get* a crazy idea like that??"

"Scott, it's true!" She threw her arms around his neck. "I know you love me. And I know it would make my parents happy."

He disengaged himself from her embrace. "I've got to get out of here."

She held onto him. "No. Don't leave me."

"Will you let go of me!" he yelled.

She backed off, staring at him in horror.

"I don't know what your problem is, but it's not going to be *my* problem anymore!" His hand was on the front doorknob. "Just...don't call me anymore. Okay?"

She ran to him. "You can't leave me! I love you!"

"Maybe. But *I* don't love *you*."

"Get out!" she raged, opening the front door and trying to push him out.

"Glad to!"

"Get out!" She pushed him as he stepped out. Slamming the front door, Rose burst into tears. "You son of a bitch!" she screamed at the closed door, her sobs uncontrollable.

Rose ran up the stairs and into her room, where she lay on the bed, crying.

A few minutes later, she got up, wiped her face, and stumbled into her bathroom.

She opened the mirrored cabinet above the sink and quickly scanned the contents.

Rose only thought about it for a few seconds before she reached for a full bottle of prescription sleeping pills and slammed the cabinet shut.

Scott was shaking as he climbed into his Porsche, drove out of Rose's driveway, and rolled down Delfern Drive toward Sunset Boulevard.

He took a deep breath, trying to calm himself, his eyes straight ahead.

Scott was feeling a little better by the time he reached Beverly Glen. Then an idea came to him. He reached for his phone, found a number, and hit CALL. It was picked up after three rings. "Hi, Christine. It's Scott."

"Hi!" She sounded thrilled to hear his voice. "What are you doing?"

"I just got done helping my dad with something," he said smoothly. "Anyway, I have a couple of hours, and I wondered if you might like to get together."

"Sure! You wanna come over?"

He smiled. "Yeah."

She lowered her voice. "We'll have to go out for a while, but as soon as my dad goes to sleep, you can come up to my room."

"Half an hour?"

"Sounds good, babe."

All the lights were out in Christine's bedroom, and Scott stood before her naked.

As she sank to her knees, he closed his eyes and leaned his head back, enjoying all the warm sensations he'd yearned for all night.

*   *   *

It was just after 11:30 P.M. when Scott pulled into his driveway. He was ready for bed now – to sleep – and was surprised to find his parents and Heather still up and waiting for him in the kitchen.

"What's wrong?" he asked, sensing something immediately.

Robert was sitting at the table. "Sit down," he said quietly. "We want to talk to you."

Scott groaned. "What did I do now?" He reluctantly took a seat across from his father.

"We got a call from Rose Leoni's parents," Robert said, his voice still ominously low. "Today...she took an overdose of sleeping pills..."

"What!"

Robert nodded. "She's at Cedars right now. In ICU." His voice cracked. "And they don't think she's gonna make it..."

Scott's Porsche ran almost every red light between Bel Air and Cedars Sinai Medical Center.

Heather, sitting next to him in the passenger seat, feared for her safety, but she didn't dare say anything.

"My name is Scott Griffith," Scott told the head nurse on duty. "I'm supposed to have permission to see her."

The woman, black, overweight, and delighted to meet someone as good-looking as Scott, quickly consulted a list, checked for his name, and nodded. "That's right." She handed him a visitor's badge. "You can go right on in. Five minutes, no more." She pointed at Heather. "You have to wait out here."

Scott turned to Heather.

"I'll be okay," she promised.

Scott slowly made his way into ICU.

Rose looked frightening.

She lay in the bed, her face completely white, several IV tubes jutting out of her arms, and a breathing tube in her mouth.

Four different machines next to her bed monitored her condition, and there wasn't the slightest movement from her body.

His legs went weak, but there was no chair.

He cautiously approached her and reached over the bar. His hand touched hers. It was warm, but he was afraid of making contact with one of the IVs.

"Oh, Rose," he said softly, a lump in his throat. "Rose, I'm sorry...I'm so sorry..."

Tears threatened, but he held them back. Just barely.

His fingers lightly rubbed the top of her hand. "I do love you...I do love you, Rose...please get better..."

He gave two of her fingers just the lightest squeeze, and removed his hand.

"I have to go now...just...don't die...okay...?"

He left the room looking about twenty years older.

Scott and Heather were sitting in a nearby waiting room.

"It's my fault," Scott muttered. "It's because of me she's lying there..."

Heather put her arm around him and held him. "No it isn't," she said gently. "She took an overdose of pills."

Scott shook his head, his hands fidgeting. "I was at her house today. You didn't hear what I said to her. Oh, God, how could I be so stupid?"

"You didn't!" Heather insisted, trying to keep her voice down. "Scott, she's got a lot of problems. That didn't start with you."

"But I didn't help any."

"What else could you have done?"

Scott looked at the ground morosely, then at Heather. "What if she dies? It'll be my fault - "

"She's not going to die," Heather hissed. "Will you get a hold of yourself? She's young, and she's strong. That's on her side." Heather looked up at a large clock on the wall. "It's almost four o'clock in the morning. What time do you have to be on the set?"

"I can't," he gasped. "I can't go anywhere, I can't leave her..."

She affectionately patted his shoulder. "Do you want me to call the assistant director?"

"Would you?" he croaked, handing her his phone. "It's Steve Winward, his number's in there."

She nodded and stood up.

"Thanks."

Ed and Judy Leoni entered. Both looked like they'd aged twenty years since the last time Scott and Heather had seen them.

Scott rose, his legs nearly giving way.

"Scott," Ed said gravely, moving purposefully towards him. "They told us you were in here."

"Mr. and Mrs. Leoni," he greeted them nervously. "How are you?"

Ed's voice was monotone. "Holding up. We wanted to thank you for coming down here. It means so much to our family. And to Rose."

Scott nodded in response.

Judy Leoni was silent.

"We wanted to ask you," Ed went on, "Did Rosie talk to you about anything that might've been bothering her lately?"

Scott shook his head, shaking. "We've only talked on the phone a few times since that party. I've been working on my show a lot."

It was evident from the look on Ed's face that he hadn't found the answer he'd been looking for, but he only stared at the floor blankly and cleared his throat. "This...this came as quite a shock to me and her mother...We just...don't understand how something like this could happen..."

"If there's anything I can do..."

Ed looked as if he were about to cry. "Just you being here is enough." His voice cracked. "Thank you."

Scott watched them leave.

He felt as if a heavy weight were crushing his heart.

10:00 A.M.

Scott and Robert were sitting at the kitchen table in the Griffith house.

Tracy and Heather were hovering nearby, until Tracy broke the silence. "If you're not going to work today, why don't you try and get some sleep?"

"I can't," Scott managed.

"Your mother's right," Robert said. "You're not doing Rose any good by wearing yourself down."

Scott only stared forlornly at the table.

"There's something else we wanted to talk to you about," Robert continued. "I've been watching the trials on that guy they're prosecuting in New York for drug trafficking. They named that girl you had over here as one of the witnesses testifying against him!"

"Yeah, Dad. I know. Gina told me about it."

"Who is this girl that she's mixed up with drug dealers?" Tracy demanded.

"She's not mixed up with them, Mom. She just knew someone who used to work for this guy."

"It sounds like she's got some bad people upset with her," Robert said. "I don't even want her in this house."

"You don't have to worry. She went back to New York, and she says she's not coming back out here."

"I know you like her, but we've got enough to worry about."

The house phone rang.

"Never fails," Tracy said irritably, reluctantly picking it up. Tracy listened. "Oh, hi, Diane..." She forced a note of politeness into her voice. "...She's right here, I'll ask her." Tracy covered the mouthpiece and looked, concerned, at Heather. "It's Lynda's aunt. Lynda didn't come home two nights ago, and she hasn't seen her since. Do you know where she is?"

Heather shrugged imperiously. "I have no idea."

Tracy slipped into the other room with the phone. "I'm sorry, Diane. Heather hasn't seen her, either..."

Scott lay on the bed in his room leafing through a copy of *Teen Celeb* magazine, laughing at an article about himself. Inside the pages, a photo of Scott swimming in his pool accompanied still shots from *Wacky Wednesday*. The lead caption read *Dream Guy – Scott Griffith: Every Day of the Week!*

Laying the magazine aside, he leapt off his bed and paraded around his room in only a pair of tight white underwear. He checked out his appearance in a full-length mirror, pleased at what he saw for once.

Ambling over to his dresser, he moved his Emmy award aside and picked up a framed photograph of him and Raquel taken a few years earlier at a formal dance at Raquel's school.

He stared at the photo a moment. She was wearing a slinky purple dress, him a tuxedo. He had been sixteen at the time.

Scott shook his head and smiled at the memory.

As he held the photo frame, he thought back to the first night they met.

Then he placed the photo back on the dresser and reached for his phone.

Scott pulled up to the familiar house in Santa Monica and parked his Porsche in the already tightly occupied driveway. He was just getting out of the car when Raquel stepped out the side door. She was wearing a short white cocktail dress and beaming. He smiled back – completely enamored by her beauty.

"Hi!" She quite naturally melted into his arms and kissed him full on the mouth. Pulling back, she murmured, "Can you do me a favor and park on the street? My dad doesn't like anybody blocking him."

He rolled his eyes. "Oh, for God's sake! We're taking right off, aren't we?"

"My mom and dad want to say hello." She kissed him again, smiling coyly. "It'll be painless. I promise."

Scott drove the Porsche at a moderate pace down Santa Monica Boulevard.

Raquel, sitting next to him, wrinkled her nose. "Can't you go any faster?"

He reluctantly increased his speed. "We have enough time until the movie starts, right?"

"I know," she husked, "But this is a *Porsche*...it was meant to be *ridden*."

Scott smirked. "So was I."

Scott and Raquel hurried from the automated ticket stations, across the nearly deserted cinema lobby, toward one of the theatres.

"I knew we'd be late!" Raquel muttered in disgust.

"It's just as well," Scott shot back. "At least this way, I don't get hassled for autographs."

"Oh, you!" Raquel laughed good-naturedly. "You so need to get over yourself!"

Nearly every seat in the movie theatre was taken.

Scott and Raquel slipped in the back.

The previews had started, so only the light from the screen allowed them to see the few remaining seats all the way up front.

A walled partition separated the back row from the rear portion of the theatre. In the darkness, nobody took any notice of Scott and Raquel.

"You wanna just stay up here?" Scott whispered.

Raquel nodded, smiling mischievously.

Scott leaned against the partition, and he and Raquel happily watched the movie standing up.

A short while later, Raquel moved behind him, placed her arms around him, and slowly snaked her hands up under his shirt. He flinched, trying not to squirm as she massaged his well-toned stomach, sneakily moving up to his chest and fingering his sensitive nipples.

He turned to face her, his back to the screen, and kissed her so long and sensuously on the mouth, she held tightly onto him just to keep from stumbling.

They snuck out of the theatre a few minutes before the end credits rolled.

"Are your mom and dad still up?" Scott asked, staring intently at Raquel's house.

"Probably," Raquel spat, following his eyes. "The kitchen light is still on." She turned to him, anticipation in her voice. "Can we go to *your* house?"

"Are you kidding? My father falls asleep on the couch. And he hears *everything!*"

The two sat in Scott's parked car. Scott was finishing off a soda from the theatre, and Raquel a half-empty bucket of popcorn. "This sucks," she commented in between bites.

Scott sighed. "You wanna just sit here for a while?"

She smiled sexily. "Sure."

He looked down Raquel's street. It was quiet and deserted, and most of the large, manicured homes were dark.

"I'm glad you called," she said softly. "I never thought you would."

He looked at her earnestly. "I would have. I didn't think you'd see me. And I wasn't ready."

"Remember the night we met? At that party?"

"As if I could forget."

She struggled to stop smiling. "I never told you why I took you up to that bedroom..."

His eyes searched her face, and it was as if he were stepping back in time. "I always wondered...why me...?"

"Because you weren't like the other boys. I knew what they were all after. You had something that *I* wanted...I always felt safe with you..."

He shifted awkwardly. "I don't know how to take that..."

"It always meant so much to me that you chose me to take your innocence...there was nobody else I admired *more* than you..."

"Why?" he couldn't help asking.

"Because of what you became..." Her hands ran down his chest. "The way you transformed yourself..."

"You make it sound like I was an aardvark..."

She giggled. "And you can always make me laugh!"

Scott beamed. "You know, it's funny you mentioned the first time we met. I remember the first time you called me up and asked me to come over your house..."

Raquel smiled at the memory.

"...and you said - " He affected her voice as best he could – "'Why don't you come over tonight? When the door to my room is closed, I can do anything I want. We can even M.L.'"

She started laughing.

"And I remember – I started freaking out! I kept thinking, 'What the hell is M.L.?' I thought it was some kind of sex game you were talking about – like S & M! And then when I got here that night, you told me what it meant: Make Love!"

Raquel was laughing harder now.

"You don't know what kind of a sweat I was in that week! I didn't know *what* was gonna happen!" Scott was almost blushing now. "So that was me. The priest right out of the seminary. You were full of surprises."

"I still am," she said seriously, moving in closer. "Especially when I'm in my A.M."

He was starting to feel short of breath. "Your A.M.? What's that?"

"Attack Mode." And she was on him. Kissing him passionately and hungrily. He responded with the fire he'd felt for her four years ago. She was starting to pull off his shirt when he stopped her.

"Wait a minute. Not here. If your mom and dad see us, we're done. Aren't they going to bed soon?"

"God, I hope so!" Raquel groaned, glancing at the house, reluctantly ceasing her attack. She grabbed at some popcorn and waved a kernel in front of his face. "Want some?"

"Okay."

She coyly fed him some of the popcorn, one bite after another – until it became too rapid.

"Easy!" he laughed, reaching down his shirt. "You're getting them all over me!"

Raquel giggled, flicking the kernels down his shirt and then in his face.

"Oh?" Scott grabbed one of her wrists. "You think that's funny? Huh?"

He reached for a fistful of the popcorn himself and started throwing it at her. She shrieked wildly, unable to contain her giddiness. The popcorn fight escalated and raged until the inside of Scott's Porsche was covered with shells and kernels.

Scott regarded the seats and floor with dismay. "Wasn't *that* fun?"

Raquel stopped laughing long enough to gasp, "Don't worry about it. I'll take care of this for you."

He stared at her quizzically. "What exactly did you have in mind? You're gonna eat all this up?"

Her voice was husky. "You'd like that, wouldn't you?" She giggled. "No. I'll be right back."

Raquel used a mini-vac to vacuum up all of the popcorn in the Porsche.

"We could've eaten all that," Scott remarked.

"Yes," Raquel agreed, "But this was much more fun!"

"If you say so," he said dryly.

She put her face in his and murmured, "I say so." She pulled away and opened the passenger door. "Besides, I think my mom and dad are asleep now, so we can go inside."

He shrugged, smiling broadly. "You talked me into it."

Raquel led Scott into a large den, flipped on the lights, and quietly closed and locked the door.

"What's wrong with *your* room?" Scott asked.

"It's too close to my parents' room. Besides, they're on the other side of the house, so if we're quiet, they won't hear us."

He indicated the lights. "Isn't it a little bright?"

"Don't worry." She switched on the large flat screen in the corner, which displayed CNN, but she muted the sound and turned on the surround-sound CD player. Raquel turned off the other lights so only the T.V. bathed the room in a soft glow.

She kissed him again, then led him over to a space directly in front of the T.V. She pulled a blanket and comforter out of a nearby closet and spread them out over the floor, then grabbed two pillows off of the couch.

"C'mon," she said, guiding him down onto the comforter.

He pulled off his shirt and kissed her. She ran her hands down his smooth, well-defined chest and reached for the zipper on his jeans. Soon they were naked and in each other's arms. He lay on top of her, his eyes probing deeply into hers, and she looked at him as if they were fifteen-years-old again.

"You're pretty sure of yourself now, aren't you?" she asked quietly.

"Yeah," he admitted, his look growing more intense. "Just relax. Let *me* be the teacher now." He trailed his tongue down her neck and toward her breasts, caressing her body as he moved further down.

They writhed on the comforter, their bodies fusing together. Then Raquel moved on top of *him*, kissing his neck, licking his earlobes, and torturing him as only she knew how.

He closed his eyes, enjoying the feel of her expert attention. His hands lightly brushed down her back, until he opened his eyes and caught sight of a news segment on T.V.

Gina was sitting in a courtroom, testifying on a witness stand.

The caption read:
GINA MOORE
WITNESS FOR THE PROSECUTION
STATE OF NEW YORK VS. LUCA SANTINELLO.

Scott sat up, nearly knocking Raquel off of him. He strained to make out what was being said, but only the music filled his ears.

"What's wrong?" Raquel demanded, glaring at him strangely.

"I've gotta go," Scott said hoarsely. "I'm sorry."

CHAPTER 13

The phone on Officer Schroeder's desk buzzed, and she picked it up absently. "Schroeder."

The N.Y.P.D. cop at the airport barked into his cell phone, "This is Alvarez. I'm at JFK now. We just searched the plane. Your witness, Ms. Gina Moore, never got on."

Schroeder gripped the phone tighter.

Cynthia Moore spoke calmly into her own cell phone. "There's nothing to worry about, Officer Schroeder. Gina is here with me now, and she'll be at the courthouse tomorrow afternoon for her briefing...No, we're declining police protection...I think we can handle it, thank you..." She disconnected the call and regarded Gina, relief flooding her.

Gina and Debbie stood in the center of the room next to Caesar.

It was a beautifully furnished apartment completely unfamiliar to the three women. A large man with black hair and a stony expression stood by the door.

Caesar turned to him. "Rocco, go stand outside the door. Shoot anybody that tries to come near it."

The man obeyed silently.

Cynthia slipped her cell phone into her purse. "That cop didn't sound too happy."

Caesar laughed. "I don't care if she's happy or not. It ain't her life on the line."

Cynthia hugged Gina tightly. "I missed you."

"I missed you, too, Mom."

Cynthia regarded Caesar as if he were a man who had returned from the grave. "Caesar...how are you?"

His mysterious dark eyes twinkled. "Still breathin'. Can't complain."

"Where are we?" Debbie asked.

"This is a safe house," Caesar explained, glancing around. "Never thought I'd be 'safin'' my own family in it."

"We had a nice flight, Aunt Cynthia," Debbie said brightly. "It's been a while since I was on a private plane."

Gina and Debbie each found their suitcases and disappeared down the hallway.

"Why didn't you let her accept that police protection?" Cynthia asked Caesar.

He stared at her in disbelief. "Did you forget what Santinello is like? It only takes one slip-up and we lose her. I wouldn't even put it past him to get to the cops."

Cynthia seemed to have difficulty breathing. "It's times like this, I *really* wish Steven were here."

Caesar grunted. "'Steven.' What a load of horse crap. Was he too proud for 'Salvatore'?"

"You know why he changed his name. To keep us safe. Not that it did any good, they got to him anyway. It isn't even keeping Gina safe." She shivered, glaring at him accusingly. "It's starting again, isn't it? The same old trouble."

His gaze sent another chill through her. "It never really stopped."

"Is it ever going to end? Or is this war between you and him going to continue until we're all dead?"

"Don't get emotional on me now, okay, Cynthia? I'm here for Gina. Until Santinello's put away, I ain't gonna focus on nothin' else except keepin' her alive."

A hush fell over the musty courtroom in lower Manhattan.

Gina sat in the witness box dressed in a conservative white blouse and black skirt.

With the judge, jury, and a few dozen spectators watching, a sharp-featured man in a three-piece suit approached the box with an inviting yet assertive expression. "State your full name."

"Gina Daniella Moore."

"County of residence?"

"New York."

"What was your relationship to Frank Dinato?"

"I was his girlfriend."

"For how long?"

"About a year."

"So you knew what he did for a living?"

"No. Not until the very end."

"Objection!" came Bobby Luchesi's voice. "Relevance."

"I'll allow it," the judge decided mildly.

"How did you find out?" the prosecutor asked Gina.

Her gaze was far away. "By accident."

While she was being cross-examined, Gina tried to face Luca Santinello down, but the hooded menace in his eyes, disguised as intent interest, forced her to focus on the proceedings.

Bobby Luchesi's voice rang with disbelief. "So you never actually saw this Frank Dinato and Mr. Santinello together?"

"Not personally, no."

"So as far as you know, Mr. Santinello and Frank Dinato have never met?"

"Objection! Calls for a conclusion."

"The witness will answer."

Gina swallowed hard before responding. "I don't know."

"Isn't it possible Frank Dinato could've known you were listening? Just playing a joke on you?"

"No."

"You testified that you were listening through the door of that hotel room. Can you be absolutely sure that you heard him say 'Luca Santinello'?"

"I'm positive."

"Couldn't you have misheard him?"

"No."

"Couldn't he have said something else? A name that sounded similar?"

"No. The door was part way open. I heard him very clearly. He said into the phone, 'They won't find me. Tell Luca Santinello he'll get his money.'"

Bobby Luchesi paced a few steps, his impassive face betraying nothing. "You were a student at Kenter High School, weren't you?"

Gina tensed. "Yes."

"But the truth is, you barely graduated, because you were out for most of your junior year, weren't you?"

"I took a few months off."

"Rehab?"

"Objection!"

"Sustained. You know better, Mr. Luchesi."

Luca's lawyer remained inscrutable. "Did you sell narcotics for Frank Dinato?"

Gina was indignant. "No!"

"Then you would've had to been one of his customers."

She locked eyes with Luchesi. "I've never taken drugs in my life."

"So why the absence? You were out of school for five months. Why did that happen if it wasn't alcohol- or drug-related?"

"Objection! Relevance."

The judge grunted. "I'd like an answer."

Gina took an uneasy breath. "After what happened in Miami...I just had some personal issues...family stuff...It was upsetting to my mother..."

Luchesi feigned concern. "Oh. So you stayed out of school to help your mother?"

"It was more like *she* helped *me*."

"With what?"

"It was just...a very emotional time for me."

"Breakdown?"

"No!"

"Ms. Moore, I can subpoena your medical records, so if you were in drug rehabilitation, we will find out about it."

Gina was fighting to breathe. "It wasn't rehab...but it was a condition...you could say..."

"What condition?"

Her voice was choked. "I was pregnant."

The entire courtroom froze.

Luca's face registered disbelief.

Luchesi recovered quickly. "You got pregnant. Did you know who the father was?"

"Of course I knew who the father was. It was Frank."

The jury was looking at her with mixed expressions.

"It happened in Orlando...that was the first time..."

Luchesi spoke with deliberate compassion. "Where is the child now?"

Gina lowered her head, tears stinging her eyes. "It was a little girl...she was stillborn...my baby died..."

Gina dissolved into quiet sobs.

Luchesi's strategy crumbled right along with her. "I have no more questions."

Despite the court officers' best efforts to escort Gina, Cynthia, and Debbie out the rear entrance unobserved, a group of photographers and reporters greeted the three women as they emerged from the courthouse. Flashes popped in their faces, nearly blinding them as they descended the cement steps.

"Ms. Moore! A comment about the trial?"

"Do you think Santinello will be convicted?"

"Are you carrying Luca Santinello's baby?"

Two of the photographers and one of the male reporters were grabbed from behind by two large men and thrown to the sidewalk.

Gina looked up and saw Caesar standing at the curb next to a waiting limo. "Come on!" he waved. "Get in!"

The way was temporarily cleared, so the three of them scurried into the back of the car, Caesar and the two men piled into the seat in front of them, and the limo sped off.

Debbie rested her hand on her cousin's as Gina closed her eyes, trying to shut out the chaos around her.

"Your timing is perfect, Caesar," Cynthia smiled.

He grunted. "Narrow escapes. Story of my life."

Debbie smiled comfortingly at Gina.

"You realize," Caesar said sharply to Gina, "This here is far from over."

Gina stared at him defiantly. "I know you don't agree, but it had to be done..."

The cell phone on top of the dresser chimed, splitting the silence in the darkened bedroom. Gina was already awake, her eyes wide open, and as soon as she heard the phone, she reached for it and quietly answered it.

"Gina??" Scott's voice was frantic. "Are you okay?? I saw the trial on T.V."

"Scott??" She struggled to sit up, feeling her way in the dark. "Hold on a second."

Debbie was asleep in the twin bed next to her, so Gina silently crept into the adjacent bathroom, closed the door, and flipped on the light.

Gina, Cynthia, and Debbie were still staying in the safe apartment Caesar had provided for them, so she prudently kept her voice low. "Scott?"

"Yes, it's me. What's wrong?"

"What's wrong is it's six o'clock in the morning here, and I don't want to wake anybody up."

He relaxed. "I just didn't know when a good time to catch you would be, and I didn't want to get your voice mail."

"It's okay," she said softly, glad to hear his voice. "I was up anyway. I just can't talk too loud."

"Oh," he said, equally soft. "Don't worry about it. I understand."

"Scott," she said tersely. "*You* don't have to keep *your* voice down."

He laughed. "Oh! You're right. Sorry."

She found herself laughing with him, beaming happily. "How are you?"

"Never mind *me*. How are *you*? I saw you on the news."

"Yes. That was a few days ago. Well..." She took a deep breath. "The trial just ended, but it looks like Santinello is going to be convicted."

"All right!"

"He should be transferred to the state penitentiary next week, so it'll be safe for us to go back to our apartment."

"Where are you now?"

"In a safe apartment. Security thought it was a good idea under the circumstances."

"I'm glad. I was really worried about you."

"There's nothing to worry about - really. It's all over. And I'm perfectly fine."

"Lady – you got guts."

"That's what I've been told."

"I also...didn't like the way we left things...you weren't just another girl with me, Gina...You were special...You still are - "

"Scott, we've been through this before. I feel the same way, but we both know why it wouldn't work out. Your life is out there, and my life is definitely back here. You need somebody who's available – whose life isn't a mess right now."

"The only person I need is you – and my agent."

She didn't crack a smile. "The other thing is, I may not be totally in the clear from Santinello."

"You told me it was over."

Gina spoke with difficulty. "I don't really know what'll happen from this point on. I'd feel better knowing you were safe."

"Wait a minute. If you're still in any kind of trouble - "

"If you love me, the best thing you can do is stay away from me."

"I can't do that - "

CALL END.

Gina and Debbie embraced tightly.

"I don't wanna go!" Debbie lamented.

"I know," said Gina. "But you can't baby sit me forever."

"Why not?"

The two looked at each other and smiled.

Cynthia stood behind them amid the chaos at La Guardia Airport. Travelers with suitcases scurried back and forth, and outside the window, another plane was taking off.

"C'mon," Gina said, leading Debbie toward the security checkpoint. "Your mom's got a great Fourth of July party planned for this weekend. It's gonna be a blast!"

"Yeah," Debbie agreed dismally.

"And wait till school starts."

"Don't remind me!"

Debbie placed her purse and carry-on bag on the x-ray conveyer belt and removed her shoes.

"It'll be awesome!" Gina assured her. "You'll have all those clothes to buy!"

Debbie looked at her hopefully. "Can you come to the gate with me?"

"Honey, you know I can't do that. See that sign? *Ticketed Passengers Only*? They mean that. Now, c'mon. We'll see you at Christmas."

Cynthia hugged Debbie emotionally. "Goodbye, dear. Have a good trip."

Gina gave her cousin one last hug before Debbie stepped through the metal detector.

Once on the other side, Debbie turned to them both. "I love you!"

Gina and Cynthia waved until Debbie disappeared from view.

The limousine came to a stop in front of Gina's apartment building on Fifth Avenue. The doorman opened the passenger door, and Cynthia and Gina stepped out.

"Good afternoon, Mrs. Moore."

"Thank you, David." Cynthia turned to her daughter. "Gina, you should at least think about what I said. It's not enough to have a degree in Business. You should also study Economics."

Irritated. "Yes, Mom, I will think a - " Gina turned and stopped. Leaning against the side of her building, looking great in jeans and a Polo shirt, was Scott. His smile lit up the entire East Side as he removed his sunglasses and strolled lazily over to them. "You know how long I've been waiting here to run into you? They told me you'd 'gone out.'"

Gina was so overcome with joy, she could hardly stand. "Oh, God! I can't believe you did this!"

"What did I do?" he asked, feigning ignorance.

"Mom," Gina said weakly, "You're not gonna believe this, but - "

"Oh, I'd believe just about anything," Cynthia commented dryly.

Gina sighed deeply. "Mom, this is Scott Griffith."

Cynthia stared at Scott in amazement. "I had a feeling."

"Excuse me, ma'am," said the doorman. "Is this gentleman with you?"

"Yeah," Gina said with mock regret. "I guess so."

Gina and Scott sat on the balcony of the penthouse as Cynthia came out of the sliding glass door carrying a tray of glasses and a pitcher of lemonade. "I thought you two might like this."

Scott smiled. "Thanks, Mrs. Moore."

"You're welcome," Cynthia said, on her best behavior. "And you can call me Cynthia." She looked at Gina. "Okay if I join you?"

Gina gestured to the empty chair. "Go ahead."

Cynthia happily sat down. "So how long are you here for, Scott?"

"I can only stay for a week. Then I have to head back and start a new movie I'm shooting."

"That sounds exciting!"

Gina rolled her eyes, but faked a genuine smile to her mother.

"And what brings you here?" Cynthia asked.

Scott hesitated, his gaze moving to Gina. "I was worried. I just wanted to make sure Gina was okay."

Cynthia smiled warmly.

"As you can see," Gina said patiently, "I'm perfectly fine."

"That was very nice of you, Scott," Cynthia trilled, not sounding like herself at all.

Gina stared at her in disbelief.

The living room phone buzzed.

Cynthia scowled. "I really should get that. It might be important."

As soon as Cynthia was gone, Gina leaned toward Scott. "What are you doing here? I told you I'm okay."

"You are not okay," he retorted. "There's still a drug dealer who wants you dead, and I'm not leaving you. Besides," he added tenderly, "I missed you."

Her face softened, and she couldn't stop the slight smile from appearing on her lips. "You really are crazy, you know that?"

He grinned. "I gotta be. It keeps me sane."

Cynthia returned, much to Gina's discomfort. "That was my assistant. I have to get back to the office." She turned to their guest. "Where are you staying, Scott?"

"As of right now...the corner of 5th and 59th. Hadn't thought that far ahead."

"If you want, you can stay in our guest room."

Both of them looked at her in amazement.

"Have fun, honey." Cynthia hugged Gina tightly before setting off.

Scott raised his eyebrows. "She's leaving you alone with *me*? Is she *nuts*?"

Gina shook her head. "Actually...I think she knew exactly what I needed."

*   *   *

Gina and Scott strolled through Central Park.

"You are gonna *love* New York!" she enthused.

"I figured that," Scott said, looking around him. "That's what it says on all the t-shirts!"

"I still can't believe I'm here," Scott remarked as they stood on the top deck of the Staten Island Ferry. "It feels like I'm dreamin'."

"What about *Right On?*" Gina couldn't help asking.

"We're on hiatus," Scott replied, staring down at the rushing water beneath them. "Till the end of September."

"You must be nuts," Gina affirmed. "You're going to shoot this movie, then go right back to work on the show?"

"We don't start shooting until next week, so I caught the first flight here. My dad wasn't happy, but I told him I needed to relax."

"You came to the wrong place."

Scott stared up at the imposing Statue of Liberty as he and Gina moved briskly toward the entrance. "This thing is so big!"

"You sound like a little kid," Gina teased.

"Well I've never been here before."

She took his hand. "Welcome to *my* world."

Gina took Scott to One World Trade Center – the former site of the Twin Towers and Ground Zero.

"You were living here when that happened," Scott commented solemnly. "Do you remember much of it?"

Gina's mind was traveling backward. "Not really. What was I? Six? I remember my mother took me out of school and sent me to live with my aunt and uncle in Rhode Island for a few weeks. I thought she was doing it so I could have *fun*."

Scott stared pensively up at the gleaming, mirrored edifice. "I feel blessed that me or my family weren't anywhere near here. Still – my dad was making *business* trips here back in those days. Network meetings. Sometimes he had to pitch new shows."

"My mom *still* tries to protect me. And in the case of Luca Santinello, I'm glad she did. I don't know what I would've done without her and my uncle."

Scott turned to her. "I wanna hear more about this Uncle Caesar of yours..."

They dined at Sardi's that evening. The restaurant was extremely busy, but the upstairs room was intimate enough to talk.

"So that whole weekend," Gina was saying, "Terry followed this guy all over the ski lodge. On the chair lift. Down the slope. In the lobby. And she really thought they were going to hook up by the end of the weekend."

Scott smiled as he finished off the rest of his minestrone soup. "So what happened?"

"Finally, it was Sunday night, and she couldn't take it anymore, so she went down to his room, knocked on the door, and asked him if he wanted to hang out."

"And?"

"He says, in this real breathy voice, 'I'd like to, but me and my boyfriend are staying in tonight.'"

Scott grimaced. "Ouch."

"*Not* one of her finer moments."

"She's not like you. You could probably turn a gay man straight."

"Like I'd *want* to." Gina sipped her soda. "Me and Terry and Shannon have been buds forever. Since high school. Maybe you can meet them while you're here."

"I'd like to."

"How about you? Who are *your* best buds? Don't tell me – Channing Tatum, Robert Pattinson..."

Scott smirked. "I've run into Channing Tatum a few times, and I talked to Robert Pattinson *once* a few years ago."

"Where?"

"The Golden Globes."

"Who's your best friend?"

"My mom."

"No. Seriously."

"I am serious."

"Okay. Other than her."

"I used to hang out with these two guys in high school. Joe and Sean. They were a year older than me."

"Do you still see them?"

Scott paled. "No."

"Do you even have a life?" she asked sarcastically. "What do you *do*?"

Scott shrugged. "Just work and - "

"Screw around."

"That's not true!"

"Oh, that is *so* true."

Scott stared out the window of the moving cab, craning his neck to see the tops of the tall buildings surrounding them. "I don't know how people live here!"

"Why?" Gina asked, unable to stop smiling.

"I've just never seen so many people in one place before! It'd be a pain driving my car here."

"Oh, your car wouldn't last an hour here. That's why me and my mom don't drive. We only have the limo."

"Oh, listen to you. 'We only have the limo.'" He mocked a British accent. "Oh, excuse me!"

"I didn't mean it that way! It just doesn't make any sense to drive."

"I know," he smiled, looking at her intently. "I missed you."

"So you keep saying."

He held her hand again, and they kissed – lightly, happily, both unable to wipe the grins off their faces.

Debbie Monroe was alone in her living room when her cell phone chimed. She immediately checked the caller ID and answered the phone. "What's up?"

"Are you sitting down?" Gina asked, as she paced her own living room.

"Should I be?"

"You're never going to believe who's here!"

"Obama."

"Scott Griffith."

Debbie almost dropped her phone. "What!"

"He was waiting here when me and my mom got home yesterday."

"I knew I shouldn't have left so soon! And...?"

"Oh, it's been wonderful, Deb! I've never been happier in my life."

"So what's the problem?"

"You know what the problem is. It can't last."

"There you go, being Negative Nancy again."

"I'm serious. He has a life, and this huge career, in L.A. And you know there is no way I'm moving out *there* again."

"Who's talking moving? Why can't you guys just stay friends and leave it at that?"

"I think he has more than staying friends on his mind."

"Yeah, for about five minutes. You know what guys are like. You want my advice? Have fun, enjoy yourself, and when things cool off, just go on with your life."

"Sounds like a plan – if it was what I wanted."

Gina knocked softly before opening the bedroom door a crack. The room was quiet except for Scott's heavy breathing.

She peered over at the bed. He was still asleep, his arm wrapped around the pillow, his hair mussed. She could tell he was naked just by the way the covers were draped over him.

Smiling, she closed the door and moved quietly over to the bed. He didn't stir. She stood staring at him, what she could see of his body. Even under her probing eyes, he still didn't waken. Stealthily, she moved to the other side of the bed and silently removed her clothes.

When she was nude, she slid into bed beside him and covered herself with the rest of the blanket. Snaking a hand along his bare shoulder, she lightly trailed her fingers down his arm, slowly moving to his magnificent chest and brushing the tips of his nipples.

He awoke with a start.

"Subtle enough?" she asked dryly.

He stared at her, momentarily disoriented. Then his lips broke into a huge smile. "What are you doing?"

"If you don't know by now, I can't help you."

He slipped his arm around her. "Where's your mother?"

"Why are you thinking about my mother?" Seriously. "At work. We're all alone."

He licked his lips, casting his eyes downward. "I'd like to kiss you, but I don't think you want me to do that."

"Depends on where you kiss me."

He started with her neck, rolling on top of her and pinning her arms to the sheet. Moving back and forth, they created their own familiar rhythm. Gina allowed herself to feel every ounce of pleasure he gave her as he moved further down. She couldn't stop herself from crying out while he worked faster.

He brought her close more than once, each time slowing down and building up his speed again. The longer he forced her to wait, the more she needed her release. He was fighting hard, too. Suffering. Wanting to give himself to her but needing it to last. Both resisted the tempting sensations, until neither one of them could hold back any longer.

They lay together for a few moments, wrapped in each other's arms, smiling and flushed.

"I could die happy," he said lazily.

"You just want to go back to sleep."

"That would work, too." He shifted position. "This is great! Not having to *be* anywhere or *do* anything."

Gina stared thoughtfully at the ceiling. "You're actually going to be shooting in *Europe*?"

"First we shoot some interiors in L.A. Then we leave for the locations. We start in Vegas, and then we head to Europe."

"You have such a hard life."

"It can be. Movies are tough. The show's easier."

"Why are movies tough?"

"Longer hours. And it takes more work to get it right. With *Right On*, they set up a scene, we're in and we're out."

"That's *you*, all right."

"Thanks a lot!"

She giggled, snuggling closer to him. Then she turned serious again. "Do you like what you do?"

"Definitely! Why?"

"I just remember how much fun it was working on *Right On*. My mother wants me to go into business or finance."

"What do *you* want to do?"

She looked at him, surprise on her face. "I don't know."

He thought a moment. "How about acting?"

"Oh, get real."

"Oh, come on," he said grandly. "I am offering you the chance to come back to Hollywood and be a star!"

"Except that I have no intention of going back to Hollywood."

"Not even for me?"

She weighed her response carefully. "Scott..." she said softly. "I can't."

The pain was evident in his face. "Is that your *final* answer?"

She nodded, throwing her covers aside. "We should get dressed."

Gina and Scott sat in Gina's living room facing Shannon Damon and Terry Harmon. Both girls were well dressed and looked stunning.

"We should take another trip!" Terry blurted eagerly.

Shannon looked at her strangely. "*Another* trip? We just got back from Florida."

"I thought you guys went skiing," said Scott.

"That was in February," Shannon explained. "Florida was in May."

He attempted to look sheepish. "Sorry."

"Yeah," Gina said sarcastically, jokingly snapping her fingers at him. "Try and keep up."

"The three of us and Debbie went," said Terry. "It was awesome!"

"Where did you go?" Scott asked.

"Orlando."

"Disney World. Cool."

"Have you ever been down there?" asked Shannon.

"Never."

"Oh, it was amazing!" Terry enthused. "We went on all the rides at the theme parks, and Daytona Beach." She indicated Gina. "We even got *her* on Space Mountain."

Scott eyed Gina. "I can believe that. Gina likes thrill rides."

She looked at him in mock outrage. "How would *you* know what I like?"

"Because I've seen how you drive."

"What do *you* drive?" Shannon asked.

"A Porsche."

Terry and Shannon nodded in approval.

"I should get down to Florida sometime," Scott mused. "I mean, who wouldn't have fun there?" He motioned to Gina. "Especially The Recluse here."

"Well," said Terry, "Anything would've been better than her *first* trip to..."

Gina silenced her with a look.

Scott glanced at Gina. "Why? When was your *first* trip?"

"When I was a kid," Gina lied. "Trust me. *Anything* is better than having to go anywhere with my mom."

A cell phone chimed.

Everybody checked their pockets.

"It's mine," said Scott, pulling his phone out and checking the ID. "I gotta take this." He stood up and headed out onto the balcony.

"It's probably The Coast," Terry quipped cheerily as they watched him exit.

Scott stepped into the night air and spoke into his phone. "Yeah, Mom, what's up?"

"Hi, honey! Are you having a good time?"

"The best! We're just hanging out now with some of Gina's friends."

"Then I won't keep you. I just wanted to make sure you're still coming home on Sunday night."

"Yeah. Five-thirty."

"Me and dad'll be picking you up. You're cutting it kind of close with that cast meeting on Monday morning."

Scott stole a glance over his shoulder. Gina and the girls were chatting intently. "I know. I wish I didn't have to come back at all."

"What are you going to do?" Tracy asked sarcastically. "Tell Ellen Stellar you're backing out and walking away from ten million dollars?"

"No," Scott replied dismally. "It's just not the best time."

"It's your hiatus. It's the perfect time. You can see Gina when you get done with the movie."

"No, because then *Right On* starts shooting on September 9th."

"So have her come out for a visit. You can see her on your days off."

Scott shook his head. "She won't." He looked through the living room window again. Gina glanced back at him. "I gotta get back in there."

"All right, handsome," Tracy said warmly. "We'll see you Sunday night."

"Yeah," Scott muttered forlornly. "Love you, Mom."

He disconnected and headed inside.

Gina and Scott strolled through the deserted airport lounge, glancing out the floor to ceiling windows and admiring the overhead fixtures.

"Where are we?" Gina asked.

"It's a hospitality room," Scott explained. "I have to wait here till they board me. So I don't get mobbed by fans."

Gina shook her head. "I would never want your life."

"I don't think I could *handle* yours." Scott stared morosely out the window. "I don't wanna go."

"We talked about this. You're not moving in with me and my mother," Gina joked.

"I just hate leaving you. What if something *else* happens?"

"I'll call the police. And I still have my uncle. You don't have to worry."

"Just don't ask me not to care. 'Cuz there's no *way* I can do that."

"Scott..."

"I mean it. This is not the end."

A man's voice boomed over the PA system. "First Class boarding for Flight 3549 to Los Angeles. All First Class passengers, please board at this time."

Scott grabbed Gina by the shoulders and kissed her. When he broke away, his intense blue eyes bore into hers. "I love you, Gina. And this is not over."

Her eyes were wide – and full of questions.

He smiled as he picked up his carry-on bag and strode toward the hospitality lounge exit.

"Yes, it is," Gina murmured, sadly staring after him.

The sound of jet engines roared in her ears.

*   *   *

Debbie Monroe sat at the computer in her bedroom when her cell phone went off. Not recognizing the number, she answered tentatively.

Heather Griffith, driving in her car along the 405 Freeway, good-naturedly snapped, "Don't give me that innocent routine! Where did you disappear to?"

"Heather!" Debbie cried excitedly.

"I'm flattered you remember me," Heather said dryly.

"Of course I remember you! How are you?"

"Never been better. Wish I could say the same for my brother."

"Why?"

"I wish I knew. He's been down ever since he got back from New York."

"You don't say?" Debbie said slyly. "Funny you should mention that. Gina's been exactly the same way."

"Really?" Heather asked hopefully, exiting the freeway at Sunset Boulevard. "What *happened* when he was there? He won't say a word about it."

"Gina said they had a great time. She wouldn't say exactly *how* great, but I got the idea."

"So what's wrong, then?" Heather wondered, gripping her steering wheel. "They had a great time, and now he's..." In realization. "Now he's miserable!"

"I don't think *Gina* is exactly ecstatic these days, either," Debbie supplied. "She's been even crankier than usual."

"Oh, that's so sweet!" Heather couldn't help gushing. "Don't you see? It means they belong together."

"Gina did tell me one thing." Debbie took a deep breath. "Scott told her he loved her."

Heather almost hit the car in front of her. "What!"

"I wouldn't make it up," Debbie said calmly.

"Oh – my - God," Heather murmured. "This – is - big."

"But I don't think it'll work out. At least, Gina doesn't. She also said she wouldn't move back to L.A. again. Not after what happened."

"We've got to get them together someplace...someplace neutral."

Debbie laughed. "Right! Like *that'll* happen!"

Heather grinned. "Don't be too sure, Deb. I've got an idea."

*   *   *

"No way, Deb," Gina said into her phone as she strode briskly down Fifth Avenue. "I'm not going to Las Vegas. I'm not going anywhere."

"I can't believe *you're* turning down a trip to Las Vegas!"

"I don't want to do any traveling for a while. I've had enough. Besides, I've got a lot of stuff to sort out here in New York."

"I wouldn't ask, but my friend, Lisa, is going to be there – you remember? The girl we met in Florida?"

"How could I forget? The groupie."

"Well she's still dating Steve Riken from X-Rated Run, and now she's opening a solo act at the Paradise Hotel. You've heard of it, right?"

"The hotel, yes. How'd she manage *that?*"

"I don't know. Knew the right person, I guess."

"*Slept* with the right person is more like it."

"And I don't really wanna go alone," Debbie said cajolingly.

"If it were any other time, Deb. I just don't think so..."

"Gina, c'mon. It's only for a couple of days, and we'd have a blast! Don't you deserve a little fun?"

"I deserve a *lot* of fun! I just don't feel like going to Vegas to do it."

"If I promise it'll be the last trip of the year, will you come?"

"Why is it so important that I be there?"

"Because Lisa's going to be performing that Saturday night, and most of the reservations are for couples. The way my luck's been going, I'd rather she not set me up. Besides," Debbie added wryly, "You'll probably be the best date I've had in months!"

"When is it?" Gina sighed.

"Week after next. Can I count you in?"

"I guess so," Gina replied wearily. "At least I can relax when you start school."

"I'm trying not to think about that. And hey – whatever happens in Vegas, stays in Vegas!"

"I'll be happy if nothing happens at all."

*   *   *

"She went for it!" Debbie cried happily.

"Ripe for the picking!" Heather chortled.

"They're probably gonna figure it out when they see each other," Debbie warned.

"Doesn't matter," Heather said dismissively. "By that time, they'll be so much in love, they won't care. Are you all set with the plan?"

"I think so," Debbie said uncertainly. "This is such a stroke of good luck! My friend, Lisa, is going to be performing in the lounge show that Saturday night."

"You see? It's fate. Just like I told you."

"I can't wait to see the look on Scott's face!"

"Trust me – my phone cam is already in position!"

CHAPTER 14

A bell on the soundstage clanged, and Ellen Stellar stepped out from behind the camera. "Scott, I need you to sound more urgent when you say that. Your father has been missing for over a year, and you think these people know where he is but they're just not telling you. You're crazed. You're beyond panic. And I need to see it in your eyes!"

Scott nodded and moved into position next to two rough-looking men.

The three of them were standing on a set that looked startlingly like a Las Vegas casino. Slot machines, roulette wheels, and two-dozen extras dressed as tourists completed the look, creating an authentic appearance even to the naked eye.

Positioned near one of the men next to Scott was Miles Morrison, almost preening in the tuxedo he was wearing. He watched Scott and the others carefully as Ellen gave them directions. Scott was also dressed in a tuxedo, the two men in blue suits.

Ellen strolled once again behind the camera, studying the set and the actors intently. "Let's go again. And Background – I need you more animated!"

The extras obediently took their places.

A young man with a digital clapboard stepped in front of the camera. "Scene Twenty-One, Take Fourteen! Marker!" He ducked out of sight.

"We have speed!"

"Rolling!"

Ellen called, "Action!"

The extras silently, animatedly assumed their roles as tourists and blackjack dealers.

Roulette wheels spun and dice rolled.

The scene began. Scott approached the two rough-looking men, threatening to reveal where their stolen money was hidden unless they revealed the whereabouts of "Todd's" father. Undaunted, the men stated that "Todd" would never leave the casino alive. At that, Scott made a run for it and darted out of camera range.

"Cut!" Ellen shouted.

Another loud bell clanged.

"That's what I want! Print that!"

The actors and extras drifted away from their positions.

"Okay, people," Ellen called from behind the camera, "It looks like we're done. We're setting up for the next shot." She turned to see a tall, handsome man standing behind her. "Oh, Scott." Scott looked in her direction. "I want you to meet Jerry Garnett."

Scott beamed as he stepped down off the set. "Hey, Jerry!"

"Scott!"

The two men shook hands.

Jerry was twenty-eight, devilishly sexy, with jet black hair down to his shoulders, and sparkling blue eyes. "What do you say?" Jerry asked, his Australian accent strong. "Are you ready to make this film?"

"Definitely. Hey, I really liked your work in *Hamlet*."

"Thanks. I'll be here tomorrow to shoot the laboratory scene."

"Great!" Scott glanced over Jerry's shoulder and noticed Rose Leoni standing next to a portable floor light, her face florid and beaming. He hesitated. "I'll...talk to ya in just a minute."

Jerry nodded as Scott moved over to stand in front of Rose.

She couldn't stop smiling. "Hi."

Scott managed to look glad to see her. "Hi. What are you doing here?"

"I just wanted to see you," she lisped, her lips quivering.

"How are you doing?"

"I'm good," she replied indignantly, as if nothing had happened. "Why?"

He nodded, smiling politely. "You look good."

Her entire face lit up. "Thanks!"

"How did you get in here?" he asked curiously.

"I know people," she replied coquettishly. Rose threw her arms around him and held him tightly. "I missed you...don't leave me..."

And they were standing in her living room and she was saying those same words...just before he walked out on her...just before...

He delicately extricated himself from her embrace, holding her by the wrists and looking deeply into her troubled eyes. "You should go. We have to get back to work soon."

"All right," she said playfully, although her expression was tight-lipped. Then she brightened. "What are you doing Saturday? We could go to the Beverly Center! I have some shopping to do, anyway."

He sighed deeply. "You know I'll get mobbed if I go there."

"That's the trouble with you, Scott," she said, pretending to be irritated. "You're just so...famous." She giggled, gazing at him affectionately. "Maybe later?"

"I can't..."

"Scott, what's wrong?" she asked. "Are you mad at me?"

"Never. I just have to get back to work."

"You work too much." She looked away. "Are you sure you're not mad at me?" Her voice sounded urgent.

"No. Are you sure *you're* not mad at *me*?"

She rolled her eyes. "Of course not!"

"Okay, people!" Ellen's voice boomed across the soundstage. "We're ready to go again!"

A loud bell clanged.

"I have to go," Scott said quickly. "I'll talk to you later."

He dashed back to the set before she could say anything else.

Rose looked around her with discomfort and waved to Scott before slowly retreating from the soundstage.

Jerry caught Scott on his way back to the set. "Adoring fan?" he asked good-naturedly.

Scott hesitated as he watched Rose disappear out the stage door. "I hope not."

Jason Kellner and Raquel Morollan lay spent beneath her silk sheets.

"Wow!" she gasped, her face still flushed. "I didn't think you'd be *that* good!"

Jason slipped his arm around her naked body and smiled. "I don't like to brag..."

"And you're so *big*!"

"I can't help that." He looked at her thoughtfully. "You know what I like about you? You're a woman. Not some little girl."

"I was *hoping* you'd notice," she said sarcastically.

"It makes you special."

She couldn't help smiling.

He stared up at her bedroom ceiling. "Can I tell you something honestly? I think you were smart to dump Scott Griffith."

Raquel tensed. "Scott?"

"Yeah," Jason snorted in disgust. "He may have won an Emmy, but as a person, he's still a loser."

"Well," Raquel said sadly, "When Scott and I stopped seeing each other, it was *his* decision – not mine."

Jason feigned shock. "No way!" Pretending to digest the information. "Then I take that back. He's not a loser. He's an idiot."

Raquel's mind was traveling backward in time. "It's okay. It was a long time ago. Scott and I are friends now."

"Friends? After the way he treated you? His only friend is himself."

"I thought you guys got along."

"We're cool with each other in public, but I've never trusted him. Believe me. My sister works with him. Eight years ago, he got me kicked off of a commercial by saying some stuff about me that wasn't true."

Raquel was genuinely surprised. "You're kidding."

"I wish I was." Jason scowled. "I still remember this girl he brought to the Emmys last year. Some blonde. She didn't have anywhere near your class."

Raquel's face clouded over as she remembered.

"You know what happened to her, right?"

Raquel snapped out of her reverie. "No. What?"

"The way I heard it, Scott got her pregnant and paid her to leave town in a hurry."

"What!!"

Jason shrugged. "I thought *everybody* knew."

Raquel stared at him in stunned disbelief.

"Can you imagine?" Jason went on. "Forcing a girl to abort your own kid? What kind of guy does that?"

Raquel didn't realize she was shaking.

"You know," Jason said mildly, "He would have it coming if the tabloids got hold of that story."

She stared at him.

"I'm saying – he's lucky you're a friend of his. If you ever wanted to pay him back for what he did, you could do it."

So many emotions were hitting her at once. But she was listening. "How?" she asked, pretending to be merely curious.

Jason expertly played it cool. "All you would need is some proof. And the way you're close to him, it would be easy for you to get."

Tracy was in the kitchen when she heard the garage door go up, then a car door slam. A moment later, Robert lumbered in carrying his briefcase, his expression grim. He laid the briefcase on the counter and stood glancing at Tracy.

Her eyes registered understanding. "Oh, don't even tell me..."

Robert's voice was calm. "Yup. They didn't renew us."

"Oh, for God's sake! Did they tell you why?"

He shrugged. "They never tell you why. They just say, 'No, thank you.'"

"Damn it! What about one of your new shows?"

Robert shook his head. "They turned down all our pitches. Even that idea you had for the one about the store detectives."

"Well what was wrong with that one??"

"They want something *new*. Exciting."

Tracy turned back to her laptop, which was open in front of her on the kitchen table. "How about nobody watching? *That'll* be new and exciting."

"No. The more I think about it, the more I think it might be time for us to make a move."

"You're quitting?"

"Not quitting. Working for myself. Breaking away from this damn network and doing things on our own."

"And going off salary while you're doing it!"

"In the beginning, yeah."

Tracy shook her head. "Geez, I don't know..." She stood at the kitchen window and looked out. "Can we do it?"

"There's Ma's life insurance policy." He glanced around. "And this house."

Both fell silent, each engrossed in their own thoughts.

Robert spoke up. "If we don't do it now, when are we going to do it?"

She turned to face him. "It's a big decision."

"Well we don't have to make it right *now*. I'm thinking about Scott. And Heather."

Tracy nodded.

"And what's Scott supposed to do when *Right On* ends? Throw himself on the mercy of any producer who'll give him a job?"

Tracy gazed at him thoughtfully. "When would we have to decide?"

Robert shrugged. "I'll stay on for a while. May as well take the money while I can get it. I might even get offered something. But by the beginning of next year, I want to start looking into it."

Tracy smirked. "Never a dull moment in *this* family."

Robert grabbed his briefcase and headed into the living room. "Your mother told you not to marry me. You should've listened."

Heather had just driven through the gate of her house when her cell phone went off.

"Damn it!"

Impatiently she hit the TALK button.

"Heather?"

She recognized the voice, but her eyes still widened in shock.

"Heather, are you there?" the girl asked timidly, after a moment's hesitation.

"Yeah," Heather managed, parking to the left of the garage. "What's going on?"

"I need you...I'm in trouble, and...I just really need you right now..."

Scott checked the caller I.D. on his phone before he answered it. "How ya doin'?"

"I was wondering why you hadn't called me," Raquel said sweetly.

"I had to leave town," Scott explained lamely. Getting to the truth, "I start shooting a movie next week."

"Awesome!"

"Yeah. It's a big budget. A lot of action."

"Sounds like something I'd *like*," she purred. "Am I gonna see you before you go?"

Shutting Gina out of his mind, Scott forced a hint of excitement into his voice. "Sure! What would you like to do?"

"Could I come over?" she asked innocently.

"Sure. Saturday afternoon work for you? We could go swimming."

"I suppose I'll have to bring my bathing suit," Raquel sighed.

Scott grinned. "My parents'll probably be around, so, yeah."

"I hope you appreciate the sacrifices I make," Raquel said coyly.

"Don't worry," Scott replied playfully. "I'll make it worth your while."

LAX was noisy as Heather entered the domestic baggage claim area. She stepped off to the side, looking around intently.

Stressed out travelers rushed past her in both directions while small babies cried incessantly, their parents doing nothing to quiet them.

Heather stared unseeingly at the circular conveyor belt loaded with eclectic suitcases when she looked up and saw Lynda Seville. Slightly thinner, a little paler, and hair shorter, but definitely Lynda. Her cherub face broke into a smile when she saw Heather, who, by comparison, looked far more attractive.

Heather started in her direction, then stopped, hesitating.

Lynda, too, stared at the floor, began to say something, then thought better of it.

Heather bravely marched up to her friend. "Are you okay?"

Lynda nodded, attempting another smile.

Heather cleared her throat. "It's good to see you." She glanced around. Do you have a bag?"

"Just a carry-on. But they made me check it, anyway."

*   *   *

Scott and Raquel spent much of Saturday afternoon in Scott's bed.

"You've gotten better," Raquel smiled.

He gazed at her affectionately. "I had a good teacher. Remember?"

"I do," she replied wistfully, staring deeply into his innocent aquamarine eyes.

The sun was shining brightly as Heather drove Lynda up the 405 Freeway.

"Louisiana??" Heather's eyes bulged.

"That's where we ended up." Lynda shook her head dismally. "He could've talked me into anything. When he said he loved me, I thought he meant it."

Heather pursed her lips, staring at the heavy traffic up ahead. "Been down *that* road."

"Heather, I want you to know I really appreciate this. I couldn't tell my aunt. If she found out, she'd throw me out of the house."

Heather sighed wearily. "*I* can't talk. You tried to warn me about Miles. And you know what happened *there*."

Lynda didn't appear to be listening. She was staring down at her lap, thinking intently. "I'll pay you back for the plane ticket. I didn't know who else to call."

Heather smiled warmly. "Not necessary. You forgive me, I'll forgive you, we'll call it even. Deal?"

Lynda's voice was choked. "Deal."

It was dark by the time Heather arrived home. She was surprised to find out that her parents weren't around, as they usually were on a Saturday night, but even more surprised when she stepped out onto the balcony off of the living room and saw Scott and Raquel Morollan swimming around playfully in the pool. Heather watched as Scott made a grab for Raquel, who coquettishly swam away from him and called out, "Bite me."

Heather's face fell. "Oh, no..."

Scott awoke much later that night and climbed out of bed, careful not to wake Raquel, who was still asleep on the other side. Slipping on a pair of shorts, Scott headed upstairs and found Heather watching T.V. in the living room.

"You're not on your phone?" Scott asked sarcastically. "The operation was a success?"

"Cute," Heather smirked, muting the T.V. and following him into the kitchen. "Raquel's spending the night?" Heather asked softly. "You know Mom and Dad are home, right?"

"Relax," Scott said, opening the fridge and pouring himself a glass of root beer. "I'll wake her up in a few hours, before they get up."

"What about Gina?"

Scott's face clouded over. "What do you want from me? She won't move back here, and I can't move there."

Heather couldn't disguise her disappointment. "I know – but *Raquel*??"

"What's wrong with Raquel? She's *here*. She *wants* to be with me. She's not going to go running off to the East Coast when I need her." Scott took a sip of his soda and sat down at the kitchen table.

Heather joined him. "So that's why you're back with her? Because she's geographically desirable?"

"We're just hanging out." In the living room, Raquel was slowly making her way up the stairs and was just about to head into the kitchen when she heard Scott say, "I'm not going to ask her to marry me..."

"I don't know how you can give up so easily," Heather remarked. "Gina's your soul mate."

"That's the same thing I thought about Rose," Scott muttered. "And Maryann..."

Raquel, still in the living room, stopped and stood listening, clutching the top of the pink silk robe she wore.

"Why can't you put that behind you?" Heather asked Scott.

"Because every time I get behind the wheel of my car, I feel guilty," Scott murmured.

Heather gently took her brother's hand. "It wasn't your fault."

"Whose fault was it? *I* was driving the car." Scott's voice was hoarse. "I can still feel Maryann in my arms...one minute, we were laughing and having a good time...The next, there was no life in her body...it should've been me..."

"Don't say that. It was an accident."

Scott shook his head miserably. "It never would've happened if it wasn't for me...I shouldn't have been driving that fast...I never should've gotten that car..."

Visibly upset, Scott got up from the table.

Raquel turned and hurried through the living room and back down the stairs.

It was early evening. Cynthia Moore sat alone in the living room of her penthouse, curled up on the couch and talking on her cell phone. The T.V. was on with the sound muted, Cynthia engrossed in her conversation.

"No, Kathy, I haven't seen her in two years...I heard the same thing...and the daughter's pregnant *again*..."

Cynthia absently bit one of her nails and glanced up at the T.V. A news program pictured a courtroom with the caption SANTINELLO RELEASED. Her mouth dropped open and she reached for the remote, jabbing at the VOLUME button.

"Kathy, I'll call you back," Cynthia said quickly into the phone before disconencting.

A female anchor's voice-over narrated, "Alleged drug lord Luca Santinello was released earlier today, following a verdict of Not Guilty, after the now-infamous trial held in New York Superior Court."

The anchor, a pretty blonde, appeared onscreen in front of the courthouse, microphone in hand.

"The case was dismissed due to insufficient evidence to support the charge that the known racketeer allegedly supplied narcotics to minors. At this time, no further charges have been filed. For WKPS News, I'm Regina Stratton. Back to you, George - "

Cynthia hit the OFF button, her hand shaking. She grabbed her cell phone and hurriedly dialed. It seemed to ring forever. "Caesar! I was just watching the news - "

"I know." Caesar paced his home office, clutching his own cell phone. There was no surprise in his voice. "I heard."

"Gina...what do we do now...?"

"There's nothing to do," Caesar said with certainty. "He won't touch her. He knows if he does, he's dead."

"How can you be sure of that?"

"I *am* sure of that," he said darkly. "You think I'm playin' games here?"

Cynthia's head was pounding as she anxiously looked around her.

"I can put some protection on you and Gina for a while," Caesar went on. "She there with you?"

Cynthia felt short of breath. "No. She left for Las Vegas this morning."

"She what! What the hell is she doin' *there*?"

"She just...she's visiting some..."

"Where is she?"

"She's at the...the Paradise Hotel...on the Strip..."

"Unbelievable. She's gotta leave town *now*."

"Caesar...if I'd known..."

"Relax. I'll get my boys on it. Just don't send her out of the *country* before I can make a call, huh?"

As soon as Raquel returned to her house and was alone, she accessed the Internet on her phone and pulled up everything recent she could find about Scott. She didn't discover anything she didn't already know until she came across a photo of him taken at last year's Emmys. He was crossing the red carpet with a beautiful blonde girl on his arm. Raquel recognized the girl immediately as the same one she'd found Scott with the night they'd broken up at the beach.

Raquel scanned the accompanying article and found the girl's name: Maryann Davis. A search of obituaries for Los Angeles County turned up a horrific caption.

MALIBU CANYON – **Maryann Davis** (1995-2012)
Maryann Davis, daughter of Mr. and Mrs. Cameron Davis of Malibu, entered into Heaven on Monday. Maryann was a senior at Malibu Canyon High School and was active in the International Club and the Cheering Squad. Maryann leaves her parents, her sister Kelly, 15, and her grandparents, Frank and Maureen Casey of Santa Ana. Memorial services will be held at St. Joseph's Church in Ventura. Donations to the American Cancer Institute of Research may be made in lieu of flowers at the request of the family.

*   *   *

Raquel's phone went off, nearly causing her to drop it. Her hands shook as she checked the caller ID.

JASON KELLNER.

She reluctantly answered it.

"I've been thinking about you," he said affectionately.

"Have you?"

"I'd like to see you."

"Well I really...I don't think I can."

"Don't you miss me?"

"I just...have a lot on my mind these days."

"I know what you mean." He forced himself to sound casual. "I was thinking about our conversation the other day. The one we were having about Scott."

"What about it?" she asked sharply.

Her reaction surprised him. "Well...it's just a gut feeling, really...I just know he's hiding something - "

"Well you're wrong. I've known Scott for years. And I saw him over the weekend. He's the sweetest, nicest guy I've ever met. And he's not hiding *anything* – except how kind he really is."

Jason was completely taken aback, but before he could say anything, Raquel went on.

"And I think you're trying to spread malicious gossip about him because you're jealous of him. He's better *looking* than you, a better actor, and much nicer than you'll *ever* be." She paused for a quick breath. "I've gotta go."

She disconnected confidently, even though her hands were still shaking.

"Scott?" Raquel's voice was exuberant on the telephone.

"Hey! What's up?"

"I've gotta see you," Raquel purred. "Can you come over tonight?"

"I'd love to, but I leave for Vegas tomorrow. I've gotta pack and study my script some more."

"I understand, but it's very important that I see you before you leave. Would it be okay if I stopped by? Just for a few minutes?"

Scott hesitated. He did have a lot to do, but he didn't want to hurt her feelings. "Well...we're just about to eat dinner, so why don't you come by after seven? I'm really not going to be able to do anything, though..."

"No worries. It won't take long. I'll see you then."

Raquel arrived at exactly seven o'clock. Scott was in his room with Tracy, who was supervising the packing of Scott's suitcase. They were also having a talk about *On the Verge*, *Right On*, and Scott's career. Scott greeted Raquel at the front door and escorted her up to his room. When they were alone, Scott asked, "Why did you need to see me? Is something wrong?"

"Not a thing," she smiled. "I just didn't want you to leave before I had a chance to say goodbye."

"I'm only gonna be gone for a week. We're just doing some exterior shooting."

Raquel's face lit up. "Why don't I go with you? We'd have a great time!"

"Sorry. I'm going to be working. Besides, *Heather's* already coming with me." He lowered his voice. "I think my mom's sending her to make sure I don't have any showgirls in my room."

"You better not!" she laughed, gazing at him lovingly.

He smirked. "I *wish* my life was that exciting."

She slid her arms around him. "It *will* be when you get back."

He kissed her, then turned to inspect the items in his suitcase. "I think I have everything I need..."

Raquel sat down on Scott's bed. "I can't wait till you get back! We're going to have an awesome time!"

He looked at her. "I'll still be shooting. And the week after next, I leave for more locations in Europe. I told you that."

"How would you like me to come to Europe with you?"

Scott thought quickly. "I'd love it! But I don't think it's a good idea."

"Why not?"

"Because I'm going to be shooting a movie, and I wouldn't have any time to spend with you."

Raquel looked crestfallen. "When do you come back?" she asked, not looking at him.

"Next month. I have to back in September to start on *Right On* again."

"I didn't realize that..."

Scott placed a few extra pairs of socks and underwear in his suitcase and zipped it up. "I'm sorry. I wish it didn't have to be this way, but this is my work. It's what I'm about."

Her smile was fraught with pain. "I know..."

"C'mon," he said sympathetically. "You're acting like you're never gonna see me again."

Raquel stood. "I know I will!" she said happily. "We'll work it out *somehow*. We always did." Her stare was intent. "Now that we're back together, everything's going to be great!"

"Raquel...it's been great to see you again...and I'm glad you're not mad at me anymore...but we're not getting back together."

Her smile faded. "What?"

"I care about you...and we'll always be friends...but I just don't think we'd work as a couple."

"How can - ?"

"I'm so swamped right now, I can't get involved with *anybody* - "

"You're breaking up with me?? *Again*?"

"We can't break up. We're just friends."

"That's not what you said the other night. What was *that* about?"

"We...were just having fun. I thought you understood that."

"Oh, I understand," she spat. "You were using me. Again."

"No."

"Yes! I don't know how you can do it - "

"It's not like that at all."

"What else would you call it? You think I'm just a slut you can brag to your friends about?"

He stared at her in amazement. "Where is all *this* coming from? I have never done that!"

Raquel fought to calm herself and took slow, deep breaths. "You're right. I'm sorry. I know that *you* know that I would never want what we do behind closed doors to get out."

It was almost like he was looking at a stranger. "Of course not."

Her voice trembled. "Just like I know that you wouldn't want anybody to find out that Maryann Davis died in your car."

He felt like all the oxygen had vanished from the room. "What?"

"I'm just saying – I can't imagine what people would think if they found out you were responsible for a girl's *death*. Your fans. The network. Can you imagine?"

"You don't know what you're - "

"It's not like it would be difficult for someone to prove if they knew where to look. But you don't have to worry, Scott. Nobody will ever hear about it from *me*. I love you. Why would I ruin your life like that?" She smiled sexily and kissed him.

He stood motionless.

"You make sure you call me when you get back from Vegas," Raquel said sweetly. She turned, started out, then stopped at the doorway, her voice tinged with authority. "I mean it – don't forget."

CHAPTER 15

The Las Vegas Strip was one hundred and fifteen degrees and alive with activity. The gigantic hotels towered against the desert skyline while swarms of vacationers poured in and out of the magnificent casinos. No hotel lobby was accessible without first going through their casino, and enormous neon marquees twinkled brilliantly in the glittering sunlight.

Each hotel/casino has a theme. The Excalibur – a medieval motif. The Luxor – Egyptian landscapes. The Paradise Hotel was a gleaming white edifice in the style of a tropical island – palm trees, waterfalls, even a huge wave pool.

Gina stared out the window of their room overlooking the Paris Hotel.

"This is really your first time in Vegas?" Debbie asked, taking some things out of her suitcase.

Gina turned from the window. "It's *your* first time, too," she pointed out, strolling over to the bed.

"Not anymore," Debbie said lasciviously, smoothing out a red cocktail dress and hanging it up.

"Is that why you wanted to come? To score with one of these male strippers?"

"I'm here for Lisa. Although..."

"Is she in her room now?"

"Should be. Lisa said we could come up as soon as we get unpacked."

Gina and Debbie stood outside the hotel room door.

Debbie pressed the room buzzer and waited.

The door was answered by Lisa McClure, wearing a skimpy white top, extra short shorts, high-heeled shoes, and holding a drink in one hand. "Deb!" she boomed in a very loud voice, sweeping Debbie into a genuine hug. "You made it!"

"Would I miss it?" Debbie retorted good-naturedly, turning to Gina. "You remember my cousin, Gina?"

"Hey!" Lisa beamed, hugging Gina also, trying not to spill her drink. "Come on in!"

Lisa escorted them inside a large suite with a sweeping view of the Strip below and the desert in the distance.

"Wow!" Gina couldn't help marveling. "You're staying here by yourself?"

"Naw!" Lisa made a face, gesturing for them to sit on a plush white couch facing the floor-to-ceiling window. "I'm here with Steve. You guys want a drink or somethin'? We got tons of stuff in that mini-bar."

Gina and Debbie shook their heads, and all three girls sat.

"So you're performing with the group?" Gina asked.

Lisa gulped her drink down. "You got it, dude! Tomorrow night, we're gonna be rockin'!"

Debbie and Gina grinned.

"And there's this one number I'm singin' – all by myself!"

"We can't wait!" Debbie enthused.

"What's up?" drawled a male voice behind them.

All three girls turned to see a skinny, long-haired guy in his early twenties staring at them through sleep-clouded eyes. Aside from a gold chain he wore around his neck, he was completely naked.

"Hi, honey!" Lisa gushed happily, going over to him and giving him a big kiss. "Remember Debbie and Gina? They stayed with us in Florida."

Steve stared at the other two girls and tried to focus. "Hey," he mumbled. "Wha's up?"

Scott leaned back in the first class airplane seat and stared miserably into space.

Heather, seated next to him, talked as if he were hanging on her every word. "This is so exciting! I can't wait till we land! This is gonna be so much better than that time when we were kids! This time I wanna play the slot machines! And see some of those shows - "

"Heather," he groaned, frowning. "I said you could come along. I didn't say you could talk all through the trip."

She smiled contritely. "Sorry. I'm just excited."

"I'm glad you're excited," he said without enthusiasm, shifting in his seat, "But this is only a vacation for *you*. Did you forget that I have to work? Besides, I promised Mom and Dad that I would keep an eye on you."

"Do I get to go to the *ladies room* by myself?"

He was taking shallow breaths. "Maybe we can see one of the shows, but I don't know how much time I'm going to have."

"Are you okay?" she asked, looking at him strangely.

"Not so good," he muttered. "I feel sick to my stomach. I think it was something I ate."

"Sorry," she said compassionately, touching his arm. In a softer voice, "Thanks for taking me on this trip, big brother."

He took her hand and smiled affectionately. "It's not like I had much of a choice."

Gina and Debbie were standing at the open door inside Lisa and Steve's suite.

Gina said, "We're gonna change right now and meet you down at the pool."

"Sounds like a plan," Lisa smiled, teetering on her high heels. "Do you mind if I just talk to Deb a sec? I wanna show her these photos I took at Steve's concert."

"Yeah, sure. Deb, I'll be in the room."

"Okay."

As soon as Gina was gone, Lisa closed the door and the two girls excitedly high-fived. "I gotta hand it to ya, Deb. Looks like sweet little cousin Gina doesn't suspect a thing."

"Oh," Debbie said worriedly, "If she finds out this is a set-up, she'll kill me!"

"You worry too much," Lisa said casually. "You gotta chill out. When's that girl, Heather, supposed to get here?"

"Any time now. I just hope this works. Gina's been so depressed lately."

"Yeah, well, if this Scott dude doesn't do the trick, I don't know what will."

A private airplane landed at McCarran Airport, and an astute-looking man in his late sixties was escorted from the plane to a waiting limousine with two young men with very large builds.

"Paradise Hotel," the older man barked at the driver.

"Yes, Mr. Santinello."

Luca Santinello stared out the tinted window as the limo traveled slowly along the I-15 Freeway toward the Strip. "Ricky," he said to one of the men, "Call Nick and Tony. Tell 'em I wanna meet with 'em tomorrow night. Make it someplace public – with a lot of people."

"Will do, boss," said Ricky, reaching for his cell phone.

The front entrance to the Paradise Hotel was blocked off to make room for the film crew. The team consisted of about two-dozen people, including Ellen, her assistant director Dave Barnes, Scott, and Jerry.

Heather sat in one of the director's chairs off to the side watching Scott and Jerry do the scene for the single camera.

Ellen's sharp eyes studied everything intently. "Action!"

The scene called for Scott to burst out of the hotel's revolving door, followed by an anxious Jerry, who pleads with Scott to let him explain why they'd both been shot at. Scott refuses to listen until Jerry gets down on one knee and declares his mock homosexual attraction to Scott in front of a large group of extras. The ploy works. Red-faced, Scott reluctantly allows a victorious Jerry to step into a waiting cab with him, and the cab tears out of the hotel driveway toward the Bellagio.

"Cut!" Ellen called at the end of the first take, and the crew and extras broke from their positions. "Reset for the next angle!"

Heather watched as the cab returned, much slower this time, and Scott and Jerry got out. "You almost made me laugh on that one!" Scott grinned. "I'm gonna kick your ass for that!"

"Don't look at *me*!" Jerry shot back. "I think you were just enjoying it too much!"

The two joined Heather.

"How was that one?" Jerry asked her.

"I thought it was great!" she enthused.

Jerry turned to Scott. "She was actually speaking to me, not you, so don't let it go to your head." He reached for a bottled water. "Man, I can't believe how hot it is here!"

"Yeah," said Scott, squinting in the bright sunlight. "By the way, Jerry, this is my sister, Heather."

Genuine disappointment. "Scott is your *brother*? I can only imagine what a burden that must be." Sexy smile. "Delighted."

Heather didn't take her eyes off him.

"Heather," said Scott, "They've got a show here called *Return to the Night*. It's supposed to feature a really good heavy metal group. You wanna go?"

"Sure!" He was making it too easy!

Scott threw Jerry a look. "I told you she would take some convincing."

"Such a complete lack of enthusiasm," Jerry agreed.

"We're going again!" Ellen called. "I need everybody back to one!"

Scott and Jerry set their water bottles down and strolled back in front of the camera.

Heather pulled out her cell phone and began texting.

Luca's limo bypassed the front entrance of the Paradise Hotel and made the first right turn onto a side road.

Luca exploded when he saw the crowd gathered around the film crew. "What the hell's goin' on here??"

"Film shoot, Mr. Santinello," Ricky explained stoically. "Nothing we could do. We're goin' in through the back."

"Idiots," Luca grumbled irritably. "A lot of crap."

Ricky put down his phone. "The two of them will meet you tomorrow night here in the Palm Grove Lounge at seven o'clock."

Luca nodded, pleased – although it was hard to tell. He grunted as the limo came to a stop in front of the back entrance and he was escorted inside.

The Paradise Hotel had three huge swimming pools, not including the wave pool.

Gina and Debbie were sprawled on lounge chairs in front of the largest one. After they'd been lying in the sun for some time, Debbie glanced over at Gina and realized that her cousin was asleep. Debbie smiled secretly and read the text that had just come in on her phone.

MY BROTHER'S READY. PUT PLAN INTO
ACTION. LOUNGE SHOW TOMORROW NIGHT.
CAN'T WAIT!

HEATHER

The Palm Grove Lounge of the Paradise Hotel was a huge three-story theatre with circular banquet tables, soft lights, and a stage that encompassed one entire wall. A closed lavender curtain completely concealed the stage area while tranquil music issued forth from hidden speakers.

The seating was at half capacity as people were still being ushered inside.

Scott and Heather were seated at a table near the front with Ellen Stellar, Jerry Garnett, and a few other people from the production.

Heather glanced behind her, scanning the room, then faced forward.

"Why do you keep doing that?" Scott demanded, looking at her strangely.

"What?" she asked, her face red.

"You keep looking behind you."

"I'm just admiring what these other girls are wearing," Heather said quickly, pretending to do so.

"Don't you own enough clothes? Your closet looks like a boutique."

"Now you sound like Dad."

"Thanks a lot!"

Gina and Debbie stood in line waiting to gain entry to the Palm Grove Lounge. Gina wore a tight fitting white dress, and Debbie a conservative blue one. Debbie's face was glowing, and she couldn't stop the smile that kept curling around her lips.

"What is *with* you?" Gina couldn't help asking.

"I'm just excited!"

"I know, but why?"

"Because we're here. And we're going to see Lisa."

Gina appeared nowhere near as ecstatic. "Well try not to get *too* exited. Or else the rest of your life will seem real boring."

When the line finally moved and the two girls were let inside, they were led to a table only a few tables away from where Scott and Heather sat.

"If we were any closer," Gina said, "We'd be *in* the show!"

Debbie smiled. "That's 'cuz we know the right people."

Gina leaned in closer to Debbie. "Is this the kind of show where all the guys take their clothes off?"

Debbie looked disappointed. "I don't know."

Gina shrugged. "Doesn't matter. I guess I'll stay, anyway."

Ellen turned to Jerry Garnett. "These Vegas shows aren't half as good as the ones I used to see here."

"When was *that*?"

"Maybe ten years ago. *Now*, it's just a lot of singing and stripping, but I remember when Siegfried and Roy were headlining. Now, *that* was a show!"

"I hear the illusionist is pretty good."

Ellen frowned dismissively.

Jerry grinned uncomfortably. "Well, if you don't care for the show, why did you want to come?"

Ellen was studying the dimensions of the stage. "There's a girl in the rock'n roll group I particularly wanted to see."

Luca Santinello had a table near the front but off to the side. "Make sure your suppliers get the cash before the product is delivered," he said to the two men sitting with him. "The receipts are comin' up short, and goods got a way of disappearin', know what I mean?"

Both men nodded in understanding as a young waitress in a skimpy outfit set their drinks down on the table and departed.

"I hope there's some hot babes in this show" one of the men commented, eyeing the stage with interest.

Luca carefully sipped his drink, his eyes darting around the immense room. "This is Vegas. What *else* would there be?"

The houselights went black, and a loud drum roll pierced the serenity of the lounge.

"Ladies and gentlemen," a deep male voice boomed over the sound system, "The Paradise Hotel Las Vegas proudly presents...*Return to the Night*...! Featuring Master Illusionist, Mark Trevor...the *Baby, That's Rock'n Roll!* Dancers...and our featured headliner – X-Rated Run!!"

Young girls cheered fiercely, their piercing cries nearly shattering glass.

The announcer continued, "And special guest performer, Valentina Ferris!"

"*Who*??" Gina asked, making a face at Debbie.

"Lisa's stage name," Debbie whispered back.

The audience clapped excitedly as the intro music swelled and the curtains opened.

From opposite sides of the stage, beautiful young men and women glided into view. The men were attired in classic tuxedos, and the women, elegant ball gowns. The performers partnered up, merging into a graceful display of adagio dancing and lyrical ballet.

The music increased its pace gradually, and as the rhythm escalated, the women casually shed their ball gown skirts and tops, until they were clad in only skimpy thongs. The men, slowly, methodically, discarded their jackets, shirts, and strip-away pants, until they were down to merely thongs and bowties.

From there, the movement progressed to a scintillating, upbeat combination of modern dance and Broadway-style jazz. When the number finished, the audience applauded wildly and the theatre went black.

"Ladies and gentlemen...the Paradise Hotel Las Vegas proudly presents...the triumphant return of master illusionist and acclaimed comic...Mark Trevor!"

More ecstatic applause as a large, round-faced man dressed in a tuxedo appeared on stage, and in time to the high-energy dance music, seemed to make a magic wand levitate in midair. Next, he conjured a beautiful female Asian assistant out of a dollhouse, then covered her in a white sheet and levitated her high above the stage floor until she disappeared from view.

The audience was exuberant!

The *Baby, That's Rock'n Roll!* Dancers were an energetic group of vocalists – four guys dressed in 50's bowling shirts and blue jeans, four girls dressed in tops, poodle skirts, and hair sashes. The eight young people danced, sang, and parodied their way through various 50's tunes. Ellen was watching one of the girls very closely.

The lounge lights dimmed.

Scott started to get up from the table.

Heather glared at him in alarm. "Where are you going??"

"To the bathroom," he said softly.

"Now??" she hissed.

He looked at her in surprise. "Yeah. I gotta *go*. You mind?"

He left her sitting there helplessly as another announcement filled the room.

"The Paradise Hotel Las Vegas is proud to present ... tonight's headliner...X-Rated Run!!"

A surge of young female screams exploded through the audience.

Luca Santinello and his companions cringed and scowled.

Steve Riken and his other band members, also skinny and long-haired, ran on stage.

Blaring heavy metal music ensued, much to the delight of the younger people and the dismay of their parents.

Gina and Debbie gleefully clapped along, resisting the urge to jump out of their chairs and dance.

Debbie barely noticed Scott Griffith leave his table and head out of the room. She tried to catch Heather's eye, but they were too far apart.

Lights flashed, and smoke filled the stage. Then the lights went out, and laser beams shot out toward the audience. The young people's excited screams grew, and the entire lounge exploded with ear-splitting applause.

A multitude of rainbow-colored lights swept over the stage as another announcement echoed forth. "Tonight's guest performer...Valetina Ferris...and her Rock Hard Rollers!"

More cheers arose from the frenzied onlookers as Lisa appeared on stage wearing a leopard-skin bikini top, bottoms, and brown fur boots. She cracked a whip in her hand as she paraded across the stage, and eight topless male dancers leaped on stage and twirled around her.

The attractive young men performed an acrobatic display of energetic dance moves while Lisa, wearing a headset mike, sang an original high-energy dance song called *Surrender Your Heart*. Her voice wasn't exceptional, and she had some noticeable trouble with a few of the notes, but the audience's response was ecstatic.

Luca Santinello sat at his table, fuming. "I've had enough of this crap," he grumbled, getting up. "A lot of noise!"

His two companions reluctantly stood and followed him out of the lounge.

It was during Lisa McClure's act that he saw her. He was just coming back from the restroom and heading towards his table when he looked over and saw Gina sitting next to Debbie. His eyes rested on her for a moment, although she didn't look in his direction. Then he smiled and headed towards her table.

It was during Lisa McClure's act that he saw her. He and his associates were just starting out of the room when he looked over and spotted her in the dark. She was sitting next to another girl and enjoying the show, unaware that he was watching her. Realizing he was blocking some people's view, he stepped out of the way and left the lounge, the other two men following him. Neither of them could see the hatred in his eyes.

When Lisa finished her number, the crowd went wild.

Gina and Debbie clapped excitedly, standing up and cheering.

The lights went down again, and Gina felt a hand touch her shoulder.

She turned.

Scott's eyes twinkled. "Any chance I could talk to you?"

"Scott!" Her eyes bugged out. "What are you - ?"

"Show's almost over. If you come with me, you can beat the crowd."

He offered his hand. Shaking, she took it.

"I'm gonna hang out with Lisa when this is done," Debbie said. "I'll see you back in the room."

Gina nodded and allowed Scott to lead her out of the lounge.

Just before the next comedian took the stage, Debbie rose, hurried over to Heather's table, and sat in the chair Scott had occupied. Debbie smiled. "I think it worked."

"I'll say!" Heather said, checking to see that Scott and Gina were really gone. "Better than we hoped!"

Luca stood in the center of his suite, gazing out the window and talking on a cell phone. "Naw, naw. The show wasn't that good...not for two-hundred bucks a pop...! I tell ya, it ain't like the old days..."

A discreet knock at the door immediately drew his attention.

"I'll call ya back," he muttered into the phone before disconnecting and slipping the instrument into his pocket. "Yeah?" he called sharply, taking a step toward the double doors.

One of them opened, and a large man in a suit stuck his head inside. "Mr. Santinello, sir? Somebody out here wants to see ya."

"At *this* hour? Who?"

A party was going on in Steve Riken's suite. Mostly young people, some even teenagers, and performers from the show. Despite the raucous music playing from hidden speakers, there were elegant buffet tables, wait staff, and lots of liquor.

Lisa was now wearing a country-western fringe blouse, tight rodeo jeans, and cowgirl boots. She made her way down a narrow hallway and knocked tentatively on one of the bathroom doors. "Deb? You okay in there? Yer spookin' me out."

On the other side of the door, Lisa could hear Debbie retching, then the sound of the toilet flushing. The door opened, and Lisa was staring at Debbie, whose face was white and her eyes clouded.

"Deb! What's wrong?"

"I don't know," Debbie said, coughing, her voice hoarse. "I just feel sick...I was fine a little while ago, and now I feel like I just wanna die!"

A thin, long-haired girl wearing a midriff squeezed past them into the bathroom and closed the door. Lisa pulled Debbie closer. "Don't go trippin', okay, Deb? What did you take?"

"Take?" Debbie scowled. "I didn't take anything! I think it might be something I ate."

Lisa placed a comforting hand on Debbie's shoulder. "Do you wanna lie down? You can use the big bedroom."

Debbie shivered. "I just wanna go back to my room. Can you get Heather for me?"

Lisa nodded, her face full of genuine concern. "I'll be right back."

*   *   *

Gina admired the view from Scott's suite as he came up behind her carrying two glasses of Coke. She took hers and continued staring out the window. "It's gorgeous!"

"*You're* gorgeous." He sipped his drink, unable to keep his eyes off her.

"You don't drink, do you?"

His gaze fell. "No. Do you mind?"

She shook her head, starting down the stairs into the sumptuous living room. "It's just a little strange."

"For a guy?"

"For an actor. I thought all you guys were into sex, drugs, and liquor."

Scott shrugged. "One out of three."

They were at the bottom now and strolling toward the couch.

He looked at her, almost like he was going to say something, and then reconsidered. "I'm really glad you're here."

Her smile was contagious. "I said I would be."

And they were kissing – almost forgetting about the glasses in their hands.

Luca's glare was hideous. "I oughta beat your ass!"

Frank Dinato was shaking. "Please, Mr. Santinello. It almost came off. I don't know what happened."

"You screwed up, that's what the hell happened!" He sipped the drink in his hand. "Someone else'll do the job."

Frank appeared to relax. "Thanks. Ya got any work?" The look in Luca's eye made him flinch. "Just some distributin'. Nothin' heavy. I ain't had a hit in weeks, and I'm runnin' low. I had to drive out here."

Luca's expression was milder, and he almost seemed to smile. "'Course. I got loyalty to the boys who been good to me." He set his drink down and moved closer to Frank. "Eddie and Charlie'll take ya to an apartment I got here. Ya can get cleaned up 'till I get some more stuff in. Soon as it comes, I want you back to work." He motioned to Frank's pocket. "Keep that cell phone on."

"Yes, Mr. Santinello," Frank said politely. "Thank you, sir."

*   *   *

Heather helped Debbie into the suite Debbie was sharing with Gina. Debbie's color was starting to return, but she still seemed a little unsteady.

Heather quietly closed the door. "How ya doin'?"

Debbie cleared her throat. "I'm just sorry I had to make you leave the party early."

Heather followed her into the suite's plush living room. "It was okay. That Steve Riken is really hot, but it still doesn't compare to Laurel Gillis' party!"

Debbie took a seat on the couch, grinning. "Oh, yeah! I will never forget the fight in the swimming pool!"

Heather sat across from her. "And of course I had to miss it."

"Where were you, anyway?"

Heather blushed. "I was with that scumbag."

"Oh. Have you talked to him?"

"Not since that day at his apartment," Heather said angrily. "I know he took advantage of me. Pure and simple."

Debbie clutched her stomach, taking a deep breath.

"Are you sure you don't want me to call a doctor?" Heather asked.

"No," Debbie said emphatically, her voice strained. "I'll be fine. And after what we went through to get Gina and Scott together, I don't want anything to mess it up."

Luca watched as Frank was escorted out of his suite by two imposing men.

The second, larger man closed the door but stayed in the room. He turned to Luca expectantly. "Any special instructions, Mr. Santinello?"

Luca's mouth was set in a grim line. His eyes narrowed. "Take care of it."

CHAPTER 16

Luca's two men kept Frank between them as they entered P6 of the hotel's subterranean parking garage.

Another man was waiting beside a silver Lincoln, and a fourth was seated behind the wheel.

Frank scanned all the men's faces.

They weren't smiling.

He looked at the one who had just opened the front passenger side door.

The man was watching Frank closely.

Too closely.

"Hop in, Frank," the guy behind him said mildly.

Frank took only one step toward the car before bolting towards the nearest exit.

Two of the men were on his heels instantly.

"Frank!" one of them called. "Where ya goin'?"

The man standing by the car door shouted, "Get him!"

Frank darted into a stairwell and flew up the stairs. He pelted to the top of the first landing and raced through another doorway onto P5. Two groups of hotel guests were heading toward their cars.

Frank slowed and fell into step alongside them.

The two men who had followed him through the stairwell watched helplessly as Frank blended with one of the vacationer groups and disappeared into an elevator.

"How the hell did he get away from you?" Luca roared into his cell phone.

"We're on him, Mr. Santinello," one of the taller men gasped, running through the parking garage. "We've got the exits covered. He won't get out."

*   *   *

Sunlight gradually filled the high-ceilinged bedroom as they lay naked and sprawled in the over-sized bed.

Scott awoke first. When he looked up and saw Gina, he slid his arm around her and cuddled closer.

Gina's eyes fluttered open and she stared at him. She looked neither happy nor surprised. Just pensive.

He broke into a smile first. "Good morning," he said, kissing her lightly on the cheek. "How did you sleep?"

"Like a baby."

"Wet and crying?"

Her eyes narrowed.

He glanced out the window. Even in the morning, the view of the Las Vegas Strip was spectacular. "I just wanna stay here all day. All *week*."

"Do you have to work today?"

He shook his head. "Even *Ellen* lets us have Sundays off." Scott moved on top of her and they kissed. "I'm all yours."

Alarm filled Gina's eyes. "Oh my God! Debbie! I completely forgot about her!"

"Relax. I'm sure she made it back to the room all right. Besides, she was with Heather. They couldn't have gotten in *too* much trouble."

"Still, I should text her."

Scott rolled off of Gina and lay beside her. "Do you want her to know exactly where you are?"

"Like they don't know! They planned this whole thing!"

Scott rested his index finger over his lips. "Ssshh. That's a secret."

"I would never *tell* them. It would break Debbie's heart if she found out you overheard your sister talking."

"It's not *my* fault. Heather's voice carries. And when I heard her mention your name, I had to find out what she was talking about."

"Is that why you called me?"

Scott hesitated. "I wanted to see you again. I wasn't sure if you wanted to see me – until you agreed to play along. Then I knew that maybe...there might be a chance."

Gina shook her head. "There was just...a lot of stuff going on with me then. Now that that whole nightmare is over, I just want to get on with my life."

"Does that include me?"

Gina grinned slyly. "Maybe...if you're lucky..."

The Las Vegas Strip lay sprawled far below them as the compact helicopter careened over high-rise hotels and neon lights. Scott, Gina, and Debbie sat in the back, and Heather sat up front with the pilot.

When they'd reached the end of the Strip, the chopper swung east and headed out toward the Mojave Desert. The ground became more arid and the horizon blurry as they flew over miles and miles of barren acreage with minimal plant life.

The roar inside the cockpit was muffling, so verbal communication was only possible through the headsets each of them wore.

"Scott?" Gina's voice was soft, although everyone else in the compartment could hear her. "We're going awfully far. You're not going to leave me out here, are you?" She sounded like she was half-joking.

"This is all part of a plot," Scott said smoothly. "To kidnap you." He pointed to the pilot. "He's in on it."

Smiling, Scott and Gina held hands as they watched the ground become more cracked and creviced. The wide-open land gave way to deep canyons and rocky surfaces.

And onward they traveled.

Debbie looked behind them.

The city of Las Vegas had vanished.

"I like the way you guys made me sit up *here*," Heather grinned from her cramped space in the front.

"It's 'cuz you're the smallest," Scott reminded her. "With *me* back here, I'm just glad this thing didn't have trouble taking off."

"How fast are we going?" Heather asked the pilot.

The man's eyes didn't stray from the sky. "We're cruising at about a hundred and fifty miles an hour."

"How long till we get there?" Debbie asked.

"We should be in Arizona in about twenty minutes."

      *   *   *

The Grand Canyon was unmistakable. Several miles wide and encompassing the entire region before them. None of the travelers said much to each other, just took in the extraordinary sight. The sky and mountains resembled a painting - the canyon itself, a special effect from a movie. The helicopter gingerly swept over the side of the canyon, enabling them to look almost a thousand feet down into the giant chasm. A tranquil river flowed through the bottom of the canyon, and it looked as though not another sign of life existed down there.

The helicopter circled the canyon once, then landed in a clearing about a hundred feet from the cliff's edge.

"Everybody stay seated," the pilot instructed. "As soon as we get clearance, we're gonna head down."

Gina and Debbie exchanged glances.

Scott grinned excitedly.

When they rose into the air again, the helicopter slowly descended into the valley until it landed at the very bottom of the canyon. A camp and tarp was already set up, and the pilot unloaded a crate of bottled water, champagne, and snacks.

Debbie and Gina climbed out of the cockpit and immediately gasped, taking deep breaths.

"Oh my God!" Debbie's eyes were wide.

Gina stared upward in disbelief. "It's like a sauna down here!"

Heather turned to the pilot, concerned. "How hot is it?"

The man was setting out rows of bottled water. "It's about a hundred twenty-seven."

"Degrees??"

He nodded. "I advise you all to drink some water and stay close to the camp. Nobody go wandering off."

Gina turned to Debbie. "My God! It was a hundred and fifteen in Vegas, and that was bad enough!"

"What about *you*, bro?" Heather asked Scott. "*You* like the heat. Hot enough for you?"

Scott regarded Heather gravely. "I *do* like heat...but this is even too much for *me*."

"We'd *better* stay close to the camp," Gina said, staring up at the mountainous canyon walls. "This heat is almost dangerous."

"I'm gonna go get some water," Debbie said, climbing back towards the tarp.

"Get me one," Gina called.

Scott stumbled up a low embankment, careful not to connect with any of the cacti.

Heather slid up beside Gina, keeping her voice low. "Can you imagine if you were ever *left* down here? What do you think your chances of making it back to civilization would be?"

Gina took another deep breath, her face flushed. "Probably none." She scowled. "You *would* have to think of something like that."

"Hey – reality."

Gina looked up and realized that Scott was standing several yards away from them – and moving further away. "Scott..." She was finding it hard to breathe. "Don't go too far..."

Seeing the panic on her face, Scott headed back in their direction, slowly making his way down the steep incline.

"Listen." Heather held up her hand. "It's so quiet out there."

Gina stared, unblinking, at the top of the canyon, then the bottom. "Yeah. Now I know why they call this Death Valley."

Heather followed Gina back up the slope. "You're so negative!"

The man standing next to Luca was a few years younger, but just as hard-edged. They stood behind a bank of T.V. monitors, each screen displaying a black and white image of different locations within the Paradise Hotel casino. The only light in the room was the glow from the monitors.

"You sure he didn't get out?" Luca asked, his eyes surveying several of the screens.

"We had all the exits and stairwells covered since last night," the man assured him, watching Luca carefully. "He tries to slip out, one of our boys'll grab him."

The helicopter landed on the tarmac at the small municipal heliport just as a pelting rain fell from the overcast sky.

Gina, Debbie, and Heather ran straight for the terminal while Scott tipped the pilot.

"We *almost* made it," Scott said, holding his hand over his face as he followed the girls inside.

*   *   *

The hotel maid unlocked the storage room filled with sweepers and cleaning fluids, and snapped on the light. She immediately noticed the disheveled man curled up and sleeping on the floor. Shrieking and shouting in Spanish, she ran from the room and reached for her hand-held walki-talki.

Frank woke up, scrambled off the floor, and scurried in the other direction.

Scott, Gina, Debbie, and Heather slipped in the back entrance of the hotel and headed for the bank of elevators. Their clothes were still soaking wet from the rain.

"Compliments of the hotel," Heather quipped. "A free outdoor shower."

"Dad wouldn't care," Scott added. "He'd say it was water he didn't have to pay for."

"I'm starved," Gina said, smoothing down her wet hair. "Where do you guys wanna eat?"

"Doesn't matter," Scott shrugged. "As long as it's indoors."

Luca nursed a cocktail as he stood staring at the driving rain against the windows of his suite. He gazed pensively into space, recalling sitting in the back of his limousine with three of his bodyguards back in New York. A cell phone had gone off, startling him. Luca had scowled, taking the phone from one of the men.

"Never will get used to these damn things," Luca had muttered, reluctantly taking the phone.

Still staring at the rain, Luca remembered his last meeting with Frank Dinato the night before. *"When it comes in," Luca had said, "I want you back to work." He had motioned to Frank's pocket. "Keep that cell phone on."*

Luca raised the glass to his lips and stopped. His eyes widened. He set the drink down on a table, pulled out his cell phone and dialed. "Santinello...lemme talk to him...Jimmy...? Somethin' I want ya to do..."

"When are you guys done?" Gina asked, picking at her salad.

Scott grabbed up his fork and began twirling his Fettucini Alfredo. "We're supposed to wrap on Thursday. We leave for London a week from Monday."

"That is so cool!" Debbie chirped. "A location shoot in Europe!"

"It's not a vacation," Gina reminded her. "He's going to be there to work."

"But still!"

Heather glanced around the elegant hotel restaurant, turning to Scott. "You're doing locations in London?"

Scott shook his head. "That's only our stopover. First we go to Madrid, then southern France, Athens, and more interior shooting in - "

"Athens!" Debbie nearly choked on her soup.

"Don't even think about it," Gina admonished, shooting her a look.

"I've never even *been* to Europe," said Scott. "This'll be my first time."

"When was the last time you said *that*?" Heather smirked.

"Did you get your passport?" Gina asked.

Scott nodded. "All done. Now we just have to shoot this film."

Gina sipped her Coke. "Should be a hell of a movie!" Teasing. "It almost sounds like you're playing James Bond."

Scott tried to stifle his smile. "James Bondage."

Jimmy Siegel strode briskly down the hotel corridor, Luca by his side, two bodyguards behind them. In Jimmy's right hand was a cell phone with a GPS display and a red dot that bleeped on and off the tiny screen.

"Your boy is dumber than we thought," Jimmy muttered, his eyes fixed on the digital readout. He pointed to the screen. "He left his cell phone on. Every time I call it, it transmits a signal to the communication relay. He's on this floor. I should have his exact location in a couple minutes."

The fire in Luca's eyes flared as all four men quickened their pace.

The signal from the phone grew louder and more frequent.

They had reached the door to a men's room.

Jimmy and Luca stopped. The two bodyguards stepped in front of them, drawing their guns and pushing the door open.

The restroom was empty.

Jimmy pushed another button on the phone.

The sound of a cell phone going off from across the room.

The four of them moved closer and stared.

The ringing cell phone lay innocently on the sink.

Gina, Scott, Debbie, and Heather piled out of the hotel restaurant and looked anxiously about.

"Do you guys wanna check out the casino?" Heather asked, her eyes gleaming.

"You guys go," Scott said. "Me and Gina are going to take a walk around the hotel."

"Oooh," Heather teased. "Sounds like they want to be alone."

Debbie nodded primly. "That's what it sounds like to me."

Scott pretended to be angry. "I'm gonna give you guys till the count of three..."

"We'll see you later," Debbie said quickly.

"Just don't get caught in there," Gina said. "You guys aren't twenty-one."

"Neither are you," Debbie retorted.

"Say it a little louder," Heather said, annoyed.

When the girls were gone, Scott and Gina headed past the lobby and down an extraordinarily wide carpeted corridor.

"It seems like we just got here," Gina commented. "Deb and I'll be heading back the day after tomorrow."

"I'm excited about this location shoot," Scott said. "But I'm gonna miss you."

Gina took his arm. "You'll be back in two months. You're going to shoot a movie, not off to war."

Scott appeared thoughtful. "Our last location is London. Then we fly back. We have to stop off in New York. I just won't come back with everybody else."

"Will you have time?"

"About a week. Then *Right On* starts shooting again."

"Then I can see you *then*."

"Maybe not."

Gina looked at him expectantly.

Scott stopped and they stood facing each other. "I want you to come to Europe with me."

Gina's eyes widened. "Are you crazy?"

"You already know I am," he said calmly. "But I'm very serious. Why should we be apart if we don't want to be?"

"I can think of a lot of reasons."

"Like what?"

"Well..." She thought carefully. "For one thing, you're there to work. When would I ever see you?"

He held her. "You forget about the nights. We'd be together."

She still seemed unconvinced.

"And I'll have some days off. Think about it – Europe! Greece...Spain...London...How many chances are we gonna get like this?"

Her face was glowing.

They resumed their stroll past the giant hospitality rooms on both sides, which weren't in use at the moment. "I can cover your plane tickets, if you want," Scott added.

"I can pay my own way, Scott, that's not what I'm worried about."

"So what *are* you worried about? Having too much fun? Spending every night with *me*? Afraid you might actually enjoy yourself for - ?"

"All right, Scott! All right. I'll go."

"You mean it?"

"Are you calling me a liar?"

He turned to her. "You know what?"

"What?"

Scott grabbed her, lifted her into the air and spun her around. "We - are going - to Europe!"

Gina shrieked and laughed. "Put me down!"

He set her down gently. "It's gonna be great, Gina! I promise you!"

She was beaming. "I know."

He hugged her tightly. "Now that I have you back, I'm not letting you go."

She feigned discomfort. "You're gonna *have* to let me go," she gurgled, pretending to be stifled. "I can't breathe..."

Scott released her and looked at her seriously. "I mean – can we try again?"

Her smile radiated warmth. "We can do better than that!"

Scott kissed her and held her. Then he looked out the exit doors leading outside the hotel. The heavy rain was still coming down. "There is no *way* I'm going out there!" Scott asserted.

"Wuss," Gina teased.

He slid his arm around her shoulder and steered her in the opposite direction. "Hey, I have an idea! Why don't we go back up to your room and think of something fun to do?"

"I don't know," Gina said with mock uncertainty. "I don't think I like the sound of that."

"Oh, sure! It'll be great! Strip Go-Fish...Naked Twister..."

The two of them disappeared back into the casino arm in arm.

Neither of them noticed the slim figure, wearing a hat and jacket, only a few feet behind them.

Frank Dinato waited until Scott and Gina reached the lobby before following them to the elevator banks.

Caesar Camarari sat in his living room barking into his cell phone. "I don't care how many degrees you got on your wall! You pull one more stunt like that, you'll be the Executive Director of a fast food joint!"

Caesar disconnected and tossed the phone on the couch.

Nina, lying at Caesar's feet, looked up, startled.

Carol sat in the easy chair across from him, leafing through a textbook on graphic art.

"Unbelievable!" Caesar spat. "I hire him to head one of our biggest divisions, and he makes a bid on a job with *my* money – doesn't even check with anybody!"

Carol nodded her acknowledgement, her eyes quickly dropping back down to her book.

The cell phone chimed.

Grumbling, Caesar reached for the annoying device. "What...? You gotta be kiddin' me...no...I'll take care of it." Caesar hit CALL END and quickly dialed another number. "Tony! Book me on the first flight to Vegas from L.A." Hitting CALL END again, Caesar sprang from the couch and glanced at Carol as he headed upstairs. "Gina's in Vegas. So is Santinello."

CHAPTER 17

Lightning broke the sky over Vegas as the thunder rumbled fiercely and the rain mercilessly thrashed the streets and hotels.

Inside the sumptuous hotel room, they took no notice of the storm as they moved, naked and entwined in each other's arms. They explored each other slowly, getting to know one another again. Changing positions, he allowed her to lead him. He lay back, looking up at her, and their bodies again melted into one.

Lightning flashed, and their kisses grew more urgent as her body responded to his. Their pace increased, and he joined her willingly, beginning their ascent. She slowed him down, fighting for control, torturing him with her teasing rhythm. He moaned loudly, spreading his legs wider, his head sinking deeper into the pillow.

His hands gripped the sides of the sheet as she continued the pressure, gradually moving faster on top of him. He couldn't stop himself from crying out.

Shoring himself up, he grabbed her and kissed her, and they fell back onto the bed. He slowly massaged her body, gently moving downward, his lips hungrily devouring hers. She caressed his fine blond hair, her hands traveling down his back and squeezing him tight. He knelt in front of her, carefully straddling her until his essence fused with hers. She joined him in his release while the rain continued to pound outside.

Heather was so intent on the slot machine she was playing, she barely noticed Debbie standing next to her.

"Heather, I'm going to go upstairs," she said weakly. "I'm not feeling so good."

There was concern in Heather's voice, but her eyes remained focused on the machine. "Not again. Are you sure you don't want to see a doctor?"

"I don't think so. I just want to go back to the room and rest. I'll call you tomorrow."

Heather glanced at Debbie, at the same time hitting the button for another play. "Okay."

Gina and Scott lay side by side, naked, in bed. The bedroom was still dark, and he held her tenderly in his arms.

"Debbie's gonna freak when I tell her," Gina said softly.

"Yeah," Scott agreed. "My dad's not gonna be too thrilled, though. But it's not like we're running off and getting married. You're just coming with me on a business trip."

"We could, you know," Gina said innocently.

"Could what?"

"Get married. I think there's a wedding chapel down the street."

"There's a wedding chapel on every block." He looked at her for a moment.

She grinned. "Scott, I'm only kidding."

"I know. But if I *did* decide to get married..."

Caesar Camarari strode through the hotel casino with a large muscular man who looked to be in his early forties.

"Did you tell him we're comin'?" Caesar asked, his eyes darting everywhere.

"He knows we're meeting, he just doesn't know why."

"He just better not have done anything yet, or he's dead."

Caesar started toward the Paradise Hotel's bank of guest elevators, but the other man redirected him. "There's a private elevator we can use. Take us right to his office."

Caesar warily followed him toward the indistinguishable mirror-paneled elevator door, which slid open when the man held up a fob. Caesar hesitated, then stepped in first. The man joined him, scanned the fob again, and touched an illuminated button marked "M." The elevator rose so smoothly, it hardly felt like they were moving.

"You realize we can only ask," the other man murmured, staring straight ahead. "We can't *make* him tell us anything."

"The hell we can't."

The man glanced sideways at Caesar, then faced him directly. "Why, Caesar? Why do you want to nail Santinello so bad? Just because he deals in narcotics?"

Caesar's face was a mask of thunder. He turned to the other man, very slowly, and stared at him for a long moment. "Ya wanna know? I'll tell ya. That scum killed my brother. And now he's tryin' to get to my brother's *daughter*! And if Santinello is in this hotel – right now – I'm gonna find 'im!"

Debbie dragged herself over to the door of the suite, despite the insistent knocking from the other side. When she opened it, Lisa McClure breezed into the suite as if she owned it. "You don't answer your cell phone, you don't return my texts. On top of that, you left my party early. What kind of a friend are you?"

Lisa stopped when she took in Debbie's disheveled appearance. Debbie was dressed in her pajamas, and her hair looked like she'd been sleeping on it for days.

"Oh, Deb. I didn't realize it was that bad."

Debbie trudged into the living room like it took every ounce of her strength to do so. "I thought it would pass, but I still feel like crap."

Lisa trailed behind her. "Do you want me to get the hotel doctor?"

"No doctors. I just want to rest."

"What do you think you have?"

"It's the weirdest thing. The slightest odor makes me vomit, and I can't seem to hold any food down."

"Are your boobs tender?"

Debbie looked at her strangely.

"Do your legs hurt?"

Debbie's eyes were wider.

"Debbie...when was your last cycle?"

"Don't even joke about that! I am *not* pregnant!"

"Well, there's only one way to find out. And I think the gift shops are still open."

"Don't be ridiculous! If I was pregnant, I would know it."

"*How* would you know it? Have you been pregnant many times before?"

"Of course not! Lisa, you know me. I would *never* do anything so stupid."

*   *   *

Heather stepped off the elevator and headed briskly down the hotel corridor.

One of the doors to the numerous rooms opened and Miles stepped out.

For a moment, they both froze, staring at one another as if they'd never met and never wanted to – he in a brown suit and tie, she in a tight-fitting black dress and diamond earrings.

He took a deep breath and started toward her. "Heather - "

She brushed past him and quickened her pace, but he wasn't having it. In an instant his strong hand was on her arm and she spun around to face him, glaring at him with malice.

"Heather, wait a minute - "

"Get your hands off me," she seethed. "Now!"

"Not until you let me explain - "

"I mean now!" she blazed, pushing him off her. "I don't care about your damn explanations! Do you get it?? I don't care!!"

She started to turn again, but he blocked her path. "You gotta listen to me, Heather! Please!"

Now his hand was on her shoulder.

Something in his voice made her stay. "I gotta talk to you."

Scott slipped on his shirt and tucked it in.

Gina entered the living room fully dressed. "Sure," she teased. "Now that you got what you wanted, you're running out on me."

"Just until we leave for Europe."

He smiled, and they kissed.

"I'm gonna check on Heather," he explained. "Then I've got to get some sleep before tomorrow. Me and Jerry shoot our next scene in the morning."

"You can sleep here," Gina said demurely.

"Oh, right! If I stay, I won't get out of here till next Tuesday."

"Bragger!" She regarded him affectionately, and they kissed again.

"Come down to the set tomorrow," he suggested.

Gina nodded. "Soon as I wake up." She followed him to the door. "I don't know *where* Debbie is. I thought she'd be back by now."

"She's probably still with Heather – prowling casinos. You know this town. It never sleeps. But *I* have to." Scott stood at the open door. "Well...I'll see you tomorrow."

"You will."

His stare was intoxicating. "I love you."

Her eyes twinkled. "I love you, too. Good night."

"You mean good *morning*."

She beamed as she closed the door behind him and headed into the living room.

Lisa paced outside the closed bathroom door inside her suite. "How ya doin' in there, Deb?"

No reply.

Lisa returned to her pacing.

The bathroom door opened and Debbie appeared, her step slow and her face white.

Lisa's mouth dropped open. "Oh, no!"

Debbie stared at Lisa, the fear growing in her delicate eyes. "Lisa, you cannot tell anybody about this," she said evenly. "Not even Gina."

To Debbie's surprise, Lisa was shaking. "No. I won't tell anybody." She followed Debbie into the living room. "Deb, I don't believe this!"

Debbie was strangely calm as she reached the center of the room.

"So...who's the father?"

Debbie's eyes widened as she flashed onto Rick, then Brian. She glanced at Lisa helplessly. "I...I have no idea..."

Gina was on her way into the bedroom when she heard a distinctive knock at the door. Groaning in mock annoyance, she hurried over to the door. Another familiar knock. "I'm coming!" she called out, reaching the door and opening it. "I thought you said you were tir - "

Frank pushed the door open, knocking her to the ground and pointing a revolver in her face. "Make one sound and you're dead!"

CHAPTER 18

Scott quietly entered his suite and realized the door to Heather's bedroom was open, even though the lights were out.

"Heather?" He moved closer to the threshold and peered inside. "Heather?" It was empty.

He pulled out his cell phone, dialed, and listened.

His sister's voice. "Hi! You've reached Heather! Leave me a - "

He snapped it off, took another look around, and headed for the door.

"Get up!" Frank growled, waving the gun threateningly at Gina.

Her eyes bulging, Gina scrambled to her feet and kept her hands visible. "Frank...please...I'll do anything you say..."

"Get away from the door!"

She backed into the sunken living room, carefully keeping her distance from him. "I thought you were dead - "

"I need money, Gina." His voice was low. "I've gotta get outta the country. Santinello is tryin' to kill me."

Gina glanced toward the bedroom. "I have some in my purse - "

"I don't mean your play money! Get your card! We're goin' to an ATM...and you're gonna withdraw the limit...you owe me...after the hell you put me through..."

Gina nodded, and the two of them started into the bedroom.

A loud knock at the door.

Gina and Frank spun around, each panicked.

Frank glared at her. "Don't even think about it."

Knocking – more urgent this time. "Gina?" they heard Scott call through the door. "Gina, let me in. I've gotta talk to you."

"Who is he?" Frank hissed.

"He's a friend," Gina whispered lamely. "He just left. If I don't answer, he's gonna *know* something's wrong."

Another forceful knock.

Gina's body moved instinctively toward the sound, but Frank held her back.

She met his fierce gaze expectantly.

His fingers pressed hard into her arm as he propelled her toward the door. She wriggled in vain from the pain, nearly stumbling as she reached the door.

Frank released her and aimed the gun at her heart. "You try one trick," he muttered, "And I'll kill you both."

Gina watched as he slowly stepped behind the door, and she opened it a crack. Scott started inside, but she stopped him. "What is it?"

"Heather's not back. Is Debbie here?"

"No," Gina said irritably, "But I've got to get some sleep right now, Scott. Check with Joannie or Jason. They were with her when she left."

Scott stared at Gina strangely, but she started to close the door.

"I've got to get to bed, okay?"

"Uh – yeah." He nodded uncertainly and stepped back.

"Thanks," she said with forced pleasantness. "I'll talk to you tomorrow."

Gina closed the door, and she and Frank stood waiting for several seconds, listening intently. They heard some movement in the hallway – then nothing.

"I think he's gone," Gina said, her voice barely audible.

Frank smirked, his eyes almost radiating admiration. "You played that one beautifully, babe. Shame you had to screw with me." He waved the gun toward the bedroom. "C'mon – let's get mommy's credit card."

*   *   *

Jimmy Siegel feigned confusion – and not very well. "I'd like ta help ya, Mr. Camarari, but we got a lot of guests comin' in and out of this hotel."

Caesar sat on the edge of the chair facing Jimmy's desk, a dark look in his piercing eyes. "Listen, Seigel. I know Santinello is here. Right now. So unless you want a death here tonight, you're gonna keep that rotten bastard away from my niece till I can get her the hell out of here!"

Gina stepped outside her room and secured the door, closely followed by Frank, who shielded the gun under his jacket. She turned and started down the hall, but Frank stopped her.

"Naw, naw. No elevators. We're takin' the stairs."

She obediently proceeded in the opposite direction, trembling with every step. The corridor was deserted, and neither of them heard a sound coming from any of the rooms.

Frank continued shooting looks down the hall to see if anyone was behind them.

When they reached the stairwell door, Frank waved her inside and fell behind her like a shadow.

Inside the empty stairwell, Gina slowly descended the hospital-white steps, trying to watch Frank and where she was going at the same time. She nearly tripped just before the first landing, steadying herself on the handrail and moving carefully.

As they reached the second landing, the stairwell door opened and one of Luca's men, Charlie, appeared.

Charlie reached under his coat.

Frank pointed his gun at Charlie.

Gina ducked under Frank's arm and bolted up the stairs.

Frank fired at Charlie, hitting him in the chest before Charlie's fingers closed on his own gun.

Charlie crumpled to the ground.

Frank looked up to see Gina pelting towards the next landing and shouted, "Get back here!"

He spun around and darted up the stairs after her.

Gina reached the landing and desperately pulled on the door handle.

The door didn't open.

She turned and fled up the following flight of stairs – Frank only a few steps behind her.

*   *   *

Luca strode through the lobby of the Paradise Hotel accompanied by two of his largest bodyguards.

From several feet away, behind a high bank of slot machines, Caesar and four tall, muscular men watched the other three men approach the elevators.

Caesar gave his four men a discreet motion with his hand, and the five of them moved in quickly.

Caesar's four men overtook Luca's two, sticking their guns into the stomachs of their adversaries and quietly moving them out of the way.

Luca's eyes widened in amazement as Caesar shoved him inside the elevator, pushed him against the wall, and pointed a gun under his chin.

The elevator doors closed behind them, and the cab started upward.

"You son of a bitch!" Caesar raged. "Where is she?? You tell me where she is right now, you dirty bastard, or you're dead!!"

Frank pushed the heavy metal door open and let himself out onto the roof of the hotel. The gun still poised in his hand, he scanned the vast unenclosed area, the lights from the other hotels twinkling all around him.

"Gina!" Frank yelled, his eyes as dark as the night. "I know you're up here! I won't hurt you! But if you make me come lookin' for you, you're gonna pay!"

Only the noise of the traffic below and the night wind answered him.

His hair blowing in his face, Frank prowled the dark rooftop, several protruding enclosures impairing his view. He stepped carefully around different pipes and vents as he slowly crossed the precarious surface.

Her back pressed against a nearby wall, Gina closed her eyes and held her breath, struggling not to move. She heard Frank's light footsteps and could almost feel him getting nearer. Her legs weakened as she scanned the area around her. There was no means of her escaping without Frank seeing her.

Frank moved stealthily in Gina's direction, although he could barely see where he was going.

A hum drew Frank's attention to the other side of the roof, and he turned and headed away from where Gina was hiding.

Gina stole a look around the corner to see Frank's retreating back. Then she slid behind the wall of the cooling unit and carefully made her way toward the stairwell door. She hit her leg on a pipe sticking out of the rooftop, but Frank was too far away to hear, so she kept moving.

Gina looked everywhere, but she couldn't see Frank. Only the Vegas lights shimmered around her. She was still a distance away from the stairwell door, but she didn't dare run. Gina was forced to traipse over more pipes and around large generators, but Frank was still several yards away.

In the distance, Gina could hear cars and people yelling, but the shouts were soon followed by obnoxious laughter. Breathing heavily, she looked up to see the stairwell entrance only a few feet away. Gina glanced behind her quickly. It was very dark. Frank was nowhere in sight.

Gina leaped over a raised beam and sprinted toward the stairwell door, not caring about the noise her shoes made on the cement. She tripped and fell, but scrambled back up again.

An iron grip pulled on her arm, twisting it back and forcing her to face him.

"I told you not to mess with me!" Frank thundered, grabbing Gina's shoulder with his other hand and propelling her past the stairwell entrance. "I didn't wanna do this, Gina...but I'm not gonna give up *my* life for *yers!*"

"No!" Gina screamed, unable to fight him. "Frank! No! Please! Stop!"

He savagely squeezed her wrist. "Shut up! You make any more noise, I'm gonna make this as painful as hell!"

She tried kicking out at him, but he was too strong. He held her fast as they reached the edge of the roof. Gina could see the lights, people, and cars below them on the Strip. It was almost like a blur dancing before her eyes.

Frank pushed her forward, but she steadied and straightened herself as best she could.

Frank's hold on her grew stronger. "This is the cleanest way to do it," he gasped ferociously, gripping her around the waist and grabbing one of her legs. "It'll be over before you - "

Her elbow caught him in the face, and he released her and staggered back. She was already a few steps away when he had her by the arm again. Gina's cries died in the wind as Frank shoved her over to the side, picked her up, and maneuvered her over the edge.

She clung to the ledge as her feet scraped the side of the building, hunching frantically to keep her arms over the railing.

Frank pulled on one of her wrists and tried to pry her hand off the bar when he was yanked from behind and smashed in the mouth. Gina looked up to see Scott standing over Frank.

"Ya freakin' pansy!" Frank scrambled up and rushed Scott, pushing him on the ground and pummeling his face. Scott squirmed away, shielding himself from the blows.

Gina hauled herself up, threw her leg over the railing, slipped, and dangled off the side of the building.

Her screams pierced the air.

Scott rolled away from Frank and leapt to his feet. He made a run for Gina, but Frank caught him by the ankle, and Scott hit the ground. Scott's fingers closed on a metal pipe. Just as Frank was pinning his arms, Scott turned his body and swung. The bar hit Frank's head, and Frank's body slumped over Scott's.

Scott pushed Frank off him, dropped the pipe and sprinted over to Gina, who was just climbing over the railing. He could hear her sobs as he reached her. "Hold on!" he gasped. His hand grasped hers and he pulled.

A tingling in his shoulder shot through Scott's body. Scott let go of Gina. The pain completely took over. Gina gripped the railing and saw Frank standing behind Scott, holding the pipe. Frank pushed Scott out of the way, lunged at Gina and raised the pipe. Scott kicked out at Frank, pushing him off balance. Frank turned and charged Scott, aiming kicks at Scott's head and stomach. Scott frantically rolled away from Frank, struggling to his feet and dodging the pipe Frank was wielding.

Gina screamed, one of her hands slipping off the railing.

Frank threw the pipe at Scott, who ducked just before it struck him. Scott dove at Frank and wrestled him to the ground, pounding his fists mercilessly into Frank's face.

Scott glanced up at Gina. She was dangling precariously by one hand. Scott sprang to his feet and sprinted over to where she hung. He looked down into her face and saw her futile tears.

"Hang on!" he shouted, grabbing her hand.

"I can't!" came her faint gasp.

"Yes you can! Come on!"

Scott felt the draft behind him and turned just in time to see Frank rushing toward him, a crazed malice in his eyes. Both of Gina's hands were on the railing, and Scott gripped them frantically.

Scott saw Frank's hands reach out as Frank's dash turned into a run. The steep drop at the end of the ledge and the lights on Las Vegas Boulevard loomed far below them.

Scott faced Frank and remained standing until Frank was almost upon him, then dropped to the ground, one hand still grasping one of Gina's hands. Frank leaped at Scott just before Scott hit the cement.

Frank tripped and flipped over the side of the building and plunged to the street.

His final yell was a sickened plea.

Through a haze, Gina could hear shouts from the ground as her hold on the railing weakened and her hand faltered. Scott caught her just in time and pulled as hard as he could. Gina's body rose half way up over the railing, then hung limp in Scott's grasp.

"Can you get a grip with your feet?" he asked anxiously, Gina's arms slipping away from him.

She shook her head, her eyes slits.

"Come on! I got you!"

He managed to get one of his arms around her waist, then the other.

Scott pulled Gina back to the other side of the railing until she collapsed, breathless, in his arms.